CHAINED

LACEY LEHOTZKY

Copyright 2023 by The Lehotzky Group LLC

First paperback edition August 2023

ISBN 979-8-9883620-1-2 (paperback)

ISBN 979-8-9883620-0-5 (e-book)

Book cover and formatting by Beholden Book Covers

Edited by Kaitlin Ugolik Phillips

Published by The Lehotzky Group LLC

www.laceylehotzky.com

MORE BY LACEY LEHOTZKY

A Choice of Light and Dark
Chained
Light

PRONUNCIATION GUIDE

Agrenak - AG-ren-ak

Béke - BE-k

Cazius - KAZ-ius

Endre - EN-dre

Északi - EE-sah-kee

Este - esh-te

Izidora - iz-i-dawr-uh

Kazimir - kaz-imir

Kirigin - ki-ri-gin

Kriztof - KRIS-tof

Liliana - lil-i-ana

Vaenor - VAE-nor

Viktor - vik-tor

Vadim - vaa-deem

Valynor - VAL-noor

Vasvain - vas-vain

Vaszoly - vaas-o-ly

Zalan - ZA-lan

Zekari - zek-AR-i

Zirok - ZIR-ok

CONTENT WARNING

Chained is suitable for audiences of 18+. It contains scenes that sensitive readers might find disturbing. Your mental health matters, and you should make the choice with which you feel most comfortable.

This is by no means an exhaustive list of trigger warnings, and you can check the author's website for the most up to date list.

Trigger warnings: Torture, kidnapping, mentions of rape and sexual assault, nightmares, flashbacks, panic attacks, suicidal ideation, graphic violence, explicit sexual content, death, and mentions of physical, verbal, mental, emotional, and child abuse.

Survivors are the strongest ones of all, and I promise if you make it to the end, you'll see just how strong a survivor can be.

A CHOICE OF LIGHT AND DARK
PLAYLIST

Hunting Season - Ice Nine Kills
Watch The World Burn - Falling in Reverse
There's Fear In Letting Go - I Prevail
Werewolf - Motionless in White
Masterpiece - Motionless in White
No Masters - Bad Wolves
I Will Not Bow - Breaking Benjamin
Fallen Angel - Three Days Grace
Infinite - Silverstein, Aaron Gillespie
Riot - Three Days Grace
TRIALS - STARSET
Don't Stay - Linkin Park
Face Everything And Rise - Papa Roach
Say You'll Haunt Me - Stone Sour
Last to Know - Three Days Grace
Without You - Breaking Benjamin
Pain - Three Days Grace
Whispers in the Dark - Skillet
Take Me Back To Eden - Sleep Token
Whatever It Takes - Stephen Stanley

To everyone who has been to hell and back and remains unbroken

***

PROLOGUE

Blood was everywhere. The sheets, the towels, and the arms of the healers were all soaked in the ruby liquid gushing from between the queen's thighs. She screamed, her voice ripping with the effort of delivering her babe into the cruel world. Her voice died out, only to have the child pick up the end of the piercing note, wailing as the Royal Healer caught her.

"It's a female!" she exclaimed, but Queen Liessa no longer had the strength to hold herself upright and had collapsed backward in a heap of sweat, blood, and tears. She was deathly pale, and the Royal Healer's helpers rushed to her side, dabbing her salty face with cool cloths and wrapping her in a blanket as chills set her body trembling.

The Royal Healer quickly cleaned and swaddled the princess, returning to the queen's side in an attempt to rouse the delirious female and hand her the babe.

Shouts rang out in the hall outside the chamber, followed by the clash of steel. The healers immediately jerked their attention toward the door. One took a tentative step forward as if she would fling herself to the lock and slam it down before the chaos outside could barge into the lavish room where the queen and the princess moaned and cried.

But she was too late.

The door broke from its hinges, splintering into pieces as males boasting thick armor shoved their way into the space, swords drawn. "Give us the babe," the lead soldier growled.

"No!" The brave healer clutched the babe to her chest, bending over her in an attempt to shield the princess and sprinting to the adjoining bathroom, slamming the door behind her.

More screams filled the room as the soldiers began slaughtering the healers one by one, merciless in their attempt to reach the princess.

"No harm will befall you if you open the door," the leader said to the Royal Healer.

The female only looked at the ceiling, offering a whispered prayer to the Goddess. Before she could finish her plea, the door at her back slammed into her, sending her and the babe flying into the stone floor. The wails of the newborn reached a crescendo just as the sword sliced through the Royal Healer's neck, spraying blood over the princess.

With one large hand, the leader scooped up the babe, tucked her under his arm, and trudged through the sea of bodies. He returned to the frenzied halls where more of his soldiers battled against the Fae both young and old.

"Leave no one alive," he threw over his shoulder, pushing into the cool night air through a side door. The full moon greeted him, along with his dark steed. He mounted the beast, spurring him into a gallop, and disappeared into the night.

I

THE RESCUE

IZIDORA

Twenty years and three hundred and sixty four days had passed since I was first chained. The guards harassed me more when that once-yearly day was upon us, finding sadistic pleasure in telling me I would never get out, that I would spend the rest of my birthdays chained in this dark cave.

The wall that moored me in place was the only friend I'd known. The rough stone around the anchor centered on that wall was the map to my infinitesimally small world, and with only a touch, I knew exactly where I was. The point where my chains tautened and I could step no further was a well-worn semi circle, rock smooth from my years of endless pacing, like an animal kept in too small a cage. At that furthest border of my existence, the remnants of a once-fine feather mattress poked and prodded me no matter which way I turned, straining against the iron that bound me, denying me the sleep I so desperately craved.

Darkness had become a friend too, in its own way. In the eternal void that surrounded me, I was safe. The moment a flicker of flame graced the granite walls, my heart leaped into my throat, racing toward freedom in a way I could not.

The torches signaled food or pain – nothing in between. Most guards were cruel, chucking loaves of hard bread or too-dry meat at me, leaving a trail of bruises along my deathly pale skin. I hardly ever saw their faces, save for the wayward flicker illuminating a wicked grin or wetted lips.

Even the ones who wanted to take from my body knew better than to bring their light with them. My chains kept me from running far, but I fought with everything I had at my disposal until they beat me into submission, shortening my chains so the jagged stone cut into my arms as they ripped my tunic open and lashed me with metal-tipped whips. The whistle that cut the air before the whip landed haunted my nightmares. Once my spirit and body had been broken, another level of torment would begin, tearing me apart until my insides bled and joined the ruby river that poured from my back.

The only way to save myself was to lock the best parts of me away behind a wall sturdier than my constant companion. I learned to eat my words, bite my tongue, and swallow my pride because I wanted to survive. One day, I would make my escape. One day, I would see what was beyond these dark walls. One day, I would be strong enough to bleed these bastards dry.

But the next day marked the ending of another year in chains, the silent midnight air ringing in my birthday, though I didn't know the date. I didn't know what I looked like. I didn't even know my own name.

KAZIMIR

For as long as I could remember, the story of the lost princess of the Night Realm was a dark whisper in the back of my mind – kidnapped the day she was born, torn from her dying mother's arms, never to be seen again. I was ten years old the day she burst into the world, a day that fundamentally changed the course of my life, too.

King Zalan had beseeched my father, High Lord Cazius Vaszoly, to find his only daughter, to return her to Este Castle where she belonged. Having lost my mother not even a year prior, he had readily agreed. His grief drove him to drown himself in the search, and at the young age of fourteen, I joined him, dreaming of the day we would return to Vaenor with the lost princess in our arms. How we would be heralded as heroes and have ballads written about our deeds. Yet twenty years after her kidnapping, we still searched.

The king was old, surpassing the lifespan of most Fae. My father was surprised he had lived this long, and we all wondered if the hope of reuniting with his lost daughter kept one foot from the grave. With each day that passed, the king hung on by a fraying thread.

Over the years, we'd had dozens, if not hundreds, of leads that all ended in disappointment. Because of that, new leads stopped being passed to the king, staying in the circle of the Nighthounds, an elite group of warriors dedicated to finding the lost princess. We never stopped cultivating that seed of hope despite most of the realm believing she died long ago. Then, we received a new lead on her location that gave us hope that maybe this one would finally be real.

A tavern in the village of Zanin had been our home the past two nights as we planned our raid deep into the Agrenak Mountains. The mountains were a desolate, uninhabited place – the sharp, snow-covered peaks speared into the clouds above. The knife-like peaks were only accessible by confident fliers with strong wings, as one wrong gust of wind could slam a Fae into the mountain's jagged rocks, leaving them flightless and plummeting thousands of feet to their death. Investigating leads in the mountains was always dangerous because scouts didn't often return.

But finally one returned.

He had discovered a cave, hidden in the tallest peak of the treacherous mountain range, guarded by Iron Fae, who were long believed to be the lost princess's kidnappers. Those bastards were the nastiest of the Fae Realms, and the only ones impervious to iron. Subduing them was challenging, as weapons of steel had no effect on them, unlike the rest of the Fae, where one cut slowly sapped our magic reserves. Thank the Goddess the Iron Fae had been blessed with less magic than the other realms, or we would all be dead.

My father looked out over the small gathering of males standing in a field just outside the city. Seven of the most skilled warriors in the whole of the Night Realm stared back, stone-faced. We knew the risks, we knew the danger, we knew our mission, we knew our enemies.

"Tonight, we have the best chance of finding the princess since the days after she was taken from us. This mission is fraught with danger and may turn out to be another false lead. However, on the eve of the princess's twenty-first birthday, I believe the Goddess will favor us and deliver her to us on this night. You are all highly skilled warriors; you know what to do."

He offered a quick prayer to the Goddess to watch over us on this mission and then hugged each of us individually. We'd been a unit so long that these males felt like my brothers, and to my father they felt like sons.

My black feathered wings snapped from my shoulder blades, and I launched into the air, leading the charge as we flew higher, higher, and higher. Checking under my arm, I spotted the Nighthounds flying in formation behind me, spread out evenly so as not to disturb the air beneath another's wings while we traversed the steadily climbing ridge. An hour passed before we spotted the highest peak, Vasvain, where Kirigin spotted the cave.

We breached the clouds, rising into a sky filled with a million stars, imbuing each of us with the strength needed to fly in and fly out with the lost princess in tow. As Night Fae, we had an intimate relationship with the moon and stars, both fueling our Goddess-gifted magic.

A light tingle brushed against my skin with our proximity to the heavens. A deeper one shook my hands as Kirigin overtook me, guiding us to the left side of Vasvain, perilously close to the Iron Realm border and a maw of glacial rocks below. He pulled up suddenly, raising his right hand in a fist.

There.

You would miss the narrow opening behind a rocky outcropping on the side of the mountain if you didn't know what you looked for. Two guards in armor that nearly blended in with their surroundings lazily held crossbows as they surveyed the landscape, wholly comfortable in their belief that they'd never be discovered.

Zekari and Kirigin, our two most agile fliers, were armed with longbows and a quiver of arrows tipped in poisoned steel. The Royal Healers infused the arrowheads with anything that might slow down the Iron Fae and provide us with an upper hand. Zekari and Kirigin would attack first, trying to draw as many guards as possible to the mouth of the cave, where we could rain arrows from a safe distance.

They dove quickly, bows drawn. We waited a beat, then followed. Shouts rang out from the cave as their otherwise peaceful night abruptly ended. Crossbows were drawn and aimed in our direction, but Zekari and Kirigin rapidly fired arrows into the necks of the guards at the mouth of the cave. One guard slipped past his fallen comrades and loosed an iron bolt from his crossbow, sinking the projectile into Kriztof's thigh.

"Fuck!" His grunt echoed between the peaks, but it did not prevent him from nailing his attacker between the eyes.

Damn, that was a beautiful shot.

No one else appeared, so with a jerk of my head, I gave the order to proceed. On silent feet, we touched down at the mouth, careful to avoid the fallen bodies.

This cave was unlike anything I had ever seen. Its high, arched walls reminded me of the temples we built to worship the Goddess. But instead of clear glass ceilings, this one seemed to reach into the heavens themselves. Dark glittering ore lined the walls, mimicking the stars high above, as the torches lining the lower parts of the walls cast both light and shadow around the space.

Tucked close together, we crept deeper into the strange cave. There were two passages ahead of us, branching off in opposite directions. With two fingers, I pointed to the passage on the left, feeling a faint tether pulling me down the path. Not one of us breathed as we turned the corner, following the flickering lights down a carved hall, walking blindly into Goddess knew what.

This passage held several smaller rooms, branching off in multiple directions. Most were filled with small cots, which lay empty. It was quiet. Too quiet.

At the end of the hall, we spilled into a large room with a central fireplace, the snapping and crackling breaking up the unearthly quiet. Pots, pans, and plates were still strewn atop the surrounding stove and tables. Across the room, a heavy iron door loomed before us menacingly, daring us to enter.

I motioned for Zekari to check the door. Picking his way carefully among the haphazard tables, chairs, and couches, he managed to move silently until he stood before the great door. He pulled out gloves made by the Night Realm's healers to withstand the touch of iron, flexing his fingers once they were snug. His hands glided over and around the intricate iron door, touching along every ridge and surface for an opening mechanism. After a few minutes, he turned back to us, shaking his head.

A dead end.

Once Zekari was tucked into formation again, we returned to the hewn passage. The torches became nonexistent twenty paces into the left-hand tunnel. A scuff of metal on stone was the only warning we received that more guards awaited us there.

Rounding a corner, twenty Iron Fae stood before us, whips, swords, and crossbows trained on my brothers and me. We were undoubtedly outnumbered, but we were the Nighthounds for a reason.

As if lighting struck that very moment, the twang of Zekari, Kirigin, and Kriztof's bows thundered through the stone hall, dropping four Iron Fae as an arrow sailed through the neck of one male and out into that of another.

Sixteen.

I threw up a shield of shimmering silver magic just before the iron bolts would have struck their targets, dropping it the moment they clattered to the ground so another volley of our arrows could fly past my ears.

Thirteen.

Only Iron Fae armed with swords and whips remained, poised and ready to strike as one. My blade flashed before my eyes as I drove forward, engaging them in a dance of blades, Endre and Viktor fighting alongside me. Out of the corner of my eye, I saw the glint of an iron-tipped whip sail my way, leaping to the side just in time to hear it crack against the wall beside me.

"Kriztof, get the fucking whips!" I shouted.

An arrow narrowly missed my other ear a moment later, sinking into the shoulder of the male a few paces behind the one with whom I was locked in battle. He fell under my blade the moment after.

Seven left.

Viktor blasted the group apart with a silver bomb, Endre timing his own shield to protect us as the Iron Fae collided with each other and the walls around us, disorienting them long enough for us to slit their throats with the daggers strapped to our thighs.

I wiped my blade clean on my dark leather pants, then resheathed it. A faint tug pulled at my middle, and I knew we were close. "Keep going."

Another fifty paces into the passage, we were plunged into darkness so thick it was unnerving even for a Night Fae. I tossed a smattering of floating balls of light to guide our way. Yet it was so dark, the only thing we could see was each other.

This had to be it.

A faint tinkle from metal rubbing against metal sounded in the distance, reminding me of the movement of prisoners in the dungeon of Este Castle. My fisted right hand flew into the air signaling the Nighthounds to halt behind me.

I felt the tug again pulling me forward.

My fist dropped, and I led my brothers forward. If this was a trap, I wouldn't let one of them lead us into it. I was the second in command, willing to fight and die for what I believed in, and this was no exception.

Suddenly, I ran face-first into another wall. Cursing, I backed away and began trailing my hand along its rocky surface. The floating lights were nearly useless in the oppressive dark.

Another tinkle, but much closer now.

Quickening my pace, I reached the end of the wall, throwing lights ahead of me to check for any errant guards. Instead, when I turned the corner, I found a female chained to the other side of the wall. Her small frame was curled up beside the wall, her back pressed firmly into its rough ridges. She was trying to be as invisible as possible. Her long hair draped over her face like a curtain, hiding her further from view. But one look at her bony arms, covered in dark marks, had me clenching my jaw hard enough to crack my teeth.

The rest of the Nighthounds caught up, fanning out on either side of me as the space opened up around us.

Endre gasped when he saw what was on the floor in front of him.

"Hey there, can you hear me?" he said to her gently.

She looked up from her tight ball, confusion pulling her brows together over aquamarine eyes as she blinked rapidly. "Yes," she whispered.

He crouched down slowly. "Is it okay if I feel along these chains and see where I can break them?"

She flinched away from him, holding her breath. "Are you going to free me?"

"Yes," he said. "We are here to rescue you."

Her eyes narrowed on him, then she leveled her glare on the rest of us. "Why should I trust you?"

The speech I'd practiced over and over in my head as I daydreamed of finding the lost princess flowed smoothly from my lips. "We have been searching for you for a very long time, and I swear to the Goddess that none of us will ever harm you. We wish to take you to safety where you will have a bed, fresh food, a place to bathe, and people to wait on you hand and foot. You will never be chained again. You will be free to run and roam and feel the starlight on your skin."

That seemed to lift some of her hesitation, and she glanced above her to a circle of iron buried in the rock wall. "That's where they break apart."

Endre pulled on his iron-proof gloves, then made to move his hand above her head. She shot to her feet and away from the wall, nearly tripping over herself trying to get out of his way. Once she had settled some distance away, he felt around the ring, searching for a weak point. After a moment, he glanced over his shoulder at me, giving me a slight shake of his head.

The princess watched that tiny exchange with rapt attention, her eyes wide and breaths short.

"We can't break them there. We'll have to try another spot," Endre said.

"No," she shot back, shaking her head and backing away again. "This is some sort of trap. You'll make me think I'm free and then it will be some cruel joke. You'll just beat me for thinking I had a chance."

Raising my hands in a placating gesture, I dropped my voice into the most soothing tone I could muster. "I understand you're scared. We just killed all the people who hurt you. Do you want some proof?"

Several expressions flitted across her face, as if she couldn't decide what to think or what to feel. The Nighthounds stood silently behind Endre and me, and I sensed them take slow steps back, giving the frightened princess more space. Her attention shot over my shoulder to their retreating forms. "Fine," she gritted out, though she stepped away again, dragging the chains with her.

Keeping my hands in the air, I turned my head to look at Viktor and Vadim. "Can you two fetch a body?"

The two threw more silvery bubble lights into the air, giving me a quick nod and retracing our steps to the scene of the battle. Their return was punctuated by the scraping of metal as the bloodied guard was dragged between them, until they rounded the corner with proof of my statement. Zekari, Kirigin, and Kriztof contributed their own floating lights to the mix, bringing more light into the void that surrounded us, giving the princess a better view of her dead captor.

She took a tentative step forward, focused wholly on the dead male, as if she couldn't believe what she was seeing. Her gaze flicked between us and him over and over, until she finally said, "How do I know you aren't his replacement? They've killed people before."

It was Viktor who provided an answer. "You see what he is wearing? The metal armor? We are wearing leather armor." He pointed to his chest, pushing more of his magic into the light spreading out from his hand. "We are different from the people who hurt you."

Her eyes narrowed once more, the scrutiny she gave us hot enough to burn. "Fine. But if you try to touch me, I will bite you." She offered no indication that she would walk closer to us, so Endre stepped slowly toward her, his gloved hands raised the entire time. She did not breathe as he approached, but she lifted her hands to him, holding them as far away from her body as possible.

Endre started on the dangling chains, working along them

until he nearly reached her wrists. With an audible swallow, he murmured, "The lock is along your wrist, and I'm going to have to use my knife to break it."

The princess opened her mouth to speak, but he interrupted her protest. "I'm going to give you my other knife, and you can hold it in your left hand while I break the shackles off your right. That way, you can defend yourself if I get too close, okay?"

She opened the palm of her left hand, turning it over in silent indication for him to give her the weapon. Gently, he lowered his hand to his side, unsheathed a dagger strapped to his thigh, and offered it to her. The princess did not hesitate to snatch it from him, holding it by the handle with the blade pointed directly at him. He repeated the motion on his other thigh, allowing her plenty of time to see that he was retrieving a dagger to unlock the iron.

The tension was palpable as we waited for Endre to complete the task, each of us barely breathing as we watched him work. Finally, a light click sounded, and the shackle dropped to the floor with a clang. She flinched at the sound, taking a stumbling step back before recovering herself and gripping the knife even tighter.

"I've got to take the other one off now, okay? Switch the knife to your other hand."

The knife shifted to her right hand, though the white-knuckled grip remained. The shackle on her left wrist fell away a moment later, and Endre retreated a few paces to give her a moment of space. Two rings of iron remained around her ankles, and breaking them would put Endre in a vulnerable position.

"Whenever you're ready, I'll take those off," Endre said to her, gesturing to her legs.

Sucking in a serrated breath, she nodded, offering one leg while gripping the knife with both hands. Endre worked quickly, careful not to touch her skin, releasing a sigh of relief when the bangle clattered to the floor. The princess offered him the other leg immediately, and I breathed out a sigh of my own. The amount of magic we were using to maintain our floating lights made me nervous about our ability to fly away from there with the princess in tow.

Once every last iron had fallen away from her skin, she jumped back, eyeing us warily. Endre retreated to my side, resheathing his knife. "Time to go," I announced, beckoning the princess forward. "I can carry you out of here."

"I can walk," she snapped, but her legs trembled like a baby deer moments after it entered the world. In a way, she was about to enter our world for the very first time.

With a quick glance behind me, I said, "Go clear the way."

Endre remained at my side while the rest of the Nighthounds went to clear the bloody mess from the passage just beyond. The princess lifted her chin as she stepped timidly toward us, but the tightness of her jaw and shoulders was unmistakable. The knife trembled slightly in her hand, when she stopped, still five paces from us. Endre and I only looked at each other, and in silent agreement, we allowed her to follow us as we led the way down the hall.

Then, so quietly that I almost didn't hear, she whispered, "Happy Birthday to me."

3

IZIDORA

Amber and smoky wood filled my nostrils as I followed the males who broke my chains. All the years in the dark had heightened my sense of smell, allowing me to discern who approached without the availability of light. The worst of my guards had smelled like rotten meat. Fitting, since that was what he often brought me. His sadistic laugh as he aimed the fetid slabs at me always set my teeth on edge. I tried as hard as I could to dodge and volley back, but the smell on my hands was enough to make me nauseous, as I went weeks without bathing.

When he wanted more from me, he would bring me a better hunk, but I had to earn it. The taste of his disgusting cock in my mouth was worse than the stench on my hands. I often refused, only to get thrown against the wall, bloodying myself as the rocks scraped my skin. He took what he wanted anyway as I numbed my body to his touch, and dreamed of the day I would watch him choke on his cock after I sliced off the small member and shoved it down his throat.

Because of my defiance, he would starve me for days until the hunger gnawed so deep in my belly that I relented, and when he finished, I immediately tore into the meat to mask the bitter taste on my tongue.

The kindest guard smelled like honey and always brought me pastries on my birthday. This year's treat was a cream-filled strawberry pastry that tasted like heaven; he even brought the light close enough for me to see the sprinkles dusting it. Despite his kindness, I did not trust him, though I knew he liked the wide smiles I gave him in exchange for treats. In my mind, it was only a matter of time before he came to me with a request of his own.

The art of manipulation was one I had learned at a young age. After all, that was how I had survived the cave – separating from my existence when necessary, fighting back against the ones who would fall back because they did not want to deal with me, and charming those who were more susceptible to kindness.

I learned long ago that who I was was wrong, and showing interest in anything only led to pain. So I became what I had to be, walling off my emotions, never letting myself truly feel the depths of my despair. Living free of chains and outside of these stone walls was my most closely guarded desire, like a dragon hoarding its most prized possession. It was as if something called to me from beyond, a distant echo weaving through the baritone voices that filled the cave at all hours.

The guards called me many names: whore, demon, bitch, worthless, and countless other damaging words that wormed their way into my brain. I accepted that maybe they were right, maybe there was something wrong with me if my life was only worth this. But there was a small spark of me that rejected the idea, that kept me fighting on the days where it all felt utterly pointless.

A group of strict and stern females came to see me monthly, taking care of my physical needs and giving me a glimpse into the world outside along with the most basic of lessons. But their presence did not always save me from the abuse of my guards. I vividly remembered the beating the nastiest of guards gave me after they left one time; a kick broke my ribs, sending air whooshing from my lungs and tears streaming down my face as I struggled to breathe.

Yet there was so much that I did not remember, and for that, I was grateful. The memories that already haunted me were more than enough.

I snapped back to the present as we entered a domed hall filled with burning torches. The strange floating lights disappeared, leaving only the firelight to guide our way, and I blinked as my eyes adjusted again to the light.

Deep male voices quipped rapidly, discussing our impending departure.

Where were we going?

It hadn't yet occurred to me to ask because I honestly didn't care. Anywhere was better than the cave. But I still did not trust that this wasn't some sort of elaborate trap, designed to break me in a new way.

"Where are we going?" I whispered.

The males stopped walking, and the taller one spun ever so slowly to look at me, then stepped aside. My mouth popped open as a gasp escaped my lips, overcome with the sight before me. We stood at the mouth of an enormous cave overlooking mountains so tall I wasn't sure where they began and where they ended. Stars of the purest white sparkled overhead against a night so black I was sure I had never really left my chains. My eyes no longer stung out here, gazing out into the darkness above and below.

"Princess," the male started, "the only way down the mountain is by flight. I need you to hold on to me as tight as you can, but I promise I won't let you fall."

Princess? This had to be a trap.

A ghost of a memory appeared before my eyes; a tub filled with cold water, and the females forcing me to play roles that made no sense. The cold stone beneath my bare feet grounded me as I took an unconscious step away from him.

My hesitation was apparent, because he spoke again. "I know you don't trust me, but you still have that knife. Hold on to it, but try not to stab me as we fly, otherwise we will both fall to our deaths."

Trust was hard for me to give away, but my only other option was to remain. Falling to my death mere minutes after being freed from my chains would be an ironic way to die. I looked at the knife, then back to him. I couldn't stay here, not when it appeared to be impossible for me to escape otherwise.

And I wanted to fucking live.

The knife clattered to the ground as I opened my palm.

The male motioned for me to approach him. Giant black feathered wings snapped from his body, and then fluffed themselves before settling down on either side of his shoulders. Sucking in a breath, I stepped forward, and he hoisted me up. Immediately, I stiffened at his touch, but I wrapped my legs around his waist, then looped my arms around his neck. The touch he offered in return was tender yet tight, and it was as foreign to me as the night sky.

He nodded to his companions and six of them leaped into the night.

Before he moved again, I asked, "What is your name?"

Better to know who I was taking this leap of faith with than die ignorant.

"Kazimir. Hold on tight." And then he jumped off the edge of the cave, hurling us into the dark night.

A scream tore from my mouth as we fell, my knuckles turning white with the force of my grip as I clung to the male.

Shit, shit, shit, I was going to die after all.

A moment later, we caught the wind and soared higher between the mountain peaks, weightless and *free*. But I dared not release the death grip that secured me to the tapered body of the male flying me into a world I had only dreamed of seeing.

A pocket of air buffeted us, and I yelped again as we were blown straight to the side and toward jagged rocks that loomed much too close for comfort. I shut my eyes, praying to the Goddess to save me from certain death. His muscled arms snaked tighter, holding me firmly against his chest as he flapped his black wings furiously.

And then it was as if the world fell away and silence enveloped me. It was deafening save for the fluid flapping of Kazimir's wings and my fearful panting. Opening my eyes, I drank in the sight of the stars passing above us and the white spire of one mountain towering over its brethren in the distance.

This all had to be a cruel dream.

"We will fly for about an hour to a small village just outside the mountains. There we will rest and eat. Tomorrow we will set out for Este Castle, where your father lives. He has been waiting to meet you your whole life."

Was this really happening?

The mere fact that I had left the cave hadn't sunk in yet, and I struggled to process the waves of emotion rocking my very core. I nodded, a long, deep breath expanding my chest, slowing my racing heart. As soon as I felt in control again, I asked the question that had burned on my tongue since we settled into our flight.

"Kazimir, what is my name?"

If he had rescued me, he must have known who I was. Any information about myself would be useful in case I traded one prison for another. At least on the open road, there was a chance for escape.

At first his brows pulled together, but then his teeth bared, clenched so violently that a muscle feathered in his jaw. I stiffened, pulse kicking into overdrive as I prepared to fight for my life.

This was what happened every time; I knew better than to voice the questions that haunted me for as long as I could remember.

Through gritted teeth, he spat, "Did no one ever call you by a name?"

Releasing a shuddering breath, I explained, "No. When I was very young I asked about my real name but they beat me in response, so I never asked again."

His face softened at my words, and he gripped me against his body as if I were a precious gem he did not want to crush. "Your name is Izidora."

"Izidora," I rolled the name over my tongue; it was pretty to me.

"I know this is a lot to process but there will be plenty of time ahead to discuss everything that's happened. Try to rest as much as you can while we fly," Kazimir encouraged.

My shoulders dropped as the mood between us changed. I may have been out of the cave, but whether I was permanently out of chains was yet to be seen. I nodded and flattened my head against his chest so I could comfortably hang on while we flew under the guidance of the stars above, toward a home I never knew existed.

INTERLUDE

The small child looked up at her caretaker with wide eyes as she was led by the hand away from the darkness of her cave. "Where are we going?" the child asked.

The female leading her thought back to her instructions, given so clearly by the king. The princess needed to be functional, yet moldable by the time she came of age. "We're going to play in the sun."

A smile as wide as the mouth of the cave they walked toward blossomed on her face, blue eyes sparkling as they adjusted to the dim light of the halls. The sound of metal tinkling against metal echoed around the space, the iron bangles around the child's wrists and ankles a permanent fixture.

The old female's weary heart twinged with sadness. The tiny princess did not deserve what was happening to her, yet there was nothing she could do to stop it. *Better to be there to help her than to leave her at the mercy of males*, the caretaker thought.

"Stay close to me, and do not go to the edge," she warned.

The princess obeyed her without question, staying far away from the mouth of the cave, but still within the beam of light that filtered through the opening. The female was not allowed to teach the child to read, yet she tried her best to engage the princess in conversation, telling her stories that pushed the limits of her remit. She hoped the guards were not listening, for the king was cruel, and she risked her own life by speaking stories of the world beyond.

The princess held a spark of something inside her, a spark of something that the caretaker knew would never be snuffed out. It reminded her of her own daughter, taken from this world at far too young of an age. It was for that reason she'd been chosen as the princess's caretaker. Living in this cave, far away from her realm, there were no memories to haunt her.

"Sweetie," she called to the little one, "would you like to hear a story about the dragon who blew apart the houses of the three little centaurs?" Another thing she was not allowed to say was the princess's name.

"Yes!" She exclaimed, turning her focus away from a pile of weathered wooden toys.

The caretaker started on her tale. "Once upon a time, a dragon flew over a forest in search of a snack..."

"What's a forest?" The little one always had so many questions.

The caretaker described a forest to her, since there were none visible from their high peak, and continued the story. The princess listened with rapt attention, crawling closer and closer until she perched in her caretaker's lap by the time the story concluded. The caretaker stroked the tiny child's long hair, holding her until she fell asleep. As the sky darkened and the sun slipped from the cave, she carried her small body back to the corner of the cave where she was bathed in complete darkness, tucking her into a small mattress braced against a rough stone wall and relatching her chains to the bangles.

No, the princess did not deserve this life, and the female

vowed to help her survive in any way she could.

II

THE ROAD

4

KAZIMIR

"She didn't know her fucking name!" I roared, smashing my fist into the worn wood desk in my room at the tavern, causing it to collapse under the force. I flung one of its legs against the wall and it shattered with a satisfying snap. Grabbing another, I broke it across my knee. Splinters were everywhere, lining the floor, digging into my skin, but the piercing pain still had yet to take the edge off the anger twisting like a hot knife in my chest.

My father watched me rage, concern etching deeper lines between his already furrowed brows. Once I was thoroughly exhausted from smashing pieces of the dark wooden furniture in my room, I heaved out a long breath. Then another. On my fifth one, my father spoke.

"She is going to have a long road ahead of her. Clearly whoever took her wanted to exercise ultimate control over her. They wanted her completely in the dark about the outside world, about who she is, and about what she is capable of. Going to Este Castle now and facing the nobles who circle like vultures is going to overwhelm her."

I sighed, running a hand over my face. "What do you propose we do?"

"Delay our return as long as possible so she can acclimate to her new world," my father said.

Este Castle was a steady month-long ride from the Agrenak Mountains, and I was certain Izidora had never ridden a horse before. Since most Fae thought she was dead, traveling slowly and stopping in cities along the way wouldn't be terribly dangerous. I nodded my head, analyzing all the possibilities. "People know that we've been searching for her all these years. I don't want to rouse suspicion when we make stops."

"Hmm," my father thought for a moment before responding. "We should give her some male clothes and a hat to hide her long hair. We can make up a reason for having a young male with us, if anyone asks."

"First thing tomorrow, I will go find some clothes for her at the market," I promised. Children's clothes would be more fitting with her small, slight frame. I reclined on the bed, exhausted from the night's events. My father stood from the one chair I hadn't destroyed and walked over to me, placing a hand on my shoulder in reassurance.

"Kazimir," he said gently, "You are always so calm and collected, I have never seen so much rage and passion in you before. What is going on tonight?"

He was right. *What had gotten into me?* "Seeing Izidora chained in the dark like that... I don't know what came over me. And then the bruises on her arms..."

My father sat beside me on the bed. "You are an honorable male, Kazimir. You would never want to cause a female harm in that way. She has suffered greatly, and we have searched for her for a long time. If we had found her sooner... well, I wouldn't have this pit of grief and guilt in my stomach."

He stood, intending to leave me to sleep as he walked to the door. With it half open, he turned toward me once more. "Izidora doesn't know what it is like to be cared for. Perhaps you can be the one to show her that kindness."

And then the door clicked softly as it shut.

I kicked off my sturdy leather boots before flopping back onto the bed, staring at the thick wooden beams crossing the ceiling. My father was right. Izidora could use all the help she could get in the coming weeks, and I would ensure the snakes of the Night Realm didn't eat her alive.

———

MORNING CAME FAR TOO SOON, sunlight spilling into my eyes and forcing me awake. A twinge in my back and shoulders reminded me of our long flight last night, so I stretched languidly as I rose from the firm mattress. Groaning internally, I surveyed the damage I had wreaked to the room in my fit of rage. A large tip would be necessary on top of repayment for the damages.

I dressed quickly, splashing cold water on my face from the basin – somehow still intact – and walked into the hall. I paused briefly outside Izidora's room, wanting to enter and behold the female for whom I'd spent more than half my life scouring the continent. From what I had seen the previous night, she was more beautiful than I had ever imagined. And I had imagined; for the years spent searching across the four realms, my daydreams of Izidora had kept me company. Soft breathing indicated she still slept, so I crept the rest of the way down the hall to the stairs, avoiding the floorboards that creaked.

Outside, the morning air was crisp and inviting. Autumn was truly upon the Night Realm. I strolled toward the town square where the sounds of haggling and the aroma of freshly baked bread spilled down each street and alley, beckoning the inhabitants to gather. I perused the food stalls, stopping to buy a loaf of bread and a hunk of cheese before continuing toward the clothing. Chewing on the loaf, I searched for simple pants, tunics, leather boots, and a hat that looked small enough to fit Izidora. Once I was satisfied with my haul, I strolled around Zanin.

The town's charm grew on me with each subsequent visit. The small wooden chalets that lined the roads were cozy and inviting. Every spot in town had a breathtaking view of the serrated, snow-capped mountains in the distance. I could see myself settling down here if I had a different life. But I was the future Head of House Vaszoly who served the whims of his king; my place was in Vaenor.

I found myself back at the tavern just as my father was leaving. "I am going to check on our horses and ask the stablehands to saddle them in about an hour. We should get going," he announced.

"I'll alert the Nighthounds and wake Izidora. Do we have enough supplies to last until the next town?" I asked.

"I will ask them to replenish our saddlebags as well," he confirmed, and then he strode toward the stables around the back of the building.

The Nighthounds gathered around a small corner table shoveling steaming porridge into their mouths.

"Want a bowl, Kazimir?" Endre inquired, his black hair even more mussed than usual, as if he had rolled off his mattress and walked downstairs without looking in a mirror.

"I ate in the town already. We're heading out in an hour, so pack up when you're finished eating, and I'll meet you outside."

With shaking hands and my goods tucked under my arm, I continued up the stairs to Izidora's room. A wave of uncertainty joined my nerves as I stood outside her door. I didn't want to startle her by knocking too loudly. I didn't want her to fear me. Sighing, I rapped softly on the door with my knuckles. "Izidora, are you awake?"

A light shuffle, and then the door opened slightly, Izidora peeking out with one bright blue eye. When she saw it was me, she opened the door slightly wider, but not enough to leave herself vulnerable. I asked, "Can I come in for a moment?"

She considered, wariness clouding her eyes as her expression remained neutral. Finally, she nodded and then opened the door, backing away toward the bed. I shut the door gently behind me and walked to the opposite side of the room so she didn't feel like I was boxing her in. Plopping my sack on the table, I flipped it open and rummaged through until I found the clothes I had purchased for her.

"We are going to extend our journey back to Este Castle. My father and I thought it best if no one knew we found you yet, so I bought these for you to wear and a hat to hide your hair," I explained.

She eased toward me, accepting the clothes from my outstretched hand, then backed away a few paces. "Will we fly to the castle?"

"No, we are riding horses. The journey should take about seven weeks. We will go slowly to give you time to adjust." A tightness fell away from her face, betraying her relief. I couldn't blame her, the previous night's flight had been intense even for experienced fliers.

"We are leaving in an hour. Are you hungry? I can bring you something to eat," I offered.

She studied me a moment before conceding. "Yes, I am actually starving."

A small grin spread across my face in response, trying to show her that I meant no harm. "Good, I will fetch some food while you change."

I gave her a wide berth as I strode for the door, aiming for the kitchens downstairs where I could order some food. As I reached for the handle, she asked timidly, "Why are you being so kind? What do you want?"

Her question hit like a stone settling in my stomach. "Everyone deserves kindness," I responded, head barely turned toward her over my shoulder. She did not need to see the pity in my eyes as I was reminded of how awful her life must have been, and how I had failed to save her for nearly twenty-one years.

Her question haunted me the entire time I waited for her food.

Ten minutes later, I knocked, a tray in hand piled with one of everything on the tavern's menu. She opened the door with caution, but her eyes grew larger than melons when she saw the banquet I carried. The door swung wide, and I entered, placing the tray on a small table in the room. "Dig in. I'll keep you company while you eat."

She perched on the edge of the seat across from me, shot me a cautious look, and meekly reached for a thick slice of vanilla cake. It received a thorough examination before she took an enormous bite. She groaned, words slipping unbidden, along with a few crumbs from her full mouth. "This is the best cake I have ever eaten."

I laughed, "Wait until you see the cakes at Este Castle. You might actually put on some weight once you start stuffing your-self with the cook's pastries."

Her cheeks flushed, and she glanced down at her too-thin body. She kept her head low as she finished the slice and I internally chastised myself for my careless words. She reached for a piece of bacon, chewing on it thoughtfully. "Tell me about the castle," she requested, still not looking up from her food.

"Well, Vaenor is the seat of the Night Realm and Este Castle is where the king, your father, resides. The city is beautiful at night. When you're flying above it, it's almost like you are flying between the stars. Now that I think about it, you're really flying in a star sandwich."

She snorted at my terrible attempt at a joke, finally lifting her gaze to meet mine. I shot her a lopsided grin aimed at disarming her. "Este Castle sits high on the cliffs at the city's edge. There are multiple towers at varying heights spilling over the edge of the cliff, all leading toward an epic point in the center. It almost looks like the mast of a ship, about to set sail across the raging ocean crashing against the rocky cliffs below. The air is fresh and briny, though the wind can be brutal in the winter. Vaenor is the biggest city in the Night Realm, always bustling with the activity of Fae coming and going. The port brings trading ships from other realms filled with fine wines, fresh fruits, and colorful crafts."

"Do you think I will like it there?" Her eyes bounced between mine, searching for any hints of deception.

I thought for a moment. "I'm not sure. It will be very different from what you are used to." I paused. "What did you do while you were..." I wasn't sure what the right words were "... in the cave?"

The haunted look in her eyes made me wish I hadn't asked, but she finished chewing and answered me. "I listened. The guards talked constantly, and everything I know about the world, I learned from their conversations. They spoke of their families and the weather near their homes, argued over who was cheating at cards, and how they couldn't wait until the females would come again so they would have some company to warm their beds." Some of her wariness slipped away as I engaged her in conversation. "The females who came to take care of me taught me a few other things, though they were strict and ruthless with their punishments when I messed up in any way. I have a vague memory of someone else when I was younger, but most of my life is a dark blur."

A surge like an angry sea rose from my gut at her confession. I quickly looked away and took a deep breath to regain control of my emotions. When I looked back, the hypervigilance had returned and her expression was hard. She sat tense to the point of stillness, as if she were a deer who had caught sight of a mountain lion.

Guilt slammed into my gut and I sighed deeply, trying to smooth over my reaction. "I'm sorry, you've done nothing wrong by sharing that. I am simply mad at myself for not finding you sooner, for not keeping you safe."

She raised a brow, still studying my face, then let go of the breath she had been holding onto when she decided that I spoke true. "Will you keep me safe now?" she tested.

"Always," I solemnly promised. Her assessing eyes showed that she didn't quite believe my statement, but she nodded anyway.

There was a knock on the door. "Time to go," my father called out.

I held out my hand to Izidora to help her rise. She eyed it like it was a snake coiled to strike, then stood without taking it.

Guess she was not ready for that yet.

I led us from the room, down the stairs, and out into the sunshine. The harsh sunlight caused her to squint and blink rapidly. With slow, visible hands, I adjusted her hat so it sat lower over her eyes. She stiffened as I touched her, not breathing until I stepped back once more.

"Thanks," she muttered, her eyes shaded from the bright morning sun.

"You can ride with me until you feel comfortable on a horse," I offered as we rounded the building in the direction of the stables.

She walked silently beside me until she hesitantly nodded her approval. The smell of sweet hay and sour manure grew stronger until we arrived at the stables, where our horses were saddled and waiting, along with the rest of the Nighthounds.

I guided her to my horse, who stood at the end of the line awaiting our arrival. Fek was a massive black beast who dwarfed Izidora's frame. His inky mane hung low over his eyes, and his muscular frame showed every bit of his Warstrider breeding. Izidora stopped short, her gem-like eyes widening as she beheld my mount. Tentatively, she reached out her hand, first touching his silky forelock, then rubbing his velvety nose, and he gently nuzzled her hand, looking for sugar. She hummed low as his whiskers tickled her hand. Fishing in my pockets, I found a few cubes and handed her one.

"Place the cube on your palm and then flatten your hand like this," I demonstrated. "He loves sugar, just like you. I think you will get along just fine."

Fek greedily snatched the lump of sugar and in two munches it was gone. Izidora stepped to his heavy shoulder, rubbing her hand over his dark hide. "He is so soft!" she exclaimed. Fek snorted his disapproval.

I grinned, happy that some of the heaviness lifted from her in Fek's presence. "Don't go saying that, he is a prideful beast. He wants to be as tough on the outside as he is on the inside." Fek nodded his head like he understood, and then stamped his foot to drive home his point.

"Okay, are you ready to ride a horse?"

Her aquamarine eyes were a swirling mixture of wonderful excitement and cautious uncertainty.

The leather groaned as I swung myself into the saddle. Then, I bent to the side and offered my arm to her. She took a breath, then gripped it with both hands. Lifting her was easy, and soon she sat in front of me, legs spread on either side of Fek's wide back. She scooted as far away as she could, and my heart dropped like a stone.

Izidora had felt more like a legend than a person over the past few years. After all this time we had found her, but despite riding mere inches from me, she felt miles away, hidden behind her guarded walls. Trying to refrain from touching her as much as possible, I gingerly picked up Fek's reins and urged him forward.

5

IZIDORA

W e rode in silence. I wasn't sure how to act around all these males whom I didn't know or trust.

Was I unknowingly trading one set of chains for another?

They seemed to be genuine...

Yet these walls, built brick by brick over twenty-one years, would not tumble down overnight. Safety came from hiding behind my mask, and not allowing anyone close to me. And those who got too close, who violated my walls, would see the viciousness with which I fought back.

The ground appeared like a distant shore from where I rode atop Fek's sturdy back, the fear of falling kept me firmly rooted in place. I settled for closing my eyes and tuning into the world around me through the senses I was more accustomed to - smell and sound.

As we departed Zanin, the smells of freshly baked bread, roasting meat, and burning wood faded along with the sound of Fae going about their day. The horses walked along a stone path leading through the twisting woods outside the town. The trees formed a tunnel, their brightly colored leaves bursting in an array of warm tones as sun streaks flitted through the canopy overhead. A bubbling creek was off to one side, the trickle of water composing a melody with the soft breeze and clip-clop of the horses' hooves striking the stone path. It was peaceful in these woods, the air fresh and crisp like a juicy apple, the scenery different yet just as lovely as the star-speckled night sky. The world that waited for me beyond my chains was everything I had imagined and more.

I was angry that I had lived in darkness for so long, fighting for mere survival instead of thriving among the nature that sang to my very soul. I was angry for the abuse I'd suffered at the hands of others, constantly balanced on a knife's edge, wondering what I was to be punished for next. I was angry at myself for not being strong enough to fight back and liberate myself, my dreams the only peaceful escape from the horror that was my waking experience.

I was sad that instead of a loving family and friends, I had caretakers who only met my basic needs – if that. I was sad that I had only just learned my name, as if they'd wanted complete control of my identity, and giving me a name would have allowed me to latch onto something concrete, something I could anchor myself to in times of defiance. I was sad that I was afraid to receive any kindness, only expecting it to be thrown back in my face with a resounding slap whose fading sting rang with a reminder of my unworthiness.

My thoughts consumed me as I relived horror after horror behind my eyes, my vacillating emotions like a barely contained wildfire, threatening to burn the whole world down if only to escape the pain. Perhaps it would be easier if I burned along with it. I was drowning in smoke as tears stung my eyes, and I shook my head to clear away the fog of memories.

We stopped suddenly, and I blinked a few times, trying to ground myself into the present as the darkness lurking within me retreated to the depths of my heart. I craned my neck to look at Kazimir, curious as to why we halted our journey.

"We're going to make camp here tonight. The sun will be going down soon, and we don't want to travel in the dark. I'm going to dismount, and then I will help you down," Kazimir explained.

With an easy grace, he swung his leg over Fek's back and landed lightly on the ground. He reached his hands to my waist, hesitating as I shrunk back involuntarily. I breathed and then straightened, allowing him to help me to the ground.

"Your legs might be sore from riding today," he noted as my leather-bound feet gently touched the lush grass.

My legs instantly wobbled, and I leaned into Fek to regain my balance.

Kazimir chuckled, "Do you need help getting to the fire?"

I took a tentative step forward, then another. On my third step, I heaved out a sigh. "I think I can make it."

Better to wobble and fall than to let him touch me again.

My less than graceful stumble to the small fire was comical, but I managed to ease myself onto a log beside it as a deep groan rumbled from my throat. The lanky male building the fire laughed at my expense. "It will get easier with time. I still remember the first time I rode a horse. My older brother bet me I couldn't ride from one end of our estate to the other at full speed without falling off. I didn't fall off, but my legs sure felt like they were going to after... I'm Zekari by the way."

I examined him closely, his story bringing a soft smile to my lips. He had an easy presence about him, one that spoke of an unhurried life and gentle confidence. "Nice to meet you Zekari."

"You're a lying bastard, Zekari, because you definitely fell off that day," another male said from behind me. I jumped, my face turning bright red and my heart thundering in my chest. I hid the terror that tore through me at his unexpected presence. The male smiled as he rounded in front of me, a lazy grin that matched his drawl. "I'm Kirigin."

He crossed to Zekari and wrapped him in a hug that turned into Kirigin messing up Zekari's hair, leading them to wrestle on the ground. Kazimir approached them, laughing as he slung his arms around both of them from behind.

"Enough, children, let's finish setting up camp before night falls." The brothers grinned from ear to ear, nearly mirror images of each other. They were both tall with dark hair and mossy eyes. Zekari was the leaner of the two. Kirigin wore his hair cropped short to his scalp while Zekari's was shaved on the sides and spiked on the top. But their facial features were identical.

Zekari noticed my assessing gaze. "Kirigin is only older by a few minutes," he explained. "We're twins."

"And don't you forget to respect your elders, little brother," Kirigin teased. Zekari rolled his eyes and continued building the fire.

Kazimir sat on the log beside me with a loaf of bread and some hard cheese. He held out his hand in offering, and I took it, glad for something to eat. While I ate, I took the opportunity to examine him through lowered lashes.

Hair as dark as night drew away from his face, as if he had run his hands straight up when he tumbled out of bed that morning rather than smoothing it back. The deep emerald pools of his eyes held a softness that spoke of years of laughter and love, the depth of color accented by his lightly bronzed cheekbones. He was wearing full leathers now, but I knew from our breakfast that morning that underneath was the corded muscle of a warrior. I felt like a rabbit next to a wolf.

His full lips pulled back into a smile, crinkling the dusting of stubble that lined his strong jaw before he turned back to the fire, where the rest of the males had taken seats on other logs.

Zekari and Kirigin sat to our right, along with Cazius, who I learned was Kazimir's father. Cazius looked like an older, more serious version of Kazimir, with wrinkles and tension pulling at the corners of his eyes and lips.

Across from us the four other males were squeezed together on a tiny log.

"Allow me to introduce the rest of our crew," Kazimir pointed to the male on the left. "That shaggy dog is Vadim. We've tried for years to get him to shave but he insists the females like him better that way, although we've yet to see the proof."

My huff of laughter surprised me, the sound slipping so easily through my lips, and Vadim winked his evergreen eyes. "Don't listen to them, they're all jealous of my luscious locks." He ran a hand dramatically across his dark hair, which was piled in a messy bun on the top of his head.

"Next to Vadim is Endre. He may look tough on the outside but he's a bleeding heart, stopping to help every injured animal we see along our journeys," Kazimir teased.

They all shared a laugh, while Endre's cheeks flamed. Despite his evident embarrassment, his peridot eyes sparkled beneath unkempt hair. The lean male with golden brown hair dusting his shoulders next to Endre piped up, "Remember when Endre saw the wounded ram outside of Salthelm? He hopped down to aid it, and as soon as he drew near it charged him. Got him right in the nuts, too! Poor guy couldn't ride for a day!" That really got them roaring, and Kazimir's hearty laugh drew one from my throat.

"That is Kriztof. If he weren't such an amazing fighter, he would definitely be the court jester," Kazimir said with a wide grin. "And next to Kriztof is Viktor, the brains of our group. Viktor is always three steps ahead of all of us. When we were all going through our basic training, no one could best him in sword fighting because he always knew our next move before we did."

Viktor tipped his head at me, grinning wide. He had a knowing glint in his sage eyes as he looked between Kazimir and me. "I hope you know that you are safe with all of us. We will protect you with our lives," he said.

The broad male was intense. I nodded, unsure how to respond to that, or how to behave with a group of males that supposedly meant me no harm. I sensed their sincerity, and I liked their casual air. They treated me like a normal person, and for a moment I almost forgot that I had been chained in the dark for years of my life.

"Nice to meet you all," I replied.

"We call ourselves the Nighthounds. We didn't choose the name, actually. After several years of scouring every town in the Night Realm for hints about your whereabouts, the people gave us the name, and it stuck. Now here we are, nearly two decades later." Kazimir looked at his brothers in arms, eyes filled with warmth.

The males joked and told stories for the remainder of our small meal. I watched them all, reading their facial expressions, gauging their moods, and listening to the words they said and did not say. Their tales came to life and I imagined myself riding alongside them as they spoke of all the adventures they'd had together. This was what I had been craving my whole life, and I hoped that one day I would have moments like this with friends of my own.

Too soon, Cazius stood. "We need to get moving early tomorrow so I suggest you retire to your tents. I know how long this can go on if I don't put a stop to it early." He shot them all a playful side-eye.

Grinning, Zekari and Kirigin stood next. "As you command!"

they said in unison, saluting him. Cazius rolled his eyes and continued to one of the tents.

Kazimir jerked a thumb behind us. "That tent is yours and mine is to the right if you need anything." He straightened, looking at Vadim. "You take the first watch – wake me when you start getting tired." Vadim nodded, and the rest of the males sauntered into their tents.

I was grateful to have my own space, but I felt hesitant to let my guard down. I was a lone female with a group of males in the woods in the middle of nowhere.

Seemed perfectly reasonable that I would be safe, right?

I planned on setting a trap just in case any one of them decided to join me.

Opening the front flap, I surveyed my tent. Inside was a small bedroll with a pillow and blanket. A fresh set of clothes sat off to one side, along with one of the saddlebags. Kazimir appeared behind me, and I jumped when he spoke. "It's not much, but there is another blanket in the saddlebag if you get cold."

I didn't know how to tell him that it was more than I had in the cave. Their kindness was almost too much for me to bear, and tears pricked at my eyes. I didn't know what to say or how to feel about all of this. So I settled for a sincere, "Thank you."

Kazimir left and settled into his own tent next to mine, a few grunts and grumbles drifting my way as he shifted beneath his blanket. Dragging the saddlebags in front of the flap as silently as I could, I set my trap. Hopefully any would-be intruder would fall on their face, giving me time to bolt or fight back. Then I grabbed the extra blanket, settled onto the bedroll, and covered myself against the evening chill. Soon the soft sighs of deep sleep and the hooting of owls were the only noises in our small camp. I closed my eyes, thanking the Goddess for this chance to explore the world and prayed that I had made the right choice, then drifted off to sleep.

———

PANIC GRIPPED my body as I ran for my life. My legs were sluggish, and a scream tore from my throat as I tried to pump them faster, to no avail. My inability to move allowed the man chasing me to close the distance between us, his dark cape flapping erratically behind him. I was suddenly pitched forward as the chain around my legs snapped taut, and shooting pain laced up my arms as I caught myself with my hands. A hand grabbed my hair, yanking roughly and dragging me to my knees. He tilted my head back so I looked directly into his hood as he towered over me. No face greeted me, but I knew his intentions were wicked. A rusty, serrated blade was at my throat a moment later. I whimpered as I realized I was about to die. I tried to pull away, but the knife bit into my neck and–

Warm blankets slipped from my body as I bolted upright, hand at my throat and gasping as I surfaced from the nightmare. I scanned the unfamiliar space around me, trying to remember where I was as my nightmare threatened to claw me back. A canvas tent sheltered me, and I lay on a small cot. Then the aroma of frying bacon and the low murmuring of male voices hit my senses. I took a deep breath.

I was safe. I was alive.

As safe as I could be as a lone female among eight powerful Fae males.

Stretching my arms and legs, I worked some movement into my stiff body, banishing the last of the nightmare. When I had them, they were so vivid, so real, that many times when I woke, my body felt as it had in the dream – tense and terrified.

To sleep unencumbered with the freedom to stretch my limbs was pure bliss. There was no way to sleep comfortably when bound in chains, each movement during the night scraping them together and jarring me awake. To sleep with a blanket was even better. For once, I didn't wake up with chattering teeth and icy skin. My tent was chilly, but beneath the two soft blankets, I was warm.

No one had bothered me overnight either, my bags lying undisturbed where I'd arranged them. Loathing to lose the warmth beneath the blankets, but stomach rumbling with hunger, I rose, deciding to face the males and fill my belly in case I needed to escape. I quickly changed into fresh clothes – also incredible – and emerged to discover soft morning light streaming through the red and orange leaves, nestling our small camp in its cheery embrace.

"Look who's awake." Kriztof's pear-colored eyes sparkled with amusement and a friendly smile showed off his straight teeth. "Bacon?" He held out the skillet, and I selected a few extra crispy slices, munching them as I surveyed the seating options.

Thankfully, only Kriztof was around, so I ambled to a log nearest the crackling fire, warming my hands without having to look over my shoulder. One by one, the other males stumbled from their tents, passing Kriztof on their way to the fire and collecting their morning meal of bacon and bread. Endre sat closest to me, rubbing sleep from his peridot eyes and brushing messy locks away from his face.

I subtly scooted away, though the male seemed to be unaware of my presence, as if sleep still had him in her claws. Through the flames, I watched the twins and Viktor eat, the three of them paying no attention to me either. Minutes passed, yet there was no sign of Kazimir or Cazius.

Before long, each male moved in a different direction to break camp, shattering our slice of peace among the trees. Viktor took down the tents, the twins packed our bags, Kriztof cleaned up breakfast, and Vadim doused the fire. Endre saddled the horses, the twins handing him bag after bag. They seemed to have a system, each male playing his part in this routine.

Though I did not trust them, I could be helpful and potentially earn some goodwill. "What can I do?" I asked no one in particular.

Vadim tossed over his shoulder, "Don't worry about it today. We're almost done here, but next time we camp, I'll teach you how to build a fire."

Learning any skills would assist in my survival. The more I knew about the world around me, the safer I would be. "Deal," I replied.

Kazimir and Cazius returned from deep in the autumn wood, heads bent together as they spoke in hushed tones. They went straight to the horses, tucking a paper away in one of the saddlebags. Their voices were too low for me to hear, but the set of Cazius's shoulders revealed tension.

I still had not moved from my earlier position, waiting cautiously to see what happened next.

"Izidora, let's get going," Kazimir called to me.

I walked to the beautiful black horse I had ridden with Kazimir the day before, rubbing his nose before acknowledging Kazimir's outstretched hand. With an internal cringe, I grasped his arm and let him haul me up in front of him, where my legs groaned in protest at the uncomfortable position. They still ached from our ride the previous day, especially with how hard I had gripped the saddle in hope that I wouldn't fall off or slide backwards into the hard body of the male behind me. With a click of his tongue, Kazimir instructed Fek to walk, and we led the way onto the main road.

I'd rather risk my neck riding alone than sit before a male with questionable intent.

"Is it okay if I ask questions while we ride today?" If I was sticking it out with them for now, I might as well learn what I could.

"I will try to answer everything I can," his rich voice rumbled behind me, his tone warm and inviting.

"Okay," I started. "What is my father like?"

Kriztof barked a laugh. "Fucking Fates, she started with the biggest question didn't she?"

With a grunt of acknowledgement, Kazimir said, "Zalan has been the King of the Night Realm for a very long time. Fae can live for hundreds of years, but he is pushing the limits of that right now. He was already an old Fae when you were born, and he has no other children. Many speculate that he has hung on all this time in hopes of seeing you at least once before he dies."

"I don't know how I feel about that," I murmured.

"There's no reason to make a judgment right now. You have time," he assured me.

Cazius added, "I have served the king for almost a hundred years. He was good to his people, in his prime. Everyone had more than enough to go around, and we had long stretches of peace with the other realms. It was only after you were born that relations became tense. He accused the other realms of colluding against him to take you. Children are rare for Fae because it takes so long to conceive. None of the other monarchs have children yet."

He dodged any explanation of my father's current state. I let it slide. "And what of my mother?" I inquired.

"Queen Liessa was beautiful and beloved by the people. She was gentle and kind. She spent time giving back to the poorest Fae in the Night Realm. Zalan was jealous of the attention she gave them and couldn't stand her philanthropy. Theirs was not a love match. Zalan saw her when we traveled through her village on the way to the Crystal Realm. He was mesmerized by her beauty and bade us to stop so he could speak with her. We stayed there for three days while he showered her with gifts and attention. When he asked for her hand, she couldn't refuse a king, so she joined our convoy to the Crystal Realm. They married once we returned to Vaenor a month later," Cazius explained.

"Do I look like her?" I asked.

"Your hair is the same chestnut color as hers, and she had the same high cheekbones and heart shaped face. There are many portraits of her in Este Castle if you want to see them for yourself when we get there. But your aquamarine eyes are a mystery to me. Most Night Fae have varying shades of green," Kazimir noted.

They spoke about her in past tense. "How did my mother die?"

A string of curses fled Kazimir's lips behind me and the whole group seemed to lose some of its luster.

Cazius was the first to speak. "I'm so sorry, Princess Izidora, but your mother died shortly after your birth. It was a hard labor, and she lost a lot of blood. Your kidnappers stole you from her dying arms."

Bile rose in my throat at the idea of bringing a life into this world only to sacrifice my own. Then to lose the baby to violent strangers mere moments later? My heart sank for my mother and the physical and emotional agony she had experienced leading up to the moment of her death.

Rather than dwell on events out of my control, I changed the subject. "What are the other realms like?"

It was Viktor's turn to chime in. "The Iron Fae are ruthless motherfuckers. I am fairly certain they were the ones holding you captive in that cave. Fire and earth are in their blood, and the finest craftsmen on the continent reside in their realm. The weapons made by their royal smiths are near priceless. They are also impervious to iron, which is the only way to bind the magic of other Fae."

From what I had noticed in my short time with these males, they all had varying shades of dark hair and green eyes, unlike the males and females I had gained a few glimpses at while I was chained.

"What do they look like? I've only seen Fae occasionally, and most were the females." Kazimir tensed behind me, his shift in energy sending my heart plummeting before bottoming out once I reminded myself he was angry about what had happened to me, not angry with me.

"The males are broad and muscular, more so than the rest of us. It often makes them slower, but their strength is unmatched. They usually have dark eyes and hair. The females are tall and lean but no less deadly than the males. Both fight in the king's army in near equal numbers," Viktor explained.

"The other realms are Day and Crystal. They are the opposite of the Night and Iron Realms because the Goddess requires balance in this world. Day Fae are fueled by the sun as we are fueled by the stars and moon. From their golden hair and darkened skin, you could mistake them for the midnight sun as they blur by you. They are vicious and relentless fighters who value a true warrior's death over anything."

"The Crystal Fae use air and water magic and are gifted with clairvoyance. You will recognize them immediately from their nearly white hair. They are ostentatious people who love finery and decorum. No talk of business before they have been wined and dined."

Viktor was thorough and serious in his explanation, and he offered up information willingly, unlike my captors who always extracted such a painful price.

My next question was precarious, but I needed to know the answer. It had weighed on my mind since we landed in Zanin two nights before. "How do you know that I am the person you've been looking for?"

Cazius cut in immediately, his voice firm with conviction. "Two things. One, the heavy guard and remote location where we found you. Two, I knew from one look at you that your mother was Queen Liessa. You are also around the right age."

A soft breeze pulled at loose strands of my hair while I processed all this new information. My legs softened around the saddle, allowing my hips to sway in time with Fek's steady walk. We traveled silently for a time, the Nighthounds content to ride to the music of the whispering wind and babbling brook.

I sensed Kazimir's desire to say something, but before he could, I blurted, "How did you find me in the dark? The guards there used torches to navigate the darkness."

"Night Fae are blessed with starlight and can create floating orbs that illuminate the way. When I heard you moving, I followed the sound until I found you," Kazimir explained.

My curiosity was piqued. "What other magical abilities do we have?"

Beside us, Endre sat straighter in his saddle, lighting up in a way I hadn't seen him do before. "Well, there's lots you can do with the magic we have. Each of us has different gifts and aptitudes since our magic is Goddess-gifted and based on the energy of the world around us. For example, I use my magic to heal the injured creatures we meet on our journeys. Each of the Nighthounds has a different set of magical skills, which is what makes us such a great team."

I wondered what magical affinities I had, and if accessing them would imbue me with the strength to kill anyone who dared lay another hand on me with ill intent.

"Will you teach me to wield my magic?"

"Absolutely," Kazimir promised. "You need to learn if you are going to survive in this world. We will teach you what we can. I am particularly gifted with manipulating shadows and blending in, but we all have an advanced level of combat magic like creating shields and casting shapes to block or redirect opponents." Kazimir's body was uncomfortably close to mine by the time he finished speaking, and I arched my back before craning my neck over my shoulder to look at him.

Holding a sincere grin on my face, I breathed, "I can't wait."

His emerald eyes glittered back at me, holding a spark of fervent hope that sent heat across my body. I hurriedly faced forward before the flush that climbed from my chest reached my face.

We stopped frequently throughout the day so I could stretch my legs and sip from the endless creek bubbling alongside the packed-dirt road. Though the road remained largely the same, bending one way and then another, time seemed to pass in a blur of autumn leaves. As the day wore on, my tense shoulders dropped further from my ears, and I relaxed deeper into the saddle. I glanced behind me at the last horse tied to Endre's black mount, her back piled with leather bags and rolled blankets.

I needed to learn to ride so I could put space between myself and the males. Though with my legs feeling more like stone with each passing minute, I wasn't sure I could ride on my own anytime soon.

"Where are we stopping next?" I asked.

"A small town called Kirody. There are many towns along the Northern Route, and you will get to see most of them on our journey. However, it is imperative that you do not reveal your identity to anyone," Cazius instructed. His somber gaze fell over the males. "I expect your lips not to be loosened with drink when we stop either."

Zekari and Kirigin groaned and rolled their eyes while Kriztof exclaimed, "Vadim always starts it!"

I giggled as the males accused each other of various offenses.

"That's enough!" Cazius shouted. "While I normally humor you, this is a critical mission. Do not fuck this up."

The Nighthounds straightened immediately under the weight of Cazius's words.

Hot breath tickled the back of my neck as Kazimir huffed a soft laugh behind me. "Your safe return to the castle is our number one priority. My father takes his duty very seriously. We've been on missions together for the better part of nearly two decades, and the fact that we finally rescued you has him taking extra precautions. Heed his words and stay close to us."

I nodded in acknowledgment.

"We should be there shortly," Cazius stated.

As we cleared a deep bend in the red dirt track, the wood-paneled homes of Kirody came into view. Tension rolled off each of the Nighthouds, each male coiled and ready to strike at the barest hint of danger. Kazimir gripped the reins tighter in his fists, the thick leather rubbing against my sides as he scanned our surroundings for any threats.

The townspeople went about their business, not paying any attention to our approaching party. We passed through a small, cobbled square in the center of the city, then halted in front of a two-story wood and stone lodge.

Cazius swung his leg over his horse's back, tossing the reins to Vadim before striding inside. Fek shifted from hoof to hoof beneath us while we waited. A few minutes later, Cazius returned, aiming for Kazimir. "We can stay here for the night, but there are only a handful of rooms available. We'll have to triple up."

"That's no problem. After we get the horses settled we can draw straws. Where are the stables?" Kazimir asked.

His father pointed down a narrow alley between the lodge

and what looked like a tavern. "Around back. There's enough room for all of them."

My weight shifted to the side as Kazimir dismounted, my aching legs unable to grip the saddle and right myself. I was almost too tired to care when his hands gripped my waist and lowered me to the ground. Handing me Fek's reins, he grabbed Cazius's horse from Vadim and guided us down the alley. The stallion shot me a sideways glance with his big dark eyes, then walked behind the other horses like he was leading me instead of the other way around. When the stables appeared at the end of the alley, I mimicked the males and handed the reins over to a young stablehand who led Fek to where the other horses were being unsaddled.

Kazimir picked up a handful of hay, breaking the pieces in half and then shuffling the pieces around so they appeared even in his fist. "Whoever gets similar sized pieces will share a room. Who wants to draw first?"

I chewed on my lip as the males selected straws from his outstretched fist. The tempo of my heart increased as that bundle of hay drew closer to where I stood in the semi-circle of males. Sharing a room with one, let alone two or three, males set my nerves on fire and palms sweating with the desire to fight tooth and nail.

But Kazimir did not offer a straw to me.

Everyone opened their palms, comparing the sizes. "Goddess damn it, Vadim snores so loud," Kriztof grumbled when he held up his straw, similar in size to both Vadim's and Viktor's.

The twins and Endre sniggered and sautered toward the slightly ajar door leading into the adjacent building.

"What about your father and me?" I asked Kazimir.

"The three of us will room together," he stated, his tone leaving no room for argument.

Trying to calm my rising panic, I inhaled deeply through my

nose and released a subtle breath through my mouth. Two days of riding in front of the male did not prepare me for the idea of sleeping in the same room as him, no barrier between us. Weariness pulled at my bones, and I didn't know if I was capable of staying awake all night to ward off any potential attacks. As my mind screamed at me to turn and run, I was corralled among the males in the direction of the adjacent tavern.

Too late to run now.

The aroma of apples spiced with cinnamon greeted us as we entered the cozy space. No other patrons graced the tables, and a fire roared in a stone hearth off to one side. I sniffed the air, my mouth watering as the warm scent intensified with each step deeper inside.

Kazimir caught my eye, and with a hint of amusement asked, "Do you want some pie?"

"Is that what I'm smelling?" Gone were my worries over my sleeping arrangement, my stomach overriding my brain.

He chuckled and approached the counter. "I'll have two pies and a round of ale please." The barmaid nodded and scurried off to the kitchen to fetch our order. Viktor found a large round table near the fire, and I sat down with a groan. My legs and ass were bruised and sore, and I wanted nothing more than to put up my feet. I dragged a chair from the table behind us and draped myself across the two, unconcerned what the others thought of me.

The barmaid arrived with a tray full of ales. Then, she returned carrying two steaming pies and slid them to the middle of our table. Finally, she brought dishes and silverware. The sweet scent rising from the middle of our table was decadent, warm, and homey. With each passing day since my rescue, I had discovered new sights, smells, and sounds, each unlike anything I could have dreamed up in the void that surrounded me all those years.

Endre pulled the pies to him and cut them into neat triangles. Heaping slice after slice of the dripping dessert, he passed plates down and around the table. Once a slice finally landed in front of me, Kazimir warned, "Wait before you attack the pie. You'll burn your mouth if you try to eat it now."

His warning came too late, as I had already shoveled the warm gooey goodness into my mouth.

My eyes bulged, and I opened my mouth to suck in cool air. The males roared with laughter, but the heat in my mouth overtook any heat in my cheeks. Viktor nudged my ale closer to me, hinting that it would help. Hands grasping either side of the glass mug, I gulped down the bitter liquid, the cool temperature easing the burn in my mouth and forcing the pieces down my throat. Ale spilled out of the corners of my mouth, and once I came up for air, I coughed and swiped with the back of my hand.

Kriztof wiped tears from his eyes as the laughter died down. "Don't be embarrassed, everyone does the same thing with their first pie."

I ducked my head, definitely embarrassed. I waited until Kazimir picked up a fork to eat his pie before attempting another bite. The sweet and gooey apples coated in cinnamon were paired perfectly with a flaky and slightly salty crust. Forkful after forkful entered my mouth until the slice disappeared completely from my plate.

"Pass me your plate, and I'll get you another," Endre reached out his hand, so I slid my plate across the polished wood surface toward him. He heaped another portion before passing it back to me. Having learned my lesson, I tested the interior with my finger, deciding it was cool enough to eat.

The males chatted amongst themselves, and I was content to sit and listen while more dessert passed between my lips. My ale remained untouched in front of me, the bitter taste not enticing enough to venture another sip. A slight dizziness buzzed in my brain, and I relaxed more than I ever had before, falling into the conversations around me.

Was this what it felt like to have friends?

A lull settled over me from my full belly and the roaring fire at my back. Sleep called to me like a siren's song, my body exhausted from riding and the excitement of the previous two days. I wanted to rest as much as I could before Kazimir and Cazius came to our room, because I knew I would not sleep with them there.

Intent on time alone, I stood but stumbled slightly into Kazimir, who caught me with a hand on my hip. Whether it was the ale or something more, I did not shrink away from his light touch.

He chuckled, "Here, let me take you to our room. I suspect that's the first time you had ale, and I don't want you to hurt yourself walking up the stairs alone."

His huge frame towered over me as he stood, and promising the others he'd return shortly, he guided me from the tavern to the lodge next door with one arm draped over my shoulders. Up the stairs on the second floor, he pulled out a key and unlocked the door at the end of a long hallway. He gestured for me to enter ahead of him, and I did, keeping an eye on him in my periphery.

"The bathroom is through that door if you want to wash up before going to bed. My father and I need to discuss a few things, so we will be up in a few hours. Feel free to pick a bed. If you need anything, we'll be right downstairs."

A bath sounded nice, especially after camping the previous night. "Can you help me draw a bath before you go?"

"Absolutely," he smiled and strode into the bathroom. Water splashed against stone, and after rummaging through my bag and finding clean clothes, I ambled into the small bathroom. Our close proximity did not even bother me.

Was that because of the ale?

Kazimir glanced up. "Stick your hand in and tell me when it's warm enough for you."

My hand swished circles in the water until it heated to the point of scalding. I'd never had a warm bath before; the water used for my monthly bathing had been nearly ice. "It feels good now," I announced.

Turning some knobs attached to the tub, he shut off the flow of water. When he turned to leave, I blurted, "I feel like a child, without knowledge of the world around me. I'm sorry I can't help with simple tasks and have so many questions."

I looked at my feet, rolling my toe over a knot in the wood floor as I waited for his response.

He took a step toward me, lifting my chin with his finger. I blinked rapidly to hide the tears forming in my eyes as his emerald pools drank me in with a glint of something I couldn't place. The touch was so gentle, so tender, so unlike any touch I'd received before. It felt foreign, but I wanted to lean into the comforting touch he offered.

But could I trust him? Could I trust any male?

"Why would we expect you to know anything, given that you spent the last twenty-one years of your life in chains? What happened to you was awful, Izidora, and I'm certain I don't know the full extent of it. I'm here when you're ready to share. But for now, go easy on yourself, yeah?"

His words struck a chord deep in my soul, one that craved validation and acceptance. I closed my eyes, willing the tears not to fall. "I needed to hear that," I admitted, my voice quavering.

"If you need anything else, I'll be downstairs or next door. Remember your hat if you do leave the room," he reminded me.

His finger left my skin, though the spot he'd touched still

burned long after. The door clicked shut softly behind him, and his heavy step faded down the hall.

The moment I was certain he was not returning, I stripped out of my dusty traveling clothes and sank into the deep tub. The warm water was almost as heavenly as the apple pie. My relieved sigh echoed around the small space as the warmth seeped into my weary bones. Only once the water chilled did I begin to move. Grabbing a lavender-scented bar from a ledge near the tub, I scrubbed every inch of my hair and skin and watched layers of grime float away until I was clean.

Once I'd dried off and squeezed as much water out of my long chestnut hair as I could, I crawled into the smallest bed, pushed against a wall, and piled extra blankets around me to create a cocoon. Back against the wall, my lids began drooping as the lavender and warm water took their effects. My exhaustion was so deep that I did not hear Kazimir or Cazius return to our room, despite my last conscious thoughts warning me to stay awake.

6

KAZIMIR

My father and I spoke deep into the night about our route to Vaenor, Izidora, and what may await us upon our arrival at Este Castle. Cutthroat nobles would try to exploit her innocence without hesitation in order to increase their station or favor with King Zalan. She needed instruction, guidance, and protection if she were to survive court intrigue. We only had seven short weeks to prepare her for what was to come.

The rhythmic sway of Fek's back while we rode lulled me into a favorite daydream, one where we returned triumphant to Vaenor, Izidora in tow, and King Zalan promptly declared we were to marry. She had fallen in love with me on our return journey and was thrilled with her father's proposition. Wine flowed freely as the whole Night Realm celebrated our engagement and shortly thereafter, our wedding.

My reverie was broken by a slight shake of the saddle in front of me. Izidora's laugh was light and airy, filling her whole body as she tipped her head toward the sky, releasing the most beautiful sound I had ever heard into the woods around us. I wanted to hear more of it, more of her.

The day's entertainment was stories of misadventures, narrated by an animated and dramatic Kirigin.

"... and then Zekari thought it would be a good idea to switch back to confuse the poor Lady even more!"

The twins used to have a game of bait and switch, seeing if those seated beside them at formal gatherings would notice if they switched places. As Knights, they were not seated among the High Houses, but the unfortunate Fae seated around them were nonetheless infuriated when they realized they had been duped.

As the laughter died down, I threw a question to the group, hoping to generate some ideas. "Navigating the politics of the Night Realm is tricky for anyone who grew up around it, let alone someone who did not. What are the most important things Izidora needs to know before we reach Este Castle?"

Endre answered first. "Don't show weakness. The castle is full of predators waiting to take you down or blackmail you."

Kriztof chimed in, "Know who can take a joke and who will want you beheaded for one." That spurred a chuckle from the group.

"She needs to know how to fight, and fight fucking well," Vadim declared.

"And she needs to wield her magic, whatever that turns out to be. The people won't respect a weak-magicked Fae on the throne," Endre added.

"Good point," I agreed. "Keep thinking. We have about seven weeks before we reach Vaenor."

I called for a rest stop. We had a long road ahead of us and I wasn't in a rush to reach our destination. Leading Fek to the stream along the road, I let him drink and graze among our other mounts while I refilled my waterskin. The crisp liquid refreshed me as I wandered through the autumn forest, a dusting of fallen leaves crunching beneath my boots. Izidora approached me as I was admiring a particularly beautiful oak tree.

"I want to learn all of that and more. I want to be strong. I don't ever want to be taken advantage of again." Her aquamarine eyes were set with grim determination. Though she still did not trust us, she spoke more often, laughed more freely, and slowly relaxed more with each passing hour. Her spirit remained unbroken, despite the horrors she had alluded to enduring in captivity. She was a fighter, and I knew she would excel at all of this and more. If being chained and abused hadn't fractured her into a million pieces, nothing ever would.

I turned to look at her, a solemn promise filling my soul. "We will make you the fiercest warrior this kingdom has ever known."

An impish grin stretched from ear to ear, a glimmer of savagery breaking through the walls she'd built. Her teeth flashed, and for a moment I saw the wildcat inside that had helped her survive. She didn't need to be coddled – it was time for her to claw her way out of the darkness. "You won't be riding with me anymore. It's time you learned to ride by yourself."

Her eyes sparkled with excitement. I wanted to keep the momentum going, to keep her spirit soaring while she flew high above her pain. Grasping Izidora's hand, I directed us to the glen where the horses grazed. Mistik, our pack horse, picked her head up as we approached, as if she sensed her new rider. Shuffling bags around until weight was evenly distributed across all our mounts, I cinched Mistik's saddle.

Once I finished, I patted her dapple gray hide and instructed, "You take care of your new rider, okay? There will be plenty of apples for you later if you do." An excited nicker rumbled from the mare, and I chuckled to myself. Izidora and Mistik would get along just fine.

Izidora stood, arms crossed, as I worked. When I motioned

her over, she approached the mare, offering a sugar cube and gently rubbing her nose. Once they were acquainted, I demonstrated how to mount a horse. "You might not be able to reach the stirrups comfortably yet, so I will give you a boost this time. But eventually you will learn how to get up on your own."

A jerk of her head and the thin line of her lips told me she was ready.

Lacing my fingers together and turning my palms up, I created a cup for her boot. She braced an arm on my shoulder as I heaved her upward, and she swung her other leg over Mistik's back. With a slightly awkward landing, she was in the saddle. She shuffled back and forth until she was comfortably seated, then I shortened the stirrups to fit her petite stature.

"Now, hold the reins in both hands. Mistik will most likely follow along, but you need to know how to direct her where you want to go. Pull to the left for her to go left. Pull to the right for her to go right. Pull back with both hands to break. Gently push your heels into her sides to go forward. Make sense?" I asked.

"Got it." The grin that pulled at her pink lips was devastating, and coupled with the fierce tenacity of her heart, I knew every previous fantasy of her was nothing compared to the real female in front of me.

The rest of the Nighthounds had gathered and mounted their steeds, so I patted Mistik one last time before mounting Fek and leading us back to the red dirt road. Izidora confidently guided Mistik forward onto the road, angling her so she could ride alongside me once we were underway.

"I'm doing it!" she exclaimed. A whooping cheer of deep voices celebrated alongside her.

My father chuckled, "Well done. Now let's see if you can stay on for a few hours."

7

IZIDORA

Riding by myself was harder than I anticipated. Walking was fine – I'd done that on Fek for three days. Mistik plodded along diligently, not needing much input from me as we traveled in a group. My legs already trembled from days of riding, but keeping my feet tucked into the stirrups proved to be yet another challenge for my weakened muscles.

Once I could steer Mistik and keep my feet in the stirrups, we trotted. The jarring landing on my ass when I missed a beat bruised it deeper, and I let out a stream of curses each time my tailbone smacked against the firm leather saddle.

But I did not give up, determined to find the right rhythm and sync with the horse beneath me. The sooner I mastered this, the sooner I had a means of escape. Princess or no, being trapped against my will again was something I had no interest in, and I wanted the skills to flee if necessary.

Viktor coached me through trotting while the others watched with barely contained laughter. "Tomorrow we will try cantering," he said as we stopped for the day.

"We're laughing with you, not at you," Kriztof teased at one point.

They all cheered once I trotted without bouncing around like a ball let loose by a small child. A moment of unbridled joy slipped past my barrier, and instead of discouraging and demeaning me, they shared in my excitement and welcomed my accomplishment. It felt like they truly wanted me to succeed. A hint of trust bloomed within my heart, and I cautiously hoped I was truly free of my chains.

A large copse of trees hid us from the worn dirt road. As I pushed up on my stirrups, preparing to dismount, my legs began wobbling dangerously, threatening to pitch me off my horse. I managed to lay my body across Mistik's back and then slid slowly to the ground, using my arms to lower myself onto shaky feet. Even my arms screamed from gripping the reins and steering the mare along the path. My whole body shook as I walked, and I felt like a newborn deer taking its first steps. I led Mistik to Endre, who tended the other mounts, and handed him the reins.

Vadim called out to me as I turned away from Endre. "I promised to show you how to make a fire at our next camp, and that time has come. Bring some of those dried branches under your feet over here."

I bent to pick up an armful of twigs and pine needles, legs protesting on the way down and on the way up. With a groan, I carried my bundle to where Vadim had cleared a spot in the earth. "Now, go find some large rocks. We need to make a circle around the fire to protect the rest of the wood."

Was he trying to punish me for something? I could barely feel my legs, and each wobbly step threatened to throw me to the ground, never to rise again. Somewhere between a waddle and a walk, I hunted the surrounding area until my arms were filled with lumpy rocks. When I returned to Vadim, a few large logs had been split and shaped into a circular tent.

"Put the rocks in a circle here." He motioned around the

outer edge of his pile. One by one, I arranged them in a circle, then Vadim adjusted a few until they were in perfect alignment. "Now, take the brush you gathered earlier and stuff it under here." He pointed to the log tent and I did as instructed.

"Now what?" I asked, hoping he wouldn't send me on another mission to find supplies that could be anywhere in the forest.

"Now, we make fire." He rubbed his hands together with a mischievous glint in his evergreen eyes.

"Don't be such a pyromaniac," called Kriztof from where he and Viktor struck tent poles into the ground.

"Normally I would use magic to light the fire, but since you haven't tapped into your magic yet I will show you another way." He drew a dagger from his boot, then picked up one of the brown-gray rocks I'd found. "You need a dagger and a rock that looks like this. Then you place them near the dried brush and strike." He demonstrated and sparks flew between the rock and dagger, dried brush catching and smoking as the sparks rained over them.

He offered the dagger and rock to me. "Your turn."

I gripped the dagger, pointing it toward the ground while holding the rock in my other hand. My first strike yielded no sparks. Frowning, I tried again. This time a little orange spark flew between the two, my heart leaping in time with the ember. My subsequent strikes were no better, and eventually Vadim grabbed the hand I used to hold the rock and changed the angle. His unexpected touch caused me to jerk my hand back and drop the rock. Yet he remained patient, not even acknowledging my reaction as I retrieved it. This time, he turned my wrist with light fingers, not lingering on my skin.

"Try it again," he encouraged.

I struck and, to my surprise, a shower of sparks dusted the dry brush, fire erupting across them.

"Bend down close and blow softly to stoke the fire. You don't want to blow so hard that the fire goes out, though."

I crouched, blowing slowly through pursed lips. The fire leaped, and more of the brush caught. Dusting my hands off, I sat back on my heels, grinning at my victory.

"Well done!" exclaimed Vadim.

A circle of tents surrounded us by the time the main logs caught fire. Blades of sunlight streamed through the trees, setting the wood aglow with soft light. I reclined against a downed log beside the fire, my legs protesting any further movement until they had time to rest. Savoring the crisp and earthy air, I deeply inhaled the scents of the surrounding forest. I always longed for adventure far away from the cave, to discover the world beyond hard stone walls and darkness. No matter what I was or was not told, a small spark hidden deep in my mind knew that life had always waited just out of reach.

I was still unsure of my place in this group, in this world outside the cave. I was still wary of trusting these males completely. But I had to admit they were growing on me. Not once had I truly feared for my life since they had rescued me. None of them had laid a hand on me in anger. None had screamed at me, demeaned me, told me I was worthless, useless, or only good as a whore. None had forced themselves on me. I even shared a room with Kazimir and Cazius without incident. They were kind, respectful, helpful, and sincere. All foreign concepts, things I had never truly experienced before.

Was this what normal Fae were like?

Then there was Kazimir.

Of all the Nighthounds, he showed the most interest in me. Always watching. Always waiting. Always the first to help. Respectful, and yet I sensed there was something more behind his attention. His steady presence was almost comforting and his smoky wood and amber scent familiar. I had been glad to ride on my own, but a small part of me missed the warmth of his large frame at my back, encircling me in a wall of safety.

I closed my eyes, tuning into the sounds of the autumn wood around me. Birds chirped and sang to one another, echoing their songs back and forth among the treetops. A small stream trickled nearby, water flowing over rock. A soft breeze rustled leaves and scraped bare branches against one another.

A deep breath filled my lungs with crackling fire, musky horse, and a hint of amber. I remained like that for a while, grounding myself through my senses. When I opened my eyes, I found others dozing in the cozy midafternoon sun.

The sun was glorious. After years in the dark, I never imagined the stunning hues that changed throughout the day, or the touch of warmth across my pale skin. It was already pinkening my hands, face, and chest as I basked in its glory.

Kazimir was awake, watching the trees around us. When he saw me stir, he motioned for me to approach. I stood, stretching my arms and stiff legs. "I thought I could teach you to tap into your magic," he said. "Let's go further out into this clearing."

Checking over my shoulder to make sure someone saw us leave, I followed him, butterflies filling my stomach as we left the rest of the group behind. The thought of unlocking the power that lay slumbering within me was exhilarating.

Once we were out of earshot, Kazimir spun to face me. "First, you must learn to control your breath. Magic responds to emotion, and control over magic starts with control over your emotions," he began, sitting cross-legged among the colorful leaves coating the forest floor.

I settled myself in front of him, adopting a similar posture, hands on my knees, spine tall, gaze soft.

"Follow my voice as we go through the exercise. Inhale for four counts, hold, then exhale for four counts, hold, then repeat. We're going to do this ten times. Any questions?"

"I got it," I replied, allowing my eyes to close softly.

"Inhale, one... two... three... four... hold... exhale, four... three... two... one... hold. Inhale..." he repeated ten times, and I settled into the steady rhythm, all thoughts and worries drifting from my mind as it melded with my body.

"Sigh out all the air left in your lungs..."

I let every last bit of air go.

"Tune into your body, and search for the source of your magic. Night Fae magic is like shimmering moonlight, a glittering silver thread that winds through your body. You should feel it in the center of your chest."

Turning my gaze inward, I scanned my body for the shimmering light Kazimir described. When I found the source of my magic, my brows pulled together in a frown. A spear of crystal wrapped in ribbons of glittering silver and bathed in white flame rested in the center of my chest.

Something must have been broken inside me.

My eyes burned at the thought. I wanted to be powerful – with both magic and strength. What if this difference prevented me from using magic? Were the guards right, was I truly worthless and useless?

Kazimir watched me, his eyes like daggers slicing my skin as he waited. With a sigh, I opened my eyes.

"Did you find it?" he inquired.

"I did, but it seems small compared to what you were talking about," I murmured. I couldn't trust him with the information that I was different. Who knew what he would think or do if I told him the truth. Perhaps they would all reject me. Perhaps they would send me back to my cave prison cell. I clenched and unclenched my fists, cursing myself for lowering my wall, opening my heart, for being vulnerable. Only pain came from that.

As if Kazimir could hear my inner spiral, he soothed, "The

well will grow the more you use it. It's like building muscle. It takes time and practice. But one day you will have a deep well to draw from."

"Okay," I shrugged, not totally believing him.

"Reconnect with your breath, then tune into that spot again. You need a technique to call your magic to the surface, which helps you ground it. I flick my fingers, but everyone's call is different. Lean into whatever feels natural for you," Kazimir instructed.

I closed my eyes, breathing and searching for the magic I had discovered before. An itch to flick my thumb against my finger emerged. When I performed the motion, the well of magic in my chest flared to life, and pure white energy flooded my palms. Beautiful starlike energy floated there, and I brought one of my hands up to my face, studying the undulating magic circling my hand and slipping through my fingers.

It was breathtaking.

Kazimir stepped closer, reaching for my hand. I was so preoccupied with the radiant light that I didn't notice him reach for my hand; the second his hand met mine, I snatched it back, and the light extinguished. We both sat in awkward silence for a moment before Kazimir cleared his throat. "Your magic is very powerful. That was incredible for your first time summoning it."

I blushed. His compliment was nice, but I had no idea how to respond to it.

"What's next?" I asked, wanting to dispel my discomfort.

"You don't have any problem summoning magic, so let's try maintaining and manipulating it by creating shapes. Let me know when you start getting tired, and we will stop for the day."

Nodding, I brought the white energy back into existence.

"Try to make a ball with the light," Kazimir instructed. I concentrated on the image of a round ball in my mind, and the white energy started to take shape. "Good, now make it bigger."

I imagined the ball growing to the approximate size of Kazimir's head. My magic flared bright and hot, too quickly, causing me to jump in and let it go. I huffed out my frustration. "I'm useless if I can't even make a damn ball."

Kazimir frowned as he knelt across from me. "You are learning something completely new. You will fail more times than you can count before you master it. I don't expect you to get every step perfectly the first time."

I nodded, hearing but not quite agreeing with his words. How was I supposed to survive in this world when I was already so far behind? Seven weeks was not nearly long enough to prepare me for the duty of being a princess and the expectations others would have for me. But I never gave up on myself, despite the biting words, stinging whips, and sharp slices that marred my skin for any disobedience. I would not give up now. "I'll try again."

This time, the flick of my fingers was all I needed to bring the white energy roaring back. I focused on the ball in my mind's eye, then slowly imagined it growing in size. The energy responded in kind, growing at a slower rate as I focused wholly on the process rather than the end result. My victory sang in my blood as it reached the correct size.

"Now try a square," Kazimir instructed.

We went on for almost an hour, Kazimir calling out shapes and sizes for me to try, before I started to feel drained. "I don't think I can go much longer than this," I finally admitted once I was unable to create the form of a leaf I'd picked up off the ground.

"You lasted much longer than I expected you to," Kazimir beamed, a hint of pride in his deep voice.

I gave him a soft smile. "Thanks for the encouragement."

Normally, my emotions were locked behind an iron wall, inaccessible unless I fought for my life. Tapping into my magic chiseled a crack into that wall, creating an opening for them to slip through and take the reins where I would otherwise completely smother them.

Would using magic continue to fracture that wall until it crumbled into dust?

What would happen when all my demons were let loose?

"You are most welcome, Izidora. Let's walk back and see if Zekari and Kirigin caught dinner," he replied.

My inner debate about whether to reveal my different magic followed us back to camp, lingering on my shoulder as I found a place around the fire among the band of brothers who had released me from my chains. Little did they know, the chains were not the only broken thing about me.

8

KAZIMIR

zidora's magic was different. There were no better words to describe it. It behaved like Night Fae magic, pure energy manipulated into different forms, and yet it looked nothing like mine or that of any of the Nighthounds. Our magic was a shimmering and undulating silver that flowed like water over our fingers. Izidora's was pure white energy, blindingly bright, and yet I couldn't tear my eyes away from its ethereal luminosity.

Her internal conflict played out on her face as she struggled to tap into her power. With all her trauma, it made sense that tapping into her magic might bring unwanted emotions to the surface. She kept a vice-like grip on anything and everything she could; letting go would be a challenge for her. Yet she managed to master everything I threw at her once she overcame her initial struggle.

As we walked back into camp, the Nighthounds were alert and chatting around the fire. I locked eyes with my father and motioned for him to follow me. He cocked a brow, and then rose, following me into his tent. As I closed the flap, Izidora settled next to Kriztof as he launched into another tale of misadventure that was certainly filled with embellishment.

My father patiently waited for me to divulge information I was still struggling to wrap my mind around.

"Izidora has powerful magic, unlike anything I have ever seen or studied," I started. "It is a pure white energy, almost as if the stars themselves have fallen into her palm."

My father frowned, a furrow in his brow deepening. "What else?" he asked.

"I was mesmerized by it, and I reached out to take her hand to examine it more closely. When I touched her hand, she jerked away from me. She clearly doesn't like to be touched." It saddened me more than I liked to admit, especially since so many of my daydreams had her falling into my arms for comfort.

He pinched the bridge of his nose, a heavy sigh escaping him. "Keep teaching her, and report any other suspicious behavior from her magic back to me. Try not to push her too hard. With everything she's been through, tapping into her magic might trigger some dark emotions in her. Perhaps that's the cause of the color and power difference."

"Have you seen anything like this before?" I asked him.

"Never," he replied, "but I know there are those in the Royal Library who might have some answers. We will speak to them discreetly upon our return."

A fierce protectiveness washed over me. "Are you certain we can trust them with this? Everything surrounding her seems suspicious to me now. Iron Fae guarding her deep into the Agrenak Mountains? The fact that they kept her in the fucking dark for so long? I'm sure there is a whole host of other shit that went down she hasn't told us yet. I don't want to put her in harm's way again," I ground out through clenched teeth.

"We cannot protect her if we do not know how to help her,"

my father snapped. "It is a risk we will have to take. However, the head of the Royal Library has done extensive research of royal records to assist us before and I trust her with this task too."

I sighed, running my palm over my face. "I will keep a close eye on her magical progress. She mastered the basic shape-making exercises we teach young Fae for months in a matter of hours. I want to see how much she can pick up before we return. Every bit will help her." I lifted the tent flap, preparing to leave when I spotted Izidora with her head thrown back in a rhapsodic laugh. So far, the others had summoned joy from her, but I wanted to be the one who coaxed that side of her out. I wanted to be the only one she smiled at. I wanted to be the only one she sought out when she was struggling. I wanted to be her everything.

I sauntered over to the log adjacent to hers, studying her face as she listened to a story narrated by Kirigin. My father exited his tent, and warmth sparked in his eyes as he joined us around the fire, taking command of the skillet as Zekari was too involved in the story his twin retold to realize the meat was burning.

As my father finished cooking, I grabbed plates and wine-skins to share. We ate meals like a family, squabbling over the best cuts of meat, arguing over who was drinking too much, and laughing with each other. Every so often, I glanced at Izidora out of the corner of my eye, wondering if she felt as welcome as I wanted her to. Her smile was genuine, but it did not quite reach her eyes. Her chestnut hair strayed over her shoulder, so I reached out and brushed it onto her back. This time, she didn't jump, but turned to me, her pink lips slightly parted and corners of her mouth turned up. My heart thumped wildly as that one smile seared its way into my memory.

She was going to be my ruin; I had to have more.

WE ROSE WITH THE DAWN, the pink-streaked sky barely visible through the canopy of trees overhead. Izidora enthusiastically joined us in breaking camp, eager to learn and help.

She and Vadim worked together to break down the tents. Her small frame was no match for the long tent poles, and she smacked Vadim with them several times in her attempt to fold and pack them away. I chuckled when she turned one way, smacking him on the ass, and when he cursed, she turned the other way and whacked him in the stomach, causing him to double over. A horrified expression formed on her face, lips pulled into an O, cheeks flushed the color of the sky, and round eyes wide. She was so damn beautiful. She dropped the poles and apologized profusely as Vadim coughed and straightened, suggesting she help Endre saddle the horses instead. Needing no more encouragement, she hurried to Endre's side to escape her embarrassment. I couldn't tear my eyes from her as she squatted to lift the heavy leather saddles then perched on the tips of her toes to hoist them across our mounts' backs.

The road was as desolate as every other day, only the pounding of our horses' hooves heard down the endless dirt path. I angled Fek toward Vadim's horse as we walked along, wanting to enlist his help in training Izidora to fight. As much as I wanted to be her one and only, I knew Vadim was a better teacher and scrappier fighter than me. He worked alongside my father searching for Izidora for years before I joined the Nighthounds, and I knew he had a vested interest in Izidora's success, almost more than any of us.

"Since Izidora seems to have a knack for hitting you with sticks already, what would you say to training with her at night?" I teased.

"You saw that, did you?" Vadim smirked. "She's got a way with a pole, that's for sure."

I rolled my eyes at Vadim's jest. "Let's see what other weapons she has a way with so she can defend herself if something happens while we're on the road."

"Alright, alright don't get pissy with me," Vadim placated. "I've been searching for her just as long as you, remember? I don't want anything to happen to her either. Although I did get to fuck some lovely females over the years while we were looking for her, so that time wasn't a complete waste. And now it's your turn."

"What are you talking about?" I questioned, heart in my stomach at the thought of him knowing about my deepest fantasies.

"Don't be an ass. I see the way you watch her," Vadim ribbed, and then sauntered away toward Endre at the front before I could deny anything. "You pitch the tents tonight, and I will teach the ways of the sword to our princess!" he shouted over his shoulder.

What was wrong with me lately?

My jaw ached from the tension of holding back my words at Vadim's double-meaning jokes. The way he talked about teaching Izidora the way of the sword had me wanting to erase his smile right off his face. He knew my interest in her as well, which only served to piss me off more. Pulling up on Fek's reins, I slowed us so we fell to the rear of our traveling party, wanting space to think and calm down.

Fuck, I wanted Izidora. King Zalan was a controlling bastard, and I didn't believe for a second he would allow us to be together. He would marry her off to someone who suited his needs, taking no care for her own. My daydreams drifted to his death, an unfortunate horseback ride or a hint of nightshade dropped into his wine. He was old enough that a death in his sleep would not come as a surprise to many. If only...

The tall trees thinned as we drew closer to another town on the Northern Route. This far removed from Vaenor, Fae cared less about realm politics and more about how their neighbors fared. The people were friendly and welcoming, though with the lost princess in tow, anything could happen. Her story was nearing a legend with more than twenty-one years having passed since her abduction.

We stopped at the first tavern with a hitching post, securing our mounts before entering the establishment. The smell of freshly baked sweets and hearty stew beckoned us. We picked through the tables filled with Fae enjoying a midday meal until we reached one at the back of the tavern, trying to keep a low profile.

Bowls of a thick stew with chunks of vegetables were served along with a few baskets of rosemary bread, and we ate rapidly, the warm liquid heating us from the inside out.

Izidora sat across from me, and we locked eyes as she looked up from her plate. Her mouth was filled with a flaky chocolate pastry, and as she chewed, she offered me a small piece. I took it from her outstretched hand, careful not to touch her skin. Her small offering was enough to stoke the flames of hope in my chest – hope that she would feel the same toward me as I felt toward her. With each passing day, she softened and warmed, hardness disappearing from her expression and cracks appearing in her barricade.

I would do anything for her, and she had no idea. She could ask me to strip naked before the whole town and I would do it. She could ask me to free climb the peaks of the Agrenak Mountains and I would do it. All I wanted was for her to look at me like I was her savior, and she needed nothing else in this world.

It was an idea I'd been obsessed with long before I ever laid eyes on her.

And I would make damn sure it would come to pass.

I popped the piece in my mouth with a grin, pushing away my dark thoughts as I enjoyed a moment of her attention. Her kindness was a breath of fresh air; she had a fiery yet compassionate spirit that shone just a bit brighter with each step away from the cave. The more distance we put between us and her prison, the better, especially if it brought her out of hiding.

"Can we go to the market after this?" she asked. "I saw some clothing stalls on the way into town. It would be nice to have another change of clothes. Especially some warmer ones."

"I think that would be alright. What do you think, father?" I looked at him expectantly, hoping he'd say yes. Despite the risk, I wanted Izidora to be happy and to experience goodness in this world.

He drummed his fingers for a moment, considering the possibilities. "I am a little leery, but I think it will be safe," he finally decided.

"Thank you!" She grinned around the remaining chocolate pastry that was shoved into her mouth.

Our meal was finished, and we paid the barmaid, who examined Izidora a little longer than I liked. Izidora still wore pants and a loose tunic with a hat, but the boyish clothes couldn't hide her femininity.

Maybe I read into the interaction, but my gut sounded alarm bells regardless. Izidora bounced as we walked to the market, and despite my trepidation, I walked along behind her. Nothing bad could happen if we were all with her.

The Nighthounds fanned out as we entered the market, traipsing through the haphazardly placed stalls to cover more area with eyes and ears. Izidora and I wandered down the colorful row of clothing stalls, stopping here and there when a richly colored fabric caught her eye. Her tiny hands trailed across thick furs of every color, collected from animals in the not too distant mountains. I directed her to a stall selling leathers, a necessary addition to her wardrobe if she planned on training with Vadim.

I asked the shopkeeper for two pairs of firm leather pants and a chest plate in her size. He fetched the items, and also threw a set of cuffs on the pile. "She will be needing these too."

Shit, we weren't fooling anybody with her current attire.

I thanked and paid him, then steered Izidora away with a firm hand on her lower back. She flinched and walked a little faster to break contact with me. I withheld the protective growl warning her to stay close to me, knowing it would scare her and only serve to confirm her belief she could not trust us. She casually browsed a stall we'd stopped at before, picking up pieces to examine them more closely. Checking around us, I marked where my brothers in arms milled about the market, each nodding when we made eye contact.

Izidora decided on two wool tunics, one the color of the ocean at night and an iron gray one that reminded me of the walls of the cave we found her in.

"I know you!" the shopkeeper exclaimed just as I turned to pull coins out of my bag.

My hand snapped up and I pushed Izidora behind me instinctively. Viktor and Vadim noticed my reaction and quickly made their way behind the shopkeeper.

She continued, "You're the bunch that always breeze through here looking for tips on the lost princess. The Nighthounds! One time I told you I saw a girl staying with some Iron Fae the next town over, and you took off like a cat when it sees a mouse!"

I remembered that night, nearly ten years before. It turned out the Iron Fae were trafficking a young girl from another continent across the sea. We saved her life that night, but it wasn't Izidora.

The shopkeeper turned to Izidora. "You must have finally found her then? It would be my absolute honor to clothe the lost princess! Your money's no good, sir." She waved my hand away, then curtseyed to Izidora while a crowd gathered around us. Among them were the rest of the Nighthounds, scanning for a clear path of escape for us.

Shit, it was too soon for all of this.

As I scrambled to think of what to do, my father stepped in. He laughed, shaking his head and said, "We have looked for our lost princess for over twenty years now, but this is not her. You can see by her eyes, they are not the green of Night Fae. Sadly, I think the Iron Fae have started trafficking again. We rescued her from their clutches, just like we rescued that poor girl all those years ago. We're simply taking her back to Vaenor so we can send her home."

The shopkeeper's face fell then reddened at his explanation. "You are such brave souls, out here rescuing females while looking for our lost princess. Please accept these clothes as thanks for what you're doing against those bastards," she swore.

I bowed my head deeply along with my father, thanking the female for her kindness. Yet my heart still galloped beneath my deferential exterior. As the crowd dispersed, grumbling that they'd gotten excited for nothing, Izidora picked up the items and thanked the shopkeeper again before we jogged to Viktor and Vadim.

"The twins, Endre, and Kriztof went to fetch the horses," Viktor stated.

"Let's meet them halfway," I urged, and we walked briskly away from the market. I kept Izidora in my sight at all times, my hand hovering a few inches from her, ready to protect her with my life.

Around the next corner, we ran into Kriztof, Endre, and the twins, mounted and leading the rest of our horses. I waited for Izidora to mount Mistik before leaping onto Fek, and we pointed our mounts in the direction of Vaenor before cantering out of town. If we looked suspicious leaving in a hurry, I did not care, for Izidora's safety was paramount.

Once we cleared the town's walls, I kicked Fek into a gallop, his powerful legs lengthening and eating up the dirt beneath his hooves. Mistik fell into stride with us, her lithe body easily overtaking Fek's muscular one as we flew along the open road. Izidora's face was exalted as the wind whipped the hat from her head, revealing those shiny locks that reddened as each blade of sun fell over them. Izidora was a natural born rider, wholly in tune with her mount, setting a blazing pace we all pushed our mounts to match.

Our mounts' sides heaved when we slowed them to a walk, more than enough distance between us and the village we left behind. My heart slowed its race and I sighed a tense breath that had been lodged in my chest since the moment the shopkeeper acknowledged us. The thrill of the ride was over, and Izidora's mouth was pressed into a firm line, tension lining her brow. She wouldn't meet my eye or anyone else's.

"Are you okay?" I asked her quietly enough that the others couldn't pick up my words with their Fae senses.

She whispered, "I wasn't prepared for that. I didn't realize so many people would be interested in me..."

"When the world knows that it is in fact you, you will never get a moment's rest," I warned. "Everyone will want to know what happened, where you were, and who took you. They will also want to know everything about you. The things you like, the things you don't, your strengths and weaknesses, and the best ways to get leverage over you. The world can be a cruel fucking place, especially for those with good hearts like you."

She ducked her head, twisting the reins in her fingers and chewing on her bottom lip. "I want to be so strong that no one can hurt me again," she paused. "But I am afraid – of the pain, of not being enough, of disappointing others. Even more than that, I am afraid of trusting people, and of myself. I don't even really know who I am, so how will others know? How do you know that I am kind and have a good heart?" Her shining eyes roamed my face, begging me to make it all make sense to her.

Her pain was like a sharp stab to the gut. I wanted to be her protector, to hide her from the cruel world so the terror of her past would no longer haunt her. She deserved to be taken care of, to feel safe, to feel loved. I would do that for her.

"Let me tell you what I know about you, after only knowing you for a few days. You are kind - you thank each person who helps you with anything. You are empathetic - you felt awful about hitting Vadim with the pole because you did not want to cause him pain. You are helpful - you don't expect others to wait on you. You are curious and always open to learning. Speaking of which, you learn quickly. Only a few days ago we threw you on a horse for the first time and you are already riding like a natural." I grinned as the image of her hair whipping in the wind entered my mind. "You did not deserve what happened to you, but it is the hand you were dealt. You can choose to fall victim to it, or you can choose to rise above it. The choice is yours and yours alone, but you are not alone in fighting your demons. I'm here to help you."

Tears welled in her eyes and she blinked rapidly, trying to hide how deeply my words affected her. "I hope one day to see myself as you do." Her voice was thick with emotion as she wrangled for control.

"It will take time. The wounds we carry on the inside never quite heal like the ones we carry on the outside," my father said from behind us. My father knew as well as anyone – the loss of my mother still weighed heavily on him, even twenty years later. He loved her fiercely, and she had loved him deeply as well.

Fucking Fates, I wanted that with Izidora. But with King Zalan in the picture, it was improbable, if not impossible.

A little louder, my father declared, "Let's make camp around mid-afternoon. Keep an eye out for a spot a little further off the road this time."

After what happened in the town, extra caution was necessary. The Iron Fae could be trafficking for all I knew, but it had been years since I'd heard whispers of it. Still, word spread like wildfire in these small towns far removed from the capital, and it wouldn't be long before the outermost parts of the Night Realm knew, the wind carrying the rumor over the ridges and into the Iron Realm. Those words painted targets on our backs and put Izidora in danger. I assuaged my fears by scanning the dense woods around us for any signs of danger, breathing a little deeper with each step we took away from town.

9

IZIDORA

My emotions were a mess. Cracking the barrier around my pain was enough to release a torrential flood of all the darkness I'd experienced. Panic gripped me when the shopkeeper recognized me. If it weren't for years of automatically clamping down on the overwhelming urge to lose my shit, I might have broken down in front of the whole town.

But snuffing out a wildfire left embers burning.

Embers that needed only a soft breeze to ignite another inferno.

Losing myself in the thunder of hooves was exactly what I needed to calm down, but since we had slowed to a walk, my body buzzed with the need to fight, to flee, to do something with this pent up anxiety that wanted to explode in every direction.

Kazimir had not left my side. His words of praise and adoration filled me with a warmth like the first rays of sun on my too-pale skin. He was a constant presence, never more than a few steps away at all times, circling me like a cougar stalking its prey. Yet I felt seen instead of threatened.

I wanted to be all of those qualities he listed and more. I

wanted to be strong, fearless, and powerful. But most of all, I wanted to be loved unconditionally for who I was.

Perhaps my father would give that to me, imbuing me with the love I missed out on during my childhood. I imagined his face lighting up the moment he saw me, my presence lifting him out of the chair where he sat anxiously awaiting my return, running over to me and wrapping me in a warm embrace. He would tell me that he never gave up hope for my return, and that I was to spend every waking moment with him so we could make up for lost time. We would sit beside a roaring fire while he told me stories of his love for my mother, about himself, and our people. I would sit and listen to him for hours like I sat and listened to the Nighthounds now. The picture I painted in my head was so beautiful, it brought tears to my eyes.

I was so lost in my daydream that I didn't realize it was already time to stop for the day. Only when Mistik halted beneath me did I come back into myself. Hurriedly dismounting before anyone realized I wasn't paying attention, I reached into the saddlebags and pulled out a shiny red apple to feed to Mistik. The mare greedily tore at the proffered fruit while I rubbed her forehead, breathing in her earthly smell. When she finished the apple, her big, black eyes blinked at me and she nuzzled into my chest. Sighing, I wrapped my arms around her neck, and she pulled me in closer with a tuck of her head, giving me an equine hug.

My eyes burned as I wondered how Mistik knew that was exactly what I needed. Touch from the males was not welcome, yet I craved the warm affection to reassure me I was worth loving.

Could I let my walls down enough to accept their touch? Could I trust them not to hurt me?

My mind tumbled the questions over and over while I absorbed as much love as possible from the dapple gray mare.

When I finally dropped my arms and wiped my eyes, Vadim jerked his head up toward the treetops, hands behind his back and walking in circles, pretending like he wasn't watching me.

"Ah there you are!" he chirped. "Are you ready to learn to fight with a sword?"

Grateful that he did not comment on my red-rimmed eyes, I nodded my head, "I'm ready."

"Let's go," he said with a wicked grin, turning toward a copse of trees and weaving through the trunks until we found a clearing that was open enough to move freely.

As I stepped into the center, I looked around at the beautiful trees soaring toward the sky, their massive trunks almost forming a perfect ring around us. The shady spot chilled when a breeze stirred the autumn air.

Vadim tossed my new leathers at me. "Put these on," he requested. "I am going to find some big sticks for us to start with." He turned and walked out of the copse as I stripped out of my wool pants and pulled on the stiff leathers. The pants were firm but as I squatted down they bent and twisted with me, allowing room to move. Rapping my knuckles against the hardened leather, I tested its strength. It protected my most vital organs but allowed me to move my arms and twist my torso. Next, I buckled the shoulder straps to secure it firmly in place, then buckled the braces over my tunic at my wrists.

Wearing leather armor made me feel like I could become a warrior. I'd fought my guards many times, kicking, scratching, and biting, but against trained soldiers, my fury was nearly useless. I was ready to learn how to be a true warrior, to fight and subdue those who sought to harm me, to protect myself without relying on anyone else.

I plaited my hair out of my face, preparing for whatever Vadim decided to throw at me. Minutes later, he returned carrying an armful of sticks. Some were longer and thicker, almost like branches, while others were short and light. He dumped the pile on the ground at the edge of the ring of trees.

"So," he began, "I'm going to teach you all about swordplay. But since you whacked me with the tent poles earlier, we're going to start with sticks instead of swords." He laughed as my cheeks flamed.

"Am I ever going to live that down?"

"Never," he replied with a grin.

He handed me one of the longer, thicker sticks and picked up another roughly the same size. Backing up a few paces, he sank into a split stance with his left leg in front and right leg behind him. He gripped one end of the stick and lifted it into the air until the other tip was about eye level.

"This is your fighting stance. Normally, we would start with other conditioning first, but it is more important that you can swing a sword than run for an hour right now. You will start from this position until we get into more advanced styles. Go ahead and plant your feet. You want to feel balanced – not too square, not too spread out," he instructed.

Shuffling my feet around then bending slightly at the knee, I mirrored Vadim's stance. Then, I gripped one end of my stick and brought the other tip to eye level.

Vadim walked over to me, circling me twice before reaching his hand to adjust my arms and legs. I grimaced at his touch but did not recoil, breathing in and out steadily as he maneuvered my limbs.

He didn't hurt me. He did not want *to hurt me. I was safe.*

"There," he said when he was satisfied with my stance. "Is that comfortable?"

"Yes," I gritted out, my arms already starting to burn under the weight of the solid stick.

"Great. Now, I want you to walk five paces to the right

without leaving your stance or crossing your feet." I did as he asked, awkwardly side-stepping.

"Don't lower your sword when you step!" Vadim called out.

Once I'd finished, he said, "Okay, now do the same thing backward." I stepped backward, remembering to keep my sword steady this time.

"To the left!" Vadim commanded, and I stepped left.

"Now forward!" he called next. I returned to my starting point, having walked in a square without crossing my legs over each other or dropping my makeshift sword.

"Excellent," Vadim grinned. "Now do the whole thing again five times."

I groaned but moved through the stepping sequence until he was satisfied with my footwork. My arms burned along with my thighs, flames licking at each muscle, making them tremble. My scrawny body was so weak, and I hated that feeling.

Wasn't there some faster way to make me invincible?

"Time for the fun part," Vadim ribbed. He adjusted my grip on the stick slightly. "I'm going to stand here, and I want you to swing your stick for mine like this." He demonstrated the movement beside me, emphasizing the footwork that went along with the stabbing motion. Then, he faced me again. "Whenever you are ready."

Leaping forward with all my might, I jabbed my stick at Vadim, connecting with his and creating a light tap between the two. A small smile pulled at the corners of my mouth, satisfied that I connected on my first attempt.

"Good job! Now do it again," he instructed. I repeated the jab, landing some but missing his stick completely on the last one. The tip of my makeshift sword smacked his hand, and he grimaced, dropping it away from his own and shaking it out.

"Oh shit I'm so sorry! Are you okay?" I apologized and

chewed my lip, hoping he wouldn't end our lessons after my mistake.

He laughed and shook his head, a lock of dark hair escaping the leather that tied it back. "Princess, that isn't the first time that's happened to me, nor will it be the last. That is exactly why we're doing this with sticks. If we were truly fighting, that would have been your goal anyway. Learn to control your strikes and you'll be able to land it on purpose next time." He winked an evergreen eye, and my shoulders relaxed.

"I guess that is true. Before too long, you'll have to guard your head," I teased.

"I sure hope so. Now, try a few more," Vadim said.

Once I'd landed a dozen more controlled strikes, we moved on to another movement. "This is a power strike, so you need to put more force into it. Use your hips to assist you." He demonstrated again, then had me move in time with him to connect my footwork with the swing. When he was satisfied, he circled in front of me again, readying to fight. Taking a deep breath, I held my stick steady, then flicked my wrist to the side, and stepped through.

A pathetic tap was all I got out of my strike, his stick not even wavering against mine. I huffed, and stepped back, readying for another attempt.

"Put more power into it this time – use your hips and shoulders to really drive forward."

After about a dozen more attempts resulting in weakening raps, I threw my stick to the ground, receiving a much more satisfying clatter. That only served to infuriate me further, fists clenching and unclenching as my mind screamed at me how powerless I'd always be. My spirit may want to fight, but I couldn't make my body work with me.

"What's the point of trying? I'll never be able to protect myself at this rate. I'll always be helpless." I pushed my hands into my eyes to stop the hot tears from flowing, pissed at myself for letting my emotions get the better of me again.

Vadim's light footsteps approached slowly, and his rough fingers circled my wrist and pulled it away from my face. "If you believe you are helpless, you will always be helpless. If you believe you can do this, then you will eventually succeed. But you have to persevere and be willing to give it your fucking all. Don't let anything hold you back." He handed me the stick again.

A few deep breaths stopped the tears, and I wiped my eyes and accepted the stick.

I was a fighter. I could do this.

He backed away, dropped into his stance, and waited for me to attack. Settling into my body and clearing my mind, I swung, my stick colliding with Vadim's and moving it with force and a loud whack.

"Just like that," he grinned.

I swung several more times, each one landing with more force than the last. By the time we finished, I was soaring on my accomplishment, aches forgotten as I fell wholly into the movements.

"That's all we'll work on with swords today," Vadim said. "We'll finish with some conditioning. A strong body creates a strong mind. You need both for a dance of swords. Let's start with some functional exercises and we'll end with balance and stretching."

"Whichever direction you need to put in more effort, tie it to your exhale," he instructed. He led me through a series of squats, planks, push-ups, and pulls using some of the thicker branches. Tying my breath to the movements made them easier, and the shaking in my muscles as I pushed myself to get stronger was nearly as intoxicating as flying down the road on Mistik's back. It was as if each drop of sweat or tremble of muscle fortified the armor I'd already built in my mind, clearing my head of worry and fear. It was so unlike the routine my guards put me through, and Vadim poured out constant encouragement, until finally I could do no more. I sank to my hands and knees as I tried to reclaim oxygen, chest heaving the earthy autumn air.

"And now for balance and stretching," he grinned wolfishly.

"Fine," I groaned, my body screaming at me to curl up among the crunchy leaves and die rather than move another inch. I grumbled as I pushed myself back to my feet despite the constant protest from my muscles.

A fluid set of poses tied to my breath lengthened the taught fibers, sending sweet relief to one aching body part at a time. Though each time I was meant to stand on one leg, I immediately pitched to the side.

"We'll work on that," he reassured me once we finished flowing through the movements. "You did good today. Go wash up in the stream and meet me by the fire."

Thank the Goddess. Sweat soaked through my clothes, my tunic clinging to my torso uncomfortably beneath the leather chest plate that was too thick to cool my heated skin. My pants fared no better, sweat running rivers down the backs of my thighs and collecting behind my knees. Each step was a tremble threatening a tumble into a tree.

My knees banged against the plush moss at the water's edge, and I cupped my hands to drink down the clean water in gulps. Once I'd cooled myself from the inside out, I splashed my hands and face, unlatching the chest plate and rolling up the sleeves of my tunic to remove any lingering salt from my skin.

Droplets traced my skin and jumped back into the water, and I took the opportunity to really look at myself for the first time in the daylight. Turning my arms this way and that, I assessed their bony edges that reminded me of the sticks Vadim collected for our training. My skin was still pale, yet there was a vitality to it as hot blood pumped through my veins.

The males were chiseled from the very stone that surrounded me from the time I could walk. Their broad shoulders spoke of years of wielding swords, their thick thighs from riding horses and running with heavy armor covering their bodies. With one look at the eight of them, you could tell that they could dominate you in every way. And yet they had not tried to harm me. Even their unwanted touches were out of protection or correction, and never in anger.

But the way Kazimir looked at me sometimes...

It sent chills skittering down my spine and heat into my core.

Groaning, I grasped the collar of my chest plate and slung it over my shoulder as I ambled back to the camp. Sunlight washed over my face as it broke through the trees, and I closed my eyes at the golden kisses.

How did I survive without this warmth for so long?

Leaning against my pack beside the fire, I tipped my head back and rested. Fatigue pulled at both my mind and body, warring for attention. There was one thing that wasn't completely exhausted, and if I wanted to ensure my safety, it needed to be flexed, too. Searching my chest for the well of magic, I found that white flame blazing as I bathed in the late afternoon sun. I stoked the flames higher and higher until I felt like I was going to burst with white light.

Pure white energy flowed to my fingertips, caressing them as gently as the sun caressed my face. It danced through my fingers, weaving and gliding among them and across my palms before twisting up my arms. Its allure was undeniable, the power that thrummed through my veins intoxicating.

A heavy thud sounded to my right, followed by a masculine gasp, and I snapped out of my reverie, immediately rocking to my feet and crouching to defend my neck and face. Endre stood before me, having just dropped the last of the bags from the horses. His mouth was skewed open, peridot eyes wide and locked on my hands, where my magic had disappeared moments before.

Panic flooded me before I could stop it; tapping into my magic opened up the floodgate that I did not have time to close before being shaken. My breaths were short, chest pressing into my knees, and I fell back on my ass, dizziness overtaking me as I couldn't get enough air.

Endre rushed to my side, Kazimir appeared on my other a moment later, and I was trapped between the two large males. Endre snapped his fingers in front of my blurred eyes, and I turned my face to him, his hands raised in supplication. "Breathe, Izidora. We're not going to hurt you. Slow it down now, breathe in and out."

His calming presence broke through the haze of panic, and I followed his instruction, lengthening my exhales until his messy hair came into focus and my blood didn't scream in my ears. Digging my fingers into the dirt on either side of me, I grounded myself into reality, finally calm enough to communicate again.

Kazimir's emerald eyes were haunted, his dark brows pinched together as he looked me over. "Are you all right?"

I nodded, blowing out another big breath. "Yeah, just startled. I was lost in thought and didn't hear Endre coming."

"Shit, Kazimir, did you know her magic was white like that?" Endre hissed

Kazimir sighed, glancing at Endre. "I discovered it yesterday when we were practicing magic."

"You know what that means, right?" Endre said.

"If you have something you'd like to share, please do," Kazimir deadpanned.

"The Goddess's Prophecy," Endre started, "states that when the one with the white light comes into the world, everything as we know it will change. I haven't read the prophecy in ages, so I don't remember the exact words, but that white light bit always stuck in my memory. It's an ancient prophecy from millennia ago. I doubt anyone thought it would come to pass at this point."

My head bounced between the two males, confusion pulling at my brow.

There was an ancient prophecy from the Goddess? And it had something to do with my white magic? And what impact would I have on the world?

The world before me spun, the males' voices becoming nothing more than senseless babble as my body tingled and vision tunneled. My elbows hit the ground behind me, and I stared numbly at the sky as my mind shut down, unable and unwilling to accept any new information. Endre and Kazimir blocked out the blue sky, their lips moving rapidly, but I did not hear them. Then there was only darkness.

10

KAZIMIR

I caught the back of Izidora's head the moment before it hit the ground. Gently easing my other arm under her knees, I hefted her into my arms, tucking her head against my chest and carrying her into her tent. Endre followed closely behind me, checking her forehead for signs of illness. She was clammy but not sickly; she must be utterly exhausted from everything that had been thrown at her in the past five days. Kneeling before her cot, I placed her on the low bed like she was made of glass, careful not to jostle her for fear she might break.

Endre tied back the canvas flaps, filling the tent with fresh autumn air. He handed me a waterskin and cloth, and I wetted it, dabbing it across her sweaty brow. She looked peaceful when she was unconscious to the world, corners of her eyes relaxed and forehead smooth. I stroked a few damp strands of hair from her face, then covered her in a blanket, tucking in the sides to make sure it was secure around her. I was loath to leave her like this, wanting nothing more than to care for her, but Endre's pointed cough had me rising and exiting the tent.

I did not stray far, dragging a few bags closer so I could lean against them and keep one eye on her and another on the fire beside me. Endre stretched out across from me, and while we talked quietly about the prophecy, my attention was not in our conversation.

My father returned after executing an extensive perimeter sweep. Given that Endre had reminded us of the prophecy moments ago, I was especially glad for our extra precautions. If Izidora was part of this prophecy, it would explain why she was kidnapped in the first place. But how would anyone know what a babe's magic would become?

I waved him over, motioning for him to speak quietly, then relayed recent events.

My father's eyes lit up as Endre reminded him of the prophecy. "It has been some time since I read of this prophecy as well, Endre, but I believe your memory of the white light is correct. It was spoken millennia ago during the Age of Prophecy, when they were spewed out left and right, some coming to pass and others not. Or not yet in this case."

My gut told me something larger was at play, and I did not like being in the dark. The irony of my frustration was not lost on me. Izidora was mine to protect, and I felt helpless from both her lack of interest in getting closer to me and not knowing who was after her or why.

"Something is not fucking right here," I stated.

Endre agreed, "That is my sense as well. We still don't know who took her in the beginning or how she got to that cave in the first place. Iron Fae do not have wings, and yet they were the ones guarding her from that damn-near-impossible to reach cave."

"It's not adding up to me either," my father added. "We must proceed with caution because we do not know who the true enemy is here. I think it would be wise if we stuck to camping instead of visiting towns until we reach Este Castle."

I chuckled softly, "Vadim is going to hate missing out on the pretty village females."

"And the twins will miss their ales," Endre joined in the joke.

The rest of the crew sauntered up then, and my father relayed our new plan. There were a few grumbles, but everyone agreed this was the best course of action.

"Let's double up on patrols during the night," I suggested. "All are guilty until proven innocent should they approach our camp."

Zekari and Kirigin shared a wicked grin at that. There was nothing they liked more than to be let loose without rules. We decided on a rotation schedule as the smoky scent of roasting birds filled our small camp, the fire sizzling as fat dripped off the animals' small bones. Feeding everyone would be difficult unless we started bagging bigger animals, since we wouldn't be stopping in taverns to fill up along the way. I checked our supplies and estimated that our current store of vegetables, cheese, and dried meat might last another week or so before we would be forced to go on a supply run.

That was a problem for another day. Izidora ducked out of her tent and ambled toward the smell of roasting birds, head held high despite her earlier exhaustion. We locked eyes as she approached, and I sat up straighter, waiting for her to take a seat next to me. Instead, she settled next to Zekari and Kirigin, who immediately jumped up to do other chores before each of them sat down in a different position next to her. She glanced between the two and stated with a grin, "You switched places." They both threw their hands in the air, scoffing, and claiming it was a lucky guess. Her unguarded giggle floated on the air, musical and light.

I ran a hand over my face, hiding a growl as she rejected me in favor of the twins. They even made her laugh with their antics. Why couldn't she laugh like that with me? Didn't she see that I was the right choice for her?

I stewed on my predicament as dinner was passed around, laughing and joking with Endre despite my heart and head not being truly present in the conversation. I would have to try harder to show her that our connection was there; it was only a matter of time before she realized it.

———

Two weeks passed in a similar manner. Rising with the sun, then riding through the increasingly bare woods through the morning, breath frosting the ever chilling air. Midday, stopping for lunch, Kriztof preparing our meal while Vadim and Izidora trained swords and built strength. Ceasing our ride in the late afternoon with just enough time for an hour of magic before the first stars winked into existence.

Dark circles lined her eyes, dulling the sparkle that mirrored the stars when she mastered something new. Her willpower was impressive, constantly asking questions, making corrections, and flawlessly executing anything that was asked of her.

Yet volatility swirled a breath below her skin, below the surface, lying in wait for the perfect moment to explode from within and burn everything down in its wake. The set of her jaw revealed the white-knuckle grip she held over herself when she did not perform to her own increasingly high standards. She threw herself off the cliff of training with wild abandon, uncaring where she landed so long as she grew stronger as she plummeted to the ground. This pace was unsustainable, yet the looming threat of discovery and pressure to prepare her for what lay ahead left us no choice.

A complaint never left her mouth, even when our food supplies ran low or when we asked her to help around camp, whether she made trips to the streams to fill waterskins or wash our clothes. More often than not, she volunteered to help with the horses, their winter coats coming in and giving them an extra soft touch. She was especially fond of Mistik, the dapple gray mare nuzzling her back as Izidora groomed her sweaty hide, eliciting a bout of laughter at each nudge toward an itch that needed a scratch. She found comfort among the beasts that did not talk back, yet I was desperate for her to seek me out when she was in need of it. I dreamed of reassuring her, holding her in my arms and pressing her against my chest like I could save her from the horrors of her past.

Our time passed too quickly for me.

We were into the third week of our journey back to the capital of the Night Realm, and each step north felt more like a march to my death: the moment King Zalan promised her to another. I wanted Izidora for myself, and I was beginning to think I would do anything to see that happen.

My obsession was locked more tightly than a chest filled with priceless treasure, unseen by my brothers in arms and my father. Yet I could not prevent the blooming love in my chest when Izidora celebrated her accomplishments, my heated eyes when she threw her head back in rapturous laughter, or my weakening knees when she treated me to an unfiltered smile.

She was a fucking goddess in my eyes, and I was made to worship her.

She was brimming with resilience and curiosity, her inner strength was unmatched. Vadim's lessons about a warrior's mindset became her religion, and she braided it into her identity like she braided her hair back for battle. She tattooed my lessons about calm control to her magic-filled palms, tying her breath to the effort of channeling her ever increasing well of pure white energy. She was enthralling to watch, her instincts sharper than a finely crafted blade and reflexes faster than the first lightning strike during a thunderstorm. Instead of falling into panic when she was startled, an impenetrable shield was aggressively thrown around her, safeguarding her against attack.

We would spar with magic, attacks aimed to knock each other off balance or subdue until a blade could deliver a killing blow. Deep into the woods, we faced each other across a bed of dead pine needles, surrounded by their towering evergreen canopies and roughly barked trunks, interspersed between the bare branches of black oaks and sharp-leafed underbrush. A few moss-covered boulders were just outside of our zone, providing cover should Izidora feel she needed it.

"Are you ready?" I asked her.

A heart wrenching smile shot across her beautiful face, and with a flick of her fingers she called her star-bright magic to her palms. "Let's do this."

11

IZIDORA

A deep breath opened the chasm of magic in my chest, the crystal spearing to life in time with a flare of white flame. Kazimir's emerald eyes were piercing and fixated on me, sending a shiver down my spine as if he trailed a finger lightly down each vertebra.

I cast a spear in each hand, ready to launch them in his direction should he move closer, wanting to keep him at a distance. They wouldn't maim him, but they would sting like a forceful slap should they make contact. The threat was more important than a direct hit.

Kazimir lifted a foot to move to the right, and without a second thought, I hurled my first white spear a little beyond his current position. But he predicted my move, backstepping to dodge the incoming projectile. The second followed a moment later, landing a hair from his back foot. His grin showed that he was wickedly pleased with my carefully thought out trap.

Before I could blink, Kazimir hurled three balls of his silvery magic in my direction, only for each to dissipate against the forceful shield that encircled my body, the low song of safety soothing my sensitive nerves. Dropping into a crouch, I let the barrier fall and scanned the area, seeking Kazimir's hulking form. Between the leaves of a bush, I spotted his black hair and telltale silver, then darted behind the nearest tree mere moments before a spear flew my way.

My heart pounded in my ears as I decided on my next attack. Calling throwing daggers to my palms, I spun around the opposite side of the trunk, the bark scraping my face as I hugged its circumference, then fired successive blades at the bush he had crouched behind moments before. Not a single blade made impact, for once they all left my palms, I realized he was not there.

I dove for cover behind the bushes to my right, duck-walking around them and peering through branches in search of my opponent. My breath stuck in my throat as I attempted to seek him out through sound and smell. A twig snapped behind me, breaking the silence. My shield was up before the sound finished cracking, and I spun on my heels, coming face to face with Kazimir, his nose a hair's breadth from my shield.

"Well done," he purred before placing his hands lazily on my shield and pushing against it with a silver glow. I held firm, firing up the crystal in my chest and fanning the white flames to add more magic into it, while thinking through what to do next. With a rebellious grin, I converted my shield into a net and threw it over Kazimir, blasting him backward and trapping him to a tree. A look of shock covered his face before he started laughing, shaking his head.

"You are surprising, Izidora. So clever." His voice was husky and sent heat between my thighs, my body momentarily taken out of the battle. He used my distraction to dissipate my net with a brush of his fingers and pushed off the tree, stalking toward me with dilated pupils that sucked me under their spell. I panted from the exertion of holding the shield for so long, yet I was not ready to quit this fight. Adrenaline still filled my veins, though my limbs grew heavier with each step back. My magic well was still filled and waiting, ready for my command.

A whip appeared in his hand, and my heart stopped altogether.

Each step of his foot was a sharp crack that bit into my back. One moment Kazimir prowled in front of me, the next, I was drowning in a memory.

A guard stood behind me. My spine arched as he unfurled the silvery rope, preparing to pull away from the string while the chains trapped me in unending agony. He raised it to strike, and I screamed, falling to my knees and covering my head with my arms.

When the strike never landed across my back, a sob broke through the protective barrier of my arms, and I curled into a ball on the ground, hugging my knees to my chest.

My fear was a potent drug that immobilized me, and all I could do was bawl as I lay on the ground, fighting for control with the voice that screamed at me to run, to fight, to do anything but succumb to the memories of the males who had punished me so brutally.

"Izidora!" Kazimir rushed to my side, his voice laced with concern and fear, placing a hand on my knee.

"Don't touch me!" I wailed, the claws of my trauma sinking in deep. My whole body trembled as I fought my way out of the darkness, nails grabbing for purchase on anything to lift me out of the living nightmare playing out over and over again.

His hand retreated instantly, and his deep timbre dropped even softer and lower as he tried to soothe me. "Izidora, listen to my voice. You are safe. You are in a forest far from the cave. The forest floor is dotted with spots of yellow from the sun. The sky is open above us, and there is endless room around us to run and roam. You are not trapped. No one will hurt you."

Opening my eyes, the trees and sky and sun were just as he described. I was surrounded by light, limbs free of shackles.

Tentatively, I released one hand then another from my knees, straightening my spine until my chest had more space to expand and contract.

"There you go, just like that," he crooned. His hand hovered over my head as if he wanted to smooth back the strands of hair that were caught in the wetness that dripped from my eyes. With a jerk of my chin, I gave him permission to touch me, and he did, caressing my cheeks and wiping the hot tears that mixed with sweat on my cheeks.

Ever so slowly, he scooted closer, until his knee brushed mine. His hand found my back, my skin automatically twitching and arching away, but he only rubbed soothing circles until the tension melted away and I no longer felt the bite in my flesh.

I had no energy to speak or move, so he sat with me in solidarity, a witness to the unbearable pain that still haunted me. All the while, he showered me with gentle caresses, showing me what comfort from another Fae, another male, could be. I wanted more, I needed more. So, I pulled on what little strength I had left and crawled into his lap.

His body went rigid while I moved, then something broke inside him, and he clutched me to his chest like he alone could hold the jagged pieces of me together, and rocked us back and forth, the cadence a balm to my terrified soul. Another wave of hot tears spilled down my cheeks as I surrendered to the warmth of his body and his scent of amber and smoky wood. His deep emerald eyes stared down at me with what I could only understand as love, his soul reaching through those deep pools and seeking to comfort my own.

"Do you want to talk about it?" he asked gently.

Talking about it would make it real. Yet, it was real. It had happened, and there was no denying it. But maybe, just maybe, sharing what had ripped apart my soul would free me from the chains that tethered the fear to my core.

"The guards... they used to whip me when I didn't give them what they wanted. They left me bloody and broken more times than I care to remember. I would numb my existence under their onslaught, painting pictures in my head of a better world beyond the void of the cave. Sometimes, I imagined the horrors I would inflict on them if I ever got the chance to escape. Anything to give me strength in those moments."

His arms tightened around me, not in a confining way, but in a protective embrace, and I clung to his powerful body as he growled out his next words. "You are the strongest Fae I know, Izidora. What you went through would have broken even the most seasoned warriors, and the fact that you survived and exited the cave with your brilliant soul still intact is nothing short of incredible."

"Do you really think so?" I whispered.

"There is no doubt in my mind," he swore.

Kazimir witnessed the darkness that clung to me and did not flinch. The shattered shards of my heart softened for this male, and in the depths of my soul, I knew something had changed between us in this moment on the earthen floor, a part of me I never knew existed flaring to life under his saccharine touch.

His gentle rocking was venerating, a soothing rhythm that abated all further tears and banished the tightness in my chest. His head buried into my hair, curling in around me and cocooning me against the horrors of my past. Kazimir did not loosen his hold, as if this moment was as precious to him as it was to me.

It wasn't until my stomach rumbled that his corded arms relaxed, and his chest vibrated with amusement. "We can continue our lessons tomorrow. Let's go get something to eat. Maybe the twins caught some rabbits today."

My head rubbed against his chest as I nodded, and he unwound his arms from around me, allowing me space to rise.

Slowly, we picked our way through the trees in the direction of the aroma of roasting meat, and I hoped no one would notice my swollen face and red-rimmed eyes.

Before we were within hearing range of our group, Kazimir halted, his hand capturing my arm as he faced me, gazing deep into my eyes as if he were trying to imprint his next words upon my soul. "We may have removed the chains from your body, but only you can remove the chains from your mind. You have an opportunity now to change your story for the better. You are not meant to be a victim. You are meant for so much more."

Then he dropped my arm and spun on his heel, leaving me among the trees to process his fervent words. He was right; this was the chance to make a fresh start, to create the life I always dreamed of, to be the person I always wanted to be. The trauma of the past twenty-one years of my life could consume me, or I could fortify myself and channel my intense emotions into something good.

The choice was easy; I would always fight for myself. It would take time, but I would see it done. What happened to me did not define me, but was simply an explanation for who I was and how I reacted. My trauma would help the world in some way, and it would not remain meaningless. Those who abused me would receive their comeuppance one day, and I would bathe in their blood as I cut down my enemies. No one would hurt me ever again.

I walked into camp with my head held high, owning the power I had over my story.

A few rabbits roasted over the fire, their gamey meat darkening with each turn of the spit as the flames licked them from below. I sat down next to Endre, who handed me a hunk of cheese and some bread, Kazimir on my other side. He nudged me with the toe of his boot as if he recognized the change in me already. This time, I did not flinch.

As I chewed on my meager meal, Endre asked, "Would you like to learn some healing magic?"

Can healing magic heal a fractured mind?

I was intrigued. "Can anyone be a healer?"

"Yes," he started, "though it takes practice to harness the right amount of magic to pour into each injury or ailment. Some injuries are more complex than others and require different treatments. I've studied it for years, so that's my job in our crew. When Kriztof took a bolt to the leg during your rescue, I was the one who healed him before we returned to Zanin with you."

My shoulder dropped as I learned that Kriztof was injured during my rescue. "Did anyone else get hurt?" I murmured.

Endre shook his head. "No, and don't worry, Izidora, we would have all gladly given our lives to rescue you that night. We still would."

His words were a salve to my guilt, though the idea that they were all so devoted to me was a little strange. Wrapping my head around the knowledge that I was royalty was challenging; the idea that one day I would rule over them was as foreign to me as the world around us. If I could learn to heal, I could be a good monarch and help others when they were in need. "I would love to learn."

"Great. When you are finished eating, I'll teach you how to heal your sore muscles," he announced.

I gasped. "Why didn't you teach me that before? I could have used that for the past few weeks."

Kazimir snorted from my opposite side, and Endre hid a shy grin beneath his unkempt hair. "One thing at a time, Izidora."

Chewing on the stringy rabbit meat, I watched Endre clean up the dishes while the others wandered off on their own, lethargic and needing some space from one another. Only Kazimir remained steadfast at my side, and for once, I didn't mind. Once Endre finished cleaning up, he returned to my side to begin our lesson, and Kazimir shuffled away to give us some space to practice.

"Tune into your magic first," he instructed. I turned my gaze inward, finding the crystal wrapped in moonlight and white fire.

"Bring forth only a tiny sliver of energy. Then you want to visualize sending it to whatever aches you have."

A tendril of white wound between my fingers. With my eyes still closed, I imagined it traveling from my fingertips up to my right shoulder and sending it under the skin. Sweet relief filled that aching joint, and I released a moan.

Endre laughed beside me. "Feels good, doesn't it?"

I opened my eyes. "So damn good. I feel brand new," I laughed. "Is this how you are able to keep going at a relentless pace all the time?"

"Pretty much," he chuckled. "Now try sending it to other places."

Another thread of white wound its way down to my left thigh, placating the strained muscle there. Then another circled my ribcage, soothing my burning lungs and that spot on my ribs that ached horribly in the cold. Over and over I sent healing magic through my limbs until my entire body was free of aches; yet no matter how hard I tried, it did not banish the haunting memories from my mind.

"That was pretty easy," I commented.

"Soreness is the easiest pain to heal," he said. "Now you can try to heal a cut on my finger." A knife that had been resting with the tip in the fire pricked his finger, pulling a drop of ruby to the surface of his skin.

My throat bobbed as I watched more blood gather on his finger. "Okay," my voice broke on the word, "What now?"

"Imagine the same light flowing to my fingertip. You have to will it to heal me. The intention is what's most important here."

I chewed on my lip, reaching for my power, then pushing a

tiny tendril toward the cut on Endre's hand, imagining the blood disappearing from his fingertip. When the brightness fell away, the cut and blood still remained.

"It is easier when you are connected to the person you're trying to heal. Rest my palm in yours."

Hesitantly, I cupped his hand with my left, holding it steady as I focused on pulling more magic into my right hand. With a deep breath, I focused on wanting Endre to be well and whole, then snaked the bright light around his fingers, bathing the tip in magic. I felt his skin knitting together through our connection, a shocked squeal escaping me when I dropped my magic away to reveal not a hint of blood remaining.

"Great work," he beamed.

"Thanks for being such a patient teacher," I replied.

"Don't mention it," Endre dismissed my compliment. "I am happy to help you. I know all of this must be hard for you."

His validation burned my eyes, and I blinked rapidly while looking at the starry night sky to banish them. I was still raw from my earlier flashback, emotions humming below the surface and ready to spill over at the slightest provocation.

"Yes, it is," I told him. "I was kept in the dark – literally and figuratively – for most of my life, chained to a wall, desperate to escape but completely unsure how. Then I am rescued and see the light. I see what normal life is like, what having friends is like, what having a family is like. All things I never had, but are now within reach. And yet I am overwhelmed with everything I need to learn. I vacillate between being strong and fearless and my demons crawling out from the cave to torture me. There are so many people, so many expectations, and so much pressure from all sides right now. I want to be what everyone wants me to be, but I have no idea who I actually am in all of this. What the fuck am I supposed to do?"

All my thoughts and fears came spilling out of me, like a

tidal wave that couldn't be stopped once it started. Endre listening to every drop of it, his peridot eyes never wavering, never hinting at judgment; he only showed me a quiet understanding that comes from an unshakable inner confidence.

"You are whoever you want to be," Endre said simply. "Don't lose sight of what you want for yourself because someone else wants a different path for you. You will never be able to please everyone, so make yourself happy instead."

"What if I don't know what makes me happy?" Another fear, whispered from that broken part of me that still couldn't quite believe that I'd escaped my prison.

"There are already a few things that make you happy, like Mistik. You will find more, and when you do, hold them close and never let them go."

Endre's acceptance was everything I needed to let the last bit of tension in my shoulders melt away, my chest loosening in time. My fears were valid, yes, but overcoming them was possible; vulnerability with these males led to reassurance rather than rejection, and through that, I would heal the scars marring my soul, even if I could not heal the ones marring my skin.

Before I lost my nerve, I wrapped my arms quickly around Endre, then retreated backward, putting space between us. "Thanks, Endre. For everything. Can you teach me more healing magic tomorrow?"

If he was surprised by the hug, he didn't show it. "Sure thing," he replied, standing and dusting his hands on his pants.

Heaving a sigh, I pushed myself upright, dragging my exhausted limbs toward the canvas tent that protected me from the elements. A heated perusal sent shivers down my spine, and as I glanced over my shoulder, I caught Kazimir watching me, and he continued without shame despite my apparent awareness. His gaze traveled up and down, slowly, as if he undressed the depth of my soul as we remained locked in a silent conversation. Feet frozen to the ground, he stalked toward me, his body closing in on mine in a way that sent a throbbing ache between my thighs. Only once he towered over me was I able to move, tipping my chin up to him, his black hair haloed by the brilliant night sky.

"Happiness is right in front of you, Izidora." His fingers drifted from his side, caressing my cheek with a reverent, featherlight touch. My lashes fluttered as his body shifted closer, his hand trailing around to cup the back of my head, supporting it as I gazed into the emerald pools that begged me to drown in them. "I will show you that with everything I have."

His calloused hands dropped from my hair, and he stepped back, sucking my breath into the space between us. "Goodnight, Izidora," he whispered, then stepped past me and disappeared into the dark canvas tent that stood mere feet from mine.

Mind spinning, I retreated into my own space, the twisting path the day had taken running over and over through my mind as I settled under a pile of warm blankets. The day had been transformative and transcendental, pushing me to look at the world in a different light, to look at these males in a different light, and opening the door for me to trust them. Kazimir may not yet know the depth of the depravity I'd experienced in the cave, but I knew that no matter what, his opinion of me would not change. And for that, I could take the risk and open myself to the happiness I deserved.

12

KAZIMIR

Izidora was becoming an addiction. I couldn't help but listen in on her conversation with Endre as I silently seethed that she chose to spill her inner thoughts to him rather than me. Confronting her before she slipped away was less than I wanted to do, but she needed to come to me on her own terms if I wanted any chance of us being together. At least our convergence after her breakdown in the darkening woods changed the air between us, and she no longer flinched at my touch.

My sidelong glances at her as we rode into Arazki drew her attention, and the closer we rode to the town between the Agrenak Mountains and Vaenor, the closer she drifted into my orbit. She chewed on her lip, sucking the pink pout between her teeth as her slim fingers clenched and unclenched around the reins.

We'd stayed away from proper civilization for days, but our supplies were desperately low and stopping in the frequently visited town was a necessary evil. In a broken and devastating voice, she'd asked me to stay close as we entered the town, revealing how rattled she truly was after our last encounter. As gray smoke drifted lazily above rooftops in the distance, Izidora rode beside me, and the whispering of her long hair played across her back like music. Her stirrup occasionally bumped into mine, and my blood sang in my veins as she solidified her place at my side. This was exactly how I wanted her.

The first Fae drifted across the road in front of us, and a sharp intake of breath and a rolling snort from Mistik had me whipping my head to the side.

"I'm right here," I reassured. A tight smile was all she offered. "Take a few deep breaths, like we practice when you call your magic." A heavy exhale was her response.

Few people braved the chilly morning; we picked our arrival with intention. Arazki was large enough that there was no market, but rather a main street lined with stores, most of which still slumbered. Warm, sweet smells floated over the musky scent of our horses as we traipsed the thoroughfare, a small smile pulling at my lips as I thought of Izidora's love of baked pastries. Dismounting, we hitched our horses and split up, each on a mission to fetch the various supplies we needed as quickly as possible.

A soft bell pealed as I opened the glass door to the bakery, and we were immediately assaulted by burnt cinnamon and warm vanilla. The baker wafted a tray filled with swirled rolls from the oven onto an open space on his counter, then gathered a nearby bowl of creamy frosting, attentively layering the sweet liquid over the steaming rolls. Izidora's eyes were wider than the buns before us as she watched the frosting melt on impact and pool around the base of each cinnamon treat.

"I'll take three of those," I said to the baker when he looked up from his craft to greet us.

"Anything else?" he asked.

"I'll take four loaves of bread as well." He gathered various loaves of bread from a shelf off to his left, returning with an armful. Opening my sack, he dropped the thick, hearty bread in one by one, thudding against each other as they filled the bag. He pulled a cloth from beneath the counter, lifting three dripping rolls from their frosting bath with a swirl of silver magic and placing them atop the cloth. I handed over my coin as Izidora snatched up the cinnamon rolls, and she waved to the baker as we exited his shop.

A stone bench framed a neatly trimmed hedge and I sat down, motioning for Izidora to join me. Izidora perched next to me, unwrapping her treats from the cloth. "Which one do you want?" she asked without looking, preoccupied with the sweets in front of her.

"Hmm, this one looks nice," I reached for the smallest of the three. The roll was gooey and warm, icing catching on the corner of my mouth as I tore a bite. Izidora did the same, spilling some creamy frosting over her chin. My finger wiped it away almost instantly, without thought, and she did not flinch. But her eyes widened, pupils flaming as I held my frosting-coated finger to her. "You can lick it off."

Her cheeks heated, but she tilted her head to suck my finger. She let go with a pop, and my pants grew painfully tight as she returned to the roll in front of her. Before my thoughts turned any darker, I shoveled what remained of mine into my mouth, concentrating on chewing and not the image of her making that sound around my cock.

The sleepy city was peaceful, and I enjoyed the silence as Izidora enjoyed the third roll. Zekari and Kirigin ducked out of the butcher's shop across the way, and I waved them over. The four of us continued to amble as more residents braved the day, yet Izidora seemed more at ease after her belly was filled with sweets. By the time we reached the horses and Endre who watched over them, my father and Vadim had returned with more wine and cheese, but Kriztof and Viktor had yet to return with vegetables. We repacked the saddlebags in the meantime, the residents of Arazki paying us no attention as they bustled about.

A few minutes passed and Kriztof and Viktor appeared from around the corner, arms leaden with bags of root vegetables and squashes, perfect for hearty stews. They laced their haul behind their saddles, then we were ready to depart. Once Arazki's walls were behind us, all our shoulders dropped in unison. Not a single incident had occurred, and I desperately hoped that bolstered Izidora's confidence and trust in people outside our small group.

She strayed further from my side during our morning ride, falling into conversation with Endre about healing magic, Izidora listening intently as he explained the intricacies of the magic craft. I tuned them out, healing not nearly as interesting to me as combat magic; training to rain blows down upon my enemies was much more my style.

When we broke for lunch, Vadim and Izidora trailed off to train with swords. Kriztof cooked thick slabs of fresh meat, something we were all grateful for after so many days of dried slivers. "I ought to give you all my meat raw instead," Kriztof joked. My eyes saw my brain as I shook off his terrible joke, glad Izidora was elsewhere. To avoid encouraging additional comments about Kriztof's dick, I pulled my father aside.

"Father, can I speak with you for a minute?" He motioned for me to lead the way, and then he followed me past the horses out of earshot of the others, hands clasped behind his back as we walked and talked.

"Yesterday, Izidora and I sparred with magic. She was spectacular, setting up traps better than any fresh Knight recruit. But when I called magic whips to my hand, she crumbled, screaming and sobbing and curling up into a ball. It was as if she crawled back into that cave and couldn't get out. I am worried about her," I confided. I left out the part about holding her in my arms, sure my father wouldn't approve of that tidbit.

He sighed. "Only a few weeks ago, we found her chained in darkness; Goddess knows what else occurred before we rescued her. There are many things that might trigger such episodes in the future, and we won't know unless she opens up or it happens. The best we can do is bring her back to reality and show her that she is safe. Honestly, I am surprised she held it together for this long." He paused, then continued, "I am worried about you also, my son. Your usual calmness hasn't been around since Zanin. I know we are all stressed about getting Izidora back to Vaenor in one piece, but you typically hold together well under pressure. It's one of the reasons these males value you as a leader."

He was more right than he knew, but not completely on target. The closer we stepped to Vaenor, the greater my fear clawed at me, terrified of losing this fantasy I had built up all these years. Searching for her was all I had; what was I to do once it was all over? Especially if she were promised to another. But I could not voice my developing feelings to him, for he would remind me of my duty and remind me that we were at the whim of King Zalan, something that constantly pricked the back of my mind.

"I will try to refocus my energy," I promised.

"Good," he said, patting my shoulder. "We should arrive back at Vaenor in another ten days, barring any complications. I expect our welcome will be tumultuous, and we need to be prepared for that."

Extricating myself from his fatherly embrace, we parted ways, him heading toward the smell of seared meat, me in the direction of Vadim's shouted corrections as he and Izidora trained. The clang of metal grew louder as I approached.

Finding a smooth-barked tree, I leaned against it, casually crossing my arms and viewing the scene before me.

Izidora's arms trembled beneath the weight of the plain sword, the metal much heavier than the thick branches she and Vadim had started with. Since her rescue, she'd put on both weight and muscle, despite our lean meals on the road. That thought sent my teeth grinding, for if her body could guzzle what little nutrients we provided her and turn them into this, she must have been given almost nothing before.

She raised the sword to parry one of Vadim's strikes before retaliating with one of her own, spinning out of the way to dodge a second counterstrike. Each movement was slowed down, no doubt to give Izidora time to feel the weight of the blade. Vadim was also a hound for perfect form, and moving mindfully through each movement ensured the right muscles were recruited to execute the strike, so muscle memory would prevail during moments where thought was not an option.

When they broke, I pushed off the tree and strode toward them. "May I?" I said to Vadim, gesturing for his sword.

"Go for it." He tossed the blade and I caught it by the pommel, then he replaced me by the tree trunk, fixing his thick locks of hair atop his head.

I turned to Izidora. "Are you ready?"

Eyes flashing with determination, she dropped into her stance, sword held high in front of her. Her fiery spirit shone through in moments like these, facing an opponent she would surely lose against if we were not merely training, but not cowing to the intimidation of that knowledge.

Facing her, I dropped into my own stance, ready to block her first attack.

She circled, eyeing me cautiously. Thirty seconds passed, and she still hadn't made a move. Circling the blade around my wrist, I initiated the dance, thrusting the sword straight toward her. With the agility of a panther, she lithely jumped to the side, swinging her own blade down to meet mine, protecting her vulnerable body. As I withdrew, she grazed her blade up mine toward the hilt, knocking the sword over to the other side and loosening my grip. Vadim had taught her well.

I regained control and swung a high arc down toward her head, pulling up before landing the blow on her exposed shoulder; but there was no need, her blade met mine in plenty of time.

"Quit going easy on me," she gritted out.

I cocked a brow, smirking. "Are you sure about that, Princess?"

"I can handle it," she shot back.

I increased my pace, Vadim shouting encouragement and assistance at Izidora, who backed up bit by bit under the onslaught of my blade. Relenting on my attacks so as to not cause her to crumble, I held my ground and forced her to move around me instead. She circled this way and that, cutting across to enter the pocket of space that allowed her to reach my toned body. I even took a few steps backward as she fought with a brave heart and pushed us back to our starting point. Her chestnut hair was a shade darker around her brow, and more salty sweat poured from her temples and soaked the light-colored tunic she wore, but still she did not stop, her face fortified with iron will.

I realized I was paying more attention to her than her movements when she kicked out her leg, tripping me as I stepped to the left. Stumbling, she deftly brought her sword up in front of my neck as I was half bent, one hand on the ground as I tried to regain my balance. She was beautiful in her ferocity as the blade bit into my neck. "I yield."

Vadim whooped as his student bested me, and soft clapping surrounded us, our performance on full display for the

Nighthounds. She leaped toward openings without hesitation, without mercy, and for that I was immensely impressed. So, I too clapped for her, then bowed low in deference.

"You will be a warrior before you know it," I beamed.

"I fucking hope so," she quipped, face flushed from exertion and giddiness.

Vadim, Izidora, and I walked over to the stream, needing to clean off before lunch. Cold water was a welcome friend as I splashed it first on my face, then cupped my hands to throw it over my back and down my neck, the crispness sending a shiver as it brushed sensitive nerves along my spine. Izidora rinsed her face a few times, scrubbing with her hands to clear the grime that was ever present while we traveled on the road. Yet her femininity never lost its luster, her aquamarine eyes shining with a depth of emotion I'd never understand, and her body and mind more resilient and adaptive than I thought possible. Vadim clapped me on the shoulder, bringing me back to the present, and I stood to face him.

He swung his arm around my shoulders, turning me toward our waiting party. "Next time, focus on what she's doing and not on her," he snickered, patting me on the chest before walking away. Fuck, I hoped that wasn't as obvious to everyone else.

Our afternoon was uneventful, a light breeze blowing through the trees accompanied by the chirping of birds as we rode along the Northern Route. We rode mostly in silence, only broken when a thought or question popped into Izidora's inquisitive mind. We taught her as much as we could about the world on these long rides, not much else to pass the time other than sharing stories or knowledge, both of which she soaked up like the sun. I'd have loved to see her in a library, where a millennia of knowledge lay between leather-bound tomes.

When we stopped for the evening, Izidora took care of the horses, feeding and watering them with so much love in her eyes, a cooing word here and there to each of our mounts as they munched on their favorite treats, a gentle caress through tangled manes to clear them of fallen leaves or twigs.

One day, she would look at me like that.

We had our usual magic lessons, joined by an excited Endre, who increased the complexity of injuries for her to heal. Both of us intentionally stabbed and sliced deep wounds, grunting with pain as she paled at our self-injury, but quickly taking to her task and healing us thoroughly, confidence growing as she surmounted step after step. By the time darkness fell, she healed dozens of lacerations on both Endre and me.

Izidora's joy leaked from her pores, seeping into my bones as we sat beside each other through dinner. Quick peeks out of the corners of her eyes dotted each passing minute, a hint of curiosity in them I hadn't seen before. We passed around the refilled wineskins, and laughter flowed as easily as the brook at our backs. This was the happiest I had seen the Nighthounds in weeks, and I was glad for the relaxed company. The stars blanketed the sky like freckles across our suntanned faces, and as I tipped my head back, I drank in their power, my body responding to their ancient call. Flying through the open night sky was my favorite place to be, especially on a new moon night when constellations became clearer without the blinding light of the moon.

The Nighthounds filed to their tents, and I stayed out for the first watch, scooting closer to the crackling fire when the wind blustered through the trees.

Izidora's wings remained hidden for now, her body not strong enough to wield their weight, for the feathered wings of Night Fae were dense and strong, a necessary evil to propel our bodies into the sky. Yet, she mastered everything we threw at her with ease, so why not start the process of teaching her to fly? My heart skipped a beat as I imagined us flying under the stars together. Her smile would shine through the darkness like a beacon calling me home. She would laugh as I chased her, then melt into my arms as I captured her in my embrace.

I had to make it happen.

A forceful breeze that carried a metallic scent yanked me back to the present. The hair on the back of my neck stood on end as I bolted up, opening my ears and scanning the trees, searching for any sign of movement.

But there was none.

Creeping to my feet, I reached for my sword resting against a nearby leather bag. A pop and sizzle whipped at my back as another wave of wind pushed through the trees. Flaring my nostrils, I scented that hint of metal in the air, every fiber of my being on high alert.

Stalking toward the edge of the camp in the direction of the breeze, I sniffed again. The aroma was gone. My gaze traveled from tree to tree, searching deep into the bent wood for a flash of metal or a rustle of leaves.

Nothing moved.

I'd been a warrior long enough to know when to trust my gut, so, eyes still scanning, I prowled to Endre's tent, lifting the flap and touching his foot to wake him. He opened his eyes and I put a finger to my lips. With a jerk of his head, he acknowledged the seriousness of the situation, quickly pulling on boots and leather and grabbing his preferred weapons – a heavy axe for his right hand and a deadly sharp dagger for his left. Once we crouched in the freshly turned dirt near the fire, I dug in with my finger to write one word.

IRON

Endre straightened, understanding immediately. His head snapped up, raking his gaze around our camp, searching for looming danger. The breeze had taken its last breath, and no more metallic scents drifted our way. After a dozen minutes, we discharged a tense breath.

"Maybe it was just a fluke," Endre whispered.

"Maybe, but I'm not taking any chances – not with Izidora," I whispered back.

"I will keep watch with you."

Back to back, our attention on the dark trees around us, we waited. For what, I did not know, but I suspected it wouldn't be long before we found out. I only wished the moon was full, to invest some extra light.

IZIDORA

My eyes snapped open. While I normally slept with one ear open, the males' changing of the guard throughout the night drifting through my hazy fog of sleep, this was different. Adrenaline ran a reckless course through my veins as I lay on my cot, listening intently, trying to discern what woke me. Only silence met my sensitive ears. But the air was thick with tension, so taut you could cut it with a knife. My fighting leathers were on my lithe body a moment later, and noiselessly, I exited my tent. Endre and Kazimir sat back to back, arms braced on knees, green eyes furiously searching the night.

I lightly padded to Kazimir. A finger to his lips, then his hand on my hip guided me to the ground in front of him, protectively caging me with his body. His soft stubble brushed my ear as he leaned in close, his voice so low I had to strain to hear. "I need you to go back into your tent. Stay there and don't come out until I fetch you."

I opened my mouth to speak, but his hand found my mouth before I could make a sound. The seriousness of our situation slammed into me, and my throat worked as I craned my neck to look at Endre, who sat coiled like a snake ready to strike. Kazimir's hand dropped away, and I crept along my prior path, crouching low to enter the flaps. Just as I reached it, a strong breeze blasted through the camp, and both males jumped to their feet. The scraping sound of metal signaled drawn swords, and I spun on my heels to find Kazimir bursting through the fire and barreling straight toward me. His massive body slammed into mine, smashing me into the rotten leaves moments before an arrow buried itself into the tree to our left.

Endre yelled, waking the rest of the Nighthounds, who flew out of their tents in various states of dress and armament. Kazimir still lay on top of me, shielding me with a wall of muscle. More shouts rang out, then the clang of steel and whizzing of arrows filled our small camp.

My breath was lodged in my throat like I had swallowed a stone of pure, unbridled fear. I knew it was the people who'd kidnapped me, chained me in darkness, here to reclaim their prize. I couldn't let them take me again. Rapid pants strangled out of me. Kazimir pushed off of me, allowing my chest space to open, yet it was just as constrained as moments before. He turned to crouch in front of me, shielding my vision and my body as chaos erupted in all directions.

"Breathe, Izidora!" he commanded, as a broad male clad in intricate metal armor strode through the trees and raging battle before us. Gulping for air, I pushed myself upright, wishing I had something sharp to defend myself with.

Zekari and Kirigin were fighting with daggers and magic, circling a group of three similarly clad Fae. They danced around, perfectly in sync with each other's movement as they took down one of the Fae by blasting him back and forth until he wasn't sure where to look anymore.

Viktor was back to back with Kriztof, swords flashing as fire-light bounced off them and fending off Fae on both sides.

Endre, Cazius, and Vadim engaged with some archers I couldn't see. Cazius shielded them, his silver magic strong yet translucent, allowing Vadim and Endre to see through while protecting them against incoming arrows. Vadim volleyed arrows in response while Endre chucked balls of light into the woods, attempting to illuminate their attackers and assist Vadim's aim.

My attention returned to the lone male who picked his way through the piling bodies as if he had all the time in the world. Kazimir stood between us, sword glinting deadly as the tip dragged into the ground. Fear dug its roots in the hard packed earth beneath my fingers, freezing me in place.

"We've been looking for you, little whore," he purred, staring at me with black, soulless eyes. His voice was like rough sandpaper, and as wind whipped through the camp again, my senses were assaulted with his smell.

Bile rose in my throat as a memory assaulted me, his grating timbre scraping against my ear as his nails scraped against my skin. The forceful rip that accompanied those nails across my back. The unwelcome entrance of him between my thighs. The crack his nose made as I threw my head back with all my strength. The blood that coated my mouth when my face was shoved into the hewn cave walls.

Rage bloomed in my chest, melting the icy prison that bound me to the ground. My teeth bared in defiance as I stood, hands fisted and filled with white hot flame. "You fucking bastard. I will kill you for what you did to me."

Kazimir looked over his shoulder at me, face half cast in shadow, and half in flame; but his eyes shimmered with barely contained rage, and he looked every bit a dark god prepared to pass judgment and exact vengeance.

The metal-clad male smirked sardonically. "Ah, you remember. I was always the best one."

Kazimir's teeth flashed white in the darkness as a feral and foreboding growl emanated from his heaving chest. The tip of his sword dragging on the ground was a dare for the male before us to fucking try to challenge him. The male bared his teeth in response, raising his sword to fight. Kazimir swung so fast I was certain he had morphed into a god, the movement too unnatural for Fae. My former captor reacted just in time, swords ringing in an angry peal as they latched onto one another. Kazimir was relentless, swinging like a madman, death blazing in his green eyes.

A burst of silver energy stabbed into the back of his opponent, whose eyes widened in surprise as he stumbled forward, off balance, and right into Kazimir's thrusting blade, speared straight through the middle. Blood gushed from the wound as he pushed it in deeper, a snarl tearing from his lips as the blade shot through the other side of the sinister male. In one forceful motion, the blade ran all the way backward, Kazimir's eyes delighted with the dripping of blood off his blade. The male fell to his knees, sword clattering away as he clutched his abdomen, ruby spittle flying from his lips.

"I'm going to draw this out, and by the end you'll be begging me to slit your throat," Kazimir purred as the patter of warm blood bounced off the carpet of leaves.

"Wait!" I shouted. Kazimir spun toward me, icy rage simmering in his emerald eyes.

"You want to show this bastard mercy?" he snapped.

"No. I want a piece," I growled, stalking forward.

His grin was wild and his eyes danced with sadistic amusement. He held out his sword, and I snatched it without hesitation, the weight nothing to me as white hot fury fueled my movements. "Do your worst," Kazimir said.

I rested my hands atop the pommel, tip in the ground, leering down upon the male who had tormented me, raped me, and abused me. It was not Kazimir who was a god fallen to earth to extract vengeance.

It was me.

The pathetic excuse for a male looked up at me, eyes glassy and panting. My hands found the hilt, and I flicked the blade off the ground and straight into his groin. He screamed, ruby rivers running from the corners of his mouth as his manhood was ripped away, just like my innocence.

"That's for raping me," I snarled. Yanking the sword out of the miniscule area, I planted a leather boot straight in his chest, kicking him flat onto his back, his head cracking against the ground with a satisfying thump. In two steps I was on top of his heaving chest, crushing his lungs beneath what little weight I had to push into him. Sword gripped in both hands, tip resting directly above his erratically beating heart, I savored the delicious fear in his eyes, the way he looked so helpless beneath me, and how powerful I felt standing above him. With a scream that held years of unreleased rage, I plunged the blade into his chest, ending his wretched life and exacting payment for what I was owed. "That's for everything else."

It was not enough; I wanted more of their blood.

Stepping down, I passed the blade back to Kazimir. His arm did not stop at the hilt; instead he yanked me to him, crushing me against his hard body as I came down from the high of killing a Fae responsible for the nightmares that plagued both conscious and unconscious dreams. The tremble began in my arms, then pushed its way up from my feet, buckling my knees before working its way up my spine and to my face, the whole thing going numb under an onslaught of tingles. Kazimir's arms snaked tighter as if he sensed the impending crash.

The clamor around us died down as the Nighthounds finished off the rest of the Iron Fae. I was suddenly faced with the whooshing sound of my heart in my ears, so loud I wondered if the males could hear its crescendo just as clearly.

Spinning in Kazimir's arms, I faced the males who fought for me, who swore to die to protect me, though I fervently hoped that did not come to pass that night. Kriztof sported a nasty gash in his thigh, his pants darkened with his spilled life force, and Vadim's shoulder was decorated with a fletched arrow. Otherwise, everyone was whole despite being covered in blood. My lashes fluttered as a wave of fatigue crashed through my body, adrenaline leaving me, along with the will to fight. I took a step toward Kriztof, intending to heal him, but stumbled, Kazimir catching me before I hit the ground.

"Endre will take care of them," he assured me.

"But I want to help. I learned this earlier," I pleaded.

Kazimir studied me for a moment before hoisting me into his arms and carrying me to Kriztof. He gingerly placed me in front of him, and I turned to my knees as I leaned on his leg.

"Don't get any funny ideas while you're that close to the crown jewels, Princess," Kriztof joked. I giggled, glad he was okay enough to crack jokes. With a deep breath, I utilized that bubble of happiness to send healing magic into his leg, knitting the muscle back together before closing the wound.

I panted with the effort, sitting back on my butt when I was finished. Kriztof saluted me and rose to his feet. "Pleasure doing business with you."

Another wave of exhaustion washed over me. I sat there blinking, while the males cleaned up the bodies of the Iron Fae, nineteen in total. We were outnumbered more than two to one, and I killed one of them without hesitation.

And I would do it again.

Yet the thought didn't scare me. Instead, the image of that awful male's eyes dimming permanently heated my core in an inexplicable way.

Kazimir was by my side an instant later, scooping me into his arms and carrying me to the nearby stream to wash off. I numbly stripped off my clothes and sat knees to chest in the freezing water, the shaking unrelenting as reality set in. Kazimir rinsed the blood out of my clothes while he called for Cazius to bring me a fresh tunic. He appeared with one a moment later, and I stepped out of the stream, pulling the soft tunic over my head, blanketing me more like a dress than a shirt as it fell to my knees. Kazimir carried me to his tent, tucking me inside his warm cot.

He brushed a hand over my hair, smoothing the wet strands from my tingling face. "I'll be back shortly. Rest."

Smothering myself in his smoke and amber scent, I let the familiarity calm me. My eyes were heavy, and I let them close as voices murmured, bodies dragged, and metal was thrown about. Sometime later, a warm body lay on the floor next to the cot, and I reached out my hand, found his chest, and passed out peacefully once more.

14

KAZIMIR

The rapid fire of my heart never slowed as I laid on the cold ground next to my cot, listening to Izidora's soft breaths. There was no way I would let her sleep alone, not when we were attacked mere hours before, unknown numbers of pursuers remaining. I did not care if she felt smothered or trapped by my attention; she was not leaving my line of sight anytime soon. She was mine to protect now, whether she realized it or not. I was in too deep with my addiction, my obsession, and nothing else would satisfy me.

How did they find us? We were so careful, avoiding towns as much as possible the last few weeks, and when we were in Arazki, nothing was amiss. Though it was common knowledge who searched for the lost princess, we'd been unsuccessful for so long that most in the town had probably ignored us for that reason.

How long ago did they discover she was missing?

The male Izidora stabbed with my blade flashed through my mind, sending a cascade of tension through my shoulders and jaw. He had raped her, tortured her, and he deserved every bit of blood she coaxed from him. I wanted to resuscitate him just so I could end his life again. Slowly.

Witnessing the bloodlust bursting from Izidora as she finished him off made my cock hard in the best possible way. Her hidden fire burst forth in that moment of defiance, and she displayed the first hints of how formidable she would become. Yet, the first kill always hit the hardest, even if we were prepared to snuff out that life. Even if they deserved it.

Dawn drifted beneath the canvas flap of the tent, bringing with it the morning song of birds. Their cheerful chirping was antithetical to my serious attitude. We needed to get moving before anyone discovered us camping next to a pile of bodies. Rather than risk an attention-attracting pyre, we decided it would be safest to scatter the dead through the woods in the morning, hoping animals would take care of hiding the evidence. It was no less than what they deserved.

There was no doubt in my mind that the Iron Realm was behind everything; they had the most to gain by taking her. Their realm was the smallest, almost entirely surrounded by mountains, and while they had the benefit of mining precious gemstones that sold for a pretty penny, they had little farmland and only a sliver of ocean access. Using Izidora as leverage was a good strategy; marrying her off to King Azim when she came of age would have forced the Night Realm to cooperate or combine should King Zalan die without naming another heir.

"Kazimir, are you awake?" my father whispered from outside the tent.

Stifling a yawn, I murmured, "Yes, just a minute." Izidora still slept, her hand resting gently atop my chest. The spot where our skin touched was warmer than the rest of my body, and I was loath to end the moment of unfiltered intimacy with the sleeping female beside me. With the slowness of a meandering creek, I lifted her hand and tucked it next to her serene face.

Sitting up slowly, careful not to smack my head, I reached for a new tunic and slipped it on before quietly exiting the tent. My father stood a few paces away, gazing at the hazy sky.

"We need to leave as soon as possible," he started. "Hurry and round up the others to help you with the bodies before dawn fully breaks. While you are in the woods, check for any sign that others might have escaped and which direction they headed. We can't take any chances."

"Yes, father," I said. I woke each male in turn, relaying his instructions, and we split into pairs to scatter the bodies, stalking deep into the woods in all directions, leaving not one body too close to another. After my third trip, Izidora emerged from my tent, wrapping her arms around her stomach to keep warm against the chill.

Cazius guided her next to the fire, fetching a blanket to cover her thin frame. By the time I returned again, they were deep in conversation, my father's brow furrowed and Izidora's striking blues shining with unshed tears. She gave him a weak smile as he stood, heading for the horses. Her attention turned to me, and she seemed to brighten in time with the sky.

"I'll be back soon," I mouthed to her.

We finished up the bodies after the next round, returning with a pile of steel armor with overlapping scales that provided the wearer extra mobility. The Iron Realm's armor was finely crafted, though this steel was too heavy for us to fly, let alone unfurl our wings, and we could not take it with us.

"What should we do with these?" Zekari asked my father.

"Bury them," he replied. Silver tendrils twisting from their fingers, the twins sent their magic into the earth, pulling on the energy buried there to dig a deep hole and lift a cylinder of dirt above ground. The rest of us chucked the dark metal into the hole, a cacophony of sound tampered by the wet earth around it, then they dropped the load of earth with a dull thud, covering all evidence of our excavation.

Izidora's back was to us as she rubbed and saddled our horses, sneaking sugar to Fek and an apple to Mistik before securing their bridles in place. The fire was already out – breakfast would be on the go. We broke down our tents, rolling them into our saddlebags and slinging them across our mounts' backs as Kriztof handed out slices of dried meat and bread.

"Glad to see you are alright," I remarked, clapping arms with him.

"T'was nothing but a scratch. Thanks to our princess, I will live to fight another day." He bowed with a flair of his hands in her direction, and she rolled her eyes at his dramatics as she mounted Mistik.

We rode side by side the whole day, an invisible rope tying us together after our joint kill in the night. The memory of my first kill surfaced; I was only sixteen at the time, a touch of youthful ignorance still clinging to my soul. King Zalan wanted me to play executioner that day, reasoning that it was time for me to grow up and face the realities of this world if I were to join my father on missions to find the princess. The king claimed a male had poisoned his food, an assassination attempt with the aim of placing the Night Crown over his own brow. In reality, the courtier had probably slept with King Zalan's favorite whore of the month, since Zalan's food tasters hadn't fallen ill. But I had to do what my king demanded of me. After that day, I truly became a Night Fae male, whatever innocence remained dashed away with the fall of the deadly sharp blade.

My father taught me to kill in life or death situations, and never for the sport of it. He understood the difference between necessity and cruelty. He pulled me aside after the deed was done to remind me of that fact, lest I fall into King Zalan's erratic reasoning.

From then, I wasn't a fan of royalty and spent as much time away from Este Castle as possible – out of sight, out of mind. But when my father's duties as High Lord called us, I was obliged to go with him. After his death, I would take his position on the council, and I had to learn how to play the political game.

The Night Realm needed a new monarch. A sideways perusal of Izidora revealed the radiant female lost in thought, eyes glassy and unblinking as she tumbled through a faraway place. She would be a beloved queen, and should she take the throne sooner rather than later, the idea of us living out our own fairytale was entirely possible.

For when we arrived in the seat of the Night Realm, we would certainly be welcomed by a nightmare. The family Izidora craved so desperately was not to be found with the king of the Night Fae, his mercurial nature only amplified by this mystery sickness that ailed him. I hoped that her return would change him for the better, but that change coming to pass was less likely than flakes of snow blanketing the Day Realm.

When I could stand the silence between us no longer, I asked, "Are you okay?"

"I don't know." Her shoulders dropped inward under the weight of her admission.

"Do you want to talk about it?"

Her teeth sank into her bottom lip. "I'm afraid of opening this vault inside me where I locked all my feelings away. My magic keeps hammering at the lock on this chest, and little by little, my trauma seeps out, bleeding into my head and heart. I want to be strong and fearless, but I have these intense emotions that compete for space in my head. The lid feels like it's about to burst regardless of how much force I put into sealing it shut."

"I'll be here to catch you when it does," I promised, angling Fek closer to Mistik so I could stroke her cheek.

Her downturned eyes popped up at my touch, and I let my

hand fall to her thigh, leaving it there as her mouth opened with another question. "Why do you care so much?"

I didn't have a good answer for her question – at least not one I wanted to share. She was my sun, and I was the moon in constant pursuit, yet never quite fast enough to catch and unite with her. Beyond my years of investment in searching for the lost princess, I'd fallen in deep with my fantasies of our lives together, only amplified by the spirit of the hellcat riding beside me. I was in over my head, and the thought of losing her to another male made me ill.

"I don't know," I lied. "I want to see you happy and safe more than anything in the world. Maybe it's because I spent so long searching for you. Maybe it's my sense of duty. Maybe it's something else." My eyes seared into hers, hoping she would read into my words, to see the possibility between us.

Holding my gaze and not backing down, she stated, "I feel good about killing him."

My brows climbed my forehead. That was not what I had expected her to say, but it wasn't hard to imagine why she felt that way. Obviously, he had inflicted significant damage on her – mentally and physically – and she received a gift most victims never get, an opportunity for revenge, turning the tables on their abuser.

"Does that make me a bad person?" she cocked her head, waiting for me to reject her.

"I don't think so. He hurt you, and you wanted to take back what he took from you." I squeezed her thigh, emphasizing that I wasn't going anywhere.

Her eyes flicked to my hand and a rosy flush shaded her cheeks, but she did not acknowledge that tug between us. Instead she spoke again. "All I could think about was how I would rather die than be chained again as you shielded me. Even as you got up, I remained frozen, fear overtaking my rational mind. But then he walked closer, and I was possessed with the need to fight back."

"You have a fire deep within you," I told her. "Don't let anyone or anything blow out that flame."

A flash of concern crossed her face, so fast I almost didn't see it, but before I could comment on it, she sighed, "Thanks, Kazimir. I needed to hear that. I worried what you would think of me if I told you how fucking good it felt to kill him. You've saved me... at least twice now, and I am starting to feel safe with you."

I nearly choked on her confession, the words unexpected yet *everything* I'd been dying to hear. My hand caressed her cheek once more, tucking a lock of chestnut hair behind her pointed ear so I could drink in more of her heart-shaped face.

"I think you are a fighter and a survivor, and that makes you all the more precious to me."

Her lashes fluttered closed beneath my words, and her head nuzzled my hand as she leaned into it. In that moment, it was only us in the autumn wood, and I couldn't bring myself to tear my hand from her face, even though I knew I should. I'd never been a greedy male, but when it came to Izidora, I was gluttonous.

She broke contact first, lifting her head out of my palm and dropping the reins to toss her long hair over the opposite shoulder, the golden rays catching it and highlighting its glossy sheen. The sun was directly overhead, not a shadow in sight, and while we would normally have stopped for lunch, fear drove us to continue down the dirt road to Vaenor. Putting distance between our mounts and those bodies was paramount. An idea struck me, and I kicked myself for not thinking of it sooner. With one last look at Izidora, I spurred Fek to catch up to my father.

"What if we head to Zirok House now to regroup, then to Vaenor after we've sent word that we found Izidora? We could use the extra manpower to guard her," I suggested. Zirok House was our family estate, surrounded by high, stone walls to ward off any potential attacks. We went there as frequently as we could because my father took great pride in helping the Fae in nearby villages. Our subjects around Zirok were the healthiest and happiest in the Night Realm, and therefore they were extremely loyal to the Vaszolys. It was perfect for our current situation.

My father glanced at the sky, judging how much daylight we had left. Zirok was far off the Northern Route and we would have to cut through the woods to reach the road that led to our home. "If we turn now, we might make it to Theszaly Track by nightfall," he calculated. "We will be safer there than on the open road."

Craning my neck to find Izidora, I asked, "Are you up for a hard ride?"

"I've got this," she affirmed.

Viktor laughed from beside us, "Let's ride hard and get there tonight. Alithaela might act pissed at us for showing up with no warning, but she will be happy to see us."

"The horses can rest when we get to Zirok House. No stops. Keep your eyes and ears open because we don't know who might be watching us." My father maneuvered his black steed toward the woods to our left, kicking him into a gallop and leading us toward our home.

The twins followed, hot on his heels, and I glanced at Izidora, grim determination flattening her lips. Digging her heels into Mistik's sides and pulling on the reins, she expertly guided the mare off the road and to race through the trees. I followed shortly after, shouting at her to ask Mistik for more speed. The drumbeat of Mistik's hooves quickened, and caught up to the twins. Weaving through the naturally spaced trees, we flew along to the shelter of Zirok House. At times, we slowed to navigate rough terrain, not wanting the horses to stumble and slow us even further. Orange light pierced our eyes through gaps in the trees as we raced west, the sun dying with the day, dropping faster and faster the deeper we wove into the woods.

We needed to reach the open plains along Theszaly Track before night was truly upon us; the openness would make it easier to spot any tails and we wouldn't run the risk of plowing headfirst into a thick oak tree.

Moments before the light of the sun winked out, the dull grassy plains appeared through the trees. My father pulled up his mount, slowing him to a walk. Our horses all foamed around their bits, hides soaked from our endless race through the trees. "Water the horses before we cross into the plains. It's going to be an all out sprint from here."

Wasting no time, we led our horses to a deep, rock-lined pool with a swiftly flowing creek dragging a constant stream of fresh water through it. They drank greedily, droplets sticking and dripping from their whiskers as they lifted their heads to look at us, a plea in their eyes to finish this grueling ride.

It was almost over. Fek had earned a year's worth of sugar cubes for his endurance on this trip. Without waiting for their breaths to even out, we remounted and trotted onto the open plain, the Nighthounds scanning in every direction, listening for the hint of a suspicious sound.

Silence greeted us. The only sounds were the heavy breathing of the horses and the occasional chirp of a bird as they settled into their slumber. Yet the hairs on the back of my neck stood straighter than the tall pines we rode through, feeling eyes from everywhere around me.

Night fell over us, coating the sky in inky paint with a single light stroke from the sliver of the moon. The stars winked to life, one after the other, greeting their children of the night and dotting the canvas around the moon. Kicking the horses in the canter, we dusted the swaying grass as we cut a path to Theszaly Track. Without the cover of the trees, I felt naked and vulnerable, giving our enemies the perfect opportunity to strike. Yet the stars hounded us from above, fueling our magic, and guiding us to safety.

My father thundered onto the hard packed road first, his mount's hooves generating the first beat before we joined him, a thundering symphony racing not against each other, but against the clock. Vadim shouted from the back, his voice lost to the wind, so I turned, craning my neck to see what caused him alarm.

A group of hooded riders appeared from the treeline, an eerie and ominous aura around them, their black mounts barely visible as they burst from the forest.

Fucking Fates, there were more of them. I had to get Izidora to safety.

"Father!" I screamed over the wind, my voice ripping with the force of my outburst. "Faster!"

He glanced back, glimpsing our pursuers, then folded forward on his horse's neck, whispering to him, asking him to give everything he had left. His mount obeyed, digging deep and increasing his speed. All our horses responded in kind, and Fek stretched his long legs as far and fast as they could carry us.

Izidora mimicked us, crouching as low as possible in the saddle and urging Mistik on with reins pushing up her neck. Her fingers wound in the mare's dark gray mane, eyes locked straight ahead as if she refused to give the Fae chasing us an ounce of her attention. "C'mon Mistik, let's fucking show them," she screamed at her mount, and the mare put on a burst of speed, leaving Fek and I scrambling to keep up with their blistering pace.

A maelstrom of hoofbeats drummed behind us as our

pursuers increased their pace, racing to catch up to us. Crack after crack sounded behind us, the Fae whipping their mounts to ask for more speed. Wind tore at my eyes as I looked at Izidora, knowing she too heard the sound. Her teeth were bared and jaw locked tight, but she did not falter despite the tears that flew back in the direction of her whipping hair.

Our horses galloped like they were floating on air, our speed so fast that their hooves barely touched the ground as they propelled us toward Zirok House. Our lead was strong, but we were losing significant ground, the Iron Realm riders gaining on us one length at a time. We'd been riding for weeks, not resting our horses nearly enough, and we were suffering the consequences.

My heart and hoofbeats pounded in my ears as we raced against the odds to get Izidora to safety.

She would rather die than be chained again.

I would never let that happen; since I had her, I would never let her go.

Soft light appeared ahead, and the outer wall of Zirok winked in the distance. Checking under my arm to gauge the distance between us, my stomach dropped when the Iron riders were twice as close as before, close enough for me to see the hammered chest plates their mounts wore.

I prayed to the Goddess that Alithaela had stationed more than two guards by the gate. They came into view moments later, and my father posted in his stirrups, balanced precariously as he waved his arms at the guards stationed there to open the gates. Slack jaws greeted our sudden appearance, and the speed of our trajectory jolted them into action. Four guards stood outside the manor's walls, and they scrambled to pull the gates open wide enough for us to pass through two at a time. I was going to kiss Alithaela when I saw her.

Half a mile to go.

I checked the position of the riders again, only to discover they were a dozen lengths behind us now. Endre and Kriztof had dropped back in parallel with Vadim, readying to defend us as we approached the gate at a blistering pace. The guards at the gate all had crossbows pointed beyond us, trained on our pursuers. Thankfully, our pursuers hadn't noticed them yet.

One quarter mile.

A tug on Fek's reins slowed him enough to allow Izidora to ride in front of us. Her safety was worth more than my life, and I would fight to the death to protect her. Mistik thundered away, headed straight toward the center of the gate. My father passed through, followed by the twins, then Mistik flew through, not slowing until she was well beyond the outer wall.

Wasting no time after we flew between the heavy gates, Viktor and I dismounted and rolled, spinning toward the gate should they attempt to follow us through. The Iron Realm's riders were within range of the crossbows, and our guards unleashed a volley of bolts. One struck a shoulder, another a leg as they sounded an alarm. Vadim, Endre, and Kriztof galloped through the gate, leaping from their mounts to shove the gate closed. Endre threw up a magical shield in front of the guards outside the walls while Vadim and Kriztof grabbed bows and blades and scaled the wall like it was nothing before dropping on the other side to defend us.

There were ten riders in all, backed out of range of the crossbows. A clamor preceded the rest of the guards stationed at Zirok House joining us at the gate. Realizing they were far outnumbered, our pursuers turned their horses abruptly and took off into the night.

"Should we catch them?" Viktor asked my father.

"Let them go," he said, exhaustion lining his voice. "They won't try anything tonight."

He barked orders to Zirok's forces, requesting an increase in the number of people on patrol. Izidora remained atop Mistik, her fingers white from how tightly she gripped the mare's mane. I patted Mistik's sweaty hide, her usually dappled fur a single dark gray color. "Thank you for keeping my love safe," I whispered in her furry ear, and she nudged her head into my chest as if to say 'you're welcome.'

Brushing my hands across Izidora's, I encouraged her to relax their grip. She relented, color flushing the skin of her hands as blood returned to them, then looked at me. Bruises marred the undersides of her blue eyes, slightly pinched as exhaustion pulled at her. She did not protest as I lifted her from the saddle, tucking her against my chest and carrying her toward the front doors of Zirok. She curled into me, resting her head near my heart as a small whimper trembled in her throat.

The doors burst open, a buxom female in a nightshift running out onto the lawn. She saw me and hurried over, the expression on her round face competing between raised brows with slack jaw and frowned brows and mouth.

"Kazimir! What are you doing here? What happened?" Her gaze fell on the bundle in my arms. "Who is this? Where have you been?" Her interrogation continued.

"Alithaela, it's good to see you too," I grinned.

She smacked me on the arm, scolding me like a child. "You nearly scared me out of my wits! I woke up to thunder and shouting, and then I saw you lot flying to the gate, another party hot on your heels. I thought we were all going to die!"

"But did you die?" Kriztof sauntered up along with the rest of the Nighthounds.

She smacked Kriztof in the stomach, hard enough to make him double over, wheezing and rubbing his bruised stomach and ego. The rest of us snickered at his expense. Alithaela was like a mother to us all, her kind and nurturing nature warming anyone she was near – when she wasn't hitting them, of course.

"And I'm not even prepared for visitors," she clicked her tongue at us. "You lot will have to make your own beds! You know where the linens are. I'll go put on some tea."

Carrying Izidora over the threshold of my home was more real than I could have ever imagined, and without waiting for anyone else, I took her straight to my rooms on the second floor. "Hey," I said softly, peering down at her. "Would you like a bath?"

She nodded, too weary to speak.

My room was exactly as I had left it, though the fire had long since died. A wood-paneled bathroom waited for us, and I placed her on the counter before I strode to the deep soaking tub and turned on the water. I opened the cabinets and pulled out soaps and salts for her, piling them near the tub in preparation for her bath. In our manor home, we had the luxury of heated water, and even a shower, something I had desperately missed during our time in the more far-flung parts of the Night Realm.

Once I'd poured a sufficient measure of both lavender salts and soaps in the water, I returned to Izidora, kneeling before her to pull off her boots. She hopped down from the counter, her tiny frame landing lightly on the black marble tiles below. Pulling at her tunic, I realized she still wore mine, her leather pants almost entirely covered since the tunic was untucked. Her bare feet padded lightly to the tub, and she reached a trembling hand in to test the temperature. I fetched some towels, piling them neatly within reach of the soaking tub.

"Feel free to use anything you find in here. What's mine is yours."

"Where are you going?" she asked, her eyes widening as I turned to leave.

"I need to check in with everyone and let Alithaela berate me some more. Do you want me to bring you some tea?" I asked.

She nodded. "Tea sounds lovely. Will you come back soon?"

My heart skipped a beat. "Do you want me to?"

"Yes." Her voice was as tiny as she was, and she bit her lower lip while she waited for my answer.

That motion and her admission had my blood heating faster than the water in her bath. Her plump pink lips were perfect for sucking, and those round aquamarine pools perfect for diving. My mind tossed images of us wrapped around each other in that tub, and I was grateful that my back was turned so she could not see my growing erection.

"I'll be right outside when you are finished," I promised, voice breaking slightly as I tried to keep my cool. Then I sped for the doors, closing them behind me before I did anything stupid. She wasn't ready; she wasn't mine – yet.

Alithaela's boisterous voice overruled Kriztof's, and a small smile tugged at my lips as I tried to guess what she was shouting at him for, imagining how red her face would be by the time I breached the kitchen entry. His favorite pastime here was riling her up with his salacious jokes.

When I opened the door, everyone surrounded a large dining table with Alithaela standing next to Kriztof, rag in hand, face red, poised to strike him with it. Kriztof held up his hands in mock surrender, while Zekari and Kirigin were doubled over, wheezing with tears in their eyes.

Alithaela saw me, threw her hands in the air, and declared, "Honestly, Kazimir, the company you keep!" She stomped to the stove, called on her magic to lift a large kettle from the flames, and poured a generous measure over rows of cups she'd set up for tea.

I strode to the counter to help her before she shooed me away. "Go sit, go sit. You've had a long journey and I expect a full report. Minus all the things that would make me worry more."

I laughed. "Then it will be a short report for you. We found the lost princess."

She dropped the kettle, cups smashing and ceramic flying everywhere. Her mouth was agape, hand covering it as she processed my words. Drops of hot water splashed onto her arm, jolting her into action; she grabbed rags to clean up the mess, and I stooped to gather broken pieces of the cups.

"I can't believe it. After all this time, I was sure hope was lost." Tears sprang to her eyes, and she sniffed. She squealed and wrapped me in a motherly hug.

Returning the embrace, I asked, "I want to take her some tea, could you make another cup?"

"Anything for our lost princess," she breathed.

"I was hoping you would say that," I grinned. "She loves sweets, and I think she would love your cookies. How quickly can you make some?"

Alithaela squealed again. "I'll whip some up right now." She refilled the kettle, placing it back over the flames before turning her magic to the rest of the kitchen, bringing all the ingredients for her cookies flying to the wood counter. A mixing bowl narrowly missed my ear, and I took that as my cue to join my brothers in arms.

Alithaela whipped up the fastest batch of cookies I had ever seen, all the while serving us more tea to warm our chilled bones. She neatly arranged the cookies on a serving tray, complete with tea, sugar, milk, and some flowers for extra flair.

Vadim reached for one of the leftover cookies cooling on another plate, and Alithaela snapped his hand with her rag. "Ouch!" he exclaimed, rubbing the back of his hand.

"Those are for the lost princess!" she scolded.

"But she's not going to eat them all!" Kriztof exclaimed.

I picked up the tray and headed back to my rooms, listening to the squabbling coming from the kitchen and laughing to myself. It was good to be home.

***

INTERLUDE

" I have taken care of her for the past thirteen years, you cannot expect me to leave her now!" The caretaker argued with a retinue of guards corralling her away from the clanging of metal and sobs echoing down the halls of the cave.

"New orders," the captain of the guard grumbled. "She'll be with us, save for one week of the month when you can return with other females to take care of her."

"I don't understand!" the caretaker exclaimed, still attempting to sidestep the male.

Another male chimed in, this one older and dressed in the fine clothes of nobility. He smoothed his dark hair back with gnarled hands, giving away his frustration. "She has become insolent in your care. You were supposed to keep her pliant, not make her rebellious."

"That is her nature," the female explained.

"Then we shall have to break her spirit." His tone brokered no room for argument.

A sob wracked the caretaker's chest, nearly reaching the pitch of her ward's. That moment of brokenness was all it took for two of the guards to snatch her arms and drag her away from the only daughter she'd ever really had. The sound of her sorrow was so loud, she did not hear the knife being drawn until it was too late.

———

"IT'S TIME FOR YOUR BATH," a stern female said to the princess, who remained with her back against the wall, head leaned back and looking up at the darkness overhead. The keeper's companions busied themselves lighting basins of oil at the far edges of the hewn cave, casting light into the otherwise dark space. The princess's eyes blinked as she adjusted to the firelight that would remain through the duration of the keepers' stay.

"Can I at least bathe without chains?" the princess asked, a hint of attitude in her voice.

The female sighed, pinching the bridge of her nose. "Last time, you tried to run. And how far did you get?"

The princess did not respond. The keeper strode towards her, towering over the princess as she demanded a response through a swift backhand across the face that drew a hint of blood at the corner of the princess's mouth. Through gritted teeth, the small female replied, "Not far. I'm not stupid enough to do that again."

The keeper raised an eyebrow, questioning the validity of the princess's words. "No, you are not stupid. But you are rebellious, and until you learn to be otherwise, the shackles will remain. Now, get the fuck up and let me unhook the chains from the wall, so you can walk to the bath. Don't try anything. You know the consequences."

The princess's lips flattened into a line, but she rose and shuffled away from the wall while her keeper unlocked the irons and dragged them across the stone ground in the direction of the tub. When the chains had almost tightened, the princess took her first step forward toward the bath with her shoulders held tensely beside her ears. The five other females attending to her had already filled it and heated the water, though it was never warm enough to chase the chill from her bones.

She sank into the tub, allowing them to scrub a month's worth of grime from her hair and skin, while they spoke of nothing of importance. The princess ignored them until they spoke to her directly. "Let's pretend today you are a High Lady. How do you greet your king?"

The princess was grateful her wet hair framed her face and hid the roll of her eyes. "Your Highness, how handsome you look today."

One of the females deepened her voice to mimic that of a male's. "High Lady, what a welcome surprise. Will you dine with me?"

"Whatever pleases you, Your Highness," she mumbled through her curtain of wet hair.

The stern female smacked her across the back of the head. "You must speak loudly and clearly when addressing your king."

The princess did not understand why she must know the correct titles and addresses for nobility, since she had never left the cave. But she complied, repeating the phrase and enunciating every word. This exchange continued until the bath was complete, but before she rose from the tub, the stern female gripped her by her sopping hair and forced her head back. "Never forget that you are nothing. You are worthless, and no king would ever want to dine with you."

The princess said nothing, waiting patiently for the other five females to dry and dress her before ambling back to the anchor on the wall, the chains relatching with a somber click. The females settled onto small poufs they dragged with them every time they came to visit, watching her as she sat with her back against the rough wall.

"Recite *The Burning of the Driftwood*," the stern female ordered.

The small female launched into the poem she'd been forced to memorize, the keepers listening with rapt attention to ensure she did not miss a word.

That was their routine; she must respond appropriately when presented with various situations regarding nobility, recite poems they forced her to memorize, learn all the ways to be elegant and eloquent, and do it all without a hint of insolence.

Her compliance, she was told, meant that one day she'd be free of these chains. Yet the princess did not believe this, for the guards told her the exact opposite, and she had been there long enough to start to believe that this life she lived was an endless hell.

III

THE REFUGE

15

IZIDORA

I sank into the deep tub, water nearly up to my chin by the time I was seated comfortably. The past day had exacted an enormous toll on me; my nerves were more frayed than my old tunics, and I balanced on a knife's edge, wondering which way I would fall. Ducking under the water, I sat for a moment in blissful silence, nothing but the beating of my own heart taking up space.

When I breached the surface, I sucked down air, my lungs seizing from holding my breath too long. Hot tears pricked my eyes, spilling out of them as I let go of the death grip I held over my emotions, allowing them to flood the bathwater and dissolve among the bubbles.

Twice in one day I was under attack. Twice in one day, I almost lost my freedom.

Yet this time, I acted instead of freezing, and for that I was proud. I was a fighter, and despite numbing out of my existence for so many years when I felt unsafe, it was a crutch I no longer needed. I could feel, and I could fight; there was no need for dichotomy between the two.

I soaked for a few more moments before grabbing a soap

and starting to scrub. The scent of roses filled the air as I worked the bar over my body, aching to scrub every last bit of blood and grime on my skin. Despite sitting in the stream the night before, I still felt dirty. I scrubbed until my skin was pink, then began washing my long chestnut tresses. By the time I was finished, blood, sweat, and tears filled my bath water, and I pulled the plug, washing them all down the drain.

I felt lighter as they disappeared in a hurricane, pulling old parts of me down with them.

Truly, I felt no remorse for killing the male – that bastard deserved what I did and more. I felt powerful taking his life, more powerful than I ever had before; I was no longer a victim, and I had the power to fight back – and to win. I got to write the ending to that part of my story, though it was unfinished for now.

I would kill every last one of them for what they did to me.

They took away my identity, my life, my family, chaining me like an animal and keeping me in the dark about this big beautiful world waiting for me. They stripped me of everything that made me Fae, leaving me questioning everything about myself. They forced me to retreat deep into my own mind to survive their abuse, becoming someone I was not.

Kazimir was right. I had a fire inside me, burning bright and aching for release. I was meant for more.

I tuned into my white flame, fueling it with evidence of my strength until it filled the entirety of my chest, so strong and sure and unable to be snuffed out. It danced around the clear crystal and intertwined with the silvery threads of moonlight, dazzling me with its performance.

A door opened and then closed softly. The tinkle of silverware followed a moment later. Kazimir had returned, and it was time for me to face the world once more. A sigh bounced off the walls, and I reached for some towels, wrapping one around my long hair before wrapping a second around my body.

A beautiful bronze mirror stood propped against the wood wall over the counter, and as I passed by it, I took the opportunity to really look at myself, studying my face for the first time. One glance in the mirror in my room in Zanin had been enough for me, not wanting to see just how awful I looked. But the image of my gaunt face, hollowed eyes, and ghostly skin would haunt me forever.

My cheeks looked fuller and my skin was lightly bronzed from all our time outdoors. My bright aquamarine eyes popped against my skin and chestnut hair. My locks tumbled over my breasts and down my back as the cloth atop my head fell away. I dropped the second towel, turning to admire the muscles developing across my frame – I looked healthy, albeit still a bit too thin.

I scrounged for something to wear in the attached closet. While walking out in a towel to sit with Kazimir would be a great way to get his attention, I wasn't sure that I was ready for it, though it was obvious he was. His touches were tender, and though I did not want them at first, he'd slipped past my walls somewhere along the way, and those touches knit the shattered pieces of my soul together.

A black tunic that I assumed belonged to Kazimir was my best option, and I slipped it over my head, the fabric tumbling to my knees. This would do for now.

I padded back into the bathroom, then opened the door into the adjoining room. Kazimir reclined on a low couch, his hands tucked behind his head. He straightened as I exited the bathroom, muscles rippling and flexing as he sat upright and dropped his arms. On the table in front of him was a silver tray laden with cookies, tea, and flowers. My eyes widened at the sight of cookies, their chocolatey scent wafting my way and making my mouth water.

The couch was plush and sank ever so slightly as I settled next to Kazimir, my wet hair falling over my shoulder as I reached for a treat. I took a huge bite, moaning as the chocolate melted across my tongue.

Kazimir chuckled, the sound like rumbling thunder in his chest. "I had Alithaela make those just for you. You should have seen Vadim and Kriztof fighting her for one. She insisted that you would want all of them for yourself."

I giggled, finishing another bite. "She was right. I want them all for myself. I think I will sleep on a bed of them tonight, in fact."

Kazimir filled a teacup, adding some milk and sugar before handing the steaming cup to me. The tea was the perfect temperature, heating me from the inside out and chasing away the last bit of tension from nearly being kidnapped – again – twice in one day. Another cookie met my stomach before I decided to play nice and offer one to Kazimir. He accepted immediately, eyes dancing as he chewed the treat slowly, watching my every move. His intense examination captured me, and our bodies slowly gravitated toward one another. A hand found my bare thigh, and my core throbbed at its nearness to that part of me that had never been shown love. My skin pebbled as the hem of the shirt slid up my thigh, and I released a shuddering breath.

With a painful grimace, his hand retreated, and air filled my lungs once more. I quickly grabbed the tea and took a sip to cover the crescendo that sounded in my chest. "Who is Alithaela?" I asked, voice a little too husky for my liking.

"She is Zirok's housekeeper and like a second mother to me. We couldn't get along without her. She watches the house while we are away, ensuring that everything is taken care of. She is also the best cook in the entire Night Realm. Possibly all the realms. Your father has tried to steal her for his own kitchen several times, but she always refuses. She likes to be in charge here, fussing over us like a mother hen." Kazimir grinned as he talked about the shapely female who had accosted us at the front door.

"She seems really nice. I would like to meet her tomorrow," I said around a mouthful of chocolate.

"You will. She is very happy we finally found you. You might be a little overwhelmed by her smothering at first, but that's just who she is. And I think you could use some of her smothering," he teased, smiling at me.

"I'll deal with whatever if she keeps making these cookies," I laughed, grabbing my fourth one.

Yes, four was a lot, but I deserved them after the day I'd had.

"You can stay here tonight. These are my rooms, the best in our house besides my father's. Only fitting for our lost princess," he winked.

I rolled my eyes. "I wouldn't know what was fitting if it slapped me in the face. You should take your rooms, I'm sure you would be more comfortable in them." I didn't want anyone to be put out because of me, and honestly, I didn't want to be in this big room all by myself. There was so much space and luxury it was a little unnerving.

What was I to do with a massive four-poster bed piled with blankets and thick furs, opposite in every way to the cave with barely a mattress for comfort? Across from it sat a large wooden desk overflowing with papers, and delicate sconces hung from the wall over it. On either end of the room, massive hearths blazed and crackled with thick logs, the one to my right holding a mantle filled with bejeweled weapons. The red couch we sat on was wide enough for two people to lay side by side, and as soft as the clouds we'd ridden under along the Northern Route. Adjacent to the low couch were a few plush chairs, one stacked with books, the other stacked with pillows, and across from us was a matching piece to this one. The whole room was warm and masculine and smelled distinctly of amber.

"Where will you sleep?" I asked Kazimir. After everything that happened, I didn't want him to be far away. This push and pull inside of me warred over his closeness, but my deepening connection to him was winning, an invisible rope begging me to tie myself to him so that I'd always be safe.

"Down the hall. There are several rooms on this side of the second floor. Endre and Viktor like to sleep on this side too. We will all be close if you need anything."

I chewed my bottom lip, thinking. It was too far for my comfort, yet sleeping alone in the same room was not a position I wanted to be in. I knew he would stay all night with me if I asked, but I couldn't bring myself to say those words.

"Will you stay in here until I fall asleep?" It was a compromise between the parts of me that were scared of being alone in the dark and the parts of me that feared the proximity of another male – though with each passing day, that fear shrunk, especially when it came to Kazimir. Weariness pulled at me, and I knew it wouldn't be long before I'd fall into the void of sleep.

"Of course, Izidora." His hand brushed a damp lock of hair over my shoulder.

I yawned, rubbing my palms into my eyes. "I think I am ready for bed."

Kazimir stood, sweeping his arm out to indicate I should go first. "As you wish, Princess." His tone was light and teasing, filling me with ease.

I giggled as I wound my way to the bed that I almost needed a stool to climb in. He pulled back layers of blankets for me, and I crawled to the middle, gathering pillows along the way and encircling my body with them before Kazimir lowered the blankets over me. I felt like I was wrapped in a cocoon of clouds, the most incredible sensation of my life. My eyes immediately started dropping, as if stones attached themselves to my lashes and weighed them down. Kazimir tucked the blankets tightly around me, and I sighed at his extra attention.

I could get used to him taking care of me.

Nuzzling my face into a fluffy pillow, I curled into a ball and lifted one lid to peer at the male who had not only saved me from a life filled with torture, but also saved me from myself.

He stroked my hair one last time, "Goodnight, Izidora." Then he sauntered to the couch and sprawled out, staring at the fire.

"Goodnight, Kazimir," I murmured, drifting off to sleep.

KAZIMIR

I lounged by the fire in my rooms, listening to Izidora's soft snores for a bit too long to be proper before I noiselessly padded out the door. I found Endre in his room across the hall, stripping off his leathers and preparing for a much deserved rest in a much deserved bed. Like a dog, I flopped onto my back in front of the fire, stretching this way and that to get comfortable.

"How is she?" Endre asked.

"Exhausted," I replied. "Shaken up, too."

"How the fuck did they find us? It makes no sense," Endre said grimly. A soft knock sounded on the door, then Viktor walked in.

"How is she?" Viktor asked too.

"That's what we were just discussing. She is shaken. I left her asleep in my bed." Another overhead stretch had my shoulders popping.

Viktor joined me on the fur rug on the floor, already dressed for bed. Endre wandered to the bathroom, returning in fresh clothes and settling on a pouf in front of the fire. Silence filled the room as the three of us digested the day's events. Out of all the Nighthounds, I was closest to Endre and Viktor. Our families were three of the seven High Houses of the Night Realm, which meant we spent our formative years training and studying together, our family homes the closest to one another as well. We shared a lot of the same opinions about the Night Realm, and they often stayed here when we all needed an escape from politics. They were the brothers I never had, and their parents were each like an extension of my own.

Endre broke the silence. "I keep wracking my brain over that prophecy. The Iron Realm wants her for something. What that something is, I don't know. If we can get a hold of a copy, maybe it will have answers."

"What prophecy?" Viktor asked.

"The Goddess's Prophecy," Endre said. "It's old, from millennia ago. I vaguely remember learning about it in our magical history class as children."

"The one taught by that teacher we all swore was older than the Goddess?" Viktor sniggered.

"That one," Endre confirmed.

"You were always a studious fucker," I teased.

"I think I slept through every one of those classes," Viktor groaned, flopping over onto his stomach to look at Endre. "He had a voice that put me right out. Sometimes I wish I had the bastard around to read to me on nights I can't sleep. I'd be out like a light in no time."

"Well if either of you had paid attention, we might know more right now," Endre rolled his eyes.

"What does it have to do with Izidora though?" Viktor asked.

"Her magic is white," I stated.

"You're fucking joking. Her magic is white? Not silver?" He shook his head as if he couldn't fathom the words coming from my mouth.

"Yep, so white it looks like she pulled a star straight from the heavens. She has a lot of power, too. Her well is endless when we practice."

"That's unusual given that she hasn't tapped into it before now." He frowned, mulling over the new information.

"She is gifted in healing magic," Endre added. "The way she knitted Kriztof's muscles back together last night was something it takes years for healers to perfect, and she did it during her first skirmish."

"Her magic must come straight from the Goddess herself," Viktor mused.

Endre pushed off his knees and rifled through some drawers until he pulled out a bottle of oaky liquor. Grinning, Viktor snatched it from him and took a long pull before passing it to me. Two gulps started me on my path to drunkenness, Endre drinking just as heavily as us. He may be the quiet one, but he held his liquor. In the morning, we would decide our next move. But for the night, I needed to kick back with my brothers.

Viktor tapped out first, heading to his usual room next door. I wished him a good sleep before rising from the floor.

Endre stopped me with a look. "You have feelings for her." It wasn't a question. Endre could see straight through us all, his keen eyes missing nothing.

With a huff, I sat on a pouf across from him, running a palm over my face. "Goddess help me, but yeah I do. I keep fighting it, but I can't stay away. Is it that obvious?"

"It's getting there," he acknowledged. "She seems drawn to you, too. She may sit and joke with us, but she only has eyes for you."

I groaned. "What am I supposed to do? I want to give her space to come to me, but *fuck* sometimes I want to throw her over my shoulder and take off. Especially when I see her in pain. All I want to do is take it away."

"I've never seen you as tense as you are now. You are the

most laid back out of all of us, always keeping your head under pressure. Something is changing in you," Endre observed.

"The other day when Kriztof made a dick joke in front of her, I almost lost it," I admitted.

"Do you want my advice?" Endre asked.

"Please," I begged.

"Don't fight your instincts. Pushing them away will only make them come back harder. Don't impose your will on her, but help guide her. She needs you."

"Thanks, Endre."

"You're my brother, and I want to see you happy."

I rose, clapping him on the shoulder, before heading to my room for the night. As I walked into the hall, I was drawn to my rooms, desperate to see the female I was falling in love with one last time before I drifted off to sleep. She hadn't moved, her chest rising and falling softly beneath layers and layers of blankets and furs. I gently shut the door and walked down the hall to an open room.

Alithaela had stoked a fire and laid out fresh clothes for me. I hurriedly washed in the basin in the bathroom, my exhaustion pulling me toward the bed. The one in this room wasn't quite as nice as my own, but I was so drained I didn't care; the adrenaline that had fueled me since the ambush was fading quickly. A moment after curling up beneath the blankets, sleep claimed me, welcoming me into its healing darkness.

———

FEMALE SCREAMS TORE me from sleep, and I bolted out of bed on instinct, grabbing my sword from the floor and throwing the door open as I sprinted in the direction of the terror. Fear gripped me as I realized they were Izidora's screams. Anger coursed through my veins at the thought of those Iron fuckers breaking into my family home to take her.

Endre and Viktor burst from their rooms a second later, ready to fight despite our semi-drunkenness and few hours of sleep. I reached the doors first, barreling straight through them and finding Izidora thrashing on the bed, tangled in a mess of blankets.

There was no one else in the room.

Dropping my sword, I ran to her side, gently wrapping her in my arms to stop her violent jerks. "Izidora, wake up. You're having a nightmare," I pleaded.

With me holding her firmly in place, her movements subsided, and she slowly blinked sleep from her eyes, a breath whooshing from her lungs as her eyes met mine. Her gaze moved behind me to Endre and Viktor, whose swords were at the ready.

Her cheeks reddened and tears sprang to her eyes. "I'm so sorry," she murmured. "I didn't mean to wake you."

"There's no trouble, Izidora," Viktor reassured. "We'll leave you to go back to sleep." Viktor shot me a knowing look, then jerked his head at Endre. They left the room, softly closing the door behind them.

Releasing my grip, I settled on the bed beside her, searching her eyes for any hint of remaining fear. "Are you alright?"

She laid back down again, curling into a tight ball. "In my dream, those riders were chasing me, but I was all alone. I was so certain they were going to catch me and drag me back with them. I felt helpless and scared." A sob wracked her petite frame, and tears spilled down her cheeks as the claws of the nightmares slowly worked their way out.

I laid down in front of her so we were eye to eye, then reached out to stroke her hair, soothing her. "You are safe, here and now. I've got you."

"Please don't leave," she begged, her jewel-like eyes pleading with me just as much as her sweet voice.

"I won't go anywhere." Not that I wanted to either way. A soft blue blanket graced the foot of the bed, and I covered myself with it before stealing a pillow from Izidora. Once I was comfortable, I faced the beautiful female I would give anything to have as my own.

Tension eased from her face, then her shoulders, then her chest as I showed her that I was going to stay. A stray tear trickled down her nose, and I wiped it away with my finger, lingering on her soft cheek. She responded with a watery smile.

"Sleep, Izidora," I breathed. She nodded her head, lids closing in time with her nods. I berated myself for leaving her earlier. How could I be so stupid? She was completely vulnerable in this large room all alone. What if someone had gotten through our defenses and covered her mouth before she could scream? I never would have forgiven myself. Our proximity fueled my desire to protect her, yet it eased the turmoil in my heart.

What would I do when the enemy was another male in the Night Realm coming to claim her hand?

She needed to know the truth about her father, and maybe once she did, she could be convinced to pry the throne from his sickly fingers, ensuring that would never come to pass. It was the only way to keep her – to keep us – safe.

17

IZIDORA

S unlight streamed through the heavy curtains and washed over my face. I blinked, the night coming back to me in pieces as I regarded the luxurious space around me. A nightmare played out in my head, translating to me acting it out in the realm of the wakeful, causing the males to burst into the room from down the hall. I recalled begging Kazimir not to leave me. A band of heat draped over my middle, and I glanced down to find a corded forearm crossing my stomach. Kazimir was still with me, sleeping softly at my back – we must have migrated positions during the night.

Yet his touch was not unwelcome; in fact, I'd never felt safer in my life. His sleep-driven cuddle filled me with serenity, and I didn't want to move out of fear of disturbing the most peaceful moment of my life. Whether our connection was from his heroism or not, I was drawn to him, utterly, wholly, completely. The other males in our group were attractive, but none of them held a candle to Kazimir. His emerald orbs on my body produced an ache low in my belly, a dull throb and soft pull toward him, as if a single look would hook and reel me in. Stolen glances were a part of our routine, and lately I welcomed them, preening under his heated regard. His attention went everywhere with me, from mealtimes when we were surrounded by others to silent moments when we rode side by side. He pushed me hard to excel, and I welcomed the challenges he threw my way. I wanted to be strong before we reached the seat of the Night Realm, and he was there every step of the way making it happen.

Kazimir stirred behind me, a low rumble vibrating against my back as the light hopped over me and into his eyes. I flipped around to face him, watching his dark lashes fan against his sharp cheekbones as he blinked sleep from his eyes.

"Morning," I whispered.

A sleepy smile spread lazily across the thick scruff that adorned his handsome face. "Morning," he replied. He noticed his hand placement and quickly jerked it back to his side. "Sorry, I didn't mean to do that."

"Don't apologize. I had the best sleep of my life next to you," I whispered, staring into the kaleidoscope of green created by the stroke of sunlight in his eyes. His black hair was a mess, sticking out all over the place. I reached my hand toward his face, stroking the soft hairs on his cheek, and he hid his emeralds as he leaned into my touch.

"I like this," I purred, my fingers tracing the scruff on his jawline.

Closing the distance between us by removing the pillow barrier, I resumed stroking his face, and he moved his hand back to my hip, sending sparks shooting across my skin. He turned his cheek into my hand, kissing my open palm. When his eyes burst open, his gaze was filled with enough heat to light the darkness of my cave. It fell to my lips, fire crackling between us as my nipples hardened beneath his black shirt, which still covered them. My body ached to rub against his, and as if he read my mind, his large hand yanked my body flush against him, my nipples rubbing against the hard planes of his bare chest. It was entirely covered in colorful ink, but I was too enraptured by the proximity of our faces to study them. My chest heaved with the intensity of the moment between us – Kazimir's face filled with adoration – and that look alone had me melting deeper into him. My petite frame was dwarfed by his physique as I wrapped my arms around his neck, and he circled his other arm around my waist. His corded muscles flexed as he stroked my back, casting shivers at the gentle yet sensual touch over the thin veil of fabric between us.

A knock sounded. "Kazimir, are you awake?" Endre asked through the door.

We both jumped, flying apart like a spider had dropped between us. Kazimir cleared his throat, though his husky tone was hard to hide. "I'll be right out."

"Meet us in the first floor study," Endre shouted, his footsteps retreating from the closed door. A snort escaped my lips and Kazimir dropped back onto the bed, shaking his head.

"That was close," I whispered.

Kazimir angled his body, pulling me against him again, his earlier lust replaced by a level of seriousness. "Do you want this, Izidora? I don't want to take advantage of you. My protective instincts are kicking into overdrive, especially after the last few days. I don't want you to feel obligated because I will protect you no matter what. I have no expectations from you." He hunted for the truth in my eyes, his own brimming with tentative hope.

Did I want this? Did I want to open myself up to him in this way, to lay in his arms during the night, share my body with him after everything I'd been through?

I chewed on my lip, considering how I wanted to respond. "I don't have a lot of experience with this..." I waved my hand around, indicating our entwined bodies. "I don't know what relationships are supposed to look like. I hear Vadim and the others talking about females they've been with, and I don't want that. I don't want anything casual, sex for one night and then never speak again. I want to be wanted. I want to be loved." My voice was insistent as I ended my impassioned speech.

"You have no fucking idea how much I want you," he growled, muscles bunching against my back as he crushed me against him. He brought a hand up to the nape of my neck, pulling my head in close to his. He glanced at my lips, then lifted his gaze to my eyes. "You have no idea how many nights I lay dreaming about this very moment." His lips brushed softly over mine. "You have no idea the lengths I would go to for you. I am not like the others. Once I have you, there will be no letting go. So choose carefully, Izidora."

He threaded his hands in my hair, keeping me close as he waited for an answer. I opened my mouth then closed it, my mind warring between yes and no, desperate to be safe and loved and yet anxious to allow someone so close to me. Without warning, his lips crashed against mine, the kiss hungry, searching, pleading. I moaned into his mouth, then parted my lips, letting in his tongue to explore mine as he deepened our kiss and roped me against him, clinging to me like I was the oxygen he needed to breathe.

He left me breathless when he pulled away, untwining his hands from my hair and mapping my back with light touches of his fingers before recalling them to his side. He pushed upright, eyes still wearing thick black rings as he explored every curve revealed by the cling of his tunic. I was licentious, grasping at his skin to pull him back to me, but he tsked and lifted my hand to kiss it instead.

"I need to see what they want downstairs. Head to the kitchen, and Alithaela will make you some breakfast."

I sighed, wanting more but also glad he was giving me an out. "Okay. Will I see you later?"

"Of course," he murmured, brushing his lips over mine once more, the act fluttering my long lashes against my cheeks. He took his warmth with him, so I snuggled back into the blankets, not ready to leave their embrace.

Kazimir fetched his sword before heading to the door, wearing only cotton pants that left nothing to the imagination in the front. He shot me a heated look over his shoulder before he exited his room. I wiggled deeper into the covers, turning my face into his pillow and inhaling his smoke and amber scent, replaying our passionate kiss over and over in my head. The intensity of my want had ratcheted up exponentially the past few days, threatening to consume me if I didn't douse the wildfire blazing in my heart.

Was this what falling in love was like?

As the sun climbed higher in the sky, my stomach growled louder, alerting me to its needs. Breakfast or stay in bed? My stomach growled again. Breakfast it was.

I searched the room for additional clothes, deciding that one of Kazimir's tunics was not sufficient for wandering the house. A green robe hung over the back of the door to the closet and I decided that would do, since there were no pants small enough for me. I pulled the lush green robe from its hanger and wrapped it around myself. It dragged on the floor, more like a gown than a robe on my small frame. I needed to find my bags after breakfast so I could have proper pants.

The elegant house greeted me when I opened the door, light spilling in from dozens of arched windows breaking up the dark oak walls that lined the hallway, its plush carpets leading me left and right, beckoning me to explore. Choosing the left-hand path, I strolled toward a large open space where two staircases spiraled to the first floor. The balcony overlooked a sitting room with a massive fireplace large enough to roast a horse.

I descended the stairs, searching for signs of a kitchen, using my enhanced sense of smell to sniff it out. A whiff of something sweet set my mouth instantly watering, so I followed the aroma into a room filled with morning light, massive windows taking the place of a wall on one side.

A plump woman dusted with white powder stood behind a long wooden table, rolling some dough with a round pin. She was deep in her work and hadn't noticed me come in.

"Excuse me," I said politely, hoping not to scare her.

She jumped anyway, sending the rolling pin flying. She curtseyed low, exclaiming, "Your Highness! I didn't know you were up. Let me fetch you some tea."

"Please, call me Izidora. I didn't even know my name until a few weeks ago. I would like to get used to that before I start getting all these formal titles thrown my way," I pleaded.

"Izidora it is, then. I'm Alithaela. You can call me Ali." She tutted, throwing a kettle over a fire and grabbing more ingredients for whatever she worked on. A round table tucked into a corner waited for me, and I took a seat, watching as she bustled about. Soon she brought me a cup of steaming tea, placing it on a saucer in front of me.

"What else would you like? I'm making some cinnamon rolls right now, but I can whip up some eggs and bacon or anything else you'd like," she offered, wiping her palms on her white frilly apron.

"Eggs and bacon, and lots of cinnamon rolls please," I laughed, my sweet tooth begging me to request a whole batch for myself.

"Let me finish up with these rolls and get them cooking, and then I will whip up your eggs and bacon," she chirped.

"Can I help?" I asked.

She looked like I had just asked her to be my best friend. "Of course you can, honey. Come here and I'll show you how it's done."

Gulping down some minty tea, I hopped off my seat and followed her to the wooden table dusted in flour. I rolled the enormous sleeves of Kazimir's robe up by my elbows, hoping that I wouldn't get it too messy.

"Oh heavens! We need to get you some clothes fit for a lady. I've had nothing but these troublesome males in this house for too long. Come, let's see what we can find you."

The rolls forgotten, we trekked through the house to the third floor. Ali opened a door, revealing a long room filled with random bits of furniture, mirrors, and trunks covered by white cloth. She seemed to know her target in the chaotic arrangement because she made a beeline for an armoire pushed against a wall on the far side of the room, dragging me along behind her as I noted all the pieces stored away.

There was a beautiful painting of a dapple gray horse that reminded me of Mistik, partially covered by a yellowed map that was nearly as tall as me. It was an intricate drawing of our continent, Északi, major cities marked in curled script I couldn't read and miniature illustrations of topography dotted the landscape around the continent. A castle marked the very tip of the northern part of the map, spearing into a vast ocean beyond its symbolic castle. I trailed my gaze further down, identifying the Agrenak Mountains at the very heart of Északi. Off to the left I saw the ring of ridges surrounding the Iron Realm, a flat surface in the center marked by that flowy writing. Beneath the mountain range that had imprisoned me for so long, the vast plains of the Day Realm covered the bottom half of the continent, large animals traced here and there throughout the realm and an illustration of a long thatched building ringing a massive tree in the heartland. Circling to the right, the Crystal Realm's massive lakes dotted the terrain, and a castle floated above the far side of the largest body of water. Gaining my bearings on the continent I called home was incredible after spending so many years wondering what lay beyond my cave's walls and the iron chains that bound me to it.

Ali called out for me, and with great difficulty, I tore my eyes from the map and jogged the rest of the way to her, the robe catching on a few pieces of furniture along the way and dragging white sheets to the ground, revealing their hidden shapes.

"These belonged to the High Lady Klariza before she passed. High Lord Cazius didn't want to see her things any longer, the poor fellow was broken by his wife's death. I kept items that belonged to her up here, just in case I might need them in the future. And looks like I was right to do that." Her kind eyes danced with amusement as she surveyed me.

"These are beautiful." I admired the rich colors hanging in front of me, reaching for the fine dresses, running my fingers over the soft fabrics. My fingers stopped on a beautiful dark navy gown, the color reminiscent of the moments following the sun dying over the horizon. The fabric shimmered as it moved, looking like stars twinkling in the sky. Ali carefully extracted it, draping it over her arm. I perused the armoire further, selecting a few simpler gowns, one in midnight black, another in a creamy white, and finally an emerald green that reminded me of Kazimir's eyes.

Ali grabbed a few silk slips and some leggings before shutting the armoire again. "These probably won't fit, but I'll alter them myself," she said proudly.

"Can I have a pair for now to cover my legs?"

"Yes, yes of course!" She handed me a black pair along with gray wool socks. They were a little big in the waist, but I rolled them a few times and scrunched up the ankles so they didn't drag on the ground. Shedding the robe and draping it over my arm since I was decently dressed, we returned to the kitchen, and she laid the beautiful dresses in a safe corner, far away from the baking station.

"Now, where were we?" she asked. I grinned, dropping the robe on a chair and rolling up the sleeves of Kazimir's tunic.

"Cinnamon rolls," I laughed.

18

KAZIMIR

I silently cursed and thanked Endre for interrupting Izidora and I. Though I had imagined the first moments our lips would lock on the long, lonely nights searching for her, I never knew it would be this incredible. Yet I didn't want to rush her into anything, because she was like a doe caught in the sights of a cougar, and one wrong move would send her bolting, racing away to safety. She consumed my every thought, my addiction, my obsession over her driving me to distraction when her safe delivery should be my only focus.

Even in my sleep, I knew she was mine – to protect, to have, to hold. My hand draped across her in the night, and thankfully there was a pillow between us, so when I woke she didn't feel my hardness. When she turned to face me, her head was framed by a golden halo, displaying her divinity. Her aquamarine eyes captivated me as she closed the distance between us of her own accord, and it took every ounce of my self control not to take her right then.

I meant what I said to her – once she surrendered to me, I would not let go. Despite my own sexual exploits in parallel with my brothers, I wanted her with an intensity I had never felt before. The females before her were merely bodies warming my bed, and I broke a few hearts along the way as one of the Night Realm's most eligible bachelors.

Courting one of the daughters of the many social climbers clambering around Este Castle was never on my agenda when I spent so much time searching for, and dreaming of, Izidora.

I adjusted my stiffness one last time before striding into the study where my father, Endre, Viktor, and Kriztof were seated around my father's massive mahogany desk, the seat between Viktor and Kriztof empty and waiting for me. "Where are the twins and Vadim?" I asked.

"They'll join us in a moment. I requested their help to create a new patrol schedule and reinforce any weaknesses they spotted in Zirok's outer wall," my father replied.

There was a pile of bacon on a side table as well as some coffee, so I reached for a cup, needing the jolt of energy after too little sleep the past few nights, and grabbed a few slices to chew while we waited. As I finished my third slice, the trio walked into the room, dragging chairs toward the desk until we fanned out around it, my father steepling his fingers while he watched us.

"Now that we're all here, let's discuss our next steps," he started. "We should send word to the king that we've retrieved Izidora and taken shelter here due to our enemies on the road. How many soldiers do you think we need to ask for in order to return safely to the castle?"

Viktor jumped in before anyone else could say anything. "Someone could intercept our message. I think it would be better to send word to the nearby towns asking for volunteers, then march to the castle together without revealing our package."

"What if we sent a raven ahead of a rider, letting the king know someone is coming with an important message, and informing him to come to Zirok if the messenger isn't received within two days?" Vadim suggested.

"But what if the rider is intercepted? They already know where we are. They could just capture anyone that leaves. Besides, flying would be faster," Viktor shot back.

"Like you said, Viktor, they already know where we are. So what information would they gain from capturing and torturing a rider? And flying is too damn risky. What happens when your magic is tapped out, and they're waiting on horseback below?" Vadim argued.

Vadim had a point, but so did Viktor. It was all risky.

"Kirigin and I can go as messengers," Zekari offered. "We can split up, leave at different times, and take slightly different routes. If there are people following us, they might get confused and at least one of us will make it. If the worst comes to worst, we can fly the remaining distance."

My father considered all of this, rubbing his chin. While we all might have a voice, he had the final say. "We'll send a raven ahead of the twins. But I want you both to be fully armed and not stray more than shouting distance away. You need to be able to get to one another quickly, so plan to meet in the skies if anything goes wrong. In the meantime, I will send ravens into the nearby villages, asking for reinforcements for Zirok House. We could use the extra eyes while we are here. If we don't hear from King Zalan, Zekari, or Kirigin within two weeks, we will march to Vaenor on our own."

It was a good plan, balanced in risk and calculated to ensure success. Este Castle was a two week ride from Zirok House, but it was possible in about half of that if you really pushed yourself. Everyone else seemed satisfied with the plan as well.

"Great," my father continued. "I will write the messages now and get them out before midday. Zekari and Kirigin, you will leave at first light tomorrow. The raven should arrive ahead of you. Please send word once you've made it safely, and once you have a plan."

"Yes, sir!" they said in unison.

"This afternoon, I want time with Izidora to prepare her with what to expect when we get to Este Castle. It will be much easier with maps and books to reference," my father said, looking pointedly at me.

Izidora was naturally curious, so she would enjoy those lessons. "I will ensure she finds her way here," I promised.

Our discussion complete, we went our separate ways, preparing for the days ahead. I wanted to find Izidora again, not even a few hours having passed and already yearning for her. Sniffing the air, I caught her sweet floral scent drifting from the kitchen, barely discernible over the smell of baking cinnamon. Amusement ticked up the corners of my mouth, and I made my way to the kitchen, her bubbly laugh beckoning me as I approached the doorway.

The scene before me was madness, white powder everywhere, especially on the black tunic Izidora must have procured from my closet. Ali stood next to her, howling with laughter, while Izidora dabbed tears from her eyes with the back of her hand, the only clean spot left on her arms. Yet she failed at preventing more flour from coating her cheeks, and that served another cascade of cackles.

They were so infectious, my own laughter joined theirs, heart swelling as the two most important females in my life enjoyed each other's company. I knew they would be fast friends with Alithaela's mothering and Izidora's kind heart. Izidora felt my gaze, her head whipping toward mine, and a wide, sheepish grin fell into place. "I just dropped a whole sack of flour with the top open. It went everywhere! Sorry about your tunic."

"Don't be," I croaked, the sight of her wearing my tunic sending heat straight to my groin. I sauntered to the round table, selecting a chair around the back to hide my growing erection. As if she heard the desire in my voice, Izidora leveled her bejeweled eyes at me, and that invisible string tugged between us again. With teeth sunk into her lower lip and mouth upturned, she shifted her attention back to the dough in front of her. Ali demonstrated how to fix the mess they'd made, and then she was back to kneading dough under her teacher's watchful eye.

"Are the cinnamon rolls almost finished, Ali?" Izidora asked eagerly. Their scent enveloped the kitchen, the air cloying with warm vanilla and burnt sugar as Ali cracked the door to the oven to check their doneness, declaring them fit for consumption and sending silver tendrils to fetch them from the roaring heat.

The baking sheet was edge to edge with swirls, and while they cooled, Ali summoned sugar, butter, and milk to create the frosting. She showed Izidora the correct portions of each ingredient and how to mix them properly, demonstrating the strokes before handing off the bowl for her to finish, the mixture turning light and fluffy as she whipped it about. Once Ali was satisfied, Izidora poured a generous helping of frosting over each roll.

The Nighthounds trickled in one by one as the comforting smell of cinnamon beckoned them to the kitchen, each laughing in turn at Izidora's flour-encrusted state, while she continued to explain the explosion that got her into this mess. Her joy was contagious, filling the whole house with light that had been missing for a long time.

After eating generous helpings, we disbanded, much left to do before we could relax for the day. Izidora was in need of another bath, and I took her powdered hand and led her through my childhood home, returning to my bedroom and the massive bathroom that was attached. I turned the taps to the deep soaking tub, wanting Izidora to luxuriate while we waited for Ali to clean up the kitchen and bring up 'proper female clothing' for Izidora.

The knowledge that company would soon come knocking was the only thing leashing my self control as Izidora padded into my bathroom, tossing her long locks over her shoulder, the tips pointing straight toward her shapely backside that was impossible to hide beneath my tunic, which fell to her knees.

I cleared my throat, glancing away before my thoughts ran away from me. "I'll leave you to it."

"Stay," she pleaded, her voice breathy and saccharine.

That tone slaughtered my self control, and fucking Fates I couldn't say no – even if I wanted to.

Unable to respond around the roaring desire in my throat, I merely leaned against the counter, crossing my arms over my chest to tuck my hands safely away. Once she confirmed I wasn't going anywhere, she bent to strip out of her black leggings, her peachy ass in the air as she stepped out of them. Tossing them to the side, she lifted one bare leg, then the other, stepping into the white soaking tub. With an unabashed flutter of lashes over her shoulder, she lifted the hem of my shirt. My eyes bulged then snapped shut, breath tight in my throat as she dropped the garment to the polished floor. I didn't dare open my eyes as water splashed and a sigh filled the space.

"You can open your eyes," she purred. I cracked one open, then the other when I saw her skin bathed in bubbles. Her chin rested on the side of the tub, a shameless smile weakening my knees as the air seemed to crackle between us.

Goddess help me, Fates damn me, I wanted her so fucking bad, and she had no clue the beast she was awakening beneath the surface of my skin.

19

IZIDORA

Kazimir struggled to keep his face neutral as I relaxed in the deep tub. Yet his eyes blew out black so thick the emerald hues all but disappeared, and his lips formed a tight line as he struggled for control. I wanted him to see me, to see all of me – from a safe distance. This was a way I could try to be intimate on my terms, slowly warming up to the idea of more between us. This tug in my gut meant something; I simply had to figure out what that was, and I could not do that if I didn't lower these walls to let him in.

He saw me, the real me, despite the facade I wore like armor. He saw my trauma and did not balk – in fact, he always knew exactly what I needed to hear when my emotions got the better of me.

I wanted him to know I saw him too. I saw the promises in his words and the happiness we could have together. I saw that he would die to protect me and do anything to keep me safe. I saw that he wanted to care for me, and I saw how he begged me to allow him to show me.

The moment felt like standing at the edge of my cave, waiting to jump into the unknown world beyond. The drop would be terrifying, but when our wings snapped open and caught the wind, it would be the most thrilling adventure of all.

All I needed to do was take that leap.

My hands trembled as I reached for a bar of soap that smelled of roses and lavender – floral, earthy, sensual. The aroma enveloped my senses before I ducked under the water and washed away the white flour that painted my face. When I broke the surface, I languidly soaped my arms with the moisturizing bar while peeking under my lashes at Kazimir, whose body had shifted a hair closer and hands gripped the marble counter so hard I was certain the stone would crumble under his white knuckles.

Heat bloomed in my core as I imagined him gripping my hips with that intensity. Emerald and aquamarine locked together as I circled the bar of soap lower and lower, mapping the way down my abdomen and below the surface. He stopped breathing as I lifted my left leg out of the water, rivulets running off the tips of my pointed toes, then rubbed the bar over my upper thigh, working unhurriedly down to my foot. Releasing the soap, I massaged the liquid into my leg, ensuring that I touched every spot at least once, especially on my upper thigh, where the kneading sent a throb even higher. I released my leg, casually letting it sink under the bubbles, then lifted my right leg out of the water, repeating the process, my arousal growing with each sensual touch.

Wetness bloomed on my thighs despite the water around me, and as I worked the bar back up my abdomen to my chest, I lightly brushed the soap over my breasts, biting back a soft moan when the soap glanced over my hardened nipple. I rested the bar on a shelf beside me, then used my hands to work the soap into a lather, cupping my heavy breasts, rubbing them in circles and occasionally brushing my nipples, eliciting a slight gasp from my lips. My shoulders were next, and I threw a glance over my left one at Kazimir as I stroked my way down to my breasts again.

Kazimir's face was anguished as he restrained himself from moving. Bubbles disappeared by the second, revealing more and more of my creamy skin as I sat higher in the water. His eyes flashed wildly, the outline of his hardness growing rapidly and straining to break free of his tight trousers. I eyed it hungrily, and he followed my gaze to what held my attention. Slowly releasing his grip on the counter, like one wrong move would spook me, he moved a hand to his cock and stroked his length up and down, smirking as an involuntary moan escaped my lips at the sight.

I turned to my knees, pressing my breasts against the cool stone of the tub, and trailed my hand down my abdomen to my core, feeling the wetness seeping out of me. Smearing some of it over my swollen clit, he palmed himself, and my whole body flushed with arousal. I dipped my hand lower, stroking my folds back and forth, grinding against my hand. A mewl parted my lips at the same time, and I sank two fingers in as far as they would go, needing the fullness as deep as possible.

He unbuttoned his pants to make room for his hand, then slipped it inside, fisting his length. My eyes danced back and forth between his hungry expression and his hand stroking in his pants, both views pushing me closer to the edge. I pumped my fingers in and out under the water, soft moans escaping my lips as the tension in my core built and built. Pressing the heel of my palm into that sensitive nub while I curled my fingers against my inner walls, I matched my strokes to his, imagining that my fingers were that thickening length that barely peeked over the edge of Kazimir's pants.

Kazimir groaned as he watched me pleasure myself, his stare rapturous and breaths labored and ragged. I panted faster the closer my release marched, grinding desperately into my own hand, aching for the relief that would come moments after my walls tightened over my fingers. Wetness gushed down my thighs as my body let go, head tilting toward the ceiling in pure ecstasy as my orgasm tore through me, breathy moans accompanying my release.

"Fuck," Kazimir swore, his hand and body jerking as he watched me come. A few furious pumps had him groaning out and tipping his head back, heaving breaths as he reached for a cloth to wipe his hand and beneath his pants.

I slid back under the water, smiling because I had taken that leap and it was utterly worth it. When I surfaced again, he held a towel for me, taking in the full view of my nakedness. I stood like a siren in the ocean, water dripping off my still tingling body as I reached for the fluffy cloth. His eyes roamed like a man starved, salivating over his next meal as his gaze drifted toward my swollen center.

Before things could escalate further, a knock sounded at the outer door.

"My arms are full Kazimir, you better open the door for me before I drop these beautiful gowns!" Ali called.

I breathed a sigh of relief. Kazimir had yet to see the scars that adorned my back, and I knew he was the type of male that would not react well to the sight. Also, I already adored Ali, but I didn't want her to find me in a compromising position on my first day here. Kazimir adjusted his pants and then strode from the bathroom, closing the door softly behind him to give me some privacy while I dried off – and probably to pretend like he had been in the other room the whole time.

Shuffling and rustling of fabric signaled Ali's entrance along with her booming voice. I dried my hair, then wrapped a towel around my body and opened the door to Kazimir's room. He averted his eyes, finding the ceiling much more interesting than the barely covered female in his space.

Ali threw a pile of fabric in his face as she exclaimed, "Give the girl some privacy! Shoo!"

Smiling, he raised his hands in supplication. "I'll be downstairs if you need me."

I smothered a snicker as he departed, Ali heaving a sigh. "Males. You can't live with them, can't live without them."

I walked to the couch, sitting in only the towel as she laid out the dresses we'd selected earlier as well as some raw fabric in soft lace and light cotton. She tossed me a pair of leggings and a white tunic. "See how these fit you," she instructed.

Beneath the fluffy wrap around my body, I pulled on the soft leggings, then turned my back to pull the tunic over my head. "Ta da!" I spun around with a dramatic flair, laughing at myself.

Ali chuckled and bent to examine the fit of my leggings. "How do they feel?" she asked.

"A little snug in the thighs, but otherwise they feel great," I replied.

Ali called silver light to her hands, the silky bands wrapping around my thighs, loosening threads here and there until the leggings melted over my skin like softened butter. My mouth agape, I looked back at Ali. "You can do that with magic?!"

"How else would I do it?" she replied smugly.

"I love magic," I enthused, and she laughed at my awe.

We spent the next few hours crafting a wardrobe fit for a princess – according to Ali. Delicate lace undergarments, soft leggings, tunics both long and short, formal dresses for dinner, and another pair of simple leather pants for training outside lay in piles across the plush furniture of Kazimir's room by the time we were finished. My current tops bunched beneath the leather chest plate I trained in, so I asked if she could make some tighter tunics that would move and breathe with me, as well as a tighter band to wrap around my breasts while training. With an excited gleam in her eye, she promised to work on a design until I could get some proper armor.

The style she crafted was practical and elegant, and I felt like they fit me well. The darkness of my cave hadn't required much by way of clothing, and fashion was not a subject with which I was familiar. The leathers I wore during our trek made me feel like a warrior, but I loved the beautiful dresses she created for me, feeling feminine and pretty in a way I'd yet to experience. They wouldn't be an all day every day attire for me, but I could see myself wearing a dramatic and elegant design for formal events in the future. Leather was much preferred for fighting for my life, something I was certain would appear again in my future, despite my fervent desire for freedom.

My thoughts returned to the male who promised and showed time and time again that he would do everything in his power to protect and keep me safe. A twinge in my heart and a pull in my low belly begged me to wander the manor until I found him. If I tuned into my magic, it was almost as if I could sense him in my periphery, knowing exactly which turns I'd have to take to reach him. Ali cleared her throat, breaking my internal monologue, and looked at me like she had just asked me a question.

My cheeks reddened as I realized I was caught thinking about Kazimir. "Sorry, my mind was elsewhere. What was the question?"

"Don't you worry, Princess, you've been through a lot lately. I asked if you were hungry for lunch?" Ali repeated herself.

I laughed when my stomach rumbled in reply. "I guess so."

"Leave the clothes here for now, we'll figure out what to do with them later. I'll make you some dessert too," she winked, knowing exactly how to win me over.

Selecting new clothes from the pile in front of me, I pulled them on then padded behind Ali to the kitchen, where we found the twins packing their saddlebags with food.

"Are you leaving?" I questioned, looking between the two youngest members of our group.

"We're going to ride to Vaenor and retrieve assistance," Kirigin replied.

My breath rushed out of my chest along with a slew of questions. "When are you going? How long will it take to get there? Will you be alright?"

"Don't worry, Princess, we can take care of ourselves. We leave at first light tomorrow," Zekari reassured me.

Throwing my arms open, I rushed over to them, and they wrapped me in a hug simultaneously, "Twin sandwich!" they yelled, pulling a giggle out of me as they crushed me between them. The twins were like brothers to me, despite our short time together.

"Please take care of yourselves. I don't know what I would do if those riders that were chasing us caught you," I begged.

"We will," they promised in unison, giving me another tight squeeze before releasing their hold.

While I talked with the twins, Ali made a plate of sandwiches and placed them on the table in front of me. The flaky bread was filled with a creamy cheese, and as I bit into one, the substance squeezed out of every available opening, nearly dripping onto my new clothing. With sharp reflexes, I caught a drip moments before it stained my black pants. The twins snagged sandwiches from my plate with a snigger right before I bent over it to save my clothes, then scampered off before Ali could smack them with her rag that she wielded like a sword.

With a huff, she took a seat across from me, entertaining me with stories of her life and her work at Zirok House while I ate. She was from a nearby village, and her parents had served the previous head of House Vaszoly, Kazimir's grandfather. I learned that she came to work at the house right before Kazimir was born, the expected babe requiring extra staff as High Lady Klariza took a step back from her duties to care for herself and her newborn son. Ali was gifted with creative magic, which was how she was able to sew clothes to fit me perfectly, and how she made such amazing food, imbuing each dish with love and spice. She never had children or a family of her own, although she considered the Vaszolys her family, and Vikor, Endre, Vadim, Kriztof, and the twins her children.

"...and now I must add you to my list of children!" she exclaimed when she finished her life story. My heart warmed with her motherly affection, filling ever so slightly that gaping hole in the beating organ that craved love and acceptance. The kindness of these Fae continued to amaze me, almost to the point of disbelief, after experiencing such significant cruelty at the hands of those who guarded my cave. The scales tipped too far into the territory of good, and in my gut, I knew something bad must be on the horizon to even them out once more.

Would I ever experience the freedom of good things happening to me?

Because the more I thought and learned about the life of a princess, the more it seemed like a different set of chains.

I didn't have long to ponder my question as Cazius walked into the kitchen, his gray-green eyes crinkling when he saw me at the table. "Ah, Izidora, I was just looking for you. Will you join me for a history lesson?"

My curiosity bubbled to the surface, imagining all the things I could learn from him. "I would love to," I replied. Maybe I would get to look at some maps too, the enormous one locked away in the attic jumping to the front of my mind.

Ali handed me a small plate of cookies on my way out the door. "You'll need those," she winked. I flashed her a wide smile and followed Cazius to part of the first floor I hadn't seen yet. My bare feet padded across plush runners lining the hallways atop polished wooden floors, oil paintings lining the forest green walls, portraits and distant landscapes waving to me as I passed.

Cazius stopped in front of a gilded door, opening it with a flair to reveal a rectangular room ringed with shelves of books, their leather-bound spines laid with filigrees of every color. Another marbled fireplace took over the back of the room, and in front of it was a redwood desk surrounded by high-backed chairs. Cazius removed most of them, tucking them against a far wall until only two remained in front and one placed between the desk and the fire. Large cushions and poufs lined the floor on the opposite side, stacks of worn books beside a pouf large enough to hold two people. I imagined myself curling up in its embrace and soaking in the knowledge held in this room, Kazimir beside me as we buried our noses in stories and histories – after I learned to read.

Cazius sat in the wide, high-backed chair across from me, steepling his fingers as he waited for me to join him. With one last perusing glance around the study, I settled into a chair opposite him, tucking my feet under me and folding my hands in my lap as I politely waited for the wisdom he would impart. He dragged a thick tome from the corner of his desk, opening it to the middle with a thwack and a dusting of loose papers. Untucking my feet, I scooted the chair closer to get a better look at what lay between the pages.

A map, colorful and detailed, spilled across two interior pages, and I leaned in, studying it. The outline was the same, but the detail was nothing compared to the beautiful map locked away upstairs. Words were scrawled across the pages, the script not nearly as flowy, but the words still indecipherable to my illiterate eyes.

"The four realms," Cazius began, "have always been separate. If you remember, we discussed the differences in each type of Fae on our ride. We all have different strengths and weaknesses to create balance and harmony on our continent. That way not one realm can become more powerful than the others and try to take all the land in Északi for themselves. Once a year, the monarchs of the realms gather for two weeks of festivities and friendly competition to celebrate our peace. It is called Béke, and Fae in all realms take part whether their realm is that year's host or not. Last year's Béke was held in the Day Realm, which means this year the Iron Realm will host." Cazius spit out the last part with a hint of disgust.

"When will it happen?" I asked.

Cazius flipped through a calendar on his desk. "In about three months," he replied. "I suspect this year will have a lot more drama than usual."

Bending over the map, I surveyed the Iron Realm with a more carefully trained eye. Cazius moved to turn the page, and I backed out of his way. The following page had more detail of the Iron Realm, so I resumed my review of the upcoming host's map.

"The Iron Realm is mostly mountainous, the majority of their people residing in the valley around Radence. Because they are gifted with earth and fire magic, they spend most of their time in the mountains, mining and crafting. The mountains allow them to maintain a level of secrecy and privacy, which they seem to prefer over more open relations with the other realms. There are only a few ways in or out, and as you can see, the terrain is difficult to navigate. King Azim, the ruler of the Iron Realm, has never taken a wife, and he has no children."

Cazius flipped to the next page. This one displayed the open plains of the Day Realm. "The Day Realm has the most territory of all the realms, their flat, grassy plains open to the beating sun year round. The few wooded areas are a respite in the scorching summer months. They grow the most food, and they are the

Night Realm's largest trading partner, and historically, they have been our closest ally. The current queen of the Day Realm, Viktoria, and her king consort, Geza, have provided us access to their lands to search for you many times. I believe she will be quite pleased to meet you."

He turned to the next page. "The Crystal Realm is as mysterious as its people. Their realm is filled with massive lakes, their shade ranging from crystalline blues near the glaciers descending from the Agrenak Mountains to a deep greenish hue near the sea. To get to the Day Realm, we must pass through the Crystal Realm's lands. The capital, Vlisa, still captivates me to this day. When you ride upon it, the city seems to rise from the water, and Blire Palace actually floats on the glassy water of the lake, held up by the water and air magic of the Crystal Fae. The palace is made of crystals, and it is truly a wonder to behold. King Airre and Queen Immonen are mated, though they have no children either. Mates are one of the greatest gifts the Goddess bestows upon us, and every young Fae prays to her, asking her to bless them with their perfect match."

Mates? Could that explain the magnetic pull Kazimir and I had to each other?

Cazius interrupted my thoughts by flipping to the Night Realm's page. "Here is your home, the Night Realm. We are here," he indicated on the map the location of Zirok House. "And Vaenor is there," he moved his finger further along the map to the very tip of a cliff at the far edge of the continent.

I studied the script there, tracing a finger over the word hanging off the tip of the cliff. "Vae-nor..."

"No, that says Este Castle." Cazius paused, then reached for a glass filled with amber liquid before taking a long drink. "Izidora... did anyone teach you to read?"

My lashes fluttered against my cheeks, and my shoulder dropped under the weight of Cazius's question. "No."

The sigh that left the male's lips was heavy and filled with sorrow. "After our history lesson, I will teach you the letters. Do not let anyone outside of our small group know you cannot read."

Meeting his forest-green eyes, I nodded. The weariness held there had only increased with each passing day – whether it was from our hard ride or something else, I did not know.

He cleared his throat, then continued. "Este Castle sits at the very edge of steep cliffs overlooking the raging ocean below. The shape of the castle and its tall turrets give it the appearance of a ship out at sea. There is a large flat deck between the two tallest spires where our astronomers set up to study the stars, looking for signs from the Goddess. We don't possess clairvoyance like the Crystal Fae, but our astronomers are second to none. On the new moon, all the lights in the city are put out so we can gather to view the stars at their brightest."

"That sounds incredible," I breathed.

Cazius smiled, "I figured you would like that tidbit. Anyway, that is an overview of the realms. Now, let's talk about Night Realm politics and history, because that is most relevant to you right now."

He cleared his throat, then continued. "Your father, King Zalan, has a council of seven High Lords that serve as his advisors on all matters. The High Houses are the highest level of nobility in the Night Realm, and we typically wield the most magical power. Second to us are the Lower Houses, who are also noble yet do not advise the king formally. It is them you have to watch out for, as most of them are social climbers, trying to acquire one of the coveted seats on the council. Most are incredibly wealthy and are not above bribery and corruption to get what they want."

I reached for a cookie. Ali had been right, I would definitely need these to get through this lesson.

"Above all else, Night Fae respect magic power and bloodline purity. Matches are often made on aptitude and strength alone, each House vying for an edge over the others and soliciting your father's blessing, if not trying to win his favor so he suggests the match beforehand. That is how House Valynor has kept its power for so long – controlling the marriages of the nobles in the Night Realm. Very few Night Fae have been born in the last few centuries with as much power as King Zalan wields, though he rarely displays his magic these days, too proud to show weakness in his old age."

"After your mother died, he never remarried. He fell ill a few years after your birth and never quite recovered. The line of succession has been in question for some time, with many of the High Lords putting forth their daughters for marriage, hoping to gain a foothold into the highest seat in the kingdom. Others angled their sons for potential nomination as heir apparent. Blood children by default are heirs, but their succession can be superseded by a sitting monarch naming another their heir apparent. But your father never chose any of them, no matter how much his council pleaded with him to give us some certainty if he were to die. Had he died, I am sure a civil war would have ensued. You can see why your appearance is going to cause issues," he explained.

I nodded. "So when I show up, schemes will be ruined?"

"Exactly," Cazius affirmed. "There are enemies on all sides now."

The hairs on the back of my neck raised, as if speaking the words into existence sent ghosts of my trauma to circle me, and the spirits of those who still sought to control me swarming. "Who is the biggest threat at Este Castle right now?" I asked.

Cazius considered my question for a moment. "Of the High Lords, House Valintin. High Lord Valintin's son is a few years older than Kazimir, the oldest of all the High Houses' children.

He has been pushing for Alekzi to be named heir apparent for years. Then there is House Luzak, who have not been shy about their designs. High Lord Luzak has been throwing his daughter at Kazimir since she came of age."

Rage boiled inside me in a flash so ferocious it took me by surprise. The thought of another female touching Kazimir set my teeth on edge, but it was not the time to unpack this knee-jerk reaction. I snapped a lid on my emotions, tuning back in to Cazius's words.

"...although I am certain many High Lords will make moves immediately to secure your hand once we arrive at Este Castle," he finished.

Hard pass.

I wanted the freedom to choose who I would marry after so many choices had been stripped from me. I would rather die than be chained to a male I did not know, did not trust, and did not love.

Could Kazimir be the answer to this?

He'd already made it plain that once I said yes, there was no turning back. I could save myself from the uncertainty if I bound myself to him before we returned. But would my father honor our wishes once we reached Este Castle?

My mouth opened to voice my question when a light knock sounded on the door.

"Enter," Cazius called out.

As if he knew I was thinking about him, Kazimir walked through the door. We locked eyes, and Kazimir stopped in his tracks before remembering himself and continuing. Lazily, he dropped into the chair next to mine. "What are we learning?"

Cazius waved him off. "Nothing that you are remotely inter-ested in, son."

"Politics," I told him, and he made a face. I quite agreed. Why couldn't we all just say what we mean and mean what we say? Why have to go through all this nonsense of wheeling and dealing to get what we want?

"Can I steal Izidora from you? Kriztof has set up a range in the garden to teach her to use a bow and arrow," he said, casually running a hand through the thick black scruff on his face.

"Very well. Politics is boring anyway," he winked at me. "We will continue tomorrow."

"Thanks for the lesson, Cazius," I grinned, bouncing out of the study after Kazimir, excited to learn to use another weapon – an endless arsenal was necessary for my safety. Down the hall, glass doors stood slightly ajar, and we pushed through them spilling into a lush garden lining the backside of the house. Our first few steps were through fruits and vegetables growing on vines, tangling around trellises, and spilling into the walkway, their earthy fragrance setting my stomach grumbling again.

Past the edibles, rows of rose bushes with deep ruby blooms greeted us, and as I reached for a perfectly petaled blossom, I cut my finger on a sharp thorn. With a hiss, I snatched my hand back, and stumbled into Kazimir, who caught my waist with a strong hand, then leaned down to speak in my ear, his hot breath plummeting to my core. "The most beautiful blooms hide the sharpest thorns. You are a deadly bloom, Izidora, and don't let anyone see your thorns until it's too late."

His body retreated, and mine followed as the string that tugged us together hummed. Without a second thought, I healed the small cut, and set my sights on rows of sunflowers stretching their necks toward the setting sun, soaking in every ounce of warmth left in the autumn air. Kazimir slowed his steps as I looked deep into the blooms the size of my head, then stooped to brush hands across plum petals of lilies and dahlias scattered at their base. When I glanced up from my perusal, Krizitof sat on a bale of hay, bow in hand, full quiver on the ground next to him, waiting with a smirk and sparkle of mischief in his pear-colored eyes. A dozen paces away sat three hay bales stacked on top of each other, a red target painted in the middle.

"My prodigy has arrived!" he exclaimed.

I rolled my eyes. "Thanks for the vote of confidence."

"Oh no, the confidence is all in my teaching abilities," Kriztof deadpanned.

I laughed, "Show me your ways, great master Kriztof."

"That's the spirit," he joked, handing me the bow. Kazimir leaned against an arbor a short distance away and watched as the jester taught me to use a bow.

"Now step up to this line with your left foot in front. Keep your feet shoulder distance apart." He adjusted me slightly, and Kazimir growled low behind us. Kriztof glanced at him with an air of annoyance but continued his instruction.

"Grasp the wooden handle in your left hand, and with your right, pull the string back toward your face, and rest your right hand on your cheek." He demonstrated the motion on the slightly larger bow he held.

I pulled my hand back like he instructed, then Kriztof adjusted the bow slightly up. "There. Now memorize exactly how your body feels in this moment, because this is where you'll return after every volley."

Memorizing every plane of my changing body, I solidified the position into my muscle memory, knowing it could be the difference between life and death one day. My magic flared a little as I stoked my inner fire, wanting it to be a raging inferno at all times. I opened my eyes and nodded to Kriztof, who handed me an arrow. Loosening my grip on the string, I plucked the arrow and nocked it into the bow.

I drew back, the fletching tickling my face as I settled into my previous position.

"Now, look at the tip of the arrow, then at the target. Visualize where you want the tip to land. Then exhale as you release the string," Kriztof murmured, his face inches from mine as he sighted with me.

I inhaled deep and long, imagining the arrow flying straight to the middle of the red target. Then I let go of my fingers and breath simultaneously, arrow sailing through the air, bow twanging as I dropped the string, and thud resounding as the arrow sank deep into the bale on the bottom of the stack.

"Agh," I wailed.

"Next time, keep the tip pointed a bit higher," Kriztof suggested, handing me another arrow.

I nocked it, lining up for the shot again. Kriztof's hands lightly touched my arms as he guided them slightly higher, then adjusted my right arm backward. Another warning growl brushed against us, and still Kriztof ignored him, but out of the corner of my eye, I watched his eyes roll.

"Try again," he encouraged.

This time when I loosed the arrow, it flew to the bottom of the target – one step in the right direction at least. Another arrow, another draw of the string, and I paused, waiting for more correction. Kriztof's body filled the space behind mine, arms coming over top to help steady them, but only for a moment before he was jerked away by the collar by a snarling Kazimir. "I'll show her," he snapped.

I pressed my lips together to suppress a smile as Kriztof backed away, hands held in surrender, though with a smirk on his face, and I got the feeling he'd goaded Kazimir for that reaction.

Kazimir's body replaced Kriztof's, his corded arms gripping mine and guiding my arms higher than before. He gently tapped my knees, silently instructing me to bend them, then he put his right hand on top of my own, helping me deepen the draw of the bow string. Heat flared at every point of contact between us, and a shiver ran through me as his breath tickled my ear, followed by murmured instruction. "Visualize again, the whole trajectory, and then let go."

Who knew firing an arrow could be so sensual?

Visualizing my goal again was more difficult when my thoughts were consumed by the closeness of this male. I inhaled, his smoke and amber scent stronger than the flowers around us, then exhaled as I released the arrow. It flew straight and true into the center of the scarlet target, generating unbridled excitement from me as I celebrated my success and as Kriztof clapped, shouting "Great work!" while Kazimir's pride painted his face.

"Let's see how many more you can get," Kriztof challenged.

By the time all the quivers were empty, I had hit the center of the target eight more times. There was something cathartic about the rhythm of grab, pull, breathe, shoot, and repeat – like power thrummed from my hands at each dull thud as the arrows sank into the bales of hay.

Kriztof walked down range to retrieve the arrows, leaving Kazimir and me sitting beside a bed of beautiful blue flowers as the last of the day's light sank low on the horizon. "Thanks for your help," I said, peeking at him from under my lashes.

"You were a natural," he replied, his voice rumbling like distant thunder beside me. He flicked a lock of hair over my shoulder, then said, "Dinner will be ready soon. You can get cleaned up while I help Kriztof. I'll see you in the dining room."

He stood, stealing a backward glance over his shoulder as he walked to the bales where Kriztof was pulling out the last of the arrows. Brushing my hands on my pants, I pushed to my feet and ambled through the dark garden toward the glass doors that separated inside from out.

Ali called for me as I opened them, so I headed to the kitchen where I found her elbow-deep in a turkey. "I'll be finished with this in a minute, Izidora, then I will be upstairs to dress you," she said.

"Dress me?" I furrowed my brows.

"You can't expect to get into those dresses by yourself can you? When you get to Este Castle, you will have a personal maid who will help you with that and your hair and makeup. Unfortunately for everyone, there is only one of me so I will have to split my time!" Her buxom chest bounced as she laughed.

"Take your time!" I called back, hurrying upstairs to hide my discomfort. Ascending the spiraling stairs, I landed on the second floor and turned toward the hall that held Kazimir's room, stopping to admire the elegant decor along the way. A tapestry here, an oil painting there, and a few delicate vases that I didn't dare touch led me to the double doors, and beyond them, my clothes remained exactly as I left them, the beautiful fabrics begging to be selected for dinner.

The twilight dress that had once belonged to High Lady Klariza pulled at me, though Ali had altered the neckline so that it dipped lower, forming a heart shape across my chest in line with the off-shoulder sleeves that clung to my wrists. She had also taken in the sides, the shimmering fabric hugging every developing curve, as I built muscle and ate my weight in sweets. A slit ran up my left leg, stopping mid-thigh so I had room to walk, but not scandalous enough to draw too much attention to my bare leg. It was the perfect blend of elegant and sexy, and I couldn't wait to see Kazimir's eyes bulge with me in it.

Would he want to pull me close to him, to kiss me with the passion he had that morning? The kiss had burned my lips all day, and I wanted more of them, especially after leaving myself unsatisfied in the bathroom.

Returning there, I sat cross-legged on the counter, fixing my long chestnut locks into small braids before weaving them into one long braid that spilled down my back. I pulled a few pieces out, framing my face and highlighting my cheeks, deciding that my clear, smooth skin needed nothing extra with the newfound brightness in my eyes.

A light knock followed by Ali's light step had me hopping off the counter and returning to the couch filled with dresses, lifting the deep blue garment toward her. "Can I wear this one?"

Her eyes sparkled as they danced over my hair. "I think that one will be perfect," she said.

She held the dress out for me to step into as I stripped out of my tunic and leggings. Tossing my braid over my shoulder, I cleared the path for her to button up the back. When her deft fingers brushed the back of my neck, she stepped back to admire her work, eyes shining with unshed tears. "You are beautiful," she breathed. "You look so much like your mother."

My eyes burned at her compliments, Ali unaware of the weight those words carried for me. I hugged her, and she sniffed, claiming something about chopping too many onions. A watery laugh was shared between us, and I knew at that moment that this was what home was supposed to feel like – a dense dessert smothered in a thick layer of love and topped with acceptance.

She dashed at her eyes, covering them with a beam from her lips. "Let's get you down to dinner."

20

KAZIMIR

I owed Kriztof an apology for my actions – my addiction to the female we had rescued was sending me spiraling in a way I never knew was possible. When Kriztof put his hands on her, I'd almost tackled him with the intent of ripping him to shreds, despite knowing it was an innocent, instructive touch. This need to possess and protect was driving me mad, but if I got Izidora at the end of it, I didn't care how it went down.

"I'm sorry I yanked you away from Izidora. I don't know what's come over me lately."

Kriztof sniggered, "Everyone knows except for you."

My stomach dropped, worried that my obsession was more obvious than I'd realized prior to her rescue. So I played innocent. "What do you mean?"

Kriztof sang, "Kazimir and Izidora sitting in a tree, K-I-S-S-I-N-G…"

I slapped a hand over his mouth, silencing him. He shook with laughter behind my hand, and I removed it from his mouth, realizing he was pushing for a reaction to see if it was true.

My secret fantasies were still safe in my head.

Kriztof rolled on the ground now, so amused by his jokes and schemes that he could no longer hold himself upright.

"Are you finished yet, asshole?" I said flatly.

He stood, wiping tears from his eyes. "I am now, brother."

Spinning on my heel and stalking back to the house, he raced to catch up to me, then fell in stride. "You know we all support you, right?" he reassured.

That stopped me in my tracks. Before, I'd worried that my brothers would judge or begrudge my infatuation with the lost princess, but hearing from Kriztof that the opposite was true was like taking a long breath after diving deep in the ocean. "How long have you known?" I still needed to confirm that they only saw the signs after her rescue.

"Since you started teaching her magic. We saw the way you looked at her, looked out for her even, always watching to make sure she was okay. Then we saw the way she looked at you. We're a group of good looking males, and none of us stood a chance against you. I know you two were trying to be discreet, but we all saw right through you. Well, except Cazius maybe, but he's always been blind to your antics." Kriztof shrugged, then resumed his march inside.

At least one of them was coming clean now.

"Endre told me last night that I should give in to my instincts," I admitted.

"Endre is the most in tune with his emotions out of all of us. That's why he fucks all the females that Vadim wants," he chuckled.

"Have you ever been in love?" I felt foolish asking him, but he was the only one available at the moment.

"Only with my reflection in the mirror," he deadpanned, then unable to contain how much he amused himself, he snorted.

"Thanks for being honest, Kriztof."

"Don't mention it." He waved me off as we parted at the top of the stairs, diverting to our respective rooms at Zirok House. After a quick wash in the basin of my temporary room, I pulled on a fresh suit, knowing that Ali expected formal dinners while we were here – meaning leathers were unacceptable at the dinner table.

When I strolled into the dining room, my father was already seated at the head of the long polished table. Another chair was placed opposite his at the other end of the massive table, presumably for Izidora. She had yet to arrive, so I milled about at that end, angling to sit beside her once she joined us. The Nighthounds trickled in, dressed smartly to avoid a rag slap from Ali.

At last, Izidora glided into the room, and the splash she made knocked the breath from all our lungs. She floated deeper into the room, the gown hugging her every curve with its shimmering fabric hypnotizing me as she sashayed her hips. Her hair was braided down her back, leaving her collarbones clear as the cut of her dress showed off her shoulders. A high slit ran up her leg, exposing most of her thigh, and my thoughts went wild as I imagined lifting the hem to reveal more of her exquisite body.

I snapped out of my thoughts as my father stood to greet her. "Izidora, you look every bit the princess you were born to be. I am honored to have you eat at my table." He bowed low, and the rest of us followed his lead. Her eyes widened just a fraction, pink flushing her cheeks as she plastered an uncomfortable smile on her lips.

My obsessive desire to save her kicked in, so I beelined to her side, tucking her arm into mine and leading her to the place of honor at the far end of the table. Like the well mannered male I was, her chair was pulled from the table, awaiting the grace of her hips before I pushed it in place again. I snatched the seat next to her and Kriztof joined me while Endre and Viktor sat across from us. Down the table, Vadim sat to my father's right, leaving an empty seat between him and Viktor for Ali, who loved being the center of attention at dinner. We'd insisted she join us a long time ago, but she insisted on setting the table with food first. The twins sat to my father's left, next to Kriztof, and we all waited for the food to appear.

A roasted turkey preceded Ali's entrance through the double doors leading to the kitchen, Viktor and Vadim shuffling apart to make room for the rosemary-scented poultry in the center of the table. She ferried platter after platter of homely food from kitchen to table, plates of root vegetables, squash, honeyed rolls, and cups of sauces arranged neatly along its length. A sugary aroma drifted through the doors, a dessert still cooking in the kitchen.

Izidora looked every bit the queen she was born to be perched at the head of the table, tracking Ali's movements as she bustled about. My eyes never left her despite the smells tugging at my attention. Kriztof's elbow found my ribs, and he whispered in my ear, "There's no turning away from your instincts now, fucker."

He was right. I wanted to pick Izidora up and carry her out of here into my bed, feast on her instead of the meal Ali had slaved over. My cock was rock hard under the table, and blood was thrumming everywhere but my head with her floral scent overpowering the herbal ones wafting around the room. I groaned internally, wondering how I was going to make it through this dinner. Viktor smirked at me across the table, watching and probably sensing the battle that raged in my body. Next to him, Endre gave me an encouraging nod, reassuring me that I could keep it under control.

A shaky breath opened my lungs, and I turned to Izidora, reaching for her hand where it rested neatly in her lap. I brought it to my lips, planting a featherlight kiss on the back before lifting my gaze to meet her aquamarine eyes. "You look stunning, Izidora."

She blushed. "Thank you, Kazimir. You look handsome as well." I don't know how long we were trapped in that moment, but Viktor pointedly cleared his throat, breaking our trance. I dropped Izidora's hand, missing her warmth immediately, as Ali descended upon us, heaping mashed potatoes on all our plates. The smile Izidora shot me after Ali walked away was one over which I would launch a thousand soldiers into battle.

A scraping chair tore my regard to the center of the table where Ali had finally settled in. "Dig in! You all look like you could use a thick meal."

Forks and knives immediately scraped as we tucked into her food, the rosemary melting over my tongue as I speared a slice of turkey. I passed a basket of rolls to Izidora, knowing she would want more than the single plump ball currently resting on her plate.

Kirigin was the first to break through the clanging of silverware and plates. "Ali, you have outdone yourself again. It's a good thing we don't live here because I would not be able to fight if I ate your cooking everyday. You'd have to roll me onto the battlefield," he joked, patting his stomach.

She preened under his praise, then dismissed it with a wave of her hand. "Now, hush, you're just saying that."

We slipped into easy conversation around the table, Ali repeating the latest gossip from the surrounding villages – who was marrying whom, disputes over land, and a baby born just last month. We regaled her with our adventures, but glazed over the harrowing details, like just how high we'd had to fly to rescue Izidora. The two of us stole glances throughout the meal, and even as I joked and laughed with my brothers, my attention was wholly focused on her. Perhaps it was the fear of her being captured again that accelerated what was already building between us, but I didn't care so long as she ended up mine in the end.

Her leg brushed mine under the table, and I almost jumped out of my seat as her bare foot traveled up my leg, over the knee, and rested on my thigh. The slice of turkey I'd just shoved into my mouth almost became my killer as she brushed the inside of my thigh with her toes, mere inches from my groin. Out of the corner of my eye, Izidora's pink pout turned into a smirk, and I grasped my wine glass and sipped it in an attempt to cover myself.

Fucking Fates, I couldn't believe this was the time she chose to initiate contact between us. Draining my wine glass, I prayed the buzz would distract me from the powerful need to claim her building in my chest. My arousal increased in time with the decadent aroma wafting from the kitchen, and when Ali went to fetch it, I almost collapsed with relief that our meal was almost finished so I could snatch Izidora up and lock her in my room until she said yes to me.

When Kriztof spotted the steaming pie Ali floated to the middle of the table, he teased the female whose pointed foot still brushed my hardness beneath the table. "Remember to let it cool before you take a bite, Izidora."

She rolled her eyes, a giggle escaping the lips I wanted all over my cock. "I'm a fast learner." She stuck out her tongue at him, and it took every ounce of willpower not to suck it into my mouth in front of my father and Ali. I pulled at my suit collar. Goddess help me.

Ali served each of us a slice topped with vanilla ice cream, which instantly melted over the sides of the steaming slice. Izidora swiped at a drip, sucking the sweet cream off her finger, but my eyes snapped shut a moment too late and I used the last bit of sanity in my brain not to snatch her up right then. Kriztof,

Endre, and Viktor sniggered at my expense there would be vengeance in the sparring ring.

"Kazimir, can I speak to you in my study after dinner?" my father asked, and the thought crossed my mind that I might have to disappoint him as I blew him off to blow on something else.

Viktor choked on his wine, and Kriztof slapped a hand over his mouth, barely stifling his amusement. Endre and Izidora both bit back smiles, not wanting to draw attention our way. I was so glad everyone got a kick out of my current predicament.

"Of course, father," I finally choked out. I looked up at the ceiling, trying to calm myself. He was clearly oblivious to what was occurring at this end of the table.

When I leveled my gaze again, Izidora was reaching for my dessert, stealing bits of fruit and flaky crust with a hint of sweet cream from my plate with her spoon. She took the head of the spoon into her mouth, turning it over and pulling it out slowly, eyes never leaving mine. Her grin flashed at me as the spoon slid out of her mouth; then she glanced at Endre, snickering conspiratorially with him. He and I were sparring first.

My father stood, ending our meal as he scraped back his chair. He thanked Ali for her wonderful cooking, then motioned for me to follow him to his study. With a prolonged look at the female who was pushing me past the point of temptation, I pushed back from the table and threw my napkin on my plate. "I'll see you later," I purred, dipping my mouth to her ear as I blew by her to follow my father.

Once I'd cleared the dining room, I stopped to adjust my pants, needing to hide my obvious erection before facing my father. Izidora, Endre, Kriztof, and Viktor burst into laughter as I walked away, the twins asking what was so funny. Their question was dismissed as the howling continued. "You had to be there," Kriztof wheezed.

Their voices disappeared as I traipsed down the long hall

toward my impending explosion. Fuck, I didn't know how long I could sit and speak with my father without needing a moment alone to take care of the agony below my belt. My father paced in front of the fire as I settled in a seat and folded my hands across my lap.

"Do you think we are taking the right action? I worry about sending only Zekari and Kirigin when we know there are at least twice as many Iron Fae riders about."

My father considered the Nighthounds to be his sons, just as I considered them all my brothers. This extended family we'd built filled the hole in his heart from my mother's absence, and I sensed that the decision to send the twins out on what could turn into a suicide mission weighed heavily on him. Losing them would be like losing his youngest children, after he'd already lost so much.

"They are both good riders, and fierce in battle," I reminded him. "I think we are doing the best we can, given our current predicament. Your wisdom hasn't failed us yet."

He gave me a soft smile, the embers reflecting off the circles under his eyes. "You know I worry about each of you."

"I know, father," I said, feeling slightly guilty as I'd been so wrapped up in Izidora that I'd forgotten Zekari and Kirigin would be riding for their lives to Vaenor the next day. Still, I believed what I said to my father, and I knew they would be okay.

"Is there anything else?" I asked.

"Two things. One, Izidora is illiterate."

My fingers clenched my knees as I hissed out a breath. "Fucking Fates. I suppose it makes sense though. If they wanted that much control over her, why teach her to read? Then she is wholly reliant on what she is told."

He nodded. "My thoughts exactly. I will begin teaching her tomorrow, but no one in Este Castle can find out."

"Absolutely not. The power-hungry cunts would immediately use that to their advantage. What was the other thing?"

"Tomorrow we will receive additional assistance from the villages. Can you get them settled and structure a watch schedule?" he requested.

"Of course. I'll have Vadim help coordinate as well." Then I rose, and he crossed the room to me, and I clasped him on the shoulder. "They're going to be okay," I reassured him one last time.

"Thank you, Kazimir," he said. With one last look at the male who'd brought me up on his own, I slipped from the study, heading for the stairs. Zekari and Kirigin were leaving the dining room, so I changed direction, wanting to speak to them before they left early the next morning.

I embraced each of them, then asked, "Is there anything else you need before you go?"

"We'll be fine," Zekari dismissed, a cocky grin on his face.

"Between Ali and Cazius, we might be too heavy to move quickly," Kirigin joked.

"We have all our armor and enough food to last us three weeks already packed," Zekari laughed.

"Just don't do anything stupid," I said.

They clutched their chests in unison, feigning insult. "When do we ever do anything stupid?"

"All the time," I laughed, ruffling Zekari's hair while he swatted at my hands. I wished them a restful sleep when we parted at the top of the stairs, and then my hunt was on – it was time to find Izidora.

 IZIDORA

Teasing Kazimir over dinner was far too fun, especially when our friends became involved, Endre whispering suggestions in my ear to push Kazimir to the limits of his self control. There seemed to be a pleasant acceptance among the males of the blossoming relationship between us, especially after our harrowing ride and the nightmare that had torn screams from my throat and sent them bursting into my room.

But the way he looked at me when I entered the dining room sent tingles down my spine, his eyes wide like he was a man starved and I was the food he'd been so desperately seeking. No one had ever looked at me like that before – like I was their only reason for breathing and they'd do anything for a moment of attention. So far, Kazimir had given me all the control over our intimacy, but tonight, I'd pushed him, testing him to see what he would do when his desire became unbearable.

Because my desire for him grew like a wildfire in a dry wood over the past two days, and I wanted him near me all the time, providing refuge from the storm that waited beyond these walls. It was as if something inside me flipped after making my first kill with Kazimir by my side, my subconscious throwing truths at me that I was finally ready to see by way of the traumatizing nightmare the night after.

The hooded riders caught up to us, their horses racing parallel as they dragged me from Mistik's back. One of them threw me over his horse like I was nothing more than a sack of grain, whipping his mount in the opposite direction, ripping screams of terror from my throat. Kazimir chased us with wild desperation, snapping Fek's reins, begging him to gallop faster. But Fek was exhausted, his hide coated in sweat, his mouth foaming from exertion, and he floundered at the penultimate moment. I screamed Kazimir's name as I reached my arms for him, tears racing down my face, fear gripping my heart like a vice at the sight of him dropping away from me. He screamed for me too, promising he would find me before slowing Fek to a walk and watching helplessly as I faded out of view.

The hairs on my arms rose as I fell into the grips of that nightmare once again; it felt so real, the dream so vivid, the emotions so heightened, that when I woke I was certain I was in the camp of the Iron Fae. But Kazimir was there instead, ready to defend me, and I caved to the pull of his comfort, begging him to stay so the nightmare would not come to pass. I no longer cared that males had hurt me before, for time and time again, Kazimir had shown up when I needed him most and asked nothing in return. When I woke in the morning after a dreamless sleep, I discovered we'd drifted together in the night, as if we could no longer fight the string that tugged us together.

Ali promised she would be up to help me out of my dress as soon as she cleared the table, yet I rather wished it would be Kazimir helping me out of it instead.

His calloused fingers drifted down my spine as he unhooked the buttons lining the back of the dress. His warm breath floated across my neck and ear as he skimmed my shoulder with his lips. His hands slowly dropped my dress, letting it pool around my feet as he trailed his fingers down my flat stomach.

A small moan slipped from my lips at the fantasy.

A light knock broke my reverie. "Enter," I called, opening my eyes.

As if summoned by my desire, Kazimir slid through the door, closing it lightly behind him. A chill wracked my body despite the roaring fire heating the room. His gaze raked over my still dressed body, lasciviously appreciating my form in the dress that was nearly painted on my skin. He circled me, his predatory gaze trained on my throat, watching the shallow rise and fall of my chest, as if estimating the effort it would take to capture his prey.

If I was going to be hunted, I only wanted to be hunted by him.

He stalked forward, capturing me and spinning me in his arms so his hardness dug into my back. I gasped at his sudden forcefulness, and he leaned down, pressing a light kiss to the crook of my neck. The wine I drank with dinner had already lulled me into a heady lust, so I leaned into his touch, encouraging him to continue. His hands moved to the back of my dress, roughened fingers slowly unhooking each button one by one, his tease tantalizingly slow as he allowed moments to pass before moving on to another.

He was midway down my back when another knock sounded and Ali's voice shouted through the door. "Are you ready for help with the dress?"

Kazimir's hands froze, hovering a hair off my tightening skin, sending a shiver to the spot. "I think I've got it!" I called back.

"Okay, come find me if you need help," she replied, muffled footsteps retreating down the hall.

Kazimir fanned a hot breath across my neck, planting his lips in the crook again. "Now, where were we?" he purred, trailing kisses along my shoulder until he reached the tip of my arm, then nipped. The wispy touches pebbled my skin, the bumps growing as he loosed a few more buttons, the time between each release painfully slow.

Moisture gathered between my thighs, and with little room to move in this dress, I could do nothing but squeeze them together to relieve the tension budding there. I craned my neck, reaching for the nape of his neck and digging my nails into his scalp before angling his lips to my own. As they touched, a soft moan slipped from my mouth to his, and he nipped my lower lip in response.

The buttons completely popped open, he let the dress puddle on the floor, a midnight ocean surrounding me and separating me from the shore upon which he stood. Absolutely nothing was hidden beneath that fabric, and the chill of the room was the cause of the shiver that started between my shoulders and worked its way to my tailbone.

Kazimir sucked in a breath as he viewed my back for the first time. I'd barely been able to stem the tears that threatened to drown me when I saw the marks that I already knew covered them, and they pricked my eyes while I waited for the male who saved me to process the torture he'd rescued me from.

His fingers traced line after line across the hourglass of my back, painting it with gentle caresses instead of the bite of whips. With bated breath, I waited for the inevitable rejection once my brokenness was laid bare. The scars on the outside were just a fraction of the ones that marred my soul.

"Tell me you want this," Kazimir croaked as his hands stilled on the last scar just above the dimples in my lower back.

"I want this," I moaned, his hands traipsing toward more sensual parts of my torso. Rough palms flattened against my waist, then trailed up my ribs and stopped just below my breasts, brushing their heaviness.

"Do you want to be touched here?"

"Yes," I breathed, and he relieved their pressure by cupping them in his palms, squeezing them lightly and rolling my nipples between his fingers. His cock was insistent at my back, and I wanted to feel the heat radiating off his body without any barriers. Pressing his hands down, I turned into him, grasped either side of his lapels, and pushed them over his shoulders. He picked up on what I wanted, flinging the jacket off and away, then working on his crisp white shirt.

His fingers deftly moved along the buttons, revealing his massive chest and shoulders as the fabric parted. Running horses chasing an eagle were tattooed over his chest, the scene disappearing over his shoulder, and I wanted to run my hands over the art, learning every detail of the colorful spread. Shrugging the shirt from his shoulders, his whole torso was bared to me, and my mouth watered as I binged his sculpted abs that dipped into a V below his waistband. The firelight flickered across his sculpted physique, casting highlight and shadow in all the right places.

My hands mapped the sinew holding him together as I felt from the planes of his chest, over his shoulder, and wrapped my hands around his neck.

"Once we start this, there's no going back," Kazimir warned, his hands finding the back of my head and tilting it up so I could see the weight of those words.

He'd said the same thing this morning, giving me an out before we dove into the deep end; but I was already in over my head, the world around me threatening to drown me under the weight of a title and a group of Iron Fae focused on keeping my head below water.

It was time to carve a path to freedom for myself, and it started in the sanctuary of Kazimir's arms.

"Then keep your eyes forward." I pulled his mouth to mine,

arching my body into his as he wound his fingers tighter into my hair, an animalistic noise slipping past his lips. His tongue swiped my lips, and I opened my mouth to him, letting him lead as he deepened our kiss. I moaned into his mouth, wanting more as his tongue twined with mine. I dug my nails into his scalp as he dropped his hands from mine and snatched up my lower back, bending me over without breaking our kiss. He lowered us to the thick fur rug laid in front of the fireplace, my body warming rapidly as it was assaulted by heat on all sides. He took some of that with him when he sat back on his heels, drinking in my body, which was half lit by the fire and half sheathed in darkness.

"You are perfection," he breathed, planting a hand on either side of my head as he leaned in to kiss me again. His large frame pressed mine into the soft rug, his bulge digging into my stomach as our passion intensified. My hips ground against his as our tongues danced like the flames beside us. I forgot about the outside world as I lost myself in Kazimir, the feeling of his tongue sliding over mine, his hard body pressed firmly against my soft one, his smoke and amber scent filling my nostrils.

Air filled my lungs when he moved his lips to my neck, leaving a blazing trail down my throat as he fell to an elbow and used his other hand to palm my breast. My pebbled nipple was swept up between his fingers, my gasp giving way to a moan as he pinched thumb and finger over it.

Mouth tracing from throat to breast, he swirled his wet tongue around my nipple then took it into his mouth, sucking lightly before letting his teeth graze over the sensitive peak. I arched off the floor, and he moved his ministrations to the other nipple, sending a rush of tingles across my skin as he worked over it.

He looked up from his task, releasing his mouth to flash me an impish smile. Too gently and too slowly he charted a course lower, his fingers gliding over my ribs and down to my hip bones, rubbing circles over them and coaxing my legs wider as he savored every moment of baring me to him. It was clear he scented and saw how wet I was from the approving growl that left his lips.

"What a good girl, so wet for me already," he crooned, and I flushed, his words fanning the flames of a deeply rooted need for affirmation.

Pushing my knees to the floor, he instructed, "Stay there." He reached for his belt, and I peeked under my lashes as he unhooked it, then began unbuttoning his pants. The outline of his hardness was so close that I could clearly see the massive bulge that waited impatiently for freedom. I laid bare to him as he stood, eyes never leaving my swollen center as he kicked his pants away, revealing his muscled thighs, large enough to be low-hanging branches on the trees we rode through in the wood. He stood over me, looking like a statue of the ideal male form carved by the Goddess herself, and all I could do was relax my legs further, bite my lip, and wait for the last bit of him to be revealed. Dropping the last piece of fabric separating us, his massive cock sprang free, standing at full, painful attention as I saw just how hard he was for me. The tip was already beaded with moisture, and something between a moan and a groan rumbled in my chest as I examined his thick girth, wondering how I was going to take all of it.

His knees hit the floor first, then his hands, and he crawled toward me on all fours, his face predatory as he set his sights on my swollen pussy. "So pretty and so open," he murmured, sending a flush across my rapidly rising and falling chest. Fingers finding the muscles of my ass, he yanked me to his face, eliciting a gasp as he blew on my hot core, the sensation almost tipping me over the edge.

"Kazimir..." I breathed, my skin too hot and too cold at the same time.

He trailed kisses along my inner thighs, winding me up before delivering a knockout punch. When he reached the apex of my thighs, he planted his lips on mine and sucked my clit into his mouth.

"Oh!" I whimpered, jerking underneath him as those sensitive nerves came to life. Taunting me with rough flicks of his tongue, I nearly begged for him to give me more so I could combust and relieve the tension building low in my belly. Without shame, I ground my hips into his face, his beard adding sensation in all the right places. I whimpered his name as I laced my fingers into the furry rug, closing in on the edge already. My walls fluttered and he stopped his ministrations, drawing a whimpering cry from my lips.

"I want to ruin you as thoroughly as you ruined me," he uttered, and then drove a finger into my soaking center and curled, stroking my inner walls with the rough pad of his finger-tip. His tongue resumed its post at the apex of my thighs, lighting those nerves on fire as he synced his movements, sending me crashing toward release.

My walls clenched around his finger, and fire blazed inside me, tearing me apart from the inside out as my orgasm took hold. "Fuck, fuck, fuck..." I moaned as I ground into his finger and mouth, riding out my high until my head tipped back and all I saw was stars.

He did not cease his movements until I was thoroughly wrung out and breathless; only then did he remove his finger, coated with sticky arousal. My thighs were slick and trembling, and he only smirked at me once he saw I was immoble from the orgasm that ripped through me.

His emerald pools were deep in lust as he looked up my body, hooking his eyes on mine. "I want to show you what it's like to be adored, Izidora. I want you to scream my name as I make you come over and over from the pleasure I bring you. You taste like fucking honey, and I will gladly drink from you, day or night. This is only the beginning."

Gripping his cock fiercely in one hand and bracing himself with the other, he jerked himself roughly and sank his mouth to my sensitive core again, eliciting wanton mewls as he dragged me toward another release.

"I want to touch you," I breathed between pants as his tongue parted my folds and speared into my core.

He stopped his lapping, looking up from beneath furrowed brows. "Are you certain?"

"Yes," I breathed, pushing off my elbows and scooting backward until I could turn to my knees in front of him. He sat back on his heels, and I tossed my braid over my shoulder out of the way as I reached my hand to the head and smeared the liquid beading it in a circle around the tip.

"Fuck, Izidora..." He jerked at my touch, and he gasped a groan as I repeated the jerking motion he'd used on himself, moving my hand up and down over the velvety soft skin. Hands on my shoulders, he guided me closer until my lips hovered over him, indicating that he wanted more from me than I was currently providing.

And I wanted to give him more. I wanted the taste of him on my tongue to replace the lingering bitterness that had forced its way there. I was no longer a victim. Rather, I was a powerful Fae, the world at my fingertips.

After a few more pumps, I lowered my mouth, flicking my tongue over the tip, tasting a salty bead of moisture dripping from him. The groan that escaped him was primal and sent a throb straight to my core. His guttural sounds filled the space around us as I circled my tongue around the tip, only serving to spur me further. He wrapped my long hair around his fist, and I opened my mouth as wide as I could, taking the whole head into my mouth and sucking like I had on the spoon at dinner.

"Just like that," he ground out, a sharp tug on my hair pulling me backward before I sank his cock again, trying to adjust my mouth to the thickness. I scraped it with my teeth as I tried to adjust, and he hissed but kept hold of my hair. Relaxing my lips and jaw, I was able to take him deeper, the length filling my mouth and making it hard to breathe.

Kazimir's hips pumped in and out of my mouth as I held it in a wide ring to accommodate him. The tip hit the back of my throat when he went too deep, and I gagged, the gurgle sucking his cock deeper before pushing it back out. The swears that escaped his lips were vulgar, and having him at my mercy like this made me feel powerful. My nose hit his stomach as he thrust in again, causing me to gag harder and sending tears to my eyes.

"You are going to ruin me with that mouth." The feral moan was enough to get me to relax my throat further, enjoying wielding this power over him. Using my hair as a guide, he directed my head up and down his shaft, flattening my tongue and sucking him into my throat as his groans grew erratic and primal.

"I'm about to come," he grunted, and I took a deep breath in preparation. Hot ropes of liquid squirted into my mouth, coating my tongue and dripping down my throat. I sucked harder as he twitched in my mouth, coaxing every last drop from him before swallowing it down like it was the best dessert I had ever tasted.

His emerald orbs flared with desire as my throat bobbed, and our disjointed panting filled the room as we stared at each other, neither of us fully satisfied and wanting more. Two strong hands lifted me from all fours on the fur rug, cradling me in his arms as he carried me like the most precious prize to his soft bed. With one hand still wrapping me against his chest, he yanked back the covers, allowing me to escape to the embrace of the soft sheets. The white silk did not have me for long, Kazimir pulling me flush with his body a moment later, wrapping his arms around my waist and nuzzling my neck.

"I'm not nearly done with you, Izidora," he breathed into my hair, calluses roughening up the bare skin on my belly. I shivered from the promises held in his words and the chill in the air as sweat dried across my skin. Kazimir pulled blankets over the top of us, trapping the heat from his body in with mine. "Sleep, and I promise I will keep you safe while you dream."

A spent sigh slipped from my lips as my eyelids fluttered and drifted closed, the shelter in his arms enough to ferry me toward sleep. My last thought before I crossed into the land of dreams was that I wanted to spend every night like this.

———

"No, please, don't," I begged the hooded figure towering over me. My knees were sliced by the sharp stones beneath them and tears streamed down my face, dropping one by one onto my bare shoulders as my body was wracked with sobs. I reached for his cloak, but my hands stopped short as the clanking of chains reverberated around us. I yanked and yanked and yanked, desperate to escape the sinister whip he held in his hands. The black leather uncurled as he backed away, a low, haunting laugh leaving the lips I could not see. He circled me, growling appreciatively at my naked form, that pointed tip grating across rocks behind him. When he stepped out of my field of vision, I trembled, waiting for the first crack to light up my back. No matter how many times I was strung up like this, that moment between losing sight of the male and the first whistle never got easier. The sharp bite dug into my left shoulder before I could draw a deep breath to fight through the mental panic, and I cried out as physical pain blended with emotional pain. He struck again, and again, my

muscles seizing with every blow as I strained against the iron. He landed three in quick succession on my lower back, and I arched wildly as I screamed and–

My eyes flew open, my breath lodged in my throat as I found myself arching away from Kazimir, as if I acted out my nightmare while I slept. Craving his warmth against my back to relax the muscles still thrumming with adrenaline, I crawled closer to him, breathing in his amber scent. When I draped his arm over my stomach, Kazimir woke, a grumble and a groan following the first hints of light beneath the heavy velvet curtains covering the windows. He kissed my shoulder and rolled out of bed, a yawn cleaving his jaw open.

"Where are you going?" I murmured, not wanting him to leave when the remnants of that nightmare still clung to my back.

"To see Zekari and Kirigin off. Go back to sleep," he whispered.

"Ugh," I replied, stretching from the tips of my toes to my interlaced fingers above my head, then turning to my knees and sitting up in bed. I wasn't going to miss seeing them off, especially as they risked their lives to ensure my safe return to Vaenor. The distraction of their departure would banish the echoes of the whip on my back. "I'm coming with you."

He tucked an errant strand of chestnut behind my ear with a smirk. "Sleep well, Princess? Your snores were cute."

I tossed a pillow at him and he caught it, grinning. My tortured dreams weren't a topic of discussion I was ready for. Their intensity and how closely they paralleled my reality was disturbing enough in my head, let alone voiced to the world. Instead, I hopped out of bed, not deigning to respond to his false accusations of my snoring. Hunting down leather leggings and a trim tunic, I dressed quickly, fetching my chest plate and cuffs for the sparring we would do later. Not even five minutes after waking my body was restless after a day of inactivity. Playing dress up and cooking the day before had been nice, but I itched to move, to push my body to its limits and reap the benefit of the stillness that settled across my bones afterward. But more importantly, I didn't want to play out my nightmares by being an easy target anyone could capture.

Kazimir reached for my hand as we exited the room, guiding me downstairs and out the massive front entry, the rocky drive ending as we turned to the stables where the rest of the Nighthounds, Cazius, and Ali already gathered. Cazius sternly spoke to Zekari and Kirigin, who wore grim expressions and black leather armor. They nodded before each embracing Cazius in turn, the latter's eyes boasting bags thicker than the ones that draped across the horses' backs. These mounts were different from the ones we rode to get here, their legs longer and bodies leaner than the muscular black beasts that befitted the Nighthounds.

"Why are they taking different horses?" I asked Kazimir as we crossed the dew-dusted lawn.

"They need to move quickly, and this breed is faster than their other mounts," he explained.

"There are different types of horses?"

"Yes, these are Sprinters. The nobles of the Night Realm like to race them for sport. Mistik is a Hunter, and Fek is a Warstrider. Their breeds are named for the jobs they are bred to do."

We reached the gathered group, Vadim and Viktor parting to welcome us into their circle. Kazimir strode forward, clasping arms with each of the twins once before dipping his head to them in a sign of respect. "Get to Vaenor swiftly and without incident."

"If I had a gold coin for every time I heard that today,"

Kirigin joked, then looked past Kazimir to where I waited to wish them well.

"I will miss both of you. See you when you get back," I beamed, stepping around the male I'd shared a bed with last night.

"Twin sandwich!" they screamed one last time, crushing me between them and forcing all the air from my lungs with a barking laugh. Once they'd thoroughly smashed me, Zekari ruffled my bed-matted hair, and I swatted his hand away.

"See you when we get back," he said, then followed his twin to their shiny bay steeds, hopping swiftly atop the closest and angling the stallion toward the waiting gate. The guards swung it open wide enough to let Zekari through, immediately breaking into a gallop as he made a mad dash away from Zirok House. We waited anxiously for a few minutes before they reopened the gates for Kirigin to depart, his mount carrying him off onto the grassy plains headed north to the capital of the Night Realm.

Cazius murmured something to Ali, who sniffed and allowed him to lead her away from the gate and toward the open doors of the manor, leaving me standing with the remaining Nighthounds.

"Let's spar, shall we?" Kazimir suggested with a wicked gleam in his eye.

Vadim rubbed his hands together, ready for a fight.

"To the ring!" Kriztof shouted, pumping his fist and strutting away in the direction of the guard house. The males placed bets on who would be the ultimate victor as we sauntered toward a bare dirt ring fenced by slats of wood. They were spaced out enough to watch the action, but thick enough to sit atop should you want a bird's eye view of the training below. Strapping on my chest plate and cuffs, I climbed to the top railing and settled in to watch. Kazimir and Kriztof hopped the fence with ease and faced off before the waiting crowd of off-duty guards that had perched across from me, or watched through the slats in the ring. Endre settled down beside me on the fence, his hair messier than mine and hanging in his peridot eyes, while Viktor and Vadim laced their hands through the panel next to us, whooping as the pair dropped into their fighting stances.

Kriztof pulled two short swords from sheaths strapped to his back, and Kazimir held a lethal looking blade, a giant emerald surrounded by moonstones set into its hilt. They circled each other, Kriztof spinning his short swords, baiting Kazimir into an attack. But he patiently waited for Kriztof to get cocky, a vengeful gleam in his emerald eyes. I sensed Kazimir's strike before I saw him swing his sword, the tip arcing toward Kriztof's thigh. Kriztof's blades parried in a clash of metal, flinging Kazimir's sword low and away as he spun into a high attack, whipping one blade and then the other in a flurry of motion. Kazimir side-stepped, the blades mere inches from his throat before swinging his blade up, centering himself, and launching a series of brutal strikes that had Kriztof backing up.

Kazimir fought with the same level of intensity that he'd used to seduce me – intense and wholly focused, letting nothing distract him from his prize. Their dance was violent and thrilling, and with rapt attention I assessed their movements, Kazimir anticipating Kriztof's blows and setting traps to lure him into opening too far and leaving himself vulnerable.

Sweat dripped from the males' flushed faces as they fought for control of the ring, but soon Kriztof's back was against the fence, Kazimir's relentless pace forcing him back one step at a time until there was nowhere else for him to go. He knocked one of Kriztof's twin blades away, flicking the tip of his sword up and under Kriztof's chin with a wicked grin.

"I yield," Kriztof admitted defeat.

Vadim whooped, and Viktor yelled, "I see you are taking this seriously today, Kazimir."

"I've got to remind you guys that you can't fuck with me," he grinned back.

Kriztof resheathed his blades, then crossed the ring to join Endre and me on the fence, tucking sweaty strands of his shoulder length hair behind his ears, then elbowing me in the ribs. "He's just showing off because you're here. I let him win to boost his ego."

I rolled my eyes while Endre pretended to laugh.

Our attention returned to the ring as Viktor jumped the fence, his long sword matching Kazimir's, though his hilt held a large lapis lazuli stone, surrounded by intricate carvings. The pointed tip traced a line in the ground as he circled Kazimir, who stood preternaturally still, only his head tracking Viktor's menacing movements. With speed contradictory to their size, the males closed the distance between them, broad swords clashing with a sharp sound that pricked my sensitive ears. Flashes of magic erupted between them as they battled for control of the dirt ring, and I struggled to track their movements or decide who gained the upper hand as the two fought viciously and without mercy. Kazimir was like a shadowed blur as he bounded around the ring, forcing Viktor to slow his strikes and defend against an opponent who was harder to pin down. Yet Viktor was a strategist, and he waited until Kazimir was over-confident before blasting him with a wave of silver so powerful it blew my hair straight back.

Kriztof whooped beside me as the shadows that clung to Kazimir disappeared and the shockwave blasted him toward the wooden barrier separating us from them. Viktor's lapis lazuli encrusted sword returned to the action, pressing his advantage and forcing Kazimir to concede ground. My hands gripped the railing as the male who did everything in his power to keep me safe was thrown into a life or death situation, this string tugging between us screaming at me to do something. I willed Kazimir to recover, my eyes never breaking contact with his hulking form as he backstepped under Viktor's brutal onslaught. Kazimir's lips pressed into a thin line, his heel digging into the ground and a cry tearing from his lips as his blade moved like lightning backed with booming thunder, clashing with Viktor's sword so hard my teeth rattled.

The force of the blow sent Viktor stumbling, and he caught himself with one arm while keeping his blade pointed toward Kazimir. But the blow was too powerful, and Kazimir easily knocked it away, pointing the tip of his sword at Viktor's heart.

Viktor grinned, his sage eyes glittering with fierce amusement. "I yield."

Kazimir grinned back, proffering his arm to hoist Viktor to his feet, the two males embracing and clapping backs, congratulating each other on a well-fought match.

Kazimir pointed his sword at Endre, the challenge apparent by the vengeful grin playing across his face. "Your turn."

Endre's boots thudded against the packed clay as he dropped into the ring. With a cool expression that betrayed nothing, he pulled a battle axe from a holster at his back, tossing it between his hands before unsheathing a lethal looking dagger from a strap on his thigh. Kazimir gripped his gem-encrusted sword high once again, readying for his next opponent.

Jumping into action before Kazimir was too settled, Endre cut left, out-maneuvering Kazimir's long sword as he danced around him, twirling his battle axe. Kazimir steadied his sword, pivoting left and right as he tried to line up with Endre again. But Endre was faster with less bulk to maneuver, and his agility put him directly behind Kazimir. My heart galloped in my chest, an audible gasp leaving my lips as Endre swung his axe down in the direction of Kazimir's exposed shoulder. At the last second,

Kazimir's sword clattered against the ground and he rolled over his shoulder and away, spinning into a crouch as Endre pressed forward.

From his position hovering above the ground, Kazimir lunged for Endre's legs, snatching one and rising roughly, bringing Endre's leg high and setting him hopping. Endre's weapons dropped as Kazimir yanked him in, grappling for control of arms and hands as they moved fluidly from one position to the next. Kazimir snuck under both of Endre's arms, spinning behind him and locking his hands around Endre's front. With a grunt, Kazimir lifted Endre into the air, flipped him over, and slammed him into the ground, the thump from his landing solid yet lighter than I expected from such a brutal throw.

Endre coughed as the dust kicked up from their scuffle settled around him. "I yield."

"That's for the ice cream trick," Kazimir grinned, holding out his hand to his fallen friend.

Endre grasped it, the males working together to haul him upright. "Next time, don't pull the throw," he said, striking Kazimir on the shoulder. The two embraced, sweat soaking their tunics and highlighting every hard plane on the males' bodies as the fabric clung to them. Males. I would never understand how they could be so brutal to each other and then act like nothing happened after.

The way they moved was breathtaking – ferocious, powerful, and unforgiving. Even without sharpened blades, they grappled and subdued each other; they didn't need weapons or magic to fight tooth and nail. This was knowledge I could have used in the cave, and yet another item on my ever growing list of learning, though I tacked it to the top as an essential survival skill.

"Show me how to do that!" I exclaimed as Kazimir approached the beam that supported Kriztof and me.

A rumble of amusement started in his chest and worked its way to the eyes that perused my leather-clad form. "You need someone closer to your size to practice on," he said. "Otherwise, you'll hurt your back."

Kriztof launched off the railing, sprinting toward the stables. "I know just the thing!" he yelled over his shoulder, rounding the corner of the faraway building, then reappearing with a sack of grain slung over his shoulder. He threw it to the ground at our feet upon his return. As I measured myself against it, a roar of laughter swept through us; he wasn't wrong, the burlap sack was about my height. My bubbles of laughter joined theirs, Kriztof beaming with pride at his successful endeavor.

"Maybe start by picking up the sack until it feels easy," Kazimir instructed. "Then we will move on to the rest."

Regarding the awkwardly slumped sack, I sank into a squat, locking my hands around it as I had seen Kazimir do to Endre. Pushing through my heels, I attempted to lift it. "Oof," I grunted as I strained to put space between it and the ground. It hovered for only a moment before I dropped it, smiling at the males. "I'll work on it."

Viktor snorted, then challenged me. "Let's go, Izidora."

Viktor was by far the broadest of the males, and I swallowed as he handed me a plain short sword similar to the ones Kriztof used. His bejeweled one was slung across his back as he hopped back into the ring. I tossed the metal through a gap in the boards, then slipped between them, retrieving my weapon and squaring up with the male who towered over me. A crowd gathered around the ring, and my palms slicked the hilt as all the eyes watched me expectantly. Flipping the blade to my other hand, I rubbed the moisture off on my pants, then returned the blade to my dominant hand, self doubt cascading over me like a tidal wave and crashing panicked questions against the walls of my mind.

What if I made a stupid mistake? Would they think less of me? Would they think I was unworthy of their loyalty? Would they turn me over to the Iron Realm so I wouldn't be their problem?

I was so caught up in my sea of self doubt that I didn't see Viktor's strike until it was almost too late. The impact rang up my arm as I swung my blade up to parry. Under the next blow, I pressed back and up with all my strength, holding Viktor's blade off my body. The force behind his blows backed me up, my limbs flooding with adrenaline as my body remembered what it was like to fight underneath the onslaught of a male whose strength vastly outmatched mine. My breath clogged my throat, and I struggled to suck down enough air to maintain a clear head and focus on the fight in front of me rather than slipping back into my worst living nightmares.

In the absence of air, time seemed to slow down as light and dark flitted in front of me, two paths I could travel down with vastly different outcomes. The path of panic freezing my feet and sending them slipping out from under me would get me captured or killed. The path of fire slicing through the dark would sharpen my focus and fuel my defense.

There was a reason my inner fire never snuffed out when I was trapped in the void.

Viktor's sword arced, and I gritted my teeth, bracing myself for impact and stoking the white hot fire inside me. That same fire erupted down my blade as it connected with Viktor's, sending sparks scattering around us. I stared in shock at the white flame licking down the short sword, and Viktor's eyes widened a fraction, but he did not stop. Ducking under a blow from above, I sprinted to the left, dancing back to the center of the ring where we were on even footing again. Cheers sounded among the onlookers, and the combination of their approval and the unrelenting flame before me renewed my energy.

Viktor grinned wickedly, a look that held no promise of

holding back as he faced me, tip of his blade dragging the ground while silver swirled in the air around him. A fierce smirk was my response to the renewed challenge, and I waited for the drive of his blade to imbue my arms with the firmness needed to hold my ground. I channeled all my willpower into winning this fight and showing myself and the others that I would not crumble under pressure or the demons that burst forth at the worst possible times. Viktor may be broad and stacked with strength, but I was light on my feet and moved faster than he did. Sucking in a steeling breath, I slipped past Viktor's brute force, cutting across his right side and whirling around so my front was on his back. I whipped my blade across his stomach, holding it steady without cutting through his tunic. The flames still coating my blade caught the threads, cloying the air with the sharp bite of burnt cotton.

Silence fell across the gathered crowd. "I yield," Viktor stuttered, disbelief lacing his tone.

The flames subsided as I dropped the blade, then fell to my hands and knees, sucking in much-needed air. My chest heaved and the crowd went wild, howls and claps surrounding me on all sides. Kazimir wrapped his arms around my middle and lifted me into the air, beaming with pride as he hugged me to him. I laughed, and the sound was so free that I swore to myself I would feel this elation over and over again for as long as I lived to make up for all the pain I'd suffered before. Once Kazimir finished spinning me, he set me on the ground in front of a much-pleased Viktor, who bowed low. "Congratulations, Princess. You continue to surprise us, and I for one cannot wait to see where your ferocity takes you."

My cheeks heated under his regard, but I did not have long to dwell on his words as I was utterly surrounded by my friends and strangers who were thrilled to see me succeed.

This limitless feeling was intoxicating, and I took a moment to savor the thrill arcing through my blood. My mental battle was just as great as my physical one, and despite my earlier doubt, I disregarded the demons who begged for attention and stepped into a more powerful version of myself. That alone was worth celebrating, so I lifted my blade, punching the air as I cheered for my hidden victory too.

22

KAZIMIR

Izidora sat breathlessly beside me, flushed from another day's worth of victories, our skin a hair's breadth from each other as we watched some of the local Night Fae fight hand to hand. Part of my duties for the past few days had included assessing the strengths and weaknesses of each volunteer from the village, then assigning them to different rotations. It was an opportunity to teach Izidora the finer points of fighting, and I pointed out moves that worked well and ones that were sure to get her killed. She watched with rapt attention, often asking questions or asking for clarification, absorbing it all like the night sky absorbs the light of the dying sun.

Yet my mind often drifted back to the battle between Izidora and Viktor a few days prior, and how I nearly went mad with the need to jump between their blades and defend her with my life. It took a white-knuckled grip on the splintered wood to let her fight her way through, and fucking Fates was she incredible. The resilience she displayed when her back was against the fence was nothing short of extraordinary, her willpower an endless well to rival her magic. She was going to be a force to be reckoned with, and the thought of bending a knee to her as my queen one day pounded against my skull and sent heat straight to my groin.

There was only one problem – no Night Fae could call flames to their swords like she did.

Mid-afternoon, Izidora, Vadim, and I walked back to Zirok House, chatting about the pros and cons of different weapons. Izidora revealed she liked shorter weapons that allowed her to move with more agility, and we promised to work with them more. With each passing moment, I loved Izidora even more, her mind as brilliant as her body, her spirit unbroken despite the abuse she suffered at the hands of the Iron Fae. Having her sleep in my bed only fueled my obsession, and despite the fact that I had yet to fully lay claim to her, there was no doubt in my mind I would do anything to make it happen – even if it meant going against tradition and decorum.

When we entered the house, my father called to us from the long hall beyond the dual staircase where his study lay. He sat behind his desk, pieces of parchment scattered across it and another resting in his hand, his crinkled eyes skimming the paragraphs.

"Kazimir, Izidora, Vadim," he addressed each of us individually. "You look like you've been having fun."

"We've been working hard, that's certain," Vadim said. "You should have seen Izidora best Viktor again earlier. I'm sure Kriztof will regale us with the story at dinner tonight."

"I look forward to hearing it," my father replied. "Izidora, why don't you wash up while I speak with Kazimir and Vadim. I thought we might pick up today with more history of the Night Realm."

"Sounds like a plan to me. Thank you," she smiled, then headed upstairs, her light trot my sole focus as she departed.

My father waved the parchment in his hands, returning my

attention to the room. "I just received this from Vadim's father, Lord Arzeni."

Vadim's family was from a Lower House whose lands were a few day's ride from here. At thirty-nine, Vadim was the oldest of our group, so I had known him for as long as I could remember. Our families often gathered here in the summer, our fathers close friends, having grown up together themselves. Vadim had been a natural first choice for the Nighthounds when my father was tasked with finding Izidora, having just reached adulthood himself and needing an outlet for his battle skills.

"What did he say?" Vadim asked.

"He said that he saw a group of Iron Fae riding through the woods near your home late yesterday," Cazius read from the parchment.

"Did he say which direction they were headed?" I asked, hoping it wasn't north.

"Southwest, away from here, thank the Goddess."

We all breathed a collective sigh of relief – that meant that Zekari and Kirigin wouldn't have crossed paths with them.

"Was there anything else?" Vadim leaned his elbows on the chair before him.

"He said, and I quote, 'Please tell my son that his mother misses him dearly and to pay a visit soon so she will stop worrying me into an early grave,'" Cazius announced.

"You should write back and request that they join us in Vaenor. I know they aren't much for staying at Este Castle these days, but they will want to be there for the return of the lost princess," Vadim suggested.

"Your sister might be a good friend for Izidora as well," I added. Vadim's sister Liliana was sixteen years younger than him, and they were close despite their age difference. She was similar in age to Izidora, whose only exposure to females so far had been Ali; it would be helpful to have a female friend who could relate to what she would go through at court. Liliana was also headstrong and continued to defy her father's wishes about accepting offers from males wanting to court her. I was honestly surprised that 'talk some sense into your sister' wasn't included in Lord Arzeni's letter as well.

"Two of the most beautiful females in the Night Realm scheming together? The Fates couldn't have planned that any better. Goddess help us all," Vadim laughed.

My father agreed with the sentiment. "I will respond to your father, asking him to join us at Este Castle and to bring your sister. Shall I also promise that you'll have tea with them every afternoon while we are there?"

"Tell them I will try, but make no promises," Vadim snorted, shaking his head.

The scent of roses and patter of small feet hit my senses before Izidora reappeared in the study. Her long hair was damp, darkening the chestnut color into a deep auburn.

"You two may go," my father dismissed us, beckoning Izidora deeper into the room. "Close the door behind you." I caught Izidora's eye on my way out, and she flashed me a smile so bright that my heart melted on the spot.

"I'll see you later," I mouthed to her. She nodded, then joined my father at his desk.

"I'm starving. Let's see what Ali has in the kitchen." Vadim led us down the darkened hall and through the large sitting room that separated the two sides of the house. "So what are you going to do when we get to Este Castle?"

"What do you mean?"

"I mean, about you and Izidora. Everyone here can see what's going on between you. You're a lost cause, Kazimir, and she has you wrapped around her finger. The females of the Night Realm will have to start chasing after me now," he said, punching my arm.

I groaned. "A lot will depend on King Zalan's mood when we arrive. Maybe we'll get lucky and he'll give us permission to marry. I wish we knew which of our allies were currently in Este Castle, because an assessment of the King's mood would be incredibly helpful."

"We'll figure it out," Vadim reassured me, though his voice was as gruff as his beard and contained what I hoped was a hint of support for what I was certain was going to have to happen to get what I wanted.

Ali already had a plate of sandwiches and cookies laid out, so we sat at the round table and chatted with her. But in the back of my mind, my worries about what was to come swirled, gaining momentum as fear of losing Izidora gripped my mind.

———

IZIDORA WORE a dark green dress to dinner, the color making her long hair shine and her blue eyes pop. She wore her hair loose, tumbling down her back, as the V cut into the back of the dress dipped far below her waist. Her hair covered her scars, but I caught a glimpse of them topping the cut of muscle forming along her back when she turned her head about. Her figure was damning, and scars or not, she was the most radiant female I'd ever set my sights on.

Unbidden images of her on all fours in front of me as I lifted the hem of her dress over her round ass and fucked her from behind flashed through my mind. That string between us tautened further as I pulled out her chair, drinking in her every curve as she rounded it and lightly sat, glancing up at me under her long dark lashes.

No one sat at the heads of the table, as we were missing the twins and didn't need the space. We all breathed easier knowing the Iron Fae were headed in the opposite direction from them.

True to Vadim's prediction, Kriztof regaled us with the tale of Izidora besting Viktor in the ring. As Kriztof embellished many details, Viktor jumped in to correct him, and they laughed and argued over who was right. The frivolity of the moment offset the distress building in my chest, where the fear of losing Izidora at Este Castle was sinking its claws in deep. My instincts were kicking into overdrive, screaming at me to protect and keep her at all costs.

I reached under the table, gently squeezing her leg, if only to reassure myself that she was still there. She laid her hand over mine, gently stroking the skin on the back of my hand as if she sensed my anxiety. The motion soothed me, my body relaxing under her tender touch. I wanted more of her. My hand trailed higher up her leg, her breath hitching as I hit the sensitive parts on the inside of her thigh. Out of the corner of my eyes, I watched her struggle to keep her face neutral, her mask slipping as my digits stroked higher and higher. There was entirely too much fabric between me and my destination.

Bunching the loose fabric, I removed the barrier between us until her silky skin was beneath my hands. Dipping under the dress, my fingers trailed lightly up her inner thigh, skin pebbling beneath my touch. A broad smile was plastered on her face, and she pretended to listen and laugh as Kriztof went on and on. Yet she revealed her true focus to me the moment my fingers brushed lightly against the lace hiding her center. Her breath hitched again, and I shifted in my seat, inching a little closer to her so I could subtly touch the wet heat already pooling at the apex of her thighs. I hummed my approval as I began to trace her slit languidly. Her smile dropped as she bit her lip to stifle a moan. One glance at Ali sitting next to her confirmed she was completely oblivious to what was taking place.

The rise and fall of her chest sped up in time with my strokes. Pink darkened her cheeks, and her knuckles turned white around the gold fork in her hands as she fought to stay silent. Her wetness soaked her thighs now, and on my next down stroke, I gently moved the slip of fabric to the side, giving me more access to her dripping core. I slid one finger along the inner lines of her folds, almost groaning myself at how wet she was. Smearing some on my digit, I migrated the dampness to her clit, swirling it and applying a hint of pressure over the sensitive nub. She jerked in her seat at the sudden sensation. Reaching for my wine, I slipped my finger inside her, eliciting a similar reaction, and sending her hand flying to her glass to cover the rising blush. The heel of my palm ground into the apex of her thighs, and my fingers pumped in and out of her.

Kriztof arrived at the part of the match where Izidora slipped behind Viktor.

Izidora's walls were pulsing now, my fingers drenched from her arousal. Curling them against her inner walls, I pressed my palm firmly into her hips and she came undone over my hand, gasping but quickly covering it with a laugh.

"...I've only ever seen Viktor yield to females in the bedroom, and I'm so proud of him for embracing his kinks right in the open."

Ali choked on her wine as the whole table roared with laughter. I smirked and removed my hand from under Izidora's dress. She shot me a lustful glare, and I mouthed to her, "Perfect timing."

Ali covered her ears, jumped from the table, and shouted, "I'm going to fetch dessert before I hear anything else!"

Viktor tried to recover some dignity, explaining how he was very much in charge in the bedroom, while Kriztof continued to talk over him, lauding Izidora's prowess in the fighting ring. It was chaos, but I wouldn't have had it any other way.

Izidora's small hand trailed across my thigh, stopping when she felt the bulge that was there only for her. Her palms wrapped around the outline in my pants, my cock straining to break free at her touch. I glanced at where Ali had disappeared moments before, our position at the table leaving us in plain view of the doorway – the thought of our actions being discovered only made me throb harder.

She slid her hand down my length and dipped between my spread legs to cup my balls. A slight shift in her body covered the view to the doorway, but I still jerked as she circled them in her palm, stifling a groan as her deft fingers worked over them. Dropping them, she flattened her palm against the outline and rubbed all the way to the tip that leaked for her, staining my pants. Her slow strokes drove me wild, especially with the threat of Ali returning at any moment.

My stifled breaths grew more erratic, my entire groin throbbing when Ali shouted for someone to open the door a little wider for her. Panic gripped me as Vadim jumped from his seat at the end of the table, walking to the kitchen door and opening it wider. Izidora did not move her hand, and when he glanced backward his eyes widened a fraction before a smirk crossed his face. Ali walked through the door carrying a cake that was taller than her head, and I breathed a sigh of relief that she couldn't see over it. She carried the massive dessert to the head of the table where there was empty space.

Izidora's pace and roughness increased as every possible emotion ricocheted through my body, my cock harder than it had ever been under the wantonness of our actions and my fear that we'd get caught since I wasn't in control. Everyone's attention focused on Ali cutting into the massive chocolate cake at the other end of the table. My balls tightened, and I gripped the edge of my seat, forcing myself to breathe and contain the moan that threatened to escape as Izidora's ministrations pushed me off a cliff.

But I failed, and the entire group looked my way. Izidora

quickly leaned forward, reaching for her wine to cover her actions. As the lust faded, I saw Ali presenting a massive slice of chocolate cake layered with creamy white frosting and strawberries. Desperate to recover from my slip up, I beamed, "Ali, your chocolate cake is the best in the world. I don't know how I go so long without it. Can I have a double helping?"

Izidora snickered into her wine as Ali exclaimed with shining eyes, "Of course you can, darling!"

She cut a second helping from the cake, bringing both overloaded plates to Izidora and me. It wasn't until she was on the far side of the table again that my chest loosened enough to take in a full breath. I shot the giddy female beside me a leveled glare, her mouth already stuffed with cake, a hint of frosting brushed along the corner of her mouth. My eyes flicked to the spot, and her tongue darted out to clean it before I could lift a finger to swipe it away.

A scraping chair beside Izidora sent us both jumping as Ali rejoined us at the table. She eyed my plate, assessing how much I had already eaten of her offering, and I tucked into the rich chocolate and candied fruit, knowing my stomach would be bursting by the time I finished my massive helping.

"Ali, thank you for another lovely meal," my father began. "Boys, will you join me in my study after you help Ali clean up?"

A few grumbles sounded around the table, but we all obliged and carried plates to the kitchen, Ali directing where the leftovers should go. Izidora slipped upstairs without me noticing, and I felt that tug again, calling me to chase her down. But my father waited for us, and I followed behind my brothers to the homey space where my father leaned back in his overstuffed chair and steepled his fingers as he waited for us to settle in.

"While we were traveling, Endre and Kazimir revealed to me that Izidora's magic is pure white. We all know that is highly unusual for a Night Fae. But now, she has bathed her sword in white flames, twice, when she was backed into a corner. Also unusual for a Night Fae. Has anyone else noticed anything out of the ordinary with Izidora?" he enquired.

"She seems to know what I am feeling before I do," Kriztof suggested. "Sometimes I feel like she sees right through me, like I can't hide anything from her."

Vadim nodded, agreeing. "She also anticipates movement like someone with decades of fighting experience."

"During our first sparring session here, Viktor had me backing up, very similar to Izidora's situation, and normally Viktor finishes me from there. But when I needed it most, I had an intense burst of energy, like suddenly all my aches were taken away and my strength was renewed," I added. "It was unlike anything I have ever felt before. And I doubt it came from me." I had brushed it off in the moment, thinking that my desire for revenge and impressing Izidora had infused me with strength, but after listening to Vadim and Kriztof, my confidence was shaken.

My father furrowed his brow, deep in thought as he considered our suggestions. Finally he said, "I have scoured these shelves searching for any mention of the Goddess's Prophecy. It's nothing compared to the Royal Library, but I wanted to get a head start if I could. Unfortunately, I have come up empty handed. Endre, does anything else ring a bell for you?"

Endre shook his head. "No. I want to know more about Kazimir's incident though. It sounds like healing magic, but she wasn't touching you. We should see if we can recreate it tomorrow."

"We haven't tried to coax her wings out, either. We should work on that. Maybe we will discover something else," I mused, leaning forward to rest my arms on the back of the chair in front of me. My stomach ached from too much sugar.

My father's sigh was that of a male who had lived too long

and seen too much. "I am nervous about bringing her to Vaenor with so much uncertainty and with her magic being so different. It will raise many questions, and we've been away far too long to know where the snakes lie in the grass."

"I asked Zekari and Kirigin to assess and provide us with some insight before we arrive," Viktor commented.

"And that's why we keep you around, brother," Kriztof joked, slapping him on the thigh.

"Yes, thank you for your foresight, Viktor," my father replied.

We caught up on a few logistical matters before dispersing for the night. I really needed to change clothes – or stay out of them, in between Izidora's thighs. Sneaking along the hallway to my room, I eased open the doors, gently closing them behind me as I scanned for Izidora. There was no sign of her in the bathroom. Checking the closet, I shuffled through some hangers, parting fabrics to discover any potential hiding spots. But there was still no sign of her, and dread settled like a stone in my gut. The couches in front of the hearth revealed nothing, and it wasn't until I crossed the room to the bed that I discovered her among the mountain of blankets and pillows piled across the massive mattress.

She was naked but utterly departed from the conscious world, her breathing even and slow. Her face was totally relaxed, not a hint of tension pulling at her brows or lips, and I devoured her peaceful beauty. Stripping out of my suit, I slid under the blanket behind her and rearranged some pillows to make myself comfortable. My cock stood at full attention at the sight of her naked body, uncaring if she was asleep or awake. I kissed the back of her shoulder lightly, then pulled her body flush against mine. She released a contented sigh as I wrapped my arm across her low belly, and I allowed her even breaths to lull me into dreamless sleep.

23

IZIDORA

The soft rays of the morning sun filtering through the heavy curtains caressed my face, rousing me from sleep.

Shit, an entire night passed without me realizing.

I didn't mean to fall asleep, crawling naked into our bed as I waited for Kazimir to join me and finish what we started at the dining table. No nightmares stirred in my time away from the world, and it had everything to do with the male whose warm body pressed against my back.

The deep rumble of his chuckle brushed against it, then his length dug in as he returned to wakefulness. His lips landed on my exposed shoulder, then languidly mapped the distance to my ear. A shudder started at the top of my head and flew down to the tips of my toes, my nipples hardening and scraping against the blanket covering them. A flick of his tongue against the shell of my ear speared an ache between my thighs, and Kazimir moved his hand from my waist to cup my breast. My breath hitched as he slid his other hand underneath me, pulling me so tight that we melted together like two chocolates left in the sun. His callouses flitted over my peaked nipples, sending a ripple of pleasure straight to my center.

His hot breath swept over my neck. "Good morning, Izidora."

I moaned as he rolled the sensitive peaks between the rough pads of his fingers, arching my back into him and squeezing my thighs together to create the friction I so desperately craved.

He tutted, "You certainly are eager this morning."

"Yes," I breathed, not bothering to deny it. I wanted the pleasure he delivered to me, sensual sensations that I never knew existed before this male barged into my life and forced me to open up to him.

His erection dug into the tight muscles of my back as he ground into me. One of his hands dropped from my breasts, painting circles down my stomach until he reached my core. My thighs parted for him automatically, craving his touch at the apex of my thighs. He dipped his fingers between my legs, feeling the wetness already spreading there, and growled his approval, a possessive sound that brought heat to my cheeks. "So fucking wet for me, Izidora."

Too slowly, he circled my entrance, wetting his fingers with the arousal that slicked my folds. He brought them in front of my face and commanded, "Suck."

His actions were filthy, and I greedily took his fingers in my mouth, tasting my arousal on his smoky fingers. I nipped the pad of his middle finger as he pulled them out of my mouth. "Good girl," he purred, and my core throbbed at his praise.

His damp digits found my nipples, his lips found my shoulder, and his rough palm flattened against my stomach, pinning me against him as he nibbled and tugged and ground into me, eliciting desperate whimpers. His palm trailed lower, finding the sensitive ball of nerves and tapping it with his finger, sending my hips jerking, though my movement was stymied by his vice-like grip on my body, and his chest vibrated against my back as he chuckled, deep and low and raw. He rubbed slow circles over my aching nub and nipple, tension building so tight inside me I thought it might snap any second. I arched my back into his cock, rubbing its hardness, trying to entice him into delivering more pleasure between my thighs.

He groaned in response, slipping his hand lower to stroke my folds. Moisture dampened my thighs as he spread my juices all around, his fingers parting me, then dipping into the wet heat and curling against my inner walls.

"Yesss..." I hissed, the sensation everything my body begged him for. He pulsed a finger in and out, while he ground the heel of his palm into my clit. I lost myself in the rhythm of his strokes, grinding myself into his hand, searching for relief from the building tension. He pinched my nipple sharply and bit my neck, and I moaned as my body alighted from his touch alone.

"Fuck, Kazimir..." I couldn't say any more as he slipped another finger inside me, stretching my pussy around his hand.

"You need to be able to take all of me," he purred in my ear, rubbing his head against me to drive his point. All I could focus on was the drilling of his fingers inside me, the digits slipping in and out, in and out, my body poised to snap beneath his rough fingers. He removed them from my center, and I whimpered, my release mere seconds away.

Kazimir flipped me on my back, bracing his hands on either side of my head as he parted my thighs with his knees, settling his hips between mine. His eyes were wild with lust as he leaned in, searing a bruising kiss to my mouth. I kissed him back, biting his lip and sucking it into my mouth. Something between a groan and growl fell from his lips, and he pinned me to the mattress with his massive body.

"You want to play rough?" he asked, his voice thick with desire.

My response was fingers threading in his hair, nails scraping his scalp as I tilted it to the side and I sank my teeth into his shoulder, licking and nipping at his hard muscles. He growled like a wild animal rising to a challenge, his rough hands everywhere all at once, grasping me to him like he'd never let me go. He crushed his lips against mine, parting them roughly as he forced his tongue into my mouth, a sharp pain lacing my nipple as he pinched it between his fingers. He swallowed my gasp with his tongue, shoving it deeper into my mouth and licking every part he could reach. I arched into him, wanting more fullness in every part of my body. Forcing some space between, I reached for his cock, finding the silky smooth skin and stroking it from base to tip. He was so big, I could barely get my hand around it all. His hips pumped into my hand, and his mouth moved to my nipple, soothing the pain with his flattened tongue.

Without stopping work with his mouth, a hand pushed my knee to the bed, opening me wider for him, then trailed up the sensitive skin of my inner thigh until a finger was poised at my entrance. He sank one digit in, then two, at the same time as his mouth returned to mine and he parted my lips with his tongue. I moaned into his mouth as his fingers stretched apart and swirled in a wide circle, pressing against all my inner walls.

Sweat slicked my body and mixed with my arousal as my moans and breath became erratic under the deft movement of his fingers in my core. A third finger joined the dance, pumping in and out and spreading around as he coaxed my opening wider to accommodate his cock.

The thought of him entering me, of us joining our bodies in that way, was thrilling and terrifying, and I feared him ripping me to shreds with the size of him. But my body continued to give way to him, and I was lost in this pleasure he delivered, the fullness exquisite. Drops of moisture hit my stomach from his painful-looking erection. Swirling the beads around the tip of his head and cupping his balls with my other hand, I matched his pace, both of us using our hands to fuck each other in rhythm.

"Fuck, Izidora, I want to be inside you so bad," he groaned, removing his hand from my core and using it to push me flat onto the bed. His emerald orbs held my gaze as he sucked on each finger individually. "But first, I need to drink from you. You taste like honey."

The anticipation of his lips on me sent my heart into a frenzy, and I was helpless as he lowered his strong jaw to my core, a smirk lining his lips. He flattened his tongue and licked my slit from the bottom to my clit, sucking the latter into his mouth, alighting those sensitive nerves and sending pleasure rippling through me. His scruff tickled the tender skin inside my thighs as he lapped at my wetness, adding sensation to an already overwhelming amount. My mind was blank except for his touch, my body burning with fervent desire. His tongue entered me, pumping in and out, and I gripped the sheets, my nails digging into my hands through them, crying out as waves of pleasure rolled over me, my core too sensitive and my skin too tight and hot.

I panted beneath Kazimir as he rose, towering over me with a satisfied smirk. He wiped the back of his hand across his mouth, removing my lingering juices, then he fisted himself, pumping once, twice, as he drank in my sweaty and flushed body. He directed the head of his cock to my entrance, then paused. My breath caught as his head nudged at my folds, and I hoped that the ocean between my thighs would help it fit.

"Are you ready?" he asked, his eyes blazing with enough heat to melt a glacier.

I chewed my lip, my body tensing as haunting memories flashed through my mind, momentarily undoing all the work Kazimir had done to prepare me for this moment. As if he sensed the direction of my thoughts, he reached a hand out and brushed tendrils of chestnut hair from my face, then lingered on my cheek.

All the breath rushed out of me before I allowed my demons to take from me what I wanted yet again. "Yes."

He pushed himself in, only one inch.

"Holy fuck," I gasped, my pussy clenching as he stretched me.

"You tell me when you feel comfortable or if you want to stop," Kazimir ground out, his muscles rippling as he fought to control his movements. His desire was balanced at the edge of a cliff, and if he didn't know my history, I don't think he would have been able to contain his lust.

I nodded, concentrating on relaxing around his girth. He eased in another inch, and I breathed through it, the fullness indescribable. My eyes rolled back into my head as another inch entered me. My core adjusted more quickly this time, and he continued his agonizingly slow march into me. The sight of him seated fully inside me had me swaying, our hips locked together completely with my knees pressed into the bed on either side.

Fuck, he was huge.

A groan swept through him, his face pained from holding back. "Fuck, Izidora. Your pussy is so tight. I'm already close to coming."

With a gentle retreat, his tip stroked my folds, then he pushed himself all the way in again, stopping only once our bones ground together. He repeated the motion again and again until my body fully relaxed and I moaned in time with his thrusts. The perfect lines of his abs flexed as he increased his pace, stroking my pussy faster and faster. He ground into me, the feeling of fullness overwhelming as his hip bones ground against the sensitive nub at the apex of my thighs, but I did not want his motions to cease.

He bent his mouth to my neck, biting as he slammed into

me. I cried out, feeling like my body would split in two blissful halves as he impaled me over and over. Digging my nails into the flexing muscles of his back, I clung to the male wringing more pleasure than should be possible from my body.

"More," I panted, unable to form sentences as pleasure built behind a dam in my body, threatening to burst with a few more powerful thrusts.

I sank into the mattress as he drove deeper and harder into me, his bulk behind each stroke.

"Kazimir!" I cried his name over and over as he fucked me relentlessly, my walls beginning to pulse with my impending orgasm.

"I want you to scream my name as you come all over my cock," he growled. He shoved his tongue into my panting mouth, stealing my breath as I whimpered under his onslaught. Pushing my hips back into him, I received that little bit of friction I needed against my clit to send me over the edge. The dam exploded, pleasure cascading through me as I called his name, and he swallowed it like it would save him from ruin. He fucked me slower, drawing out my orgasm as the world around me dropped away and all that remained was the sensation of his length filling me to my navel.

When I returned breathlessly from the heavens, he ground into me one last time before roaring his release. "Fuck, Izidora..." he growled, still twitching inside me as he emptied himself.

We locked eyes, Kazimir still seated inside me, and I wanted to remain that way forever. The sunlight glinted off his emerald eyes as I played with his sleep-tossed black hair, and those orbs sparkled with adoration as he brushed his lips over mine again and again. Too soon, he withdrew, the lack of fullness almost an ache, and I immediately missed its warmth. Pulling me to his chest, he cradled me like a precious doll. His racing heart slowed into a steady rhythm as I laid my head on his chest, and he kissed the top of my head, the tender touch filling me with serenity.

Kazimir broke the silence. "We're going to try a few things with you today to test your abilities. How do you feel about bringing out your wings?"

Popping my head up to study his expression, I excitedly asked, "Does that mean I'll be able to fly?"

"Maybe," he chuckled. "You have definitely gotten stronger, but flying might still be a stretch."

I pouted. "But I want to join you in the sky."

He kissed my forehead, "You will."

When he ripped the covers back a moment later, I groaned, snatching them back. "It's too cold!"

Kazimir was merciless, and merely laughed as he ripped them away again. We fought for control over the covers before I gave up with a sigh. "Fine, I'll get up. Throw me something to wear?"

A set of skimpy blue lace floated my way. "More than that!"

He threw me leather pants and a tank top, shooting me a disappointed frown. "You'll need this for when we get your wings out."

I hastily ran from the bed and pulled on my clothes, then grabbed a long-sleeved tunic for warmth before yanking on my boots. "Ready commander," I said sarcastically with a mocking salute.

"Let's get you some food first." He scooped my lower back to his stomach, planting a kiss on my cheek. We walked to the kitchen hand in hand, still locked in that blissful space after joining together in the most intimate of ways. The aroma of freshly burnt cinnamon and vanilla wafted through the doorway, and my mouth was watering before we even sat at the table.

Endre and Victor were already there, plates piled high with eggs, bacon, and cinnamon rolls.

Ali bustled over, carrying more plates piled with food, and placed them in front of us. "How did you sleep, darlings?"

Kazimir and I shared a knowing look. "I was pretty tired from yesterday's excitement, so I slept great," I replied.

"Eat up, you've got another big day ahead of you. We've got to get some more meat on those bones!" Ali exclaimed, her mothering in full effect this morning.

Her concern made me feel cared for in a way I thought I'd never experience. How did I get so lucky to be rescued by these males and welcomed into their lives like I'd always been one of them?

I dug into my plate, cinnamon rolls first obviously, and followed up with a large helping of scrambled eggs.

"Cock of the morning to you, my dear brothers," Kriztof announced as he entered the kitchen. I rolled my eyes at his terrible attempt at a joke, and Kazimir choked on his coffee, while Endre and Viktor snickered. I guess it was no secret what had occurred between us this morning. My cheeks heated at the thought of them listening to us. But hadn't we pretty much done the same thing in plain view the previous night?

Kazimir appeared more bothered than I did. "I think I'm finished eating now," he said, then he stood, taking his plate to Ali. "Izidora, meet me in the garden after you are finished eating?"

I nodded, still stuffing my face with cinnamon rolls. I would have plenty of meat on my bones if Ali plied me with sweets at every meal – her treats would be sorely missed when we went to Este Castle.

Were Zekari and Kirigin safe?

What would my father say when they informed him that I was

alive? A hope bloomed in my chest that he would be overjoyed and eager to see me. My mind painted a masterpiece of our reunion, the male who sired me embracing me with as much enthusiasm as Ali had embraced the Nighthounds with when we'd arrived at Zirok House – running with open arms, both concern and excitement overflowing with our arrival. My father was supposed to be fairly ill, but I hoped that just maybe the thought of seeing me would bring him running from the castle, too.

Endre finished his breakfast at the same time I did, passing our emptied plates to Ali and pushing back from the table with the goal of reaching the garden. We had spent a lot of time together on the road taking care of the horses, but I hadn't had much one-on-one time with him since we arrived. His gentle nature soothed me on the days I struggled to adapt and adjust to my new surroundings, and he understood the healing nature of horses, encouraging me to connect with Mistik when I was struggling.

"How are you, Izidora?" His peridot eyes assessed me as he opened the door to the garden, indicating that I should walk ahead of him.

How was I? Such a simple yet loaded question. Blissful, because of Kazimir. Anxious, because of our return to Vaenor. Excited, because Cazius had taught me my letters. Fearful, because Zekari and Kirigin were in danger. Happy, because I felt friendship and family for the first time in my life.

"I feel... a lot." I shrugged as I walked past him and into the brilliant morning sun.

"That's to be expected. These fuckers are not very in tune with their emotions, but that does not mean you have to be like them. After everything you've been through, you need to feel. The only way out is through."

His words resonated with something deep inside me, but before I had a chance to respond, Kazimir appeared around a thick hedge filled with blooming roses. He smiled as he saw me approaching, his affection undeniable. "Are you ready to see your wings?"

"Yes!" I exclaimed. When I had flown through the Agrenak Mountains in Kazimir's arms after my rescue, I had been too terrified and overwhelmed with the sudden change to appreciate the freedom of the open skies. The males had flown around countless times on our ride and each time they leaped into the air, I yearned to join them and soar among the stars. I was more than ready to spread my wings and discover the world from above. Pulling my long-sleeved tunic over my head, I stripped to the tank top that would allow me to bring out my hidden wings. Heat flashed in Kazimir's eyes as he devoured my figure.

Endre's gaze bounced between us, then he cleared his throat to begin my instruction, Kazimir obviously distracted. "First you must tap into your magic."

Shutting out the world around me, I found that clear crystal wrapped in moonlight and white fire. I filled my lungs with fresh, floral air then exhaled slowly as I relaxed into the pool of my magic.

"Good. Now bring your attention to your shoulder blades," Endre directed. Kazimir touched a spot right in between my shoulder blades to guide me. A spark jumped at his touch, my magic eagerly seeking his hand, and he did not back away, his steady presence grounding me into the task at hand.

"Imagine your wings springing from your back, like you've seen us do before," Endre said.

I visualized the process, the tingling sensation mounting. Nothing had happened yet, but the pressure on my back was painful, forcing a grimace to my face as it became nearly unbearable.

"You're almost there," Endre encouraged.

I sent a tiny drop of my magic to the spot between my shoulder blades, hoping that would be enough. Kazimir pressed firmly, encouraging me to focus more attention there. My back itched unbearably, and I wiggled under Kazimir's fingers, trying to scratch it.

"Does your back itch?" he asked. I nodded in reply. "Good, you are almost there. Keep going."

Pushing more magic to that spot, a true electric shock sparked between Kazimir and me, knocking him backwards as my wings burst from my shoulders. I cried out, my back tearing as they unfurled, and tears burning my eyes as their weight settled. I sucked in a few steadying breaths, attempting to calm my racing heart as I adjusted to their weight.

Endre's jaw was slack as he took in my wings, and I sensed Kazimir returning to my back. "They're exquisite," he breathed.

I craned my neck, trying to get a glimpse of them. Feathered wings whiter than the snow that clung to the jagged mountain peaks fluffed behind me, their tips pointed straight toward the clear sky above us. I turned a little, wincing as they moved, admiring them from different angles. The morning sun caught them, the feathers glittering like gemstones, and as I turned the other way, an icy shade of blue that matched my eyes reflected off the tips of a few of the largest feathers.

I was in awe of their radiance, and that something so beautiful could emerge from me. Kazimir gently stroked the feathers of my right wing, and a wave of pleasure crashed through me, my toes curling in my boots. It was so sensual, and I wondered if all Night Fae were aroused by the sensation. As if reading my mind, Kazimir said, "Yes, our wings are incredibly sensitive. Many Night Fae take to the skies during their love-making."

My cheeks and core heated at the thought of Kazimir and I intertwined among the stars over Zirok House. Kazimir and Endre unfurled their wings as I continued to admire mine. Kazimir's wings were the darkest black, sprinkled with emerald to match his own eyes; Endre's wings were a midnight blue that reminded me of the hour after sunset. Yet the tips of their wings arced down, the feathers pointed to the ground while mine pointed toward the sky. Theirs sprung wide, while mine were tall and thin. I chewed my lip, eyes bouncing between the three sets of wings surrounding me, a kernel of uncertainty worming its way into the recesses of my mind.

"Do you think you can flap your wings?" Endre looked over the diamonds on my back with a finely tuned eye.

Visualizing my ice-white wings moving backwards and forwards through the air, they moved ever so slightly, causing me to wince again. "It's a bit painful," I admitted.

"You are likely going to be sore tomorrow. With your small size and lack of muscle tissue, it's going to take some getting used to," Endre explained.

I ducked my head, letting my long locks fall in front of my face as I stared down at my feet. I wanted to be stronger, and I was working so hard to get there. Endre sensed my shift in mood, stepping forward and taking my hands as he bent down to look into my eyes. "You are getting stronger every day. I am so proud of how far you've come already. It's not your fault that you have catching up to do. Get stronger and show those bastards that they can't fuck with you again."

Kazimir stepped to my side, careful not to touch my wings, and threw his arm over my shoulders, squeezing me to him. "You are learning faster than we all thought possible. We want to help you, and we want to give you a realistic picture of what to expect with everything. Overconfidence is just as detrimental as self doubt."

I lifted my gaze, looking each of them in the eye as I straightened my shoulders and decided to believe in the progress I was making. I would fight through the pain if it made me stronger. "Let's do this."

Both males satisfied with my attitude, Endre said, "Try flapping your wings one more time."

Flapping them was easier this time than the last. Although my muscles burned with the effort, it wasn't nearly as painful as before. Kazimir and Endre decided that walking the garden with them extended would be enough effort for me for the day. We strolled through the rose bushes, chatting about the theory of flying. They told me how to use updrafts and downdrafts to my advantage, how to hold my body so my wings took less drag, and how to land gently so I didn't break my legs. "... it will make more sense once we actually get you in the air," Kazimir finished.

We returned to our starting point, and I wondered what was next – and if hiding my wings away would be as painful as bringing them out. "How do I put them away?" I asked.

"Imagine you are folding them on top of each other behind your shoulder blades. I find it easier to tie it to an exhale." Kazimir demonstrated, exaggerating the motions so I could follow along.

I took a deep breath in, visualizing my wings folding in on themselves, and then exhaled slowly. A snap popped against my shoulder blades as they disappeared, and a gasp tore from my lips as my aching shoulders lightened. The wings' heaviness was more apparent once they were gone.

"Bring them out one more time before we move on to sparring," Endre instructed. I groaned, knowing that the extra practice would do me good, and at the same time my shoulders protested me putting any more weight on them. Bringing magic to that point between my shoulders again, I pressed forward, the pressure building as I increased my focus until finally my wings burst from my back, catching the light and dazzling.

That was so much easier than before.

I sucked in another breath and hid them away on my exhale.

"You did really well today, Izidora. Keep practicing taking them in and out, and we'll get you in the sky in no time," Endre beamed, and brushed dark hair away from his eyes.

Kazimir and I would fly together sooner rather than later, escaping from the confines of the house and seeking freedom among the stars. Even when we arrived at Este Castle, flying would be how I found my freedom from the responsibilities that came with being a princess – responsibilities that sounded more like the occasional chains when Cazius explained them to me. I sighed, following Endre and Kazimir to the fighting ring across the manor grounds, Viktor, Vadim, and Kriztof already there and shouting feedback as guards sparred with and without weapons. When they noticed our approach, they dismissed the guards back to their posts or barracks. I shot them a quizzical look, and Viktor gave me an explanation. "A few days ago when I sparred with Kazimir, he stumbled but recovered more quickly than he ever has before."

I remembered that moment, how I had been terrified for him and willed him to recover his stance.

"We have a hunch that you were able to influence his strength from afar. We want to test that today, but without eyes around. We trust these males, but only to a certain extent. Your safety and well-being is our utmost priority, and we want to help you without revealing things that might turn out to be dangerous for you."

That made sense to me. Viktor was always ten steps ahead of everyone, and I appreciated the insight into his thoughts. "What do you want me to do?"

"I'm going to fight Kazimir again, and I want you to repeat whatever you did before." Viktor's sage eyes were serious, and I swallowed nervously.

"I'll try my best," I replied.

The two squared off, and I perched on the railing beside Endre, watching them trade blows back and forth. Kazimir was intentionally losing ground, forcing a similar situation, and I focused all my attention on him, willing strength into him. I doubted what I did then would be of any use, because that day I had felt as if his life were in danger and acted out of fear. In line with my assessment, nothing changed and Kazimir continued to back up.

"What are you trying?" Endre inquired.

I shrugged. "Pretty much wishing he had more strength."

"Try pushing it from your body into his, like I taught you to do with healing magic," Endre suggested.

I turned my attention back to the fight, letting Kazimir consume me, mind, body, and soul. My feelings for him flared to life, that invisible string between us thrumming as I surrendered to the flow of his movements, the clash and clang of metal as their swords connected, and pushed strength toward him, imagining his blows raining heavy over Viktor.

Endre sucked in a breath, noticing the difference before I did. Their swords clashed with enough force to snap my teeth shut, and Viktor backstepped with each step forward Kazimir took. In three long strides, Kazimir had Viktor against the fence, and my startled gasp broke my focus, Kazimir's strength relenting and causing him to drop his sword.

"Did you feel it?" I exclaimed as I clambered down the fence and ran toward him.

He smiled broadly at me, tucking a lock of hair behind my ear. "I did."

Endre was beside us in a beat, Kriztof and Vadim not far behind. "What exactly did you do?" he grilled.

"I focused on Kazimir and dug deep into my emotions before

pushing strength his way. I think I needed to feel intense emotions to make it work," I guessed.

"Let's test that theory. Izidora, focus on Endre this time," Viktor instructed.

Kazimir, Vadim, Kriztof, and I returned to the fence. Viktor and Endre fought intensely, Endre moving lightly around Viktor as he attempted to use brute force to slow him down. As I focused on Endre, I thought about his kindness, his understanding, and how he seemed to always know what to say to make me feel better. The love I felt for him rose, and I channeled the emotion, willing him strength to stand face to face with Viktor and fight.

Endre's flurry of activity slowed as his strikes connected harder and harder. He grinned wickedly, feeling the strength I pushed toward him. Viktor gritted his teeth, defending himself fiercely, but he was no match for Endre and my will. Endre disarmed him a moment later with a forceful blow from his axe, Viktor yielding immediately as his sword clattered to the ground. They embraced, pounding each other's backs, then turned to the rest of us.

Sweat was pouring from my face like a faucet as I let go of whatever magic allowed me to fill these males with extra strength.

"How much of your magical reserves did that take?" Viktor addressed me.

I turned inward, assessing. "I'm down about half I think."

Viktor rubbed the stubble on his chin with the palm of his hand. "Are you up for trying one more thing?"

"Sure." I wanted to help them in whatever way I could.

"Take strength away from me. See what you can do to slow me down." He motioned to Vadim, who dropped into the ring, drawing daggers from his thighs. As they squared up, I focused my attention on Viktor, thinking of how honest he was, how I wished I could think like him one day. I pulled on feelings of admiration and appreciation, then imagined his feet sticking to the ground like they were trapped in quicksand. Nothing happened. I furrowed my brow, refocusing and redoubling my efforts.

I huffed when nothing changed again.

Endre asked, "What are you doing now?"

"I'm imagining pulling him into the ground to slow his feet," I replied, wiping sweat from my forehead with the back of my sleeve.

"Hmm," Endre mused. "What emotions are you calling on?"

"I only have positive ones for Viktor. Why?"

"Can you try bringing up some negative ones? Maybe imagine him as someone else for a minute?" Endre suggested, his tone tentative, like he worried that intentionally calling on the dark emotions that swirled in my mind might set me off.

But I was far stronger than them, and I could walk in the darkness without succumbing to it. I pictured the Iron Fae I had killed, the hatred and bloodlust that drove my sword though his heart filling me like an intoxicating liquor. Then I pushed that energy to Viktor, willing his feet to become immoble. He stopped mid-step, the foot that was poised in the air slamming against the packed dirt out of his control. Grunting, he strained to lift his feet again, but his attempts were in vain. "What the fuck!" he cursed.

Lightheaded from the effort, I released my hold on him in time, my magic feeling completely drained. I swayed where I sat, the world before me going sideways, and Kazimir caught my waist to steady me. His hands never left me as he hopped off the fence, then brought me to the ground with him, guiding me to sit in the plush grass. Everyone crowded around, much too close for how vulnerable I felt. As if he sensed my anxiety, Kazimir glanced among his brothers in arms. "Can we give her some room to breathe?"

A few mumbled apologies, but Viktor had a cunning edge to his eyes. "That was brilliant. Can you imagine harnessing that in a fight? Izidora sits a safe distance away while she freezes everyone in place and we can cut right through them."

"Except that nearly took everything out of her," Kazimir snapped, glancing down again at me and running a hand over his face.

"Magic is a muscle, she can train it," Viktor replied sharply.

"Hey, both of you knock it off," Vadim yelled, then he turned to me. "Izidora, both Viktor and Kazimir have good points. But is this something you want to practice?"

I had recovered a little during the exchange. "I think if I had some water and more energy I could do it more."

"But do you *want* to practice it?"

I thought about what he was really asking me. Would I want to practice a magic that could make it easier on my friends to cut down our enemies? That would essentially chain those enemies in place, unable to defend themselves? No, as much as I wanted my own vengeance and to protect my friends, I didn't want to do it at the cost of becoming like the monsters who abused me.

"I would rather practice filling you with what you need, rather than taking away from someone else," I announced. Vadim nodded his approval, and I was immensely grateful for his consideration.

"Can we just chill for a second and recognize that Izidora can influence people in a way that I have never seen before?" Kriztof looked between the males who ringed me, waiting for someone to acknowledge the strange power I had – one that filled me with more trepidation with each passing moment.

"It's nothing I ever imagined was possible," Viktor admitted.

"But you realize that she could be used as a weapon against us if they picked her up again, right?" Kriztof pressed.

"Which is why we must protect her at all costs," Kazimir growled, a threat and a reminder in his words.

I didn't want to be used as a weapon by anyone – I only wanted to be who I wanted to be without hiding myself from the world. I was done cowering in fear, hoping that something would change. I was powerful, and despite the difference in my magic and wings from those of the males, I did not plan on letting it go.

"Can someone tell me what the fuck is going on?" I snapped, anger and fear swirling in my chest.

Kazimir crossed and uncrossed his arms, looked up at the sky, then swung his gaze to me. His hesitance only served to anger me further, and I quirked a brow and narrowed my gaze at him, waiting for him to reveal whatever he was hiding. "Izidora, you remember the discussion we had with Endre about your white magic?"

I nodded warily.

"Well after you sheathed your blade in white flames, in addition to influencing me, we think you might have other abilities that we have yet to discover. None of these abilities are typical for Night Fae – or most Fae. We want to protect you above all else, but we can't do that without knowing all the facts or what you are capable of. I know you are still discovering everything for yourself too, which is why I am only telling you now. Is there anything else you haven't told us that might be helpful?"

The very source of my magic was different – yet it was beautiful and everything to me. I had become protective over those white flames in the past few weeks, calling on them when I needed strength the most. At the time of its discovery, I had been ashamed to tell Kazimir that I did not find moonlight, fearing they would dump me back where they found me for not being who they thought I was. But maybe it was time to reveal the truth. I studied the ground as I thought about what to say.

When I looked up, the males were watching me expectantly. "When I tap into my magic, I don't find only moonlight," I admitted. Raised brows, frowns, and slightly parted lips painted everyone's faces, and my heart started to gallop faster than when we raced to Zirok House. Panic creeped up my throat, but I swallowed it down. "When I look inside to find my magic, I find a clear crystal bathed in moonlight and white flame."

"Fucking Fates," Kriztof blurted, mouth hanging open. Endre's face was pale. Viktor's mind was clearly whirling. Vadim smacked Kriztof. "Thank you for your eloquence, as always."

I dropped my head, but Kazimir bent down, fingers lifting my chin to meet his gaze. "Why didn't you tell me sooner?" he pleaded, his eyes tight at the corners.

A hollow pit formed in my stomach. This was why I should have kept it secret – there was something wrong with me. I was defective, broken, useless. All the words of my captors crashed to the front of my mind, riding on a wave of grief stemming from the fear that I would lose everything I so recently gained – freedom, power, friends, *family*. My eyes burned and I snapped them shut, unwilling to shed the tears behind my lids and unable to look Kazimir in the eye – the male who made me feel free, safe, and *loved*. The thought of losing him stole the breath from my lungs, and I choked back a sob.

His hands rubbed circles over my back, reminding me that he was still there. "Because I thought something was wrong with me, and you would take me back because I wasn't the lost princess you had been looking for. But I see now that it's true, so I can find my own way — probably will get picked up by the Iron Fae along the way anyway – and I won't be your problem anymore."

The hateful words hadn't finished crossing my lips before

Kazimir crushed me to him, stroking my hair. "Don't ever say that. There is nothing wrong with you, and we would never let you go back to them."

His validation broke me, tears carving rivers in my cheeks as they washed away the shame and guilt that rose so rapidly only moments before. I sobbed into his chest while more hands touched my back as the other males lent me their strength, and I did not wish their touch away – if anything their reassurance and acceptance flooded my eyes further. My fingers curled into Kazimir's sweaty tunic as I clung to the male who kept me safe and protected, fear of losing everything I'd gained stemmed for now.

"Thank you," was all I managed to say through choked sobs, exhaustion fully settled in my bones from the day's events and the massive drain on my magic.

Kriztof cleared his throat. "I'm sorry, Izidora. I reacted poorly. You are probably the most badass female I have ever met, and the fact that you have so many types of magic is pretty fucking awesome actually. I'm jealous."

My laugh was watery, and I blinked at him through bleary eyes. "Thanks, Kriztof."

"Do you want me to carry you back to the house?" Kazimir murmured in my ear. I nodded, and he scooped me into his arms, carrying me to the house like on the day we had arrived. His heartbeat soothed my nerves, the gentle sway as we walked like a lullaby.

Ali's buxom figure greeted us at the door. "Is she alright?"

"Yes, but I think she could use some cookies," Kazimir replied. I smiled into his chest; he knew me so well. Carrying me deeper into the house, we entered the sitting room overlooked by the balcony and framed by halls leading to the kitchen and Cazius's study. "Which cushion do you want?"

He opened his arms, allowing me to slide to the ground and

select my seat. A fluffy pouf that could easily fit two people adjacent to the fire caught my attention, and I flopped onto it, releasing a sigh as its soft material enveloped me. With a metal poker, Vadim stoked the fire, blasting heat into the open space and chasing the chill from my exhausted bones. The Nighthounds, minus the twins, kicked off their boots and huddled beside the hearth large enough for all of them to lounge in.

We relaxed while we waited for Ali to return, and when she did, she carried plates full of cookies. Those alone were enough to rouse me from my cocooned embrace, and I captured a whole plate for myself. Ali returned with glasses of milk, handing them out one by one. I regarded mine for a moment as the males dunked their cookies in the cold liquid before shoveling them into their mouths.

Repeating their actions, I moaned as the gooey chocolate melted in my mouth, cooled by the white liquid. They were geniuses. My belly filled with sweets, and my mind and body thoroughly spent, I snuggled deeper into the pouf, curling up before the fire like a loyal hound. The males chatted among themselves, and I let my mind go, deciding a nap was in my best interest. As I drifted off, my pouf sank lower, and Kazimir's amber scent filled my nostrils. Uncurling only long enough to snuggle closer to him, I sighed contentedly, then slept.

24

KAZIMIR

Dinner was less formal than it had been, everyone dressing down after our mid-afternoon nap. A succulent roast bled onto our plates, the dark juices coating the surrounding hearty vegetables in meaty flavor. The savory spices melted over my tongue, and I used a dark brown roll to sop up the last of the salty juices once my food had disappeared, devoured in hurried bites after how much energy we'd expended over the last few days. As we finished our family meal, my father dabbed his mouth with a napkin and cleared his throat to garner our attention.

"Tell me more about what your magic looks and feels like, Izidora," my father prompted.

"Well, there is a solid, clear crystal at the very center of my chest," she started. "Around it, there are tendrils of silvery moonlight, not quite touching, but wrapping it all the same. And then there is a white flame forming a ring around both that feels almost protective. Kazimir once told me not to let my inner fire go out again. When I need a boost, I turn to that part and feed it more energy. That's what I did right before the flames appeared on my sword."

"Interesting," my father mused, his mind working over what she had said. "And when you pushed strength into Kazimir and Endre, what part did you pull on?"

Izidora bit her lip, eyes turned upward as she thought. "When I pushed strength into Kazimir the first time, I reacted instinctively for fear for his life. I reasoned that I needed to use strong feelings to repeat the process, and that's what worked."

"Can you pull those strong feelings and focus on your magic well for a moment?" my father asked.

She nodded, her lids closing but her eyes still roaming beneath them, as if she searched her heart for something solid to cling to. I knew exactly where she was in the process of looking inward at her magic after studying her for so long; any moment, she would open her eyes and call that heavenly light to her fingertips. I wanted to be inside her head, craving to know her every feeling, including the feelings she had for me, because I'd kill to have them match my own. Even our magic wanted to connect, mine seeking hers with my fingers between her shoulder blades, the silver begging to be released as it pushed against my skin. That spark that blew me back took more than my breath away, and when she lent me her strength, I felt unstoppable. And when I claimed her with my cock that morning, I felt more alive than any time I had flown among the stars. She was my addiction, my obsession, and I couldn't bear the idea of not having her all to myself when we got to Vaenor.

She opened her eyes, the wide orbs filled with realization. "My most intense emotions make the crystal fill with light."

"Positive or negative?" My father rested his elbows on the polished wood table, his hands folded together as he leaned forward.

"Both," she said. "But positive brings white light, and negative brings darkness."

"Do you think it's possible Queen Liessa had Crystal Fae blood?" I wondered.

"Perhaps, but that doesn't explain the fire," he said, rapping his knuckles on the table, thinking deeply. Fae from different realms did not often mate with one another; each realm had a purist mentality, wanting to keep their magic undiluted and strong, especially among the noble Fae. But Queen Liessa was not from a noble house, and her village was near the border with the Crystal Realm.

"There is much to think about," my father murmured, reclining back in his chair. "Let's keep all of these developments between us for now."

"You should see her wings," Endre added, uncrossing his legs and leaning forward to look him in the eye. "They are breathtaking."

"Would you like to show them off?" I hid a smirk beneath my hand as Izidora's shy smile pulled her mouth up at the corners. While she did not like to be the center of attention, the legendary lost princess would be bombarded with constant attention the moment we set foot into Este Castle. After her breakdown earlier, she needed us – needed me – to show her that it was safe to be in the spotlight.

A scrape of wood on wood signaled her rise, and the strapless cut of her red dress left most of her back bare, perfect to stretch her wings. Tendrils of red fluttered behind her as she rounded the table, taking her place at the head of it where there was enough space to unfurl those gorgeous feathers. Shifting in our seats, we waited for her to reveal what was hidden between her shoulders.

Her sharp intake of breath sounded more like a thunderclap in the eerily silent room. Her lips pinched as she focused on calling them forth, and like the lightning that precedes the thunder, her glittering white wings burst from her back.

"That was even faster than last time. Good work Izidora," Endre cheered.

Her face was brighter than the stars under his praise, and Ali squealed, jumping from her chair and running to Izidora, inspecting the feathers as they glittered under the bubble lights that floated above us. "You look like the Goddess herself," she cried. "You are so radiant, Izidora, and I wish your mother was here to see you now."

Izidora pulled Ali in for a hug. "Thank you," she breathed, her voice thick with emotion.

"Come on, give us a twirl!" Kriztof hooted from the opposite end of the table. With a giggle and lift of the hem of her dress, she spun slowly, flashing her devastating figure and the razorlike tips of the biggest feathers as they pointed toward the sky. Kriztof whistled, and I growled a warning at him; he winked at me and continued as Izidora turned the same color as her dress.

"I need to modify the midnight blue dress to accommodate your wings," Ali's mind started working. "You must wear that for your arrival at the Night Realm!"

My dick and I agreed completely with that assessment. She would look every inch the queen she would someday be in that dress. Add in her angelic wings, and the whole realm would bow beneath her. Treasonous ideas filled my brain, and with a pounding heart, I knew what I needed to do.

Nearly knocking over my chair, I stalked toward Izidora, heat filling my gaze as I devoured her with my eyes. Her body stiffened as that tug called us closer, and her aquamarine eyes locked on me, her breath catching as I took her hands in mine, then knelt, bowing my head so all I saw was her bare feet atop the mahogany floor.

"Princess Izidora of the Night Realm, you have my undying loyalty. My sword is yours, to protect and defend both you and the realm. I pledge myself to you from this day forth."

A collective gasp filled the room. Pledging myself to her in that moment superseded my oath to her father. It broke all customs, and I put myself at risk for doing it. But I wanted Izidora more than I feared her cruel father, and before we left Zirok House, I would ensure she knew how awful he truly was. Izidora would be an infinitely better ruler – and she could decide what was to become of us if she were queen.

She had only demonstrated kindness and thoughtfulness in her dealings with those of lesser stations. She treated everyone equally, from my father to the guards we sparred with every day and the gardeners who tended to our vegetables. Fae were won over and inspired by her without even asking for it, exemplified by the cheers that rang out as she'd bested Viktor. Despite all she had to learn, she only needed to know that I was beside her, keeping her safe always, to succeed.

Heavy boots stomped behind me, and moments later, Endre and Viktor knelt, repeating my pledge, followed by Vadim and Kriztof. The Nighthounds saw what I did, and by my pledging first, they saw their leader making a call they could get behind. My father had told me repeatedly that these males looked to me for direction and followed me because they trusted me to do what was right for us all. While my initial kick was entirely self-ish, the end result of Izidora and myself on the throne would benefit all Night Fae.

When I lifted my head to my future queen, I tried to convey that my pledge contained more than just my sword. My heart, my mind, my body, my soul were hers, too.

Her grip on my hands was bruising, and she shifted from foot to foot. "I don't know what to say," she whispered.

"You don't have to say anything, Izidora," I soothed, standing, and the Nighthounds rose behind me. "Stay true to yourself, and we will follow you to the ends of the earth."

Her delicate throat bobbed, and her chin dipped in acknowledgement. Ali wiped tears from her eyes as we returned to our seats, the angelic female remaining at the head of the table, hands running over each other as her teeth found her lip. My father offered a hint of approval with a dip of his head, though I understood why he didn't join us. As head of House Vaszoly, defecting to Izidora would put us in more jeopardy should anyone at Este Castle become aware of his change in loyalty. It didn't take much for a head to end up spiked on the gates, and everything stripped from what remained of the family.

"I am grateful to each and every one of you, first for rescuing me, second for continuing to protect me, and third for accepting me as I am now. I know I am behind where I need to be. I know I still have so much to learn, but I am working every day to be better than I was yesterday. And I promise to continue to do that as long as I live." Her speech wavered, but her chin was high as she regarded each of us.

"You will make a fine queen," my father told her.

With a slight quirk of her lips, she returned to her place beside me, bumping the chair with her wings and falling into giggles. "I was so overwhelmed that I forgot all about these."

I rubbed the sore spot between her shoulder blades as snorts and barks of laughter bounced among our family, and she folded them away with a hint of reluctance. As she sat, she reached for my hand under the table. Giving it a light squeeze, I reassured her of my undying support and sent her the love I could not say out loud. I loved her before I even knew her, and there was no denying it any more. My fantasies led me to this moment for a reason, and I'd rather die than let her go. It was time to lay the groundwork for these treasonous desires to come to pass.

———

THE SECOND IZIDORA and I were out of sight, I threw her over my shoulder and sprinted upstairs like an animal, locking the door behind us as we burst into my room. The roaring hearth was my destination, and the moment we were upon my favorite couch, I slid her to the ground and guided her into the position in which I wanted to begin my worship. Her bright face was to the flames, and I swept her hair over one shoulder, trailing my tongue along her exposed skin, tasting the salt with a hint of floral as I made my way to her neck. She bared her throat to me, sending tension straight to my groin as a guttural groan followed the path of my tongue. Her neck and ear were next under my ministrations, and after I was finished soaking her, I blew cool air across her bare skin, watching as goosebumps pebbled her milky flesh.

"Bring out your wings," I ordered, stepping back to give her space.

Her white wings flared from her back, muscles flexing while adjusting to their weight. They looked like diamonds from this angle, the firelight bouncing off each individual feather and scattering light throughout the room, painting twinkling stars across every surface. Softly, I brushed a hand along the ridges of the right one, and she moaned, a loud, heady sound that I immediately wanted to hear again.

A possessive growl tore through me as she melted under my touch. She was mine, and she was surrendering to me. It took every ounce of my willpower to rein in my darkest fantasies of how I would fuck her senseless, take her every possible way, drawing out her pleasure while she screamed my name until the stars winked out as a new day broke over the horizon.

I stroked Izidora's left wing, inducing a shudder across her marked back, pebbling her skin, then rubbing the pebbles away as my hands found her tense shoulders and massaged them, easing the ache from holding up her lofty wings.

She moaned, even louder than when I touched her wings. "That feels incredible."

"I thought it might," I smirked, then whispered in her ear, barely above the exhalation of my hot breath. "The only place I want you sore is in between your thighs. I want you to feel that ache as we train tomorrow and remember who worshiped so thoroughly at your altar. I want your every step to remind you of me."

"Fuck, Kazimir..." her voice went hoarse as my nostrils flooded with the floral scent of her arousal. Those filthy words turned her on, and she pressed back into me, silently begging me to continue.

The laces of her dress were removed slowly, each thread pulled to its maximum before I moved my hands lower. She whimpered as I took my time, not giving her what she so desperately craved. Her wings fluttered as I rubbed my knuckles lightly against her spine and planted featherlight kisses on her exposed skin, each undone lace breaking the hold the red silk had over her body, until the very last was removed and she stood in a puddle of rose petals. She stepped out of it like she had portaled into my bedroom from the heavens, and I fell to my knees before her, grasping her hips and spinning her to face me. Not a scrap of fabric covered her core, and something between a growl and a groan escaped my lips at the sight of her bared to me. I reverently kissed her hip bones as I teased my way to her the apex of her thighs, gripping her firm ass to hold her in place.

Her arousal replaced the scent of burning wood as my hands crept down the back of her thighs and around to the front, where my thumbs rubbed circles over the tops of them, parting her legs enough to witness the wetness leaking from her. My mouth and fingers met at the apex, and I lightly nibbled on her sensitive nerves. She released a breathy moan, my hair tugged beneath her delicate fingers as I pushed her thighs wider, gaining access to her dripping core. Her slit was soaked, and I rubbed my fingers over it, teasing her opening. My thoroughly wet digits entered my mouth, and I groaned around them as her taste spilled across my tongue.

"I need to taste all of you," I said huskily, latching on to her clit and sucking it into my mouth. Her moans were helpless and competed with the crackling fire as I circled my tongue around the sensitive nub.

My fingers continued to work over her slit, rubbing back and forth as she tried to adjust herself so my fingers would slip inside her. I pulled my hand away, gripping both her hips instead while I lapped at her core. Her moans were pleading as the friction of my fingers subsided. "Please, Kazimir..."

I hitched her leg over my shoulder, my scruff roughening the silky skin of her inner thigh as I brought her swollen pink core closer. My tongue parted her drenched folds, and I sucked them into my mouth like they were candy. Drinking from her source was more divine than any ritual consumption of wine, and groans vibrated against her center, sending flutters through her walls.

Our gazes locked while I tasted her, and her panted pleas were almost enough to send me over the edge. My erection rubbed painfully against my buttons as I knelt before my deity. "You are my goddess, and I plan on worshiping you just like this every night." Her eyes blazed as if the adjacent fire had jumped into them with the heat of my promise, and I drove my tongue into her pussy, fucking her with it and curling it into her sensitive areas. Her cries were pure ecstasy, so I did it again, my tongue unrelenting and my scalp scratched by her nails as she pulled my face deeper into her core, begging for more pressure. Her walls pulsed as my feral growls vibrated her body, and I worked faster, desperate for a taste of her come all over my tongue.

"Fuck, Kazimir..." she mewled as her orgasm ripped through her. Her walls throbbed as she came undone all over my tongue, and I drank down every last drop of her sweet nectar. She braced both hands on my shoulders, her body trembling as she returned to this earth. I seized my opportunity to hoist her into my arms, and her legs wrapped automatically around my waist. I kissed her forcefully, parting her lips and giving her a taste of herself as my tongue ran against hers and around her soft mouth. Her hands locked around the back of my neck as she ground against my aching cock, the barrier of my clothes still between us. Walking her to the bed, I tossed her onto her back and stripped out of my clothes, ripping buttons as I hurried to get to her. Popping up to her elbows, she parted her knees, a sliver of her pink slit visible. It wasn't enough. Her teeth found her lip as her aquamarine eyes drank in my chiseled physique, brushing over my sculpted pecs, down my abs, finally dipping below my waistband where I was hard as a diamond for her.

"You like what you see, Princess?" I purred, unbuttoning my pants, revealing my hard length to the goddess whose legs lay open for me. I fisted myself a few times to relieve the ache that threatened to ruin this moment before it began.

On hands and knees, I crawled to her, the bed dipping beneath my weight, my attention solely focused on her beautiful pink lips. Her legs were not nearly wide enough to accommodate me, and I made quick work of parting them to my liking, eliciting a gasp as her knees fell apart. My mouth was on her an instant later, and I tasted her from bottom to top, over the apex of her thighs, around her belly button, between her breasts, ending at her collarbones. I pinned her beneath me, moving my lips to her neck where I planted a nipping kiss at her pulse.

She moaned again, grinding against me, trying to line up with my throbbing cock. "Please..." she begged, wanting to be filled.

I tsked, "Patience is a virtue."

"Good thing I am not a virtuous female," she panted.

Fuck, my mind went straight filthy as I imagined how many ways I could take her with no inhibition. That was enough to rub my head at her entrance, running it up and down her slit to wet the shaft.

"Since you put it that way..." I pressed her nub with my thumb before sheathing myself with one powerful thrust.

"Fuck!" she screamed, but I didn't give her time to adjust as I slid my length to the tip and pounded her once again. Three more spears inside her sent her cries to a crescendo before the slick sounds of our joining mixed in, and I reined in my desire to continue these merciless thrusts.

"Do you like it when I force myself all the way in, acting as impatiently as you?" I ground out, stilling my hips and rubbing them in a circle against hers.

"Yes..." she hissed, raking her nails down my back, drawing blood. The metallic scent only spurred me on, and I traced her shoulder with my teeth, biting her pulse as animalistic desire coursed through my veins. My thrusts were brutal, and I gritted my teeth to distract from the ache building within my balls. She took every bit of what I had to offer and more, pushing back into me just as hard as I drove into her, our bodies moving as one. I'd never had a female that could take this dark side of my desires, and in my wildest fantasies about us I'd never imagined she could either. The thought of losing this left me distraught, and my wings burst from my back unbidden, flaring over us like a protective shield to hide our carnal pleasure from the world.

Her eyes widened, moving beyond me to the black feathers stretching and moving as we did. Mapping the ridges of them with her fingers, she set me trembling in more than one way. "Keep doing that and I will come sooner than I'd like," I ground out, holding back my release with quickly fading willpower.

With an impish grin, she continued her strokes, my hip bones grinding forcefully into hers as I paused to grasp her lower back and angle her hips higher. My cock reached the deepest part of her core, and she whimpered as I slammed into her, another wave of wetness spilling from her pretty thighs. She pleaded with me, writhing as sweat dripped between us. Her walls clenched harder and harder each time I seated myself to the hilt, her release moments away.

"Come with me, Izidora," I commanded, staring into her soul as I showed her what it was like to be worshiped like the goddess she was.

"Kazimir!" Her orgasm ripped through her, and her scream was wanton, the sound stroking my ego, and I emptied myself inside her with a roar, her walls milking every last drop of hot liquid from me.

Izidora panted beneath me, sweat slicking her body as she regained her breath. My wings still flared protectively around us, a perfect cocoon that I was loath to break. I leaned in to kiss her as reverently as the Goddess-crafted deserved.

Our combined juices spilled onto her thighs and the bed as I exited her warm center, and already I was powerless to the desire to have her again. Reluctantly, I sheathed my wings, and Izidora did the same, rolling onto her side with an arm under her head to face me. Her body glowed from our fucking, and she looked more radiant than should be possible. The words racing through my mind begged to be given a voice, to tell her how she consumed my every thought both in that moment and before I had saved her, to confess my love for her and plead with her to have me. She studied my face in that curious way of hers, and I felt as though she could hear my internal struggle, despite the easy expression on my face.

She broke our silence. "Earlier when you said you want to worship me every night, did you really mean that?"

"I do," I swore. Her eyes narrowed slightly as she looked for any insincerity, though she found none.

"So, this isn't some passing fancy for you?" she pressed.

"You are everything to me." And had been for years.

She chewed on her lip as she thought, and my cock hardened again as I imagined sucking that lip into my mouth, biting it hard enough to draw blood and tasting her sweet life source. I blinked to erase the image from my head as she opened her mouth to speak.

"You are everything to me too," she confessed. "There are so many things I do not know right now, but that is one that I do."

My body nearly collapsed under her words, everything I'd been dying to hear and more passing between her lips. She was undeniably mine, and my blood sang as the female I'd dreamed about for so long admitted how deep her affection ran.

My goddess, my queen, my everything.

She scooted closer to me, hooking her leg over my waist and laying her hand on my chest. "What does your tattoo mean?" she asked.

"It's from a child's tale about letting wild things stay wild. My mother used to read it to me when I was little. Fae and nature are intimately connected – our magic is given to us by nature and in turn we give it back. When Fae have tried to bend nature to our will instead of coexisting with it, the Goddess fights back. She is the caretaker of all life."

Her big eyes blinked slowly as she listened to my tale. "I know very little about the Goddess or our world. I learned some when I was a child but not enough to understand how it all works together. How have Fae tried to bend nature to their will?"

"In our history books, many Fae have tried to use their elements to vastly change the land around us. The Crystal Realm tried to stop their glaciers from melting, but the Goddess retaliated by drying up all their lakes. Then the Iron Fae tried to create more mountains to guard their homeland, and the Goddess retaliated with rock slides that killed many of their people. The Day Realm tried to plant too many crops and the Goddess sent pests to eat them. The Night Realm birthed too many children and the Goddess sent a sickness to our kingdom. But it is not only the Goddess who rules, but also the Fates. Where the Goddess blesses us and delivers balance and harmony to the nature around us, the Fates sow chaos and write the destinies of the Fae. Though nothing is ever set in stone, each choice we make pushes us down a path, and the Fates determine where these paths end."

"That is awful," Izidora commented.

"It is balance. Too much of one thing will destroy the whole system. Fae tend to forget as the millenia wear on, but when we stray from our path, we are quickly reminded of it. Even the Goddess and the Fates are in balance, harmony and chaos acting as two sides of the same coin."

She flicked her chestnut hair over her shoulder. "If I am part of the Goddess's Prophecy, then I must be here to bring some sort of balance?"

Running my hand over my face, I considered her statement. "I guess so. We need to find out what it says exactly. Hopefully the Royal Library will have some answers."

Her eyes widened. "The Royal Library? Like at Este Castle?"

Izidora's excitement was contagious. "Yes, it is the most beautiful library you will ever see. Imagine the shelves in my father's study, but a hundred times larger. You could lose yourself for days among the stacks of books. There is a team of Fae working in the library around the clock to preserve the books and to help those seeking knowledge. With your curiosity, I think you'll find yourself right at home there."

Her smile brightened even further. "That sounds incredible. I can't wait to learn more than my letters so I can learn our histories for myself. One more thing to look forward to besides meeting my father."

My heart twinged. I know how much meeting him meant to her, but she couldn't get too excited or attached if my plans were to work. While we had avoided revealing our explicit dislike of King Zalan, it was time to sow the seeds of discontent in her heart, to reveal the cruelties of the male who had sired her. In my gut, I knew something was off with her story, and she would be much safer if her father was not lording over her; if she was supported by me and the Nighthounds, I could protect her. I had pledged myself to her, and I planned on upholding that pledge until my death.

I kissed her softly on the forehead, then pulled her closer. She laid her head on my chest, and soon her breaths softened as she drifted off to sleep. My mind was still spinning, trying to process everything that had happened and plan what should happen next. Izidora was mine to protect, mine to touch, mine to have, and I was never letting her go.

25

IZIDORA

I woke the next morning – once again nightmare free – curled up in front of Kazimir, his deep breaths lifting wayward strands of my hair. The male who swore himself to me – along with his brothers in arms – had promised me so much more than his sword these past weeks. Yet in the back of my mind pieces of the puzzle did not quite add up. With my mention of reuniting with my father, Kazimir had momentarily blanched, and another piece had fallen into place.

I'd been told time and time again that the Night Realm was a brutal place, filled with cutthroat noble Fae, and even picked up hints that my father might not be as great as he once was.

But did I know the whole truth?

After living in darkness for so long, my whole world was smaller than the room I currently occupied and my knowledge was limited. I trusted these males to teach me what I needed to know, but if they were only giving me half-truths, how was I any better off than before?

My jaw worked as everything clicked into place.

I finally saw between the words everyone had danced

around without explicitly expressing their inner thoughts. My father was not a good male, and saying those words aloud was dangerous, repercussions of a type with which I was intimately familiar. The Nighthounds' unplanned pledges were given freely in the safe space of Zirok House, but if anyone were to uncover their new allegiance, they might lose their lives. My eyes burned at the thought of each of them succumbing to a fate I'd wished upon myself one too many times, and the weight of their decision pressed into my chest so forcefully that I could not fill my lungs with air.

Yet my fists tightened at the thought of them keeping so much from me, especially knowing how I felt about discovering the world around me.

How could one ever be certain what was real and what was not if their only source of information was looking through the lens of others?

I wanted to hear Kazimir say what I was thinking out loud; I was owed the whole truth. Rolling over, I roughly shifted until he started to stir.

Sleep still tugged at his lids, his black hair falling in his face as he cleared his throat. "What's wrong? Where are you going?"

He was immediately alert when I narrowed my eyes at him, my mouth set in a firm line. "I want the full truth."

Kazimir's eyes widened, showing off more of those deep emerald pools, before he schooled his face into a neutral expression, waiting for me to explain myself. When I offered up no words, he asked, "What's the matter?"

"My father. King Zalan. How do you really feel about him?"

His eyes glittered for only a fraction of a moment before his face returned to passivity. With a sigh, he pushed himself upright, pulling me into his lap. I pushed away from him, wrapping a blanket around my naked torso, and stared him down waiting for the answers I deserved.

His fists and jaw tightened at my rejection, but he let me be. "I'll give you the whole truth and my own opinion. There are many reasons why we stay away from Este Castle as much as possible. The power-hungry nobles are a large part, but the other is your father. His moods change in an instant, and he has become more erratic the sicker he has gotten. He was ruthless and paranoid before he met your mother, but after he married her it increased significantly. He started executing people with very little reason, mostly to instill fear and show his power. Speaking as we are is enough to send us to the gallows. Reputation is everything to your father. He wants to be seen as powerful, so he takes actions that he thinks make him look powerful. He wants to be seen as in control, so he takes actions that he thinks make him appear in control. He wants to be respected, so he takes actions he thinks will garner him respect.

"But his whims have the noble houses dancing to the tune of the day, and some fall out of favor only to quickly rise again. Some of the High Lords try to steer the realm in a better direction, but their pleas fall on deaf ears. My father gave up on change years ago, and his assignment of finding you in many ways saved his life. When he does appear at court, he prefers to be neutral on as many things as possible and lay low as much as he can."

"So you fear him?" I interrupted.

"In a way, yes. He has a lot of control over our lives – our magical power only gets us so far. He pits the High and Lower Houses against each other, the threat of a Lower Lord taking a Higher Lord's place keeping us in line, while the promise of moving up keeping a Lower Lord subject to his whims. It is a game I want no part of."

Constantly catering to the whims of capricious males was all I'd experienced prior to my rescue. It was exhausting, and there was no freedom to be had when one wrong step could send you tumbling into an abyss there was no way out of. The guards in my cave were always on rotation, and not knowing who or what I would receive on any given day was what kept my shoulders glued to my ears, waking at the slightest sound, and never truly resting out of fear. Kazimir and I may have lived different lives, him with wealth and opulence, and me with darkness and grime, but our internal experience was still the same.

The hard wall I had rebuilt in an instant came crumbling down, and my posture relaxed as I heard the unsaid words coming from his lips. But I was not finished with my questioning. "And you believe I would be different?"

Kazimir braced his hands on the bed behind him. "Yes, we all do. You treat each person with respect. When we spar in the ring, you laugh and joke with the common Fae like you joke with me or Kriztof or Endre. I can see how much they admire you already from that alone. And to me, that is what makes a good ruler."

"Even though I killed that male without hesitation?" My brow raised as I awaited his response.

"Kings and queens have to show their strength and decisiveness too. He hurt you in more ways than I can imagine, and you took your vengeance. Most Fae would respect you more for that. There is a difference between ending lives to instill fear like your father, and ending lives when you are in mortal danger." His regard bounced over me, and yet I felt his search was borne of hiding something rather than discovering something.

Chewing my lip, I leaned forward, resting my elbows on my knees and face in my hands. "What do you think he will be like when we get to Vaenor?"

He ran a hand over his face, then returned it to brace himself. "I have been worried about that since the day we saved you. Part of me thinks he will throw a huge celebration and spare no expense on your return, playing the part of a grieving father whose long lost daughter is finally home. Another part thinks he will use it to pit his courtiers against each other. And still another worries that he might marry you off to someone immediately after our arrival for his own political gain. I honestly don't know what to expect, and that is what worries me the most."

"Would he really do that? Marry me off right away?" My stomach dropped at the thought of being wedded to a male I did not know.

What if they were old and cruel like my guards had been?

"It is a possibility, and a strong one at that." Kazimir leaned forward, mirroring my posture with his elbows on his knees, a tightness pulling at the corners of his mouth. There seemed to be this suspended tension between us, as if he wanted to coax that question perching on the tip of my tongue into the air around us – a question that might change the direction of our relationship.

"But what of what I feel for you?" I whispered, our heads creeping toward each other.

This time when he wrapped his arms around me and pulled me in, I relented. His hand found my hair and pressed me against the steady thump in his chest – the heart that beat for only me. "He might use that against you, to manipulate you into doing what he wants."

What kind of person would take away another's happiness simply to meet their own goals?

Not the type of person I wanted to meet, let alone dine with or hand over control of my life to. I wanted freedom, not more shackles that this male seemed poised to place on me. My initial assessment after my rescue had been correct; I was trading one set of chains for another.

Unless...

"What can I do to stop that from happening?"

Kazimir's body tensed, his breath catching and the thrum against my ear momentarily ceasing. "You can become queen."

It was not a path I felt remotely prepared for, but I was a survivor, and no one was going to take my freedom, my choices from me. If becoming queen was what I had to do to survive, then so be it. Those four words hung in the air around us like a noose around a condemned male's neck, waiting for the final drop. Kazimir's body trembled ever so slightly as he waited for my response, every muscle wound tight and no air leaving his lips.

"Thank you for telling me," was all I could manage as I caved to the pressure of the moment, unable to voice an opinion one way or the other. The way his body relaxed around me felt more like disappointment than relief, though he kissed the top of my head, then rested his cheek there.

"I swore last night that I would protect and defend you with my life. That includes when we get to Este Castle," he reminded me.

Pushing off his chest, I straddled him, and he wrapped his strong arms around my small waist, trapping me against him. Our mouths met hungrily, desperately, and I tried to forget about the expectations that lay in wait beyond the locked door. There was only the smoky taste of him in this moment, and the rapid thrumming of my heart as I lost myself in him.

My stomach rumbled, breaking the moment of peace, but Kazimir's warmth did not leave as I broke our kiss. "Let's go get you something to eat."

Unwinding us, he hopped out of bed, then scooped me up and carried me to the closet. Grabbing my favorite fighting clothes, I strapped in, letting the change that came with dressing for battle steel my spine against the panic that clawed up it, trying to drag me into its void. I found my inner fire, fueling it instead of my fear, and decided that no matter what happened, I was going to fight like a wild cougar with fangs and claws for what was right for me.

26

KAZIMIR

Late in the afternoon, my father called us to his office. "I've just received a raven from Este Castle, from Zekari and Kirigin."

In the weeks they'd been gone, my father's black hair had peppered with more gray, the lines on his face etching deeper with each passing hour without word from them. His shoulders drifted from his ears as he reread the letter, my own following suit with the knowledge that the two youngest members of our unit had arrived safely.

"What does it say?" Viktor leaned against the polished desk, almost attempting to snatch the parchment from my father's hands.

He glanced at Viktor's outstretched hand with a hint of amusement. "They arrived without seeing a single Iron Fae on their way to the castle and believe it will be safe for us to depart tomorrow." His eyes scanned a few more lines. "They relayed our news to King Zalan."

The sound of silence was deafening as we shrunk forward, hanging on every word my father read. The next few words could make or break Izidora, especially after our conversation about her taking the throne a few weeks prior. Fucking Fates, her desire to be in control of her life was my savior, opening up a line of suggestion that would have been otherwise difficult to navigate.

"He was pleased with the news and is planning a royal feast in about three weeks to announce her return. They expect that he will invite every noble house to join, as well as the wealthy merchants living in Vaenor." My father continued to read.

"So is that a good thing or a bad thing?" Kriztof questioned.

"I'm thinking both," replied Viktor. "He wants to show off his wealth and power while setting up for something else. If everyone is there to witness his decree, then it holds more weight."

My jaw nearly popped with the force of my grinding. I hated that Viktor was probably right; his instincts were usually spot on.

"What sort of trick do you think he will try to pull?" I asked him, my heart gripped in a vice as I imagined the aging king announcing Izidora's engagement to one of the other High Houses' sons.

Rubbing his clean-shaven chin, Viktor looked out the window behind my father, eyes vacant as he thought. "The most likely are marriage pact, succession announcement, or public execution."

"Why stop at one? Maybe it will be all three," Kriztof scoffed, his disdain for the king on full display. Kriztof's family had been stripped of their title after his father was executed for refusing to fuck one of King Zalan's harem before the whole court, his wife included. If Izidora knew his story, she might lean more favorably in the direction I wanted her to take.

My father interrupted us as he finished the letter. "They also added that High Lords Valintin and Luzak seem to be in the king's favor right now."

I groaned, banging my head on my hands as I dropped them to the table in front of me. Alekzi, High Lord Valintin's son, was a few years older than me and likely to be Izidora's betrothed if he was truly in Zalan's favor. His slimy face flashed through my mind, and I imagined the light going out in his eyes as I strangled him. Izidora was mine, and no one would get in the way of that.

"Did they say anything about our fathers?" Endre questioned, glancing at Viktor. They both came from High Houses, and their fathers were our allies in a castle crawling with snakes. They chose to spend most of their time in Vaenor, feeling a sense of duty to steer the realm rather than allow it to fall into ruin.

"No mention of them," my father reported. "But it seems we must make haste to Este Castle. With all of us and some guards going, it will take longer than Zekari and Kirigin going alone. Pack your things and prepare to leave at first light tomorrow."

"I'll let Ali know we are leaving," Kriztof said, darting from the room – probably needing space, with the mention of another grand feast, like the one where he'd lost everything, triggering his trauma.

"I'll round up the best fighters and let them know the plan," Vadim offered, excusing himself.

Only myself, Viktor, and Endre remained, and Endre shot me a pointed look, peridot eyes jerking toward my father. He wanted me to confess my feelings for Izidora; whether my father chose to remain oblivious or really did not know, I wasn't sure.

I sighed, running a hand through my hair. "There is something I need to tell you, father."

He quirked an eyebrow but waited for me to continue.

"Izidora and I have grown... close in our time together," I started. Viktor sniggered, clearly amused at my description of our relationship. I shot him a look, then continued. "My impulses can be a bit challenging to control at times. I wanted you to know before we arrived in Vaenor that... we have been together."

Fuck, how was I supposed to say all of this in a way that didn't make me sound like I would rip anyone's head off for looking at her the wrong way, even though that was definitely what would happen?

"Say what you mean, son."

"He almost beat the shit out of Kriztof for touching her arm when he was teaching her to shoot a bow and arrow," Endre said for me.

"And I can't fall asleep unless I bury my head in a pile of pillows to block out all of their sounds," Viktor added.

I looked up to the ceiling as my two best friends ratted me out. One day they would fall in love, and I would have my revenge.

"Is this true?" My father honed in on me, and sweat dripped down the back of my neck under his acute assessment.

"It is. I tried to fight it, but I gave in shortly after we arrived home," I admitted in a whoosh of air.

The corners of his eyes crinkled with amusement. "I am happy for you, son."

I blinked, brows dipping slightly when I did not receive a tongue lashing. "Are you not worried about us being torn apart when we get to Vaenor?"

"It sounds to me like your feelings are very intense. So, no, I am not worried," he replied.

Endre and Viktor appeared just as confused as me, Viktor shrugging as I caught his eye. "Let's go tell Izidora the good news," Endre suggested, digging me out of the hole he'd created.

"Thank you, father." I bowed my head and followed Endre and Viktor away from the study, where my father continued to pore over the letter and other documents needing his attention since our last visit to Zirok House.

LACEY LEHOTZKY

Once we were out of earshot, I said, "Thanks for the vote of confidence in there."

Viktor smirked, "Don't mention it. Happy to help."

"And you definitely needed help," Endre added.

I rolled my eyes. "I would have gotten there eventually."

"No, you wouldn't have," Endre laughed. He was right, but I couldn't let him know that.

"For what it's worth, I don't think you have anything to worry about either. I know her father would have to give you permission to marry, but once he sees you two together I am sure he will allow it," Endre reassured me.

Catching both their arms and glancing around us to ensure we were alone, I dropped my voice. "There is another way to ensure we stay together."

Endre sucked in a breath, and Viktor's sage eyes hardened. "If you say the words…"

"There's no turning back. Yeah, I fucking know, Viktor. But I'm getting desperate, and you are my closest friends – brothers, really. I can't lose her."

Viktor blew out a breath after a glance at Endre. "Does she know?"

"She started asking questions during our time here."

"So you've primed her?" Endre narrowed his eyes at me.

"In a sense. She didn't fall one way or the other, but with the right encouragement or information, she could. We should have her talk to Kriztof," I whispered.

"She's too young," Endre hissed.

"But she's not stupid or cruel, and she'd listen to our fathers' advice. The realm would be better off with her," Viktor argued in a hushed tone. "Kazimir would be king, and I trust him to lead us in the right direction. He hasn't led us astray yet. He has my loyalty."

Endre shifted from foot to foot as Viktor stared him down,

daring him to disagree. "You know I'm loyal to both of you – and Izidora. But I don't want to push her too hard too fast. You've seen what happened before."

"She's so much stronger than that now, Endre. While we've been here, she's thrown herself into training and learning at all hours of the day. Let's get her on the throne and make everyone happy, yeah?" I grasped him by the shoulder, and he nodded his agreement.

"This stays between us," Viktor warned, his tone laced with the threat he did not need to supply with voice. If anyone discovered our plan, we were dead.

I embraced the males, arms over their shoulders, and corralled them down the hall to where I knew Izidora waited, that faint tug between us always pulling me to her.

As we approached the doors to my room, I said, "Let me go in first."

"If you're not back in one minute to let us in, I'm calling Cazius to listen at the door with me," Viktor joked, all tension from moments before banished.

Endre groaned. "You are as bad as Kriztof."

I left them bickering and slipped through the door, hoping Izidora was dressed. An oversize robe wrapped around her slight frame as she sat in front of the mirror in the bathroom, brushing out her long hair. The front of the robe hung open, revealing the shape of her breasts while her legs peeked out from under a scandalously high slit. Heat flooded my groin, and I closed my eyes, gulping in a breath and trying to regain control.

"Why are your eyes closed?" she trilled, her voice light and sweet and *everything*.

"We have something important to tell you, and Endre and Viktor are waiting outside the bedroom door. If I look any longer I won't be able to let them in," I croaked.

She snickered, and I opened my eyes as she shucked off the

robe, giving me a perfect view of her backside as she walked to the closet. My mouth watered as she sashayed her hips before disappearing into the fabric beyond. Returning to the other room, I opened the door for Endre and Viktor.

"A few more seconds and I would have shouted for Cazius," Viktor laughed, shouldering past me into my room and flopping on the gray couch closest to the fire. I suppressed a smile, the memory of what I had done to Izidora there flashing before my eyes. If he knew, he would relocate his ass. Endre stepped past me, his peridot eyes still holding some hardness, but his support was there. We settled in, waiting for Izidora to appear, and when she did, clothed, she sat on my lap, regarding the three of us with hawk-like eyes.

"So?" She arched a brow, waiting for someone to tell her the news.

"We received a raven from Zekari and Kirigin," I started.

"Are they alright? Did they make it to Vaenor? Are they coming back now?" she asked in a rush.

"Yes, they made it safely. They saw no Iron Fae on their journey. And we are going to them. Tomorrow, actually." I rubbed circles over her back, anticipating the tightness that would wind up her body as our timeline shortened.

"So soon? Don't we need to prepare?" She paled, a hint of fear opening behind her aquamarine eyes as she allowed me into that walled off part of her.

"It won't take us long to pack the things we need, and I am sure Ali will spend all night baking if you want treats for the road," I reassured her, though there was not much I could do, and that alone killed me. I wanted to ferry her away into the night so she never had to experience the hurt that waited for her unless she said yes to the proposal the three of us would shortly make.

My words did not soothe her. "Did they say anything about my father's mood?"

Viktor glanced at me, and I silently conveyed that we could broach the subject through this line of questioning. "Zekari and Kirigin said he is throwing you a massive feast and inviting every noble house in the Night Realm. It will be held in a few week's time," Viktor explained, sitting up and opening his posture to appear non-threatening.

Izidora's chest rose and fell rapidly beneath the overflowing tunic that covered her breasts. Plucking her face between my fingers, I spun her head gently so she looked only at me. "We have to ask you something... and I want you to answer honestly, Izidora. We're still loyal no matter what you say, understand?"

She nodded, her body completely tensed beneath my palms.

"Do you want to be queen? Not eventually, not in a few decades, but now. Because if you do, we will make it happen, and you will be safe with us by your side. You will have the tremendous responsibility of ruling the realm, but you will have the support needed to get through, and you will be free to make the choices you want to make for yourself."

My eyes flicked to Endre and Viktor, the former pushing his hair out of his eyes, the latter studying the female in front of me with intense scrutiny. The rise and fall of Izidora's chest grew rapid, her breasts heaving despite the loose tunic she wore. My hand dropped from her face, allowing her space to breathe, and I yanked her to my chest, smoothing her hair and rubbing her back as she succumbed to the panic. Gently rocking back and forth with her wrapped in my arms, I soothed her. "Breathe, beautiful. Follow my breath."

But it was no use. Tears soaked my tunic as her breath hitched higher, short gasps all she could manage as her emotions overwhelmed her. I let her crumble as I crushed her against me, showing her that she was not alone, that she was supported, that she was safe. No one uttered a word as she broke apart, instead giving her the space she needed to process and feel. We remained motionless for many moments before her breathing evened out and I relaxed my grip on her. My hands found the wetness on her cheeks and wiped away every last drop with the tender care she deserved.

"It's just all so much and so soon," she whispered.

Endre leveled his gaze with her, leaning forward and resting his forearms on his elbows as he spoke. "And we are here for you every step of the way. You are not alone."

"You are stronger than you think, Princess. There are not many Fae who could go through what you've been through and be the person you are today. Remember that," Viktor added.

She nodded weakly, lids dropping as she gulped down a shaky breath.

"I was going to wait until we were at Este Castle to tell you this, but Vadim's family will meet us there. His sister is only a few years older than you and just as headstrong as you are. We thought she would be a good friend for you to have." I smoothed a few stray hairs out of her face, and she opened her eyes, smiling through another sheen of tears.

"That is a great gift. Thank you, Kazimir," she croaked, her voice thick and raw after her breakdown.

"So you will have more than us to help you, if you want it." I left the door open for her to answer the question that had just sent her into a mess of panic.

Her head swiveled between the three of us, as if the answer lay in one of our eyes. She wanted validation in her choice, and thinking of what we would gain by being together, I showed her what she searched for with a small dip of my chin.

"If my father is truly as cruel as you say he is, then I want it. I don't want others to suffer like I did, under the oppression of fear and unable to express their truest selves for fear of retaliation."

Her words landed like a fallen tree, the crack of the splitting trunk ringing with a finality that would end in either success or our deaths.

"That decision does not leave the four of us, understood?" Viktor rubbed his palms across his pants before brushing back his already perfectly styled hair.

"Understood," Izidora echoed.

"It's not that we don't trust the others, but rather that the less involved, the safer for everyone," I clarified.

"So, what's next?" she asked, that spark of white fire flaring in her eyes.

I grinned wickedly. "We put you on the throne."

———

THE FOUR OF us concocted a damn good plan, one that would look like a natural progression from the outside, while we would know the true intent. As Endre and Viktor rose to leave, Endre pulled Izidora in for a hug, his peridot eyes telling me to chill as he addressed her. "What sweets do you want for the road? Kriztof went to tell Ali we'd be leaving, but I'll make sure she knows what you want to eat."

"Definitely cookies and cinnamon rolls," she grinned, then thought a moment longer. "We should just bring her with us."

We shared a laugh, all wishing the same thing. Endre and Viktor departed, promising to tell Ali to fire up the oven and bake enough of each to last Izidora a month at Este Castle.

"What clothes do you want to bring?" I asked her after they left, hoisting her over my shoulder and carrying her to the closet, her tiny fists pounding into my back as bubbly giggles left her lips.

After returning her to her feet, her fingers trailed along the row of dresses hanging and flowing across the floor. "How much can I bring? All the dresses Ali made me are so beautiful."

"Bring them all. It's not a terribly long journey, and I'm sure we will need another packhorse anyway," I winked.

She gently folded the decadent dresses into a neat pile, and I fetched more leather bags from deeper in the closet. A pile of her favorite pants, tunics, and tank tops waited beside the dresses by the time I'd gathered what clothes I wanted.

"When we get to Vaenor, I will take you to a store that can make clothes to magically accommodate your wings. They are very secretive about their process, but you'll never have to worry about ripping your shirts," I said. I hoped giving her things to look forward to would help ease her anxiety about this transition. "Or we can have a tailor make backless shirts that show off your beautiful body," I suggested, my fingers painting her spine. "That would be my preferred choice."

She bit her lower lip, trying to hide a mischievous smile. "And would you be able to control yourself if I wore those around the castle?"

"It would be one way of announcing you as mine," I purred, my dick stirring at the thought. Her gaze drifted to my growing erection, and pink dusted her cheeks as I laid bare my desire for her.

"So you want the whole realm to know who I belong to, huh?" She sashayed toward me, swaying her hips like a cat stalking its prey.

I watched her hungrily, my hands snaking around her waist when she was close enough, pulling her soft flesh against my hard body. "My instincts are screaming at me to make you mine, to let everyone know not to touch you. They have been since I first saw you." My confession and nip of her shoulder elicited a wanton gasp.

"Do you want me to proclaim you as mine? Is that why you want the throne for yourself?" My nose nuzzled the sensitive point beneath her ear.

"Yes," she breathed, angling my face to the spot on her neck where her pulse fluttered.

My self control snapped like a rope stretched too tight for too long, and I sank my teeth into the spot, her life thrumming beneath my tongue as I soothed the bite.

"Kazimir..." she moaned, the sound nearly bringing me to my knees. Lifting her lithe body into the air, she wrapped her legs around my waist and I walked her to my bed. I threw her down once my knees hit the edge, ripped her leggings off, and dived in between her divine legs to taste her sweet center within the span of seconds, unable to control my lust.

She cried out as I latched onto her core, her thighs trembling and soaked already. My tongue licked her slit, stopping to circle over her clit and then repeating the motion until her hips bucked wildly underneath me as she tried to get friction where she wanted it. Spreading her legs wider with my hands, I opened her hips to give myself better access. My hands drifted up her torso, taking the tunic with them, revealing her bare breasts as the fabric disappeared over her head. I hummed my approval into her pussy, then rolled her hard nipples between my thumbs and forefingers. Her back arched off the bed in time with her breathy gasp, and I planted a hand on her stomach to hold her still, while my other fingers found her heat. Lapping at her like she dripped the finest wine, I slipped one finger in, then two, and pumped them in and out, swirling them around until I found that spongy spot on her inner wall. My digits rubbed roughly against it, setting her walls spasming around them.

"Fuck me, please," she begged, her moans desperate as I drew her to the edge. She was going to come several times before I was finished with her, a reminder who she belonged to before we departed for Vaenor. I sucked greedily on those sensitive nerves at the apex of her thighs while stroking her with two fingers, faster and faster, matching my movements to her rapid breaths. Slipping a third inside her, she whimpered, riding my hand and face.

"Tell me you are mine," I snarled from between her thighs, only releasing her for a moment to voice my command.

"I'm yours," she gasped breathlessly, her walls clenching around my fingers.

"Good girl. Now come for me."

Her mewls were as decadent as the come that flooded my tongue, and seeing the sheets curled in her small hands as her orgasm ripped through her was the cherry on top. Her whole body convulsed, and she screamed my name as she exploded on my fingers.

Before she came down from her high, I pulled them out and brought them to her plump lips. "Taste yourself," I ordered.

Her bright blue eyes flared as she sucked them into her mouth, obediently cleaning them off and releasing them with a pop. Wild need tore through me at the sound, and my shirt and pants went flying. Our naked bodies were flush a moment later, and I kissed her deeply, sucking her tongue into my mouth before releasing it to nip her lower lip. No matter where my mouth was on her, she tasted divine. My hands palmed her breasts, so soft and full beneath my grasping digits. Her nipples were sharp, but my teeth were sharper, and I grazed them over the sensitive buds before soothing them with my flattened tongue.

She groaned, threading her fingers in my hair and holding me in place above them. Continuing to graze and lick around them, I fisted myself, trying to relieve some of the pressure building in my balls. Her body was so tight beneath me, and it only served to build this unending tension in my chest.

I had her where I wanted, and I wasn't letting go. My future queen's sparkling aquamarine eyes held my gaze, and the world around me fell away as she hypnotized me with her blue depths. She smiled wickedly, then reached between us to stroke me, knocking my hand away and pumping my shaft with her tiny fist that could scarcely get a grip. Her thumb smeared beads of wetness around the head, and I claimed her mouth, stealing her air as I ground into her hand.

"Fuck, Izidora..." I groaned, wanting to be inside her wet heat. "Tell me you're mine again."

"I am yours," she promised, her voice breathy and lustful.

That was all it took to unleash the frenzy inside me, and I lined myself at her entrance, tapping her clit once, twice, then seating myself fully with one powerful thrust. Without giving her time to adjust to my girth, I slammed my hips into hers again, then relentlessly pounded her into the bed. Her nails found purchase on my back as she moaned my name, scratching lines so deep I was surprised they didn't bleed. It only encouraged my onslaught, and wetness pooled underneath us, a mixture of arousal and sweat gathering below our thighs. I was a male possessed by a demon that forced me to protect what was mine at all costs.

My wings snapped from my back along with a roar, and I pulled out of her soaking center, lifting and flipping her so that she was on all fours in front of me. Her peachy ass graced the air, her puckered hole winking at me. Biting the juicy fruit, I marked her skin with bruises and indentions, my fingers rubbing circles over her clit as I worked on my claim. Once I was satisfied, I thrust back into her wet heat, my wings flaring protectively around us. Tracing around to her front, my fingers dipped between her thighs, finding that nub again and applying pressure. The moan that escaped her was primal, and her glittering white wings burst from her back unbidden. She pressed back into me, whimpering as I placed more friction over that bundle of nerves while I brutally drove into her, over, and over, and over, slapping resounding around the room as my thighs met her ass.

Her breath was erratic as she approached the peak of her pleasure. I used my free hand to stroke her wings in the sensitive spots I knew would make her come.

"Fuck, Kazimir, don't stop," she begged, mewling under all the sensation I gave her.

Her ass ground into me, and I let her fuck me while I pleasured her in every way.

"Such a good girl, taking all my cock like that," I purred, my fingers flattening against the apex of her thighs, letting her ride my hand and my cock. My balls tightened as she pushed even harder into me, and I had to flex my glutes to stabilize us as she rode me into oblivion. Wrapping her long hair around my fist, I yanked her head up, creating a deep arch in her back that took me to new depths inside her. She couldn't get away as I held her in place with my cock, hand, and fist.

"You are mine," I growled, sinking my teeth into the crook of her neck, marking her there like I had on her ass. "Come with me," I commanded around my bite.

I roared so loud that the walls around us shook, roping spurts of hot liquid filling her and dripping down my thighs as she screamed my name, her walls milking every last drop from me as we rode that high together. My hands dropped to either side of her, careful not to land against her feathered wings, and I panted over her back, spent from the force of our carnal fucking.

We stayed like that, breaths evening out, until finally I had the energy to remove myself from her. I banished my wings and she did the same, then rolled onto her back to look up at me, her dark lashes brushing her pink cheeks and sweat coating her forehead.

My hands braced on the bed beside her heart-shaped face, I

brought my lips down, brushing them over hers and stealing what little breath she had regained. Then I rested my forehead on hers, drinking in the bright soul I saw in the depths of her aquamarine pools. "I love you, Izidora."

A blink of dark lashes momentarily hid her eyes from me, but when they reopened, they were filled with the sentiment I'd been fervently hoping to see. "I love you, Kazimir," she echoed.

I crushed her against my chest, happiness filling me so completely that I thought I might explode. She wrapped her arms around me, and we stayed locked in that blissful embrace until our bodies grew cold. With one final kiss, I removed myself from the bed, tossing a fluffy robe to her before we finished packing and preparing ourselves for what lay ahead.

As we lay in bed on our last night at Zirok House, I rested easier knowing that the next day we would enter the world with our hearts laid bare to one another. No matter where we went, she was my home, for she was my insidious bloom, and I couldn't wait to see her sitting on the Night Throne at Este Castle. I kissed her shoulder softly before drifting off with my arms wrapped tightly around her.

INTERLUDE

"Get the fuck up," the guard told the nearly-grown female, her back firmly planted against the rough wall. He remained a healthy distance from her, circling well beyond the edges of her reach and lighting a series of oil-filled basins to bathe the room in what little light such a cavernous space would allow.

She lifted her head from where it rested on her forearms, giving him a sharp glare. "What's the point? Why don't you just kill me?"

The guard shook his head. "Even if I knew the answer to that, I wouldn't tell you."

The female blinked rapidly as her eyes adjusted to the light, then, with the slowness of someone who had all the time in the world, she stood, bare feet padding across the ground to the point where her chains grew taught and she could go no further. The guard took a cautious step back. "You know what to do, so get to it."

The princess bared her teeth at him, then began the once-weekly routine the guards kept her to, if only to keep her body from deteriorating completely. Jogging to her wall and back, weighed down by her chains, she counted twenty passes before she dropped to the ground and went through a basic training routine, working through each muscle group in her body in a halfhearted attempt to keep herself fit.

"If you don't put more effort into it, I'll make sure to give you half rations this week," the guard sighed, knowing that food was always a great motivator for the princess.

She paused her routine, her blue eyes narrowed on him. He knew she did not trust him, for she did not trust a single one of them, despite there only being a few males among them with violent intent. He was not one of them, he was proud to say.

The princess considered him for a moment. The guard revealed a large, damp cloth and fresh clothes from behind his back that he hoped were visible in the dim light. That seemed to appease her, and she began putting more effort into her work. By the time she finished, he had laid the clothes and towel within her reach, and he had grasped his torch. "I'll leave you to change while I fetch you some food."

She said nothing, and when he disappeared around the corner, the princess hurriedly stripped out of her dirty clothes, ran the wet cloth over her damp body, and redressed. Minutes passed before the male returned with a tray of food, and she kicked him her sweat-soaked clothes before he slid the tray to her across the barely visible boundary line of her chains.

The princess ate every last bite, then pushed the tray in his direction before crossing to the mattress that one of the other guards had placed out of her reach in a cruel attempt to break her. Without a word, he doused the oil basins and left the princess alone.

IV

THE RETURN

27

IZIDORA

P ain – there was so much pain. My hands and knees scraped the wet ground, and my chest heaved as another tidal wave smashed through me, ripping my very soul apart in its wake. My spine arched to the depths of the ocean floor, so close to snapping as the wave retreated to my tailbone. Through blurred eyes, I searched my surroundings for the source of the riptide. Only darkness, my old friend, kept me company, and I screamed, the sound blistering my throat as another surge of torture swept up my spine, breaking against the crown of my head. Sweat dripped from my brow and mixed with salty tears as I pushed the ground away, as if the simple act of standing would save me from drowning in pain. A tsunami tore through me and my neck snapped back with such force that I finally glimpsed the source of my agony. A hooded figure floated a hair's breadth from my bare feet, and his only distinctive feature was red eyes that glinted in the darkness like a fish's scales when they caught the light of the sun. "Please, stop whatever you are doing," I begged as another swell rose from my center, snapping my head straight once more. Hot breath brushed across my ear, his haunting voice filling my mind. "Not until you submit."

I barely managed to swallow the scream that lodged in my throat as I bolted upright and out of the excruciating nightmare.

Not real. Safe in bed. Alive.

My breath quivered in my throat as I released it like a slow stream of smoke, my racing heart nearly galloping away with me before I could suck down another breath. Kazimir's back was to me, the soft rise and fall of his chest contradicting my own. Thank the fucking Goddess he still slept and did not awake to my distress. Tucking myself against the warmth of his broad back, I curled in on myself, eyes wide and tracing the outline of the gilded wall beyond the bed as I tried to forget those haunting red eyes.

Yet with every flutter of my lashes against my cheeks, those sinister embers stared back at me. A blanket of dread covered me as the events of the previous day rushed back into my mind. In only a few hours, we'd return to the road headed to Vaenor, and my father, who more than likely planned to marry me off the moment I returned. I swallowed down bile at the thought of that male who did not know me exerting so much control over my life.

Never again would I be a victim at the hands of a male.

I would forge a path for myself – and I would gladly kill to make that happen.

Queen Izidora.

The thought scared me less with the threat of execution by marriage hanging above my head; but if we failed, the deadly sharp blade would hang there regardless.

Better to die trying than to surrender to the whims of a crazed king.

I was an insidious bloom, thorns razor sharp and deadly; but more than that I was *willing* to kill to save my life.

A series of solid raps roused Kazimir from sleep, a grumble

and groan preceding a full-body stretch and a warm hand feeling around in the dark for me.

He rolled to face me, his secure arms pulling me to him as he sucked in a deep breath with his nose buried in my tangled hair. "Are you ready?" he mumbled against my head.

"Yes." The word was true, despite my heart threatening to leap from my chest. I could feel both anxious and ready – the two emotions were not exclusive. The road looming ahead was hard and fraught with uncertainty, but as long as I had Kazimir, Endre, and Viktor, I would be okay.

———

THERE WAS a dusting of frost coating the lawn outside Zirok House, where I stood among the Nighthounds, Cazius, and our additional guards. Ali's plump face was stained with tears as we said our goodbyes. She embraced us individually, smothering us in her love one last time. When at last she arrived in front of me, my throat refused to work around the thick lump lodged there. She was the first female to care for me immediately and uncondonditionally, just like a mother should, and I was loath to part with her warmth and cheer.

"Before you go, I have one last surprise for you," she said, pulling a soft package from somewhere in her apron and handing it to me. A fur-lined cloak the same color as the deep navy blue dress that I loved so dearly was nestled among the wrapping paper. The velvet fabric was luxurious against my hands, so I pressed my face into it and rubbed my cheek against the softness.

"It's going to be a cold journey with winter coming, and you need a cloak fit for a princess," she beamed through the waterfall dripping from her eyes.

Tears overflowed and swept down my cheeks as I pulled her

into me through a sob. "Thank you for being like a mother to me, Ali."

"It was so nice to have a lady in the house again. Please come visit soon," she requested.

"I will be back as soon as I am able. I need your cooking to keep putting on muscle!" I spoke in jest but the words were true nonetheless.

She shook out the cloak, and I turned so she could wrap it around my shoulders. As I spun around with a dramatic flair, she clasped her hands in front of her mouth, green eyes dancing with delight. "A true princess," she breathed.

The moment I turned away from her to walk to Mistik, my heart ached with the loss of her. It was only temporary. When I was queen, there would be nothing preventing her from living with us in Este Castle.

Mistik crunched on a dark red apple I swiped from the kitchen while I waited for everyone to finish their goodbyes. Mistik's whiskers tickled my hand, then my neck as she nuzzled me and hooked me in for a hug. I buried my face in her mane, breathing in her familiar musky scent, trying to calm my nerves.

Our traveling party had doubled in size, yet the unbridled fear rising from the memory of riding for my life through these gates did not depart. Though Zekari and Kirigin had assured us we would be safe, I didn't trust the Iron Fae not to set a trap to lure us out. With a shaky breath, I pulled myself atop Mistik, surveying the sprawling grounds of Zirok House one last time and turned my mare toward the gates, waiting for them to be pulled open before us.

They groaned open, the first of the new guards digging their heels into their mounts to start our journey north. I waved to Ali one last time before returning my attention to the road in front of me, holding my head high as I rode toward my destiny.

The mood was somber as we traversed Theszaly Track. The

long dirt road cutting through the open plains would eventually reconnect us with the Northern Route that led to Vaenor. Cazius estimated our travels would take about three weeks given the size of our traveling party, and he informed me we would stay in some of the Night Realm's largest cities along our way.

With ravens ferrying invitations and preparations underway for the feast, the whole Night Realm would know I was alive and well in a very short time. I expected to experience exuberant reactions from the Night Fae as we rode through towns both large and small, and I mentally rehearsed how I was going to behave and what I was going to say.

Kazimir rode to my left, his posture relaxed as he swayed atop his mount. Fek's long mane shone under the morning sun, and his coat glistened as if the stablehands had spent all night polishing him. Mistik looked equally as shiny, her tail braided and plaited. My new cloak spread over the mare's haunches, the deep blue pairing perfectly with her dapple gray coat. It was the perfect shield against the early morning chill, the fur lining trapping heat from Mistik's hide and blanketing me in bliss.

Kazimir caught my eye and shot me a heart-melting smile. Our time together the previous night had been nothing short of incredible, and hearing those three words spill from his lips with the most fervent sincerity pebbled my skin even now.

I was loved.

"How do I look?" I asked him, dramatically sweeping my arms like a dancer atop a horse.

"Like a princess," he praised, grinning widely at me.

"All I am lacking is a crown," I replied.

"I'm sure Kazimir will let you look at his jewels later!" Kriztof called from behind us. He sported a shit-eating grin that broke through my resolve not to laugh, and he offered me a mocking salute. "Happy to be of service. Both now and later."

The look Kazimir leveled at him was nothing short of lethal, which caused Endre and Viktor, who rode on either side of Kristof, to howl with laughter. Viktor dabbed at his eyes while Endre clutched his stomach, and their amusement was contagious, catching me in its clutches and tearing giggles from me. Our somber morning march turned into an afternoon as bright as the shining sun thanks to Kriztof, whose smile was wide though his eyes were tight.

"How long has it been since each of you were in Vaenor?" I asked.

"Not long enough," Kriztof grumbled, his words carrying an obvious, unsaid weight.

"For me, it has been around a year, but my family was there over the summer," Vadim said.

"The three of us were there briefly during the summer, which is how we picked up the tip of your whereabouts actually," Endre replied, jerking his head at Viktor and Kazimir, causing his black hair to fall into his eyes.

"Are more people there during the summer?" I asked.

"Yes, mostly because the weather is nice and Fae love to sun themselves on the beaches beneath the cliffs. During the winter, the wind is harsh and biting. Most noble Fae retreat to their country homes to escape it." Viktor illustrated castle life to me, and I could almost picture myself wearing a golden tan after bathing in the sun for months on end.

Vadim sported a wolfish grin enhanced by his scraggly beard. "The beach is my favorite place to be in the summer. I can pick a lady without having to be disappointed when I get her alone later."

I snorted. "So why weren't you there last summer?"

"He was breaking hearts with Zekari and Kirigin near the Iron Realm border," Endre teased.

"And we got the final piece of the puzzle for Izidora's whereabouts, fuck you very much." He clutched his chest like the words offended him, but his evergreen eyes danced with amusement.

"What is your sister like?" I asked Vadim.

He shook his head. "Oh, no. I am not going to encourage your friendship. You two will break more hearts combined than I ever will."

"His sister is almost as pretty as you." Kriztof pulled his lips between his teeth suggestively, slicking back his shoulder-length hair. It was Vadim's turn to deliver a death glare. "You know every noble male in this kingdom has dreamed about her before going to bed."

Viktor roared with laughter, but Endre's smile briefly slipped. There was something beneath that, and I intended to find out.

"That is not something anyone wants to know about their sister," Vadim groaned.

"Please tell me. You males are great, but having a female friend would make me happy too," I begged.

"Fine, fine. But if you two bring the whole castle to its knees, I am not to blame," he sighed dramatically. "She is more stubborn than a mule, but she is fiercely loyal to those she loves. Honestly, it might be my fault that she is so fierce. I trained swords with her when she grew up. She is also too smart for her own good. She can twist your words until even you don't remember what you said anymore. She and Viktor got into it a few years ago and it was like watching the king's lawyers."

I liked her already.

We turned onto the Northern Route past midday, stopping to water ourselves and the horses at the stream that I learned spilled from the Agrenak Mountains into the ocean beyond Este Castle. Among the thick tunnel of trees along the Northern Route, blades of golden light sliced through the nearly bare branches, dropping lower and lower until a kaleidoscope of colors was upon us, painting the dying sky in stunning purple hues.

"We'll stop in Zezka for the night. There should be plenty of space for us at The Saturn," Cazius announced from the head of our traveling party.

"How long until we arrive?" I shouted over the distance between us.

"It's over that hill." He pointed a gloved hand along the darkening dirt to a sloped uptick in the ground in the distance.

Opening my mouth, I blew out a shivering breath. My gut twisted and knotted, but Kazimir's warm hand found mine, giving it a gentle squeeze. "Everything will be alright. You know what to do."

I nodded, then focused my mind on what I'd rehearsed a dozen times over the course of the last night and day. My teeth still chewed on my lip as we approached the hill, and my hands fidgeted over Mistik's reins. But the mare was calm when I could not be, and she plodded along beside Fek without incident.

As we crested the hill, I sucked in a breath, eyes widening a fraction, as I drank in the scene before me. A sprawling city filled a small valley, its lights twinkling into existence like the stars overhead in the descending darkness. Lazy gray smoke curled from chimneys, mingling with their cloud counterparts in the sky. Mothers called their children home for the night, and Zezka's taverns roared as they filled with patrons. The herbal and savory scent of stew drifted on a light breeze, lifting wayward strands out of my eyes as we cleared the outskirts of the city. Wood chalets lined the streets as we rode further through Zezka, toward a vibrant square at the heart of the city.

No one paid us any attention, the people consumed in their day-to-day lives and accustomed to travelers cutting through their city seeking the capital of the Night Realm. The square opened up, lights in every color flickering all around us as others danced through the streams of water flowing from a massive fountain in the center of the square. The marbled orb turned slowly, slightly off center as water dripped from within it. I gaped, enchanted by its movement.

"What is that?" I gasped.

"Saturn," Kazimir responded. "It moves in time with the movements of the planet. Those lights are magically enhanced to represent its moons."

I couldn't stop staring in wonder at the creation, my attention snapped to it until Kazimir touched my leg. Our whole party had already dismounted and waited for me to join them on the ground. With a slip of pink on my cheeks, I sheepishly slid from Mistik's back and handed her reins to a young male waiting in a smart tunic and pants.

We entered the marble building, a grand foyer opening in front of us. Black marble with veins of silver the color of the males' magic crawled up the walls to a glittering chandelier, each light hanging from the thinnest of threads above us in a pattern that reflected the night sky.

"High Lord Vaszoly, so pleased that you have graced us with your presence once again. Would you like your usual rooms?" A female with painted red lips beamed at him as she sank low into a curtsey, showing off her ample cleavage.

"Yes, please, and extra rooms for the rest of our company," he replied airily. His usual warmth was gone, and I wondered if this was his "High Lord" act.

"I will ensure each of you is well taken care of," she promised, licking her lips as she regarded Kazimir. Without thinking, I bared my teeth as she undressed him with her eyes, causing her to pale when she noticed my aggression.

"Your Highness," she gasped, nearly hitting the floor with her curtsey. She didn't move from the position, and I looked at Kazimir for help, losing all the knowledge Cazius and the females had imparted about protocol with the rising panic clawing my throat. He motioned for me to speak and release her from her curtsey.

"Please rise, and you may call me Princess Izidora," I said warmly, only feeling a little guilty about baring my teeth at her.

Trembling, she stood as commanded. "Your hi - Princess Izidora, welcome to The Saturn. It is an absolute honor to host you here. I will have our maids prepare the best room for you. We don't often have guests of your status here, so I apologize that it will take a bit to prepare. Let me get you a bottle of our finest wine while you wait." She darted behind a wall, hissing orders at whoever was hidden there, returning a few moments later with a bottle nestled in the crook of her arm. "Please follow me into our private lounge, you must all be exhausted from your journey."

The lounge had black wallpaper that swirled stars into roses, while poufs and deep couches lined the space. At the opposite end of the room was a glass bar that stretched across an entire wall, and behind it was an oil painting of the hotel's namesake in a heavily gilded frame. She led us to a large sectional in the center of the space, uncorking the bottle and placing it in the middle of a gray and white marble table. "I'll grab you some glasses and be right back," she promised.

Cazius, Kazimir, Viktor, and I sat on one side while Endre, Vadim, and Kriztof sat across from us. My head whipped around as I searched for our other companions. "Where did everyone go?"

Cazius leaned around Kazimir and Viktor to answer my question. "They are not allowed in here."

I furrowed my brow. "Why not?"

"Because they are not noble. This lounge is for the exclusive use of nobility and Knights. You will find many places such as these the closer we get to Vaenor," he stated.

I huffed, making a face. After what I'd learned the previous few days, I knew it was better to keep my opinions on the matter to myself for now. Our hostess returned with glasses, pouring a measure into each and handing them to us. "If you need anything, I'll be in the foyer. I will fetch you when your rooms are ready." She curtseyed one last time and departed.

"Cheers to the royal treatment," Kriztof said, lifting his glass.

"Cheers!" We exclaimed in unison. I took a sip of my purplish red wine. Its bold flavor washed over my tongue – chocolate and cherries. Reclining against the fluffed cushions, I kept my glass in hand, sipping a little too fast. The alcohol was relaxing me, and tension melted from my shoulders.

I blew out a long breath. The female's reaction was the first in many tests, and I had no choice but to approach each challenge with the intent of overcoming if I wanted to be free. I only hoped I wouldn't get overwhelmed with recognition upon our departure the next day. One Fae prostrating themselves before me was bad enough. I didn't want a whole city to do it, especially if I were to freeze like I had earlier. It was not a good look.

A male appeared in the doorway, bowing low to us before he approached. I sat up, straightening myself, trying to appear regal. "Good evening, Your Highness, My Lords, my name is Jozef and it is my highest honor to welcome you to The Saturn."

What was with people and their honor?

"I am the owner of this fine establishment, and when my assistant told me the wonderful news that we would be hosting the lost princess tonight, I simply had to see with my own eyes." He bowed low again, remaining there, and I realized I was meant to release him. "Please rise, Jozef. Thank you for your hospitality," I said with as much formality as I could muster; it felt so strange, like I was living another person's life.

"When we heard the news of your rescue, our whole city

cheered," he continued. "I almost didn't believe it. But now, here you are, sitting in my hotel."

My fingers twined in my cloak as I sat awkwardly, unsure how to respond, but Cazius saved me.

"Thank you, Jozef, for your kind words. I am afraid we are all a bit road-weary, so I hope you can excuse our quietness," he hinted.

"Of course, My Lord, all is excused. I will fetch you personally when we have prepared your rooms."

The overly excited male finally left, and I threw back the rest of my wine, catching a few drops that dripped out of the corner of my mouth with the back of my hand before they spilled onto my beautiful new cloak. "I feel so awkward," I whispered to Kazimir.

"You'll get used to it," he replied. "This is just the beginning. Like forming shapes with your magic. Soon you'll have to build shapes and then fight with them, and after that, you'll have to use complicated healing magic to placate the masses. But you will learn, just like you have learned everything else."

I knocked my shoulder into his. "Thanks for believing in me."

His lips brushed my forehead, then returned to his glass before anyone saw.

"I'm going to get another bottle. It's time to get drunk," Kriztof declared, marching from the room, empty bottle in hand. He returned a few minutes later with a full one and poured a measure into each of our glasses. My stomach rumbled, and a craving for Ali's cookies called out from the gnawing pit. But they were stuffed safely in my saddlebags, which I had left on Mistik.

"Where are our bags?" I asked.

"They will be waiting for us upstairs," Endre replied. "Fancy service, huh?"

"Very," I nodded, then downed my second glass, the purple liquid burning my stomach when it hit nothing but more wine. My head swam a little too much as the alcohol flooded my veins, but it stopped my skin skittering. The moment we polished off the second bottle, Jozef reappeared as if he had been perched beyond the doorway, waiting for his next opportunity to pounce. "Please follow me," he requested with a sweeping bow.

A grand marble staircase led to the second floor, where we walked straight to a set of white double doors. He grasped both handles, flinging his arms wide to reveal an opulent room with floor-to-ceiling windows looking out over the city. In the center sat a large round table overflowing with fresh flowers. To the right, another set of double doors led to a bedroom with a draped four-poster bed sprinkled with ruby rose petals. I wandered further into the space, a black marble bathroom with a tub large enough for three people catching my eye. Beside it, there was a glass cage with holes lining the wall and ceiling. A full-size mirror hung on the opposite wall, large enough to capture me and Kazimir, who I did not realize trailed behind me.

His emerald orbs caught my eye, a smirk pulling at his lips and flashing white in the massive mirror. That faint tug pulled us together, and his hand swept my hair over my shoulder, his body framing mine and showing me just how petite I was next to him. "I will fuck you in front of this later." His voice was hoarse, and heat pooled in my low belly at his promise.

Tearing away from the mirror, we returned to the main room where three smaller doors lined the opposite wall, and Viktor, Vadim, Endre, and Kriztof played rock, paper, scissors in front of them. As I approached, Viktor lost the round, his head thrown back with a cackle of laughter. "Now I can get a decent night's sleep tonight!"

"I'm taking the one closest to the exit!" Endre did not hesitate to jump into action, racing for the white door closest to where a horror-stricken Jozef stood, mouth slightly agape as he discovered the Nighthounds' antics. Vadim was fast, and he and Endre grasped the handle simultaneously, a battle of wills ensuing until Endre shouldered past him and shut the door with a maniacal laugh.

"Would you like dinner brought up?" Jozef stammered, his wide eyes bouncing between me and a cool Cazius, who relaxed in a chair with a book in hand as if these males were of no concern to him.

"Please," Cazius replied.

Jozef bowed, then closed both doors simultaneously as he darted from the room.

Our bags were piled in a corner, and I searched mine for Ali's cookies, too hungry to wait for our evening meal. With a glance over my shoulder to make sure the greedy males weren't watching, I stuffed two in my mouth, nearly moaning as their gooey goodness filled it with ecstasy. She cut the sweet with a hint of salt, and the flavors came to a perfect crescendo as I chewed the cookies. I slunk to a nearby couch after hiding them away again, unwilling to share my treats with any who witnessed the crumbs falling from my mouth.

Jozef returned with a young female, both laden with silver serving trays topped by rounded bowls. The two arranged them around the edges of the round table, careful not to crush any petals beneath the heavy servingware. One by one, they revealed the contents beneath the gleaming lids, each lift performed with dramatic flair. There was roast duck, bacon-wrapped steaks, steaming mashed potatoes, earthy vegetables covered in a creamy sauce, freshly baked bread, and crispy lettuce mixed with fresh berries. It was more than enough food for us – more than enough food to feed our traveling party, in fact.

Jozef stacked plates and silverware between the salad and

steaks, then faced me and swept into a bow. "Do not hesitate to ask for anything else, we are only a ring away." He indicated a silvery rope hanging near the door.

"Thank you, Jozef," Cazius dismissed the overly excited male with a wave of his hand.

We filed around the table in a semi-coordinated dance, collecting plates and circling until they were filled with food. There were plenty of seats in the open space, so I took the first free one and popped a slice of roasted duck into my mouth, quickly followed by a rosemary roll and some vegetables. I didn't look up from my meal until it was done, and with a contented sigh, I lounged against the soft cushions, belly full and eyes heavy.

Cazius and Viktor departed, heading to a shared room down the hall, and Kazimir shamelessly threw me over his shoulder the moment the doors closed behind them. He smirked at Endre, Vadim, and Kriztof as a giggle burst from me, and I helplessly pounded his back, watching Kriztof cover his ears before the double doors swung shut and cut off my line of sight.

My back was on the bed in an instant, Kazimir snatching my waist into his arms and arching me off the soft surface. I gasped then giggled as he bent his face to my neck, dusting it with his breath. "Now I've got you all to myself, and I want to play."

Heat pooled between my thighs at the promise of him between them. I wanted him to tell me he loved me as he pounded into me, nearly splitting me apart over his length. "Then let's play," I purred, my fingers scratching against the scruff I loved so much.

His tongue found the shell of my ear, and I dug my nails into his scalp to hold him in place as he nibbled and licked the sensitive area.

"You're mine, Izidora. Be a good girl and tell me you understand," he growled, and I trembled beneath the possessive sound.

"I understand," I breathed, grinding my hips against the hardness that dug into mine.

"Fuck," he hissed. "I want to drown inside you."

He dug his hands into my ass, lifting me from the bed and carrying me into the bathroom. My legs wrapped around his waist, and I rocked my hips against him with each step, hands threaded in his hair while he sucked on my neck. The marble counter was cold against the back of my thighs, and I only got colder as my tunic was ripped over my head. Kazimir's joined mine on the floor, and his lips captured mine with the roughness of a male whose control slipped away by the second. Having that power over him was more intoxicating than the two glasses of wine filling my belly.

His probing tongue parted my lips, licking them before moving onto my tongue, our mouths so connected I wasn't sure whose air we breathed. As we rose into a dizzying high, he released my lips and placed his on the tops of my breasts, sliding the lace fabric covering them aside and sucking a nipple into his mouth. The fabric pushed them together, giving me more cleavage than I had, and Kazimir licked the space as he pinched my hard peaks between his fingers, eliciting a wanton moan that started in my core and exploded in my chest.

He broke away, leaving my lashes fluttering against my cheeks as I adjusted to his absence. A few squeaks opened my eyes, finding Kazimir turning knobs outside the glass cage and water cascading from the holes in the ceiling and wall. Steam filled the room as he stepped out of his pants, his heated regard never leaving my heaving breasts. He crooked a finger at me, drawing me to him as if he pulled on that rope that tied us together. I hopped off the counter, swaying my hips as I strode toward him, wanting him to devour my newly muscled curves.

He stood at full attention now, his eyes hungry as he drank me in. The lace dropped to the cool ties beneath my feet as I stared into his emerald orbs, then my fingers hooked around my waistband, slowly teasing my pants over my hips before stepping out of them and into his broad chest. He grabbed my hips possessively before crashing his mouth against mine once again.

A hot, watery breath brushed around us, the open glass beckoning us to enter. Kazimir led me into the rolling mist before shutting the door behind us, cutting us off from the world beyond. The blissfully hot water soaked into me at once, the spray inescapable in this cage when Kazimir took up more than half of it. Kazimir's tongue roamed my mouth as he pressed me into the tile at the back of the space, hand drifting toward my dripping core. The contrast between his warm body and hot water with the cold tile against my back was divine.

Too slowly, he massaged my clit, and I bucked my hips, trying to get more friction where I wanted it. His digits dipped lower, rubbing my slit as he wet his fingers with my arousal, then returned the rough pad of his finger to the apex of my thighs, applying more pressure against the nub and my body, trapping me in the pleasure only he could provide. I groaned as he continued to tease me, my nipples like diamonds against the planes of his chest. They ached to be touched, and I arched into him, brushing them against the tattoos that marked his skin. He sensed my need and twisted one between his fingers, causing me to cry out at the painful sensation, but my cries turned into mewls as he dipped three digits into my core, spreading my folds wide.

The fullness only created tension in me, the strings of my pleasure pulling taught around his hand. Over and over, he pumped his fingers into me, twisting my nipple painfully. Each curl inside me lifted me higher until I stood on my tiptoes as he thrust them into me. I was completely trapped against the wall at the mercy of his deft fingers, and something about that spurred my desire until I was panting with the need to come. His teeth found my neck, sucking and licking the water dripping from my skin.

"Kazimir…" I moaned, half begging for him to continue his maddening movements and half begging for him to bring me to release.

"You are so wet," he groaned. "So wet for me, and only me."

"Yes, only you," I gasped as his fingers sank deep into me, touching that spongy spot against my inner walls. They clenched around his hand, the tension finally breaking and waves of pleasure crashing through me. He ground the heel of his hand into my sensitive nub, bringing me to the highest point of my climax, and I screamed his name. "Fuck, Kazimir!"

Without waiting for my orgasm to subside, he withdrew his fingers, forcing my legs apart as his knees hit the tile. My still-pulsing core was assaulted by his mouth, his black scruff tickling my thighs and his tongue sweeping over my sensitive clit. My hands found his soaked hair in an attempt to control the overwhelming sensation. He let me direct him further down, where he lapped at my wetness, and my pussy melted like chocolate under his mouth. The pressure between my thighs built, the tension ready to snap again only moments later. With a nip of my sensitive nub, he cut the rope and tore his name from my lips as my thighs shook with my release.

He stood over me as I returned from the heavens, looking like a god as water ran down his chiseled abs to his swollen length. I wanted to taste his saltiness. Knees against the cold tiles, I gripped his shaft with my hand, looking up at him from beneath wet lashes. The steam was so thick, his wild expression was barely visible, but I wanted to exert a drop of power over him before I took him in my mouth. Lip between my teeth, I stared at him, pumping his hardness and cupping his balls, eliciting a feral snarl and two hands braced against the wall behind me.

"I want to see how much you can take, Izidora," he crooned.

Parting my lips, I flicked my tongue over his dripping head, batting my lashes like butterflies. His groan spurred me, and I closed my lips around it, swirling my tongue before bobbing my head up and down his shaft. I needed it slick before I could swallow him down. Breathing through my nose I relaxed my throat, sinking lower until my nose nearly brushed his stomach. I gagged as the back of my throat was assaulted, my muscles tightening around him, provoking a string of curses from him. "Fuck, Izidora..."

Kazimir fisted my soaked hair, taking control of my head as he fucked my mouth. His domination sent fire straight to my core, and my thighs dripped water and arousal between my slightly parted legs. Tears sprang to my eyes as I continued to gag, but I didn't tell him to stop as I watched him become an animal before me.

He pulled out with a pop, lifting me and spinning me and pressing me against the fogged glass with the barely contained madness of a male in the throes of passion. There was so much rolling mist I couldn't see what lay beyond, and the thought of someone watching this male devour me made my blood sing. As my hard nipples pressed against the cold glass, I imagined what we looked like from the outside, my breasts and hands imprinting the clear wall, Kazimir's dark hair and muscular body standing over me as he lined himself with my entrance.

In one powerful thrust, he was buried inside me, and I cried out at the sudden fullness. His hands found my hips as he pounded me into the glass, more of my body pressing into it as he slowly, brutally, powerfully thrust over and over again. Water drenched us both from the overhead spray, the falling drops on my back a gentle contrast to the fury between my thighs as

Kazimir split me apart. He trailed his hand down my spine, kicking my legs apart as he opened me further to him, angling himself to the depths of my core, his cock rubbing against every sensitive spot and nerve.

"I want to hear your pretty voice as you come all over my cock. Tell me I'm your hero for saving you and delivering you into a world of pleasure," he commanded as he pounded me from behind, wet slapping growing louder as he increased his pace.

"Fuck, Kazimir, you are my hero," I moaned, and his cock thickened inside me, a moment from bursting and filling me.

"Yes," he hissed, fingers digging into my hips, driving me higher and higher until I was certain I would fall to my death and never recover.

My world turned on its axis as I plummeted, my walls spasming around him and milking his shaft as he roared his release, hot ropes of liquid coating my insides. Our combined release dripped down my thighs as he removed himself from my aching core. Sweat soaked my skin more thoroughly than the waterfall coming from all directions, and when I gulped down air it was more akin to soup.

"Let's get cleaned up now," he hummed, grinding his hips into mine one last time before backing away and giving me space to wash off.

"What is this?" I asked him, gesturing around us.

"A shower. It takes a very gifted Night Fae to create one, which is why they are such a luxury," he explained. "I have one at Zirok House, but I never use it because I don't have a glass barrier like this one to prevent water from splashing everywhere."

Lifting miniature bars of soap to his nose, he sniffed them individually before choosing one and pulling me against his chest so he could wash my body. The aroma of flowers and fruit mixed with the mist trapped in this glass cage.

He gently soaped my legs, massaging them as he worked over every inch. Removing soreness with magic was nothing compared to this male touching every inch of my muscles and releasing the tension held there. Working his way up and over my legs and ass, his fingers painted swirls across the skin of my stomach, mapping his way to my breasts and cupping their heaviness before moving on to my arms. Over my shoulders and down my back, he gripped and grabbed the muscles, working knots inside of knots as he washed me. With a nudge to the spray, I rinsed the bubbles away, my attention on the movements of that white bar across his torso, covering every inch of the warrior's body in front of me. He joined me in the rain, kissing me softly as the water washed away the world around me.

There was only him.

Cold drops replaced hot ones, and the rolling mist lagged with the temperature change. I shivered as Kazimir opened the door and turned the knobs, ceasing the flow of water. He handed me a plush white robe, and I immediately wrapped it around myself, stepping past him to grab a fluffy cloth for my long chestnut locks. The brilliant lights in the bathroom allowed me to discover myself as I stared at my reflection in the wall-sized mirror.

Kazimir appeared behind me, bending his head to plant a kiss on the top of mine. Dropping my robe, I spun and flexed, admiring my changing body. Fighting and flying had sculpted my arms and back while riding built my legs. Scars still lined my skin, the largest of them splaying across my back, but not a bruise remained from the males who had abused me. Chestnut locks tumbled to my waist and ribs, covering my breasts on the way down. Aquamarine orbs stared back at me, twinkling with happiness, highlighted by a rosy flush from our romp in the shower. I smiled at Kazimir in the mirror, my full pink lips spreading wide over my white teeth. "You are stunning, Izidora." His emerald eyes screamed his love for me, but I wanted to hear those words.

"Say it again," I whispered.

"I love you, Izidora," he hummed against my hair, then grabbed my hands and led me down a path of ruby petals to the bright white decor on the massive four-poster bed. Heavy velvet curtains the color of the hour before dawn shut around us, cocooning us in a luxurious enclosure. Kazimir laid back and pulled me to his chest, and my shoulders dropped as I relaxed into the male who saved me – my hero.

"Are you two finished yet? We'd like to get some sleep!" Kriztof's teasing tone crawled through the door and curtains separating us.

I snickered unabashedly.

"Yep. You can go stroke yourself in your room now!" Kazimir shouted back.

Grumbled curses from the males sharing the suite preceded the slamming of doors. I would miss our camaraderie when we got to Este Castle, for showing our closeness would only lead to the deaths of all the people I loved. Viktor, Endre, Kazimir, and I were taking an insurmountable risk, and the weight of their lives on my shoulders had not left, despite my momentary distraction.

But there was nothing left for me to do today, and I needed energy to face what was ahead. Closing my eyes, I let go, surrendering to the void of dark dreams that surely awaited me.

28

KAZIMIR

Shouts jerked me from my sleep. The heavy white blankets pooled around my waist as I bolted upright, scanning our surroundings, heart pounding in my ears as adrenaline coursed through my veins. Yanking back the velvet curtains separating us from the world, I searched for the source of the disruptive noise. More curtains covered the windows, and I stalked over to them, shrugging into my robe. Once I'd secured it around my waist, I lifted the soft material of the curtains, revealing the square we'd traveled through the previous night, packed with Fae, some holding flowers, others with children on their shoulders. Their chanting swelled, and my senses finally caught up enough for me to hear what they were saying.

"Long live Princess Izidora!"

"The lost princess has been found!"

Fuck. All of Zezka knew of her presence, which meant every Fae in the Night Realm between here and Vaenor would know the lost princess was riding in their direction. Izidora squinted at me as the bright light streaming through the windows blinded her. She scrambled out of bed, throwing her robe on to cover herself.

"What are you doing? They can see us!" she exclaimed.

"We're fine. These windows only allow us to see out. Come, take a look." I offered my hand to her.

She took it, walking to the window.

"Oh my Goddess," she breathed. "How many people is that?"

"Hundreds, probably."

A knock sounded on our door, Endre's voice following it. "Have you seen outside?"

When I unlocked and opened the door, Endre, Kriztof, and Vadim were standing at the windows, surveying the gathered crowd.

"We've seen it," I replied grimly. Endre caught my eye, and I gave him a curt nod, the first step in our plan falling into place beautifully.

"Well, get dressed because I'm sure Cazius and Viktor will be knocking at any moment," Vadim suggested.

I nodded, retreating and closing the door behind me.

"Put on a dress," I instructed Izidora as I rummaged through my bags for a formal tunic. She chewed her lips as her tiny hands dug around for a dress, selecting a long-sleeved black one that left her shoulders bare with a dip in the back to make room for her wings. It hugged her curves down to her waist where it fell in strips of textured fabric to the floor.

She plaited her long locks just the way I liked them, and my cock stirred at the thought of wrapping my hand around her braids and riding her from behind. Digging my nails into my palms, I brought myself back to reality, needing my blood to be in my head so I could think.

Cazius and Viktor had arrived by the time we re-entered the living space. "What's the plan?" I asked, still buttoning my tunic sleeves.

"We need to get moving soon if we want to stay on schedule," Viktor said.

"The crowd presents a problem," I pointed out.

"Yeah, yeah I am aware," he replied.

"I think it is an opportunity for Izidora to win some favor," my father said. He looked her over, noting the dress she'd selected and her long hair braided down her back. "She needs something else..." He drifted to the table overflowing with flowers.

Endre and I followed his train of thought and joined him at the round table, selecting flowers in dark red hues. Viktor walked behind Endre, his lips pursed as he restrained a grin. It was almost as if we'd planned this moment, rather than it happening organically. Izidora's hand brushed mine as she arrived among the flowers, and Endre plucked blossoms from my hands, placing them strategically in her hair. While he worked, I wove a cascading crown of flowers to circle her brow. He stepped back, scrutinizing his work, before indicating that I should place the circlet over her head.

I couldn't contain my smile as I placed the crown of blossoms over her chestnut hair. One day, it would be the Night Crown I placed there – the day I also made her my wife.

Kriztof let out a low whistle. "She definitely looks like a princess now."

Izidora walked to a mirror hanging on a side wall. She gasped at the transformation in her hair. Roses so dark they looked like freshly drawn blood lined the crown of her head. Endre pulled a few strands out from her braids, and they tumbled loosely across her cheeks, framing her face. In the braids that trailed down her back, Endre had woven in dahlias and green vines dotted with tiny moonflowers. She looked like a goddess of the night, a legend borne from the whispers between drunken lips come to life.

When she faced us once more, I bowed my head and proffered my arm. "Princess, would you like an escort to greet your people?"

Her throat bobbed, but she kept her chin high and placed her hand in the crook of my arm. "I'm ready."

"I will exit first to introduce you," my father laid out his plan to Izidora. "Then you will walk forward, but drop Kazimir by my side. Vadim, Viktor, Endre, you all stand behind us. Kriztof, please keep watch from wherever you think best to spot any potential attacks. With any luck, this glimpse of you will disperse the crowd, and we will be able to eat in peace before continuing on our way." He strode to the door, opening it for us to walk through in formation. Kriztof skirted around us, disappearing down the stairs as he went to scout the area.

"Breathe, Izidora," I whispered to her. Her nails dug into the sensitive underside of my arm, and her chest barely moved despite my reminder. With a nudge in her ribs, she sucked down a breath, nodding to me that she would be okay.

"Just imagine you are talking to us," Endre encouraged.

"Be yourself," Viktor added.

"Picture them all naked," Vadim suggested.

She barked a laugh at the last suggestion, and I sent a look of thanks over my shoulder at Vadim for easing some of her tension. As we descended the stairs, Izidora's bare feet slipped from beneath the black gauzy fabric of her dress.

"Did you forget something?" I teased, looking pointedly at the ground.

She smiled sheepishly, "I'm starting a new fashion trend, obviously." That sent a snort around us. "But really, I was so nervous I forgot until I stepped on this cold marble."

Jozef darted into the lobby to meet us, bowing so low his nose brushed the ground. "My sincerest apologies, Your Highness, My Lords. I have no idea how word got out." I didn't believe him for a second. "Would you like me to clear some space for you?"

"If you will, Jozef," my father commanded.

The male, who was dressed far too finely for the hour with an accidental crowd outside, snapped his fingers, and several young males exited through the front doors, pushing back the crowd. The Night Fae roared and backstepped, their excitement palpable; and to think, most of these people believed her dead only days ago.

My father sauntered ahead of us, maintaining his slow pace while Izidora gulped down a handful of steadying breaths. Her eyes shut and lips moved as she repeated her words over and over, waiting for her moment before her people. A cheer soared from the crowd as they saw my father step into the soft morning light. We paused our advance, for the moment remaining shadowed in darkness.

He held up his hands in supplication, and the crowd hushed as quickly as it had roared. "I am High Lord Cazius Vaszoly, and at long last, I have the honor of presenting our lost princess to her people. Please welcome Princess Izidora Valynor!" he exclaimed, flourishing his arm and sweeping into a bow.

Plastering a wide smile on her face, Izidora stepped into the light, the soft morning rays shining on her flower-plaited hair. She waved shyly, and the crowd went wild. Fae cried her name, others dabbed their eyes, many bowed and curtseyed, but the overall mood was ecstatic. I stepped to my father's side, Viktor, Vadim, and Endre a step behind me, and spotted Kriztof to our left, hugging the side of the building.

Izidora closed her eyes and lifted her face and arms toward the sun. Her glittering white wings burst from her back, spreading out as large as they could as she flapped them gently to show off their sparkle. Females cried with their beauty, and a wave of kneeling Fae filled the square, awed by the legendary lost princess in front of them.

"Please rise." Her voice was honeyed as she greeted her people. "Thank you for taking time out of your day to come to see me. I am so happy to be going home at last."

My heart warmed as I watched her address the crowd. She was a natural; she knew exactly what to say, and still was authentically Izidora. How did I get so lucky that she agreed to be mine? After all these years of searching and fantasizing, I finally stood with her steps away, knowing that she loved me as I loved her.

"If it weren't for these males," she swept an arm in our direction, "I would never have been found. Please, thank them with me." She clapped in our direction, beaming as the crowd joined in. My father bowed low, and I followed his lead as did Viktor, Endre, and Vadim behind me. Hoots and hollers burst from the crowd, screams of appreciation for the Nighthounds who never gave up.

Their approval was more intoxicating in reality than in any of my daydreams.

"Now if you will excuse me, I am quite hungry after our long journey, and I have some cinnamon rolls waiting for me!" She waved as she backed our way, the crowd still cheering as we reentered The Saturn, closing the doors behind us and shutting out the roars that chased us to the black marble lobby. The moment the doors clicked shut, Izidora collapsed into me. I caught her around the waist and gingerly lowered her to the ground.

"Are you alright?" I checked her forehead.

"Get us some water," Viktor snapped at Jozef.

Glad it wasn't only me who felt like doing that.

Izidora was pale and trembled beneath my hands. Kriztof burst into the lobby, catching sight of us crowded around her.

"What happened? I didn't see any sign of danger out there," he questioned.

"I'm fine, just dizzy," she mumbled. Jozef returned carrying a glass of water. Kriztof snatched it from him and handed it to me before shooing Jozef away with a leveled glare.

"Here, take a few sips," I encouraged. She did, then gulped down the whole glass, color returning to her cheeks as she drank.

"That was a lot. You probably got overwhelmed," Endre empathized, taking the empty glass from her hands.

"I felt like I wasn't even there while I was speaking, like I was watching myself do it," she admitted.

"Well, you did fucking great!" Kriztof celebrated. "I've never seen a crowd respond to a monarch like that."

Vadim elbowed him in the ribs and cut him a sharp look.

"Do you think you can walk now?" I asked Izidora

"I think I can manage," she replied. I grasped her hands, helping her to her feet. She wobbled for a moment but steadied herself. "I could kill for some cinnamon rolls though."

We all laughed and traipsed the marble staircase in the direction of the finest room in the hotel. I parked Izidora on a couch while I went looking for the cinnamon rolls Ali had baked for her. They were well hidden, for they did not appear before my extensive search was interrupted by the arrival of Jozef and two females carrying trays of breakfast. They laid eggs of all types, bacon, sausage, sticky buns, mushrooms, and plates of fresh berries around the round table dusted with wayward leaves and petals. Jozef carried one himself, and as he approached a seated Izidora, three growls halted his steps. Eyes bouncing between Viktor, Endre, and myself, he opted to reveal his package at a safe distance. With a flourish, he lifted the gleaming lid to reveal a giant cinnamon roll doused in chocolate frosting.

"I had my chef make this, especially for you, Your Highness," he said, bowing low. I gave him one point back in his favor.

"Thank you," she smiled, waving her hand at an empty space on the round table.

He placed the tray there among the fresh berries. "Please let us know if you require anything else."

"I'll make you a plate," I said to Izidora, then proceeded to load the whole pastry onto a plate and surround it with eggs and bacon before topping off the roll with a handful of fresh berries. She picked up a fork to devour her treat, and I tossed a napkin her way, seeing exactly where that frosting was about to land.

We ate quickly, ready to get out of Zezka, and as we finished our meals, we peeled off to change into more comfortable riding clothes.

"You should leave the flowers in your hair. It gives you an air of royalty even with your leathers on," I suggested.

"I quite agree," she laughed, patting a few disrupted blossoms into place once a long-sleeved tunic covered her chest.

My father rang the bell to summon Jozef. "We are ready to depart," he announced as Jozef appeared in the doorway.

"Certainly, My Lord, I will have your bags collected and horses ready shortly." Jozef bowed and scurried away to carry out his orders. Young males came to collect our bags, and we grabbed one last bite of food before making our way to the stables. Our horses were waiting, coats still gleaming, as a stablehand held each at the ready. Izidora walked to Mistik, and the stablehand's eyes widened larger than saucers as he realized whose horse he held.

He bowed deeply to her. "I brushed her mane out early this morning so she would look pristine for the road," he blurted.

"What is your name?" Izidora inquired.

"Cad," he replied.

"Thank you, Cad, she looks very pretty."

His mouth was slightly askew as she smoothly mounted Mistik, patting the horse's shoulder as she greeted her. Cad scampered away, followed by the rest of the stablehands, as we maneuvered our mounts out of the stables. The crowd had dispersed – thank the Goddess – and only a few lingered around the square as we rode toward the fountain in the center. Riding an arc around the celestial imitation, we returned to the main road.

As we left Zezka behind, shouts rang out behind us.

"Long live Princess Izidora!"

"The lost princess!"

"The future queen!"

And when we crested the hill out of the valley, my shoulders dropped in time with my breath, Endre, Viktor, and Izidora mirroring me. Our first hurdle was cleared, but we still had many days until we arrived in Vaenor.

———

EVERY TOWN we passed through or stopped in over the next three weeks greeted us with the same ecstatic reception we received in Zezka. Our pace slowed to a crawl, and we ended up behind because of it. Izidora continued giving speeches, thanking us for her rescue. In time, the crowd shouted our names with as much enthusiasm as hers. Hearing her call me her savior over and over made me even more crazed for her – in a way that was almost alarming to me.

The people adored her, and Kriztof was right – I'd never seen a monarch so well-received. He and Vadim ventured to a tavern along the way and overheard the locals discussing the beauty and kindness of their lost princess. It was everything we needed for our play, laid out like a perfect hand of cards. The Fates and the Goddess must be working in tandem to make this happen, for it was unnerving how smoothly everything unfolded before us.

My stomach was in knots at the thought of Izidora being snatched from me the moment we crossed the threshold to Este Castle. We would not be able to be together like we had these past few weeks, and I almost lost my nerve when a panic attack overwhelmed her that morning before we departed. It was far too tempting to snatch her and ferry her away into the night, never to be seen again, so I could have her all to myself and protect her from the cruel world we were about to enter.

She fought her own internal battles and won most of them. Her confidence grew with every successful speech, and her humility with every well-wisher shouting her praises. At her behest, we stopped to train daily, and a little bit of that anxiety leached from her in the moments after her breath stuck in her chest from overexertion. Her pace was relentless, but she stared down every challenge, bending it to her will and forging her victories and failures into plates of armor that protected her very being.

Armor that was essential to our plan of seating her on the throne.

She was a delicate bloom intended to distract from the thorns hidden beneath her; thorns those who stood against us would soon have embedded in their bellies.

Before breaking through the treeline outside of Vaenor, we stopped to change clothes and freshen up. The shimmering blue dress Ali made for Izidora was pulled over her hips as I created a shield with the matching blue cloak, her figure hidden from wandering eyes. Endre braided a crown of baby's breath and lily of the valley, the small pinpricks of white in her cascading chestnut hair complementing the shimmering blue fabric that was like liquid over her body.

"I wish Ali could see me now," she murmured.

I kissed her forehead. "I know."

She turned to walk back to the group when I caught her waist and pulled her close. Inhaling her rose and fresh wood scent, I imprinted it on my memory, then kissed her longingly, pouring all my feelings into one last kiss. Her arms circled my neck and she clung as tightly to me as I did to her. That tendril between us vibrated with nervous energy as she pulled away.

"I love you," I whispered, my forehead against hers, my eyes pleading with her to feel the anguish that eclipsed my soul.

"And I love you," she promised, her aquamarine eyes shining with unshed tears. She blinked rapidly, looking up at the tree-tops overhead to prevent them from spilling down her cheeks. I couldn't breathe around the lump in my throat, my heart yanked in every direction as all the possible scenarios ran through my head. I did not drop her hand until we returned to the group who had turned their backs to give us privacy. I helped Izidora onto Mistik, smoothing her skin-tight dress in place once she was seated side-saddle. Walking away to mount Fek was one of the most painful experiences of my life, claws of agony ripping into my heart with each step away from her.

We rode in silence, our time as a lighthearted family gone and replaced with the grimness necessary to handle what lay waiting for us. For Endre, Viktor, and myself, that meant risking our necks to put Izidora on the throne; for Izidora, that meant playing a deadly game without knowing the rules.

My father sat stiffly, his spine straight and chest proud as he led our group to the outskirts of the Night Realm's capital. The first homes dotted the horizon, and Izidora lifted her heart and chin, inviting in the confidence and strength she needed to see her first courtly battle through. Her wings snapped open behind her, the sharp white feathers opening toward the heavens as if they invited the Goddess to look down upon her. Which, if our luck was to be believed, She had.

The roars reached us long before our horses' hooves clopped against the stone bridge that spanned the width of the river around Vaenor. Izidora plastered on a smile so wide that it actually reached her eyes as her people swelled with excitement at the arrival of their lost princess. Her hand waved genially from side to side, as she locked eyes with the Fae lining the road that led straight to the castle. Young and old, peasants and merchants, male and female waited for a glimpse of Izidora's triumphant return. Many threw flowers in the road ahead of us while others shouted words of affirmation to their lost princess. They all cooed over her glittering white wings, stunning in their appearance on the brilliantly sunny day.

She smiled and thanked them, laughing as many males attempted to sing her songs of love and promise. Those songs boiled my blood, and I gripped my reins and clenched my teeth to prevent myself from challenging those who would seek to claim the female I loved.

Our progress to the castle was hindered by the well-wishers who wanted to see their lost princess's beauty and grace for themselves. Many mothers asked Izidora to touch their children, hoping that whatever had saved Izidora would in turn help their own. She obliged many, shaking their hands and stroking the hair of their children from atop Mistik's back. No matter what she did, she did it with her whole heart, and I was awed by her strength of character.

We rounded the last twist in the cobbled street, and at last Este Castle lay before us, its spires reaching to sun itself as raging waves crashed against the cliffs in the distance. An expansive courtyard at the front of the castle was filled with Fae dressed in their finest attire, an erected platform in the dead center holding a lone male, whose beady eyes never left the female riding beside me.

29

IZIDORA

There he was. My father stood atop a raised dais in the middle of the courtyard. I studied him as we approached, not dropping my smile.

Standing in the bright sun, he did not appear sickly. He wasn't tall, but he wasn't short either. His round belly spilled over his pants, and a formal jacket was buttoned over it. Jewels dripped from his body like fat raindrops, a string of rubies inlaid in black squares hanging from his shoulders, and a crown of black metal inlaid with diamonds rested on his head – the Night Crown that would soon be mine. Rings of every gemstone hung on his fingers, and a scabbard at his waist was completely covered in an intricate design. He glittered almost as much as my wings when the sun streamed over him.

He had green eyes so dark they were nearly black and gray hair streaked with an occasional black strand. As we drew closer, the signs of age began to show. His face was splotchy and blood vessels had burst in his nose and eyes, while his hands were spotted and withered. He might have been handsome once, but no longer.

Nausea churned in my belly as we pulled our horses up

before him. As subtly as I could, I inhaled through my nose, needing to steady my ricocheting heart. Tension rolled off Kazimir beside me, and with the Nighthounds surrounding me, I felt as if I were drowning in anxiety. Only Cazius seemed calm in front of us, opening up a path through the waves of fear.

He bowed his head to his king. "Your Majesty, it is my greatest honor to announce that I have found, at last, Princess Izidora Valynor."

Strained seconds passed as we waited for my father to respond. A grin spread across his jowls, the look a mixture of happiness and wickedness.

"High Lord Vaszoly, I never doubted you for a second." His plump hands joined together, a slow, menacing clap that sounded more like a death knell than celebration. It wasn't until the rest of the court hovering around the platform joined in that the sentiment turned positive. As the noise died down, his regard fell over me like a coiled whip poised to strike at the slightest provocation. But I was no longer a victim chained in a cave; I was an insidious bloom, and I was a survivor. He would not hurt me, for survivors were the most dangerous ones of them all, with an undying will to live that surpassed the strength of those who had not suffered.

"My beautiful daughter, come to me so I can embrace you at last," he commanded.

Smoothly dismounting Mistik, I handed my reins to Kazimir and strode toward the dais. My wings fluffed of their own accord, scattering sparks of light all around me as I approached the platform. Dipping into a deep curtsy, I showed my father the king the proper respect, even if my teeth clenched as I looked at the ground.

"Rise," he ordered, and I did, meeting his gaze without blinking. I didn't dare breathe as he left his platform and circled me like a wolf hunting its prey. "You are indeed as beautiful as they say, and you look so much like your mother."

"Thank you, father," I said coolly. He kept some distance between us, his critical gaze and coldness making my heart ache. I was prepared for this side of him, but a small part of me hoped he would express more joy or warmth at my return. Instead, he looked like he was performing for the noble Fae surrounding us.

His indifference served my agenda; putting a knife in his heart would be much easier when I felt nothing but hatred toward him.

He stepped back onto the dais that raised him over the heads of the Fae surrounding us. "My daughter has been found at last!" he roared, and those within range of his voice cheered. "For twenty-one long years, I have been worried to sickness over her. I knew she was out there, somewhere, pining for her father. But today, I feel whole once again! And now, I will get to be the great father I always knew I could be. Come, let's explore Este Castle, brought to its current glory through my efforts!"

I worked to school my expression. *Did he really just make my return all about him?*

He grinned that awful smile again and stepped off the dais in the direction of the castle. "Come daughter, I wish to give you the grand tour."

My skin crawled at the thought of spending time with him alone. Bile rose in my throat, but I swallowed it down as I painted a pleasant expression on my face. "Of course, father."

But I soon discovered we would not go alone. Dozens of courtiers followed along, oohing and aahing as King Zalan boasted about his additions to the castle. Thankfully, Cazius, Kazimir, Endre, and Viktor were at the back of the group, watching closely, or I would have screamed at the idiocy of his sycophants. The Nighthounds were right – these people were power-hungry and willing to break their spines to win any sort of favor.

After seeing what felt like two dozen lavishly decorated drawing rooms, we finally wound up the spiral staircase of the biggest tower toward the Royal Library. My mouth dropped as I stepped from the landing into the mouth of a chamber so large I was certain it would swallow me whole. The warm wood-paneled walls were bathed in soft amber light as the setting sun bounced brilliantly from the arched windows that were placed sporadically throughout the four-story room. Two wrought-iron staircases spiraled to each floor, one on each side of the massive room, rising higher and higher into the stacks of books in concentric circles on each floor.

The space smelled both musty and soothing, like old books and ink with a hint of lavender. A peaceful silence filled the space, and it felt sacrilegious to intrude with our large party. A female behind me muttered, "It's just a library full of books, why is she so excited about it?"

I locked eyes with a busty female who looked to be a few years older than me. She had medium-length black hair and dull green eyes. Her companion was similarly built with choco-late brown hair that spiraled away from her head. Kazimir was beyond them, and he dipped his head in approval as I opened my mouth to respond to her insult.

I needed some sharp words to drive a point. "Because books lead to knowledge, and knowledge is power. Seeing as you are lacking knowledge, I'm assuming you are also lacking power?" I raised an eyebrow at her. Viktor grinned wickedly beside Kazimir.

The black-haired female scoffed and crossed her arms but remained silent. My father moved us further into the library, droning on about the rare volumes he had locked away under the most skillful librarian in all of the realms, hand selected by himself of course. I tuned him out as I drank in the expansive space. The energy of thousands of lives lived in these books, the authors' souls whispering to mine. This was a spot I would definitely return to in the coming days, dragging Kazimir behind me so he could teach me to read the ancient tomes.

Too soon, we exited the library and entered the adjoining tower. This was the astronomy tower, where the most brilliant astronomers to ever grace Északi lived and worked. They too were hand selected by King Zalan. *Imagine that.*

Spiraling toward the earth, we entered a long hallway that led to a ballroom large enough for multiple fully grown dragons to wander about freely. The ceiling held hundreds of crystal chandeliers, each in the shape of one of the night sky's constellations. The gray stone floor was partially covered by thick black rugs, and a dozen fireplaces warmed the room. In front of each fireplace, fur rugs large enough to fit ten people stretched across the floor, and I shuddered to think what the beast looked like before being killed for its skin. To the left, a stage edged half the room, instruments piled along its walls with their owners currently absent. In the middle, a glass cage, not unlike the shower at The Saturn, stood silently with an air of despondency clinging to it, and a stone settled in my gut as we approached it.

"...and this is where we will host the feast in your honor tomorrow night," my father finished saying.

"The space is beautiful," I told him, and it was not a lie, though the words were still bitter rolling across my tongue.

"It is the largest ballroom in all the realms. Whenever I host Béke, the other monarchs always compliment it and admit they wish they had one of this size," he boasted.

His bragging continued as we traversed the space, the cost to build the space, the years that passed while his architects constructed it, the wings he had to add to replace the rooms lost to his grand renovation. Through the double doors on the other side of the room, we took a left and approached those wings, stopping first in the one belonging to the High Houses. I made a mental note of our location in case I needed to find Kazimir, Endre, or Viktor later. The next wing was built for the Lower Houses, whose apartments were smaller in the equally sized space.

Finally, we reached the Royal Wing.

"I had the apartment closest to the edge of the cliff prepared for you. I shouted for my servants the second I received word of your impending arrival and insisted that only the best should adorn the room of my long lost daughter," my father publicized.

Servants swung the doors open, and our entire entourage entered the room. Irritation skittered across my shoulders as they shoved into a space that was meant to be mine, but I said nothing, instead bowing my head in supplication to my father while working my jaw. I explored the space, the females in tow, oohing and aahing at the furs lining the floor, the velvet curtains, the intricately carved four-poster bed large enough for six males, a marble fireplace big enough to roast them in, and the luxurious soaking tub and shower in the ensuite bathroom.

Floor-length windows framed the back of the space, providing an unobstructed view of the roaring ocean below. The waves crashed against the steep cliffs, sending spray in all directions and occasionally dotting the window. In the distance, white sails caught the harsh wind in the open waters, buttery sun reflecting off of them on this cloudless day. Fae cast nets over the side of the ships, hunting for the large fish that lived in the deep ocean. The view was incredible, and the sight of the ocean was one of the most amazing I had ever seen. Its vastness was incomprehensible, glittering blue stretching beyond the horizon into unknown lands beyond.

A tug in my low belly pulled a smile to my lips as Kazimir

approached, his forearm bracing against the glass as he gazed at the sea with me.

"It's breathtaking, isn't it?" he asked.

"Yes," I breathed, at a loss for words.

"Our rooms have a view of the cliffs, too, but nothing this spectacular."

When I returned my attention to our entourage, I caught my father staring at Kazimir and me, his calculating gaze assessing my every movement. Averting my eyes, I darted toward the open closet that was more like a hallway with its depth and breadth. Rows and rows of fabric waiting to be shaped into the finest dresses hung along the rails attached to the stone walls.

"I was hoping you would find that!" my father exclaimed from behind me, making me jump. It took every ounce of willpower to breathe and hold myself together as my heart escaped through my throat. "I bought up all the finest fabrics in Vaenor and had them brought here. Tonight, the cloth weavers from Wings and Darkness will be here to craft whatever you like. My daughter will have the finest custom dresses ever seen in this realm!"

The females gasped, jealousy oozing from their pores. My father shot them a wicked grin. "Now ladies, don't you worry. Some of you will become my daughter's ladiesmaids and you will have to look the part as well. We will see who pleases me the most."

I wanted to throw up over the soft fur rug beneath me. *None of these females were coming near me.* Instead, I plastered another appreciative smile on my face and said, "My king, you have given me more than I ever deserved. I thank you for your generosity."

He preened under my praise for his actions like the peacock he was.

"It is no less than a daughter of mine deserves," he replied. "And we have reached the end of our tour. I will have some servants fetch you some food and wine while you settle in." He motioned for our entourage to depart and noble Fae trickled out of my rooms, bowing and curtsying to my father as they passed him, some complimenting him for his fine taste. Cazius, Viktor, Endre, and Kazimir were the last to depart, the latter catching my eye and sending me strength.

Only my father remained.

Viktor had reminded me before we rode into Vaenor that the Fae who speaks first loses. So I bit my tongue and waited for my father's words. King Zalan strolled to the fireplace, and then to the windows, his hands resting on his rotund belly. After several minutes, he broke the silence. "High Lord Vaszoly treated you well?"

Not a question of where I was, who took me, or what my life had been like up until this point. Not a confession of how much he missed me or how glad he was to finally see me. No, it was a question driving a high-stakes game where everyone's life was on the line.

I opted for a generic answer with enough detail to sound legitimate. "High Lord Cazius's kindness after my rescue knew no bounds. He ensured my safety, even taking me to his family home when my captors pursued us." I emphasized Cazius's name, noting that my father had not specified which Vaszoly in his question. This was a game I wasn't willing to lose.

"Very good," he mused. "I'm sure you will be happy to have female company after so many weeks with those males."

I withheld a grimace. If the female company was from the ones who followed us around like pups begging for scraps, then I would rather spend my time in the barracks adjacent to the courtyard. But I swallowed my true feelings and reminded myself of who was standing before me and what I stood to lose. "I've not spent much time around females, my king, and I would appreciate the opportunity to befriend some."

He tsked, "We have no friends. Only subjects to control. Clearly, you have much to learn about how a kingdom works."

His criticism was a slap to the face, and my inner fire begged me to unleash sharp words in his direction. His judgment was harsh and demeaning, and I fought a mental battle with myself to hold my tongue. The small child still chained in the cave wanted her father to love and approve of her every word; but the female breaking free of those chains wanted armor against those who sought to hurt her.

"I will appreciate any time you spend teaching me the ways of this kingdom," I gritted out.

That seemed to appease him, and he nodded in agreement. "With your return, I feel much more youthful than I have in years. I believe I will still be around for years to come. That should give me plenty of time to decide if you are worthy of the throne."

Worthy of the throne? Was this some sort of contest now? Did I have to perform every single day while he dangled wealth and power in front of my nose, just like he did to the High and Lower Houses? My treasonous thoughts ran wild, and I forced my face neutral, unwilling to lose in my first few hours in the seat of the Night Realm.

"I will do my best," I said flatly, out of energy to deal with his bullshit.

A servant arrived carrying a tray laden with cured meats, cheese, and fruit. He bowed deeply in the doorway before bee-lining to a wood table in the sitting area. Another servant appeared with bottles of wine and glasses, repeating the process until the table was filled with wine and small bites.

My father and I said nothing during the whole process, the tension in the air palpable. He waddled to the table, popped a grape into his mouth, and chewed slowly, his regard sweeping me in a way that made my skin crawl. "The cloth weavers will be here in a few hours. I will see you at dinner."

I curtsied to him, not rising until the entry doors swung closed behind him.

Fucking Fates, that was stressful.

Flopping onto a couch, I yelped and sprang up, so exhausted I had forgotten about my wings. With a weary breath, I banished them, then flopped down again. I reached for one of the uncorked bottles of wine and took a long swig. Fuck a glass, I needed to drink straight from the source. I realized too late that it was champagne, and bubbles flooded my nose and mouth as I choked on the dry liquid. Spluttering and coughing, I leaned over my knees, trying to keep the liquid off my beautiful dress. Tears sprang to my eyes as I continued to clear my airways.

Stifled laughter floated from the doorway. Vadim stood with a young female only slightly taller than me, her straight chocolate brown locks falling to her waist, and her seafoam green eyes shone with amusement. A wide grin splayed across her heart-shaped face, showing off rows of straight white teeth. A blood-red dress cut low in the front hugged her curves and the sheer sleeves displayed her toned arms.

She bounced in my direction, snatching two glasses and the bottle from my hand before plopping next to me on the couch. Vadim followed, sighing like he knew this was going to end badly. She poured two generous helpings, shooting a glare in her brother's direction as he dramatically dropped into a chair beside us.

"I'm Liliana." She handed me a bubbly glass with her introduction.

I grinned, knowing that we were indeed going to be fast friends. "Izidora," I replied.

She clinked her glass with mine. "I know," she laughed, then drained hers in one gulp. I mirrored her, the bubbles sticking firmly to my throat this time.

"Where is my glass, Lil?" Vadim asked.

"You are a grown male and can serve yourself," she scoffed, flicking her hair over her shoulder as she trained her seafoam eyes on me, lips pressed together to contain a bout of laughter. Her expression was enough to burst my bubble, and giggles flooded the air as we fell into laughter together. Vadim rolled his eyes and fetched himself a glass while we attempted to rein in our mirth.

"I went to fetch her after you went off on your grand tour," Vadim drawled. "She couldn't wait to meet you either. I absolve myself of all responsibility for you two." He held his hands up in mock surrender.

"I've heard so much about you," I said to her.

"Only bad things I hope," she winked.

I snickered. "I was warned that together we would bring Este Castle to its knees."

"Do you want to go see the real parts of the castle?" Her eyes held a wicked gleam as she wiggled her eyebrows.

"They are going to kill me." Vadim buried his face in his hands.

"Let's do it," I exclaimed. She giggled and grabbed my hand, pulling me to the door with Vadim hot on our heels, his wine discarded.

"You two cannot go anywhere without me!" he called as we burst into the hall.

My hair whipped behind me as we raced away from Vadim, one hand hiking my dress higher to run freely and the other holding the hand of my friend doing the same. I felt wild and free as we laughed our way through the castle. This was how life was meant to be lived – no games, no tricks, only light and laughter.

The white fire that lived in my chest swelled as my unbridled joy fanned its flames, the crystal shining like an invisible star behind it. Liliana abruptly yanked me to the left, and we slid into an alcove filled with a chaise. She hopped on the red velvet, reaching for a spot on the ceiling above it. Vadim's pounding footsteps grew louder as he caught up to us, curses flying from wall to wall as his steps slowed. Stone ground against stone behind me, revealing a small crack in the otherwise flawless wall. Liliana dug her fingers into the imperfection, widening it inch by inch.

"Let me do it." Vadim elbowed Liliana aside, and slid the hidden door open wide enough for us to pass into a narrow passage, then released the edge, the door closing of its own accord with a dull thud. Liliana threw balls of light in the air to illuminate our path, the orbs bobbing and floating around us as we wound into the belly of the castle.

"Where are we going?" I whispered.

"To the secret lounges. It's where all the young noble Fae hang out to escape the bullshit our parents do every day. Except Vadim no longer counts as a young noble Fae," Liliana teased.

"What matters is how you feel on the inside, and keeping up with you two has reinvigorated my youth," he laughed back.

The passages forked ahead of us, and Liliana confidently took the left route. In a few steps, we were upon another door, and she felt along the wall for another lever. Once she located it, the door cracked open, and Vadim squeezed past to pull it into the hidden pocket in the wall.

"Thanks, brother, you're such a gentlemale." Liliana patted his cheek as she walked past him.

I sniggered as he rolled his eyes, feeling the familial warmth in their teasing. A squat room appeared before us, its inhabitants all young Fae engaged in various activities their families would not appreciate. Some played cards at a round table, piles of gold coins stacked around them, and a few pairs locked lips in a dark corner away from prying eyes. Liliana's bubble lights joined the others floating against the low ceiling, dancing and playing with the other young Fae who cast light in the otherwise pitch-black space.

My shoulders were tight as I realized how trapped I was should that door fail to open again. Before my breath became trapped in my chest, two familiar faces caught my eye, and my relief at seeing my friends won out over my anxiety. "Zekari! Kirigin!" I shouted, running toward them. They looked up from their cards when they heard their names.

Zekari vaulted over the table, knocking a few piles of gold across the wood, then swept me into a hug. Kirigin jogged up a moment later, joining our hug and crushing me between them. "Twin sandwich!" they yelled in unison.

I tried to laugh but all the air was knocked from my lungs as they continued to smash me between them. They let me drop to the floor when I pounded on Zekari's chest. "I'm so glad you both are alright!" I rejoiced once I caught my breath.

"You don't have anything to worry about with us. We can take care of ourselves," Kirigin grinned. "But look at you!" He took my hand and twirled me so my dress sparkled under the floating lights. "You are every bit the princess we knew you would be."

All eyes snapped to me, and my cheeks heated, less visible in the dim light. "Introduce me to everyone?" I asked Liliana as Zekari and Kirigin embraced Vadim.

"Of course," she beamed, dragging me to the couches closest to the card table. The young Fae rose and bowed to me as we approached.

"Please, don't bother with all that," I addressed them. "And you can call me Izidora."

"I'm Mari, House Tozov," the female closest to me introduced

365

herself. The female beside her said, "I'm Viara, House Zalko."

"Nice to meet you both," I smiled at them.

Two males a little further away said, "I'm Luzan, and this is my brother Ivan. We're House Riztok," the taller one said, gesturing to his brother next to him.

"Did you get your knighthood yet, Ivan?" Liliana asked.

He rolled his eyes. "Honestly, Swordmaster Ryzard is a tyrant. I should have had it ages ago, but here we are."

"Ivan needs to stop leaving his left side open. He'd be dead on the battlefield in an hour," Luzan teased.

"I'm baiting people!" Ivan defended.

"I'll believe it when you defend strikes there, brother," Luzan laughed. We fell into easy conversation as I learned about their families, each of them belonging to Lower Houses. Mari was the oldest in her family and had three younger siblings.

"Children are rare, but the Goddess blessed my parents with four," she explained.

"Or they just couldn't keep their hands to themselves," Ivan joked.

"Ew, like no one wants to imagine their parents fucking, Ivan," she retorted.

"Mine only did twice and that was it," he swore, his joke pulling laughter from the group.

"So you hang out here whenever you are at Este Castle?" I asked.

"Pretty much. That way we are out of sight and out of mind. It's safer this way many times," Viara shrugged, and I got the sense that their families weren't the power-hungry type. I immediately liked Mari and Viara; they were both honest and easygoing.

"Shit, what time is it? I need to get back to my rooms before the seamstresses arrive," I said to Liliana.

"We should probably get going then. I don't know what time

it is," she said. We stood and hugged Mari and Viara goodbye.

Vadim had joined the card game, and he grumbled about losing his hand because of us before he opened the passage for me and Liliana. We waved to Zekari and Kirigin, promising to find them later. The three of us raced back to my rooms, finding them empty.

"Thank the Goddess," I said, flopping onto one of the chaises near the fire. We weren't missed. I grabbed another bottle of wine and took a few swigs before passing the bottle to Liliana, who lay next to me. Three sharp raps on the outer door had me sitting up with a groan.

"And that's my cue, you two have fun playing dress up," Vadim teased before opening the door for three females I assumed were the cloth weavers.

Liliana stuck out her tongue. "Catch you later, Vadim."

Vadim surveyed the three females on his way out, his tongue wetting his lips as he looked them up and down appreciatively. Liliana shook her head at her brother's antics. The females regarded him in a similar manner, eliciting a snort from me.

Once the four had finished their perusal of each other, the three females approached Liliana and me, their stylish black dresses sweeping around them as they dipped to the floor.

"I am Ezi, and this is Kari and Riza," the tallest female said. The three looked entirely too similar, with short-cropped black hair and ice-green eyes framed by round faces.

"Are you sisters?" I inquired.

"Yes, Your Highness," Kari, the female in the middle, replied. Her dress revealed her long legs and pointed shoes but swept into a long train behind her.

"Please, call me Princess Izidora," the females seemed to relax with my informality. "Forgive me, this is all very new to me, and I am still learning about the ways of Fae. What do you need me to do?"

"First, I will take your measurements, and Kari and Ezi will sketch designs to show you. Then we will retrieve the fabrics and begin crafting your gowns one by one. I think we should start with the gown you will wear at the feast tomorrow night." Riza laid out the plan, and I admired the cut of her dress, random scraps of sheer fabric draped by lace showing off bits of her creamy skin.

"Thank you, Riza. Where would you like me to stand?" Another knock sounded, and five young males walked in carrying mirrors, a pedestal, and heavy-looking bags.

"Ah, there they are. We have brought everything from our salon to give you the full experience," Ezi stated.

The males constructed a semi-circle of mirrors adjacent to the open doors of my closet, then rolled the pedestal to the middle. Heavy leather bags were piled between the pedestal and a set of easels had been erected facing the stage. A measuring tape floated from an unzipped bag and into Riza's palm as she studied me. "Can you please hop up on the stand?"

Every angle of my body was visible in the mirror arrangement; it was strange to see myself at all, let alone to this degree. Once Riza finished noting my measurements, Liliana appeared at my side, clapping her hands excitedly. "This is going to be so fun. I've always wanted to have the Wings and Darkness experience."

"Why haven't you?" I asked.

"Well, the waitlist for an appointment is like a year long, if you can even afford to pay them for their services. They make the finest gowns in the Night Realm. The fact that they are here on a moment's notice is huge." She threw her head back to emphasize her last word.

My eyebrows shot up my forehead. A year felt like an eternity to me, though for most Fae it was probably not too long; after all, most lived for hundreds of them.

"Thank you for explaining, and thank you Ezi, Kari, and Riza for accommodating me into your busy schedule," I said graciously.

Kari and Ezi stood behind the easels, multicolored pencils spread between them. Their hands moved quickly as they sketched designs, flipping pages over each other as they finished a drawing. Riza pulled fabrics from the depth of my closet, hanging them on a rack to my left. Liliana dragged a pouf behind me and sipped a glass of champagne as she watched the proceedings.

I stepped off the platform to admire the fine fabrics; their vivid colors and rich textures were sensational beneath my palms as I walked the length of the rack. A blood-red fabric caught my eye, its glossy sheen stopping me in my tracks.

"Do you like this one?" Riza asked.

"Yes, the color is so rich," I enthused, pulling the swatch away from its brethren and into the light where I could study the weave.

"The color will compliment your hair and eyes," she noted, lifting the ends of my hair to examine it more closely. She crooked a finger and spun on her heel. "I want to show you a few other fabrics."

A few steps away, a glittering gold fabric jumped out among the pastels, and Riza shoved them aside to reveal the full swatch. "Oh, I love this one as well," I told her, admiring the glint of the fabric against the sun that streamed through the windows behind us.

"I thought you might," she smiled, then silver tendrils lifted a bolt of white fabric from the piles of bags between us and the easels. When it landed in her hand, she unwrapped it, revealing strips of cloth inlaid with white feathers that matched my wings.

My mouth and eyes widened as I looked between the two rolls of fabric, and an idea popped into the back of my mind –

the gilded fabric overlaid with the feathers would fit nicely in with our plans. "How did you make this?"

"Tales of your beautiful white wings spread fast, and my sisters and I knew we had to make a dress to match them," Riza beamed. "We've kept the feathered fabric under wraps until now because we wanted you to be the first to see it."

"It is incredible. Can you put them on the gold fabric?" I asked.

"Wait, I want to see!" Liliana trotted around the rack, eyes popping open at the sight of the white feathers. Her hand brushed the silky material, bringing it against the shimmering gold and assessing. "They're so soft. You have to wear them tomorrow night."

A smile bloomed on Riza's kind face. "I think they would look beautiful together, especially for the feast tomorrow night." Silver snaked from her hands and removed the extravagant fabric, carrying it away to the mirrors.

"Princess, I've finished a sketch for you," Ezi called, and the three of us circled the growing mess to join Ezi at her easel. "How do you like this?"

Liliana's hands covered her involuntary gasp as Ezi turned the sketchbook to us. The gown was glamorous. A bodice was constructed from the glittering gold fabric with a heart-shaped neckline, while two pieces of fabric draped my arms, attached by the finest of points to the bodice, leaving my shoulders bare. The skirt hugged my legs down to the mid-thigh before flaring out in a wide trumpet made entirely of white feathers. This dress showed off my every curve while making a statement that I was here to take up my place in the kingdom. It was feminine and sexy, powerful and regal, everything I needed to be at the feast.

"I love it. What about jewelry? I'm afraid I don't have any, and I'd love to have a crown on my head when I make my first appearance before the Night Realm."

Furious scratching of pencil on paper filled the space behind us. "Come see this," Kari beckoned us to her side. Peering over her shoulder, I gaped at the sketch of my head with a white and gold headdress spiking out in all directions like a halo. Delicate gold chains connected across my temples with a third trailing down my part, meeting on my forehead where a large oval diamond in an intricate setting rested above my brow.

This headdress made me look like a queen.

It was perfect.

The pieces of our plan fell into place with such little effort, it was almost as if we had divine intervention.

The Goddess's Prophecy...

The prophecy had slipped my mind as my focus shifted to our treasonous plot. I wondered if Cazius and Kazimir were scouring the Royal Library as we designed my ensemble. I wanted – needed – answers about my magic, because the more I saw of the Night Realm, the more I was convinced I was different.

This dress and these jewels would make a statement, one that I hoped would set me on the path to the throne. I was not afraid of what was next; only ready to see myself sitting there, power filling my veins and the realm kneeling before me as I gained ultimate control over my life. My people deserved better than my father, and I could give that to them while protecting myself.

"I love it. Let's do it."

Stripping to only my undergarments, I returned to the stand, body tense while my scars were put on display for the whole room.

"Izidora..." Liliana's seafoam eyes shone in the mirror, and I had to lift mine to the ceiling to prevent tears from spilling down my cheeks.

Glasses clinked behind me, and Liliana nudged my side,

handing me a full glass of bubbly wine. Through blurred lashes, I accepted the drink, taking a gulp to steady my nerves for the questions she was sure to ask.

The sisters, to their credit, busied themselves with other tasks while my new friend took my hand and caressed the back of it.

"Vadim mentioned where they found you, but not much else. Do you want to talk about it?"

"Yes. No. I don't know." I shook my head, throat working as I tried to speak around the knot there. With the back of my free hand, I wiped my cheeks and sucked in a shuddering breath. "I was chained in complete darkness for Goddess knows how long. Males guarded me my whole life, and some were kind, though others were not. These scars are from the whips they would use on me for misbehaving or for refusing to give them what they wanted."

The whole room emptied of air as my words hung between us.

"I didn't know what I looked like until we arrived in Zanin. I didn't know my name until Kazimir told me. But something in the back of my mind begged me to hang on, to survive the pain because something waited for me beyond those stone walls. And now I'm here." I choked on the last word, pent up emotions spilling over like an overflowing tub until my face was soaked in salty wetness.

Liliana crushed me against her as I broke apart, dripping tears onto my shoulder. "There is nothing I can say to make it better, Izidora, other than I'm here now and I'm not going anywhere. You don't have to face anything alone again."

Sniffles filled the room, and through blurry eyes, I watched the three sisters drying their eyes too. Riza approached the stand, her magic undulating through her long fingers. "I know I could not have survived what you did, Princess. The fact that you are standing here now is humbling, and it is my greatest honor to craft this dress for you. It will be my finest work, for I have the most beautiful muse."

Validation from Liliana and Riza filled me with a spark of hope for my future. Sharing my story won allies, and I needed as many of those as possible. "Thank you," I croaked, wetting my mouth with wine before handing off my glass to Liliana, who returned to her pouf to watch the magic unfold.

Once Riza began crafting the piece, I understood why the sisters had a long waitlist and people willingly paid loads of coin for their services. The shimmering fabric melted to my body, silver tendrils weaving in and out and around the garment as it formed around me.

Kari rustled around in one of the many large bags, pulling out white and gold metals and chucking them to the floor with a clink. Once she was satisfied with her haul, her magic wrapped around the metals and bent them, forming each piece of the halo that would adorn my hair. The band floated to my head several times as she made adjustments to the fit.

"How are you able to work the metal? I thought only Iron Fae could bend the earth to their will," I asked.

"We are gifted with creative magic, which means we can craft any substance," she explained. "However, we keep our metal crafting a secret because it takes so much energy. But this will be worth it."

"Your secret is safe with me," I promised.

Riza circled me, icy green eyes bouncing up and down the bodice. "Can you take out your wings please, Princess?"

Tapping into my magic was almost second nature now, and my wings burst into existence with ease. The skin around them pinched beneath the fabric, so Riza adjusted the cut lower to accommodate them.

"The stories don't do them justice. This was a great choice

indeed." She leaned forward to admire the bottom feathers closely. Satisfied with the bodice, Riza began working on the skirt, Ezi joining her to meld the feathers to the glittering gold fabric. Soon, the skirt fanned around me in equal distance to my wingspan and I glittered like a precious diamond as the sun dipped lower on the horizon. Liliana's pink cheeks were scrunched under her wide smile, and her excitement filled my stomach with butterflies.

Kari finished her work on the halo, then began crafting the setting for the large diamond.

"Is it possible to weave roses into the pattern?"

A beautiful blossom with hidden thorns.

"Of course, Princess," she said, then altered her shape until the white stone was surrounded by unfolding petals. She plucked the halo from her workstation and attached the blossom to the delicate chains. Turning it over in her shaking hands, she tweaked pieces here and there until she was satisfied with the overall look.

She unplaited my hair, removing the delicate flowers that had been braided into it before our arrival at Este Castle. My hair swept down my back to reveal my neck and collarbones, and I dipped my head to accept the headdress from her delicate hands. She pinned it in place, and when I straightened, I didn't recognize the female who stared back at me in the mirrors.

She was the Goddess reborn. She turned from side to side, the mirrors highlighting every sparkle adorning the glamorous gown and her angelic white wings. The diamond centered on her forehead topped off the look with an ethereal flair. She was every part goddess, queen, and Fae, alluring in her celestial beauty.

Liliana bounced up and down beside me, her seafoam eyes overflowing with excitement. Ezi, Riza, and Kari stepped back to admire their work, soft smiles pulling at the corners of their mouths and shining eyes.

"So, what do you think?" I twirled dramatically, fluttering the trumpet skirt.

"Perfection," Kari breathed.

"You'll have every male tomorrow falling to their knees," Liliana cackled, head thrown back.

It was hard to believe how much I had changed in the past few months. Gone was the untrusting, scared female who was abused and chained in darkness. The female who looked back at me was confident, strong, and powerful, worthy of a gown of such seraphic beauty. But more than that, she was loved. Kazimir searched for me for years, then risked his life to save me, and finally loved me with the purity of the diamond gracing my brow.

After carefully extracting me from the glamorous gown, Kari and Ezi flipped through their other designs, suggesting patterns and colors and cuts that would flatter me. I deferred many decisions to Liliana and the cloth weavers, trusting their judgment over my own. It was dark by the time they finished my new wardrobe.

"Do we have time to make one more?" I asked.

"Certainly, Princess," Ezi stated.

"Liliana, which fabric do you like?" I tried to hide my smile from her, but it was no use.

Her face heated and she stammered, "You are way too kind. I don't need any more dresses."

"Nonsense, I need my ladiesmaid to look as good as I do."

She bolted from the pouf and tackled me in an exuberant embrace, nearly knocking me from the pedestal in the process. "Do you mean it?"

"Absolutely. I can't think of a better person to have by my side," I swore.

The three sisters observed our joy with soft smiles on their faces; we'd had quite the emotional ride since they walked through the door. "I think this would look lovely on you." Riza pulled a shimmering nude fabric off the rack. It would subtly match my dress the next day at the feast, showing our alliance.

Flopping against the pouf, I released a heavy sigh, my back thanking me for the support as I sank into its embrace. Liliana stepped atop the pedestal, remaining motionless as Riza and Ezi crafted the fabric. The glittering nude dress was completely backless, two long thin straps disappearing over her shoulder and attaching to the scooped neck on the front of her gown. The front molded with her body, the skirt flaring low on her hips before trailing behind her, and a long slit reaching up her left thigh.

"You look amazing!" I exclaimed when Riza and Ezi stepped back, their work complete. Liliana grinned from ear to ear, and I bounced to her side to examine the gown up close.

Vadim knocked on the door, his heavy footsteps encroaching on our space until he spied his sister on the platform. "No way are you going anywhere in that," he swore.

My lips curled over a snort, but when Liliana and I locked eyes in the mirror, we fell apart, her head thrown back in an unguarded laugh and my shoulders shaking around my giggles.

"Quit being such a fun sucker," Liliana retorted. "Plus, you should see what Izidora will be wearing. Kazimir will carry her out of there faster than you after you get discovered by your lover's husband."

"Who told you about that?" Vadim demanded.

"I have my ways," she flicked her wrist dismissively. Tears spilled down my cheeks as they bickered, unable to breathe from laughing so hard.

Ezi, Kari, and Riza finished packing their supplies and sent for servants to fetch their equipment. I thanked them individually, glad to have spent time with these fascinating females.

"Let's get to dinner, shall we?" Vadim said after the sisters departed.

My stomach rumbled in response.

With a snicker, he held out his arms, and Liliana and I each grasped one side, allowing him to escort us through the castle. He led us down a familiar hall, and when we rounded the corner, I spotted a small dining room from early in my castle tour. The Nighthounds milled about, speaking with one another and other members of court. When Kazimir saw me, that familiar rope settled around us, tightening around my waist as I unconsciously dropped Vadim's arm and walked to the male I loved.

"Hi," I breathed.

"Hi, yourself." His rough hand found mine and brought it to his lips, planting a featherlight kiss there. "I see you met Liliana," he observed with a wry grin.

"Yes, we've had quite a lot of fun today," I said as she and Vadim approached us.

"From the look on Vadim's face, I can only imagine," he chuckled.

"Nice to see you again, High Lord Kazimir," she said warmly.

"Lady Liliana, always a pleasure." He inclined his head to her.

"What are we waiting for?" I inquired.

"King Zalan. He is the first to enter the dining room. Then the High Houses, then the Lower Houses. Dinner starts when he arrives," Vadim answered.

"So how do you know when to show up?" I quipped.

"We try to arrive about thirty minutes before eight, when dinner is slated, and hope King Zalan shows before eight-thirty," Vadim shrugged. My brows climbed my forehead.

Fae waited for up to an hour for my father to arrive? That was ludicrous and disrespectful to his subjects.

Endre and Viktor sauntered up through a narrow passage in the crowd outside the dining room doors. They inclined their heads to Liliana and me as they joined our circle. Endre stared at Liliana a little too long, then swallowed and averted his gaze. My earlier suspicions were correct – he liked her. I smiled to myself and planned to ask him for details later.

Armored footsteps echoed down the stone hallway, and the crowd fell silent and split like a knife had been sliced into a cake to allow the soldiers to pass. In the center of the heavily armed guards was my father, King Zalan. The company faced the doors, then the two at the front grasped the handles and threw the double doors wide.

King Zalan glanced around. "Where is my daughter? She shall walk with me."

Fuck. I groaned internally as I stepped away from my friends. "I am here, my king." I couldn't stand to refer to him as father as I learned more and more of the bullshit he shoveled over everyone around him.

His guard parted as I approached, and I curtsied to him, as was required. He held out his arm formally, and I grimaced as I hovered my hand over it, barely able to touch him. My body seized up as it felt under threat, and it took every ounce of my willpower to breathe through my nose and school my features instead of unleashing the scream that wanted to escape from my throat. With no other acknowledgement, he led us into the large dining hall.

Three tables lined the space, parallel to one another, and at the furthest table sat an elaborate chair in the center, taking up enough space for two. My father approached it, dropping his arm as two servants pulled out the heavy chair for him. He dropped into it lazily, then one of the servants pulled out the one to his left for me. I perched on the edge of my seat, too tense to recline like the male next to me.

The formality of the event felt like a performance, each noble playing their part in pleasing their king. The High Houses filed in, taking residence in the seats around us, while the Lower Houses filled the two tables beyond us. I assessed the arrangement, analyzing why my father had chosen to sit here rather than at the place of honor at the head of the table. From this angle, we could see everything – where everyone sat, who they spoke to, and what they ate or drank. He was in control, and no one had any privacy. Cold trickled down my spine at the realization.

A servant approached, bowing low until King Zalan released him. "What would you like to drink tonight, Your Majesty?"

"I will drink whiskey, and my daughter will have wine," he stated. My hands fisted in my dress as the male ordered for me, taking away my choice. I'd had enough of that to last a thousand lifetimes.

The servant made a note, then covered the rest of the High House table. I glanced around the room, seeking out my friends. Endre and Viktor's families were off to my left while Kazimir and Cazius were at the opposite end of the table. Beyond our table, Liliana and Vadim sat with their parents at the table closest to us, chatting with Viara, Mari, Ivan, and Luzan's families. Too many unfamiliar faces stared blatantly at me, and each time I caught a stare, I plastered a soft smile across my mouth.

Out of the corner of my eye, I spotted the females who tried to belittle me in the library seated to my right. The dark-haired one stared longingly at Kazimir, and I had to restrain my lips from baring my teeth at her. Her curly-haired friend whispered behind her hand, eliciting a giggle from the dark-haired one as their attention fell over me. I crinkled my nose and looked away, not deigning to provide them an ounce of my energy.

My wine arrived, and I swigged the dark liquid, hints of berries and spice coating my tongue. My father hadn't addressed me once since we'd arrived. Drumming my fingers on my leg, I decided to make polite conversation with the Fae around me.

"What is your house?" I asked the female to my left.

"She is Malina of House of Valintin," the older male across from me answered for her. "I am High Lord Tomaz Valintin, and this is my son High Lord Alekzi."

"Pleased to meet you all." I was not pleased, especially as Alekzi's attention rested a little too long on my chest.

Viktor lifted his glass to his lips, making a slice across his neck that screamed *don't trust these Fae*. I subtly acknowledged him. We had to tread a fine line with our plans.

"How was your trip to Este Castle?" Malina asked politely.

"Lovely, I enjoyed seeing so much of the kingdom. It was everything I imagined it would be and more." I turned up my charm. "Where is your family home?"

"Not far from here. We were recently gifted a new estate about a day's ride from Vaenor. Your father is a wise and benevolent king," High Lord Tomaz flattered my father, raising his glass in thanks in his direction.

My father accepted the praise with the grace of someone who thought much too highly of himself. "One must know when to reward and when to punish as ruler. My daughter, you will soon learn who is loyal and who is not. Those who are loyal reap the benefits."

My opinion on who was loyal and who was not differed greatly from King Zalan's. "Is it situated along the coast?" I inquired.

"My room has a lovely view of the ocean. We even have a small beach you can fly down to. I would love to show you sometime." Alekzi's hazy green eyes dilated with sinister delight with his insinuation.

Bile rose in my throat as I read between the lines of that statement. Endre and Viktor did the same and stiffened without looking our way. "I have heard the beaches near here can get crowded during the summer. Perhaps all the High Houses will have to gather for a more private beach experience."

The food arrived, saving me from any further awkward encounters. A massive roasted boar carried by four Fae was placed before my father, almost blocking his view of the room. The boar's face was still intact and it stared right at me with dead eyes. Whether the animal's dead eyes or Alekzi's wandering ones made me more uncomfortable, I was not certain. I shifted in my seat and glanced at Endre, whose lips were pursed in a thin line. My father's chair scraped back and he leaned across the expanse, his thick belly nearly sending his glass spilling across the table, and carved the beast.

He sent the best cuts to select families around the tables, and I made note of their faces – more likely foes than friends. My serving was next, and he piled slices on my plate as I cringed away from his middle, before delegating the rest of the work to the servants.

No one touched their food during the entire process, which took many minutes. When the servants finished delivering meat around the room, they took the boar and its head with them. King Zalan lifted his glass, and I fisted my skirts, waiting for his lips to part. "My subjects, I am so pleased my daughter has returned to me. Tonight we eat well, but tomorrow we shall feast as the lost princess has finally returned!"

"All hail King Zalan!" came the resounding reply.

The level of worship my father required was sickening, and far more than anyone should receive.

Cutlery clinked as our dinner companions dug into the food in front of them. I scooped some venison and squash onto my plate, covering the venison in an aioli sauce. Chewing the gamey meat slowly, I observed the interactions around me. I needed to know the players in this game better than I knew myself. High Lord Tomaz prattled away with my father, and the male beside him, High Lord Luzak, joined in the conversation after dabbing his lips with a bright white napkin. Cazius leaned forward on his elbows, listening to the conversation, but his eyes were pinched in the corners and the edges of his mouth dipped in a frown.

No one bothered to engage me in conversation – even Alezki, who seemed fixated on adding value to his father's conversation, only to be dismissed at every turn. I pressed my lips together as our plates were cleared, and the young male slumped into his chair, arms crossed.

Silver platters lined with cookies were brought around, and I selected a large cookie topped with whipped icing and sprinkles in a star-shaped pattern. My teeth sank into the decadent dessert, the sweet icing hitting my tongue first, followed by the subtle hints of cinnamon from the crumbly cookie. It was gone in two more bites, and I politely dabbed my mouth with a napkin afterward, only to feel the burning stares of Fae around me. The cookies on the plates around me only had a bite or two taken from their round shapes.

Was I not supposed to eat it all?

Endre and Viktor hid their faces with their hands as I caught on to the trend. This was the stupidest rule, and the first I would change when I became queen. The Night Fae deserved better than the nonsensical ruler currently occupying the seat beside me.

Filled with confidence and fueled by indignation, I clinked my knife lightly against my wine to get the room's attention. "I want to thank King Zalan for this incredible meal. His generosity with me upon our first day together has known no bounds. I am grateful for the opportunity to dine with you all as well. I have never eaten such good food in my life, and I am particularly fond of sweets now that I can eat on my own terms. Please enjoy your cookies in my honor tonight." My jab was subtle when I wanted to land a knockout punch, but I could not reveal my strategy on the first day. "King Zalan also had the great idea of surrounding me with ladiesmaids. His wisdom and sound advice have helped me select my first, Lady Liliana Arzeni." I lifted my glass to her, but my father's broke beside me, sending shards scattering across his plate and into his dessert.

This was my first move in a dangerous game of chess; I undermined him, but the way I did it was framed in a way he couldn't refute. His chair dragged against the floor like the scraping of my chains as I crawled away from my assailants – too slow and with great malice.

"My daughter has good taste. She must get that from me," he chuckled, but the sound was hollow.

I plastered on a smile so sweet that it put my cookie to shame.

"To King Zalan," I toasted.

"To King Zalan!" Everyone cheered.

The thrum of my heart was erratic as I threw back the rest of my wine and used the glass to cover my lips so I could take a breath. Tension rolled off my father, sending cold sweat down my spine for the remainder of our meal. My anxiety rose with each passing minute, and I prayed dinner would be over soon.

A white napkin slammed over white frosting sprinkled with glass, and my father announced his departure. His guards shoved off the wall behind us, surrounding him like a swarm of bees and ferrying him into the hall. He left me where I was without a word, the insult reading clear as day.

I took my cue to exit, walking slowly in hopes my friends would catch up to me. Liliana bounded to my side, followed by the Nighthounds, and we hurried to my rooms before anyone spotted us. The moment we were safely inside, I turned the lock, then dragged a heavy marble stand holding an expensive-looking vase in front of the door – an alarm should anyone enter the chambers.

"Remind me to teach you how to magically lock them," Kazimir said as he kissed me lightly on the forehead.

His absence during the day had been like a profound stab in my soul. For the first time since my rescue, I had gone nearly a day without his constant attention. Since we were reunited, I melted into his embrace, wrapping my arms around his waist and sighing into his chest. He scooped me up and carried me close to the fire, where we nestled in an oversize pouf.

"Where are Kriztof, Zekari, and Kirigin? I didn't see them in the dining hall." Kazimir's hands massaged my shoulders, releasing the tension stored there in addition to a groan.

"They are Knights, so they get certain status, but not enough to join us at regular dinners. They will join us tomorrow for the feast, though," Kazimir explained.

"No need to worry about them. They can take care of themselves," Vadim reassured.

"I can't help it," I admitted. "I care about you all and it would kill me if anything happened to you."

"That's what love is. But you have to take care of yourself right now. You can't help anyone unless you are taken care of first," Kazimir soothed, then put his lips to my ear. "The fact that you care so deeply is the sign of a good monarch."

"Can we tell Liliana and Vadim?" I whispered back.

His scruff brushed my cheek. "Let me tell them." He crooked a finger at our group, and they gathered closer until we were shoulder to shoulder and heads ducked together. "We want to put Izidora on the throne."

Vadim released a low string of colorful curses. "We?"

"Endre, Viktor, and myself have been working on it. Are you with us?"

"Fuck, yes," Liliana breathed, squeezing my hand.

"You planned this without me? Vadim's voice cracked on the last word, unable to hide his hurt.

Viktor leaned forward, placing a steady hand on Vadim's shoulder. "We didn't want anything to happen to you, should our plan have been discovered."

Vadim shrugged off Viktor's hand, then narrowed his eyes at the male. "I'd rather die with you than be kept in the dark. We're the Nighthounds, and we stick together."

"You're right, brother. We should have included you in our plans," Endre said softly. "Will you help us now?"

Vadim scratched his beard, then with a sigh, asked, "What do you need from me?"

"Help us win support from the Lower Houses, but do not breathe a word of this outside this huddle," Viktor hissed.

Liliana threw her hand in the middle of our circle, joined a moment later by Endre, until one by one our hands joined in the center, Vadim laying his on top of the rest. Tears threatened to fall from my eyes as we swore to a pact that might end with all of our heads on spikes. "I couldn't do this without you."

"No, you couldn't. We are a team, and it takes a team to bear the weight of all of this. That's why we can be so effective – because we are all here for each other," Kazimir swore.

Heaving out a breath, I dried my eyes. "Now that we got that out of the way, who wants to explore these massive rooms?"

"I'm game!" Liliana jumped up first. "Let's play hide and seek. Then if you decide to hide from the world we will all know where to find you."

I laughed, "That's going to suck if I really don't want to be found."

"I'll count first. You all have until 100 before I come looking." She faced the fireplace as we scrambled to our feet and raced in all directions. Endre and I reached the curtains simultaneously, momentarily fighting over who would get to hide there. He won, and I darted into my bedroom in search of another spot.

The canopy above my bed looked like it was thick enough fabric to hold my weight. I scrambled onto the bed, scurried up a pole, and stuck a foot onto the canopy, testing if it would hold my weight. It held as I put more pressure, so I slid my legs toward the center and rested my head near the edge so I could peek over the top.

"... Ninety-eight, ninety-nine, one hundred. Here I come!" Liliana shouted. I covered my mouth with my hand, trying to stay silent. It felt so childish, all of us running and hiding, but it was also exactly the type of lightness I needed to feel better at the moment.

Liliana strode into my bedroom, making a beeline to the bathroom. "Found you!" she exclaimed.

Vadim swore, "Why did you have to find me first?"

"Because you always hide in the bathtub. So predictable. And you call yourself a warrior."

He scrambled out of the tub with a huff, trailing her into my bedroom. I held my breath as she checked under the bed and then opened the closet door. She walked through, and a muffled "Aha!" emerged along with a sheepish Viktor.

"I was hoping to disappear in the fabrics," he laughed.

"You need better camouflage," she snorted.

They pushed through to the other closet door, the faint creak reaching my sensitive ears as they returned to the sitting room. Curtains rustled like leaves in the autumn wind as Liliana searched for the others. It was only a matter of time before she found Endre.

Her shriek was followed by the cackling of males. "Don't scare me like that!" she squeaked, and a resounding thump landed out of my line of sight, but I had to assume she smacked Endre's chest.

That left only Kazimir and me.

I stifled my laughter so as not to be discovered. Minutes passed as they continued their search, bouncing from room to room with no sign of Kazimir. My nose started to itch, and I felt a sneeze rising from the depths of my chest. I tried to shove it down, but it burst from me regardless of my wishes.

"Achoo!" I sneezed, and the bed shook with the force of it. Footsteps pounded closer until my friends stood with hands on hips in front of me.

"How did you even get up there?" Liliana teased.

"Carefully," I confirmed, sliding down the pole to meet them on the ground.

"Okay, Kazimir, you win! You can come out now," Liliana shouted.

But Kazimir did not appear or call out for us. I furrowed my brow, scanning my room before following Liliana into the sitting room. My face began to tingle as thoughts of someone snatching him without our knowledge flooded my brain. Frantically, I ran through the closet, tearing fabric down in my wake.

"Izidora!" His deep voice yelled from my bedroom. I sprinted my way through the closet and burst through the dresses, almost knocking him over as I wrapped him in a hug.

"Please don't scare me like that," I begged.

His head rested on top of mine. "I didn't mean to scare you. But look what I found." He motioned behind him, where another secret passage lay open.

"Woah, how did you find that? And where does it go?" Viktor asked.

Kazimir shrugged. "I tripped and caught myself on the wall. Then this opened."

"So where does it go?" I repeated the question.

"It connects to the other passages hidden in the walls. I didn't explore too far, but I never knew some passages led to the Royal Wing. They must have been installed in case of emergency. The good news is, one branch leads to the High House wing. I need to figure out exactly where it comes out, but it should help us meet more secretly if needed," he finished.

Viktor clapped him on the shoulder. "This is brilliant, brother."

I was excited, too. The knowledge that I could secretly move about if I needed or wanted to lifted the trapped feeling from my body. "Will you show me the branch to take now?"

"Follow me," Kazimir motioned. We filed after him in a single line, the passage barely wide enough to accommodate the broad-shouldered males around me. We threw up bubble lights to brighten our path, and after about five minutes we arrived at a hub with spokes branching off in every direction. They all looked the same, and I scanned the area, hoping for a sign as to how to navigate. Kazimir selected the spoke two to the right, leading us down another narrow passage before arriving at a fork.

"I believe the left leads to the Lower House wing, and the right to the High House wing," he whispered. On my right, the passage abruptly broke left after a few paces. The left side trailed off into the distance, and I was unable to see much beyond the darkness.

We reversed our direction. When the spoke opened up in front of us again, Viktor whispered, "Two to the left?"

"Yes," Kazimir hissed.

Minutes later, we saw the light and spilled into my bedroom.

"Where did you touch?" I asked.

"Here, just beside this painting." The door clicked open again when I placed my hand along the smooth surface. I seared the image of its location in my brain, a safety step necessary for me to stay sane in this room.

"It's getting late, we should probably go before it gets suspicious," Endre pointed out.

I was loath to see my friends go, but he was right. Liliana and Vadim departed first as their parents' apartment was the farthest from my rooms. Endre watched them until they were out of sight, then motioned for Viktor to scurry away. My heart broke as I realized Kazimir was leaving too. This would be the first night I spent without him in weeks, and I couldn't bear the thought of sleeping without him.

"Don't go," I begged, eyes burning as I tugged on his arm. My body tingled as panic sank its claws into me, tearing air from my chest and ripping tears from my eyes. "I can't... I'm scared... I need..."

He pulled me into his chest. "Shh, everything will be alright. Endre and I will go together, and then I will try to find my way back through the passage, okay?"

"Okay," I said weakly, my lungs not filling with nearly enough air.

"I love you," he whispered against my hair.

"And I love you," I whispered into his chest.

Kazimir did not break eye contact until the doors closed behind them. I rearranged my makeshift security system, then went to my room, closing that door too. The desk chair was shoved beneath the handle, preventing anyone from opening it from the outside.

Hiccuping, I stripped out of my gown in my closet and searched for soft leggings and a tunic to wear while I waited for Kazimir to return. I ripped some fabric from another tunic, tying it around the door handle on the living room side and securing it to one of the dressers in the closet. No one would get to me without me knowing.

I snuggled into the unfamiliar bed, straining my ears for a click in the wall that indicated my beloved male's return.

30

KAZIMIR

Leaving Izidora hysterical in her room tore me to shreds. My soul screamed at me to stay and protect her, to save her at all costs. She needed me more than anything, and I left her. Endre's firm grip on my arm was the only source of grounding as he dragged me to the High House wing. Our family's apartments were adjacent on the first floor, so no one saw us as we slipped into mine.

My father stared absentmindedly into the hearth with a glass of wine in hand. The purple liquid swirled in a hypnotizing circle, the dancing flames reflecting across the crystal glass. Endre marched me to the couch and planted me there, breaking my father from his reverie.

"What happened?" my father asked, looking between us.

"Izidora had a panic attack right before we left. She didn't want to be alone," Endre explained as I buried my fingers in my hair.

My father's aged hand steadied my shoulder. "Is it difficult for you to leave her when she is upset?"

I nodded, fighting an internal battle to remain seated rather than tear the castle apart to get to her. My forearms bunched and corded and my whole body vibrated with the force of my efforts to remain seated. Endre quietly exited the apartment, returning moments later with Viktor.

"I promised I would find a way back to her," I choked out.

Viktor understood what I meant immediately. He jerked his head to Endre, motioning for him to follow. "We will find it and be back," he promised.

Once the door shut behind them, a heavy sigh escaped my father's lips. "I looked all afternoon for information regarding the prophecy. The head librarian and I scoured texts both new and old for any sign. We found books where information had been, but the pages were ripped out or burned. It was like someone did not want the information to be discovered again."

"Who would do that?" I croaked, grateful to my father for the distraction from the situation at hand.

"Someone who stands to benefit from that information. But we don't know when these pages were taken or burned. The librarians don't have any memory of anyone inquiring about it. It could have been before Izidora was born or as recently as this week. Though they would have needed to know where the information was prior to this week, because it was difficult to track down the tomes." My father pinched his brow between his fingers.

"That makes before Izidora was born more likely," I stated. "Fucking Fates, what if that is why Izidora was taken in the first place?"

"Then whoever it was had more knowledge than we do now. There must be something in the prophecy that would tip them off..." my father trailed off.

"What do we know about Izidora now that could have been apparent before she was born?" I pressed.

My father shook his head. "That I do not know. It is hard to know anything about a child before they are born, save for the approximate time they were conceived and the approximate time they will be born."

"What about Queen Liessa? Could it have been something about her?" I was frantic as my protective instincts surged like a tidal wave from the depths of my belly and crashed into my chest.

"Breathe, my son. You cannot think straight if your head is not clear," he commanded.

My nostrils flared as I tried to inflate my lungs, but they were crushed under the pressure of the ocean drowning me.

"What do you know about mates, Kazimir?"

"Only that they are rare and everyone desires one," I gritted out.

"As you know, King Airre and Queen Immonen of the Crystal Realm are mated. King Airre saved Queen Immonen from an avalanche when he was surveying a melting glacier seventy years ago. They did not accept their mating bond for ten years after that because King Airre was promised to another. The two tried to deny their bond for ten years because they did not believe they were chosen to be mated. King Airre always found an excuse to postpone his nuptials, and after the tenth excuse, his betrothed broke their engagement because she knew he was mated to Queen Immonen, even though he himself was blind to it," my father elaborated.

I blinked a few times, failing to see how this was relevant.

"Anyway, they both realized what they had been denying and accepted the bond. Once it snapped into place, they both felt great relief. The people accepted Queen Immonen immediately after they announced they had been mated. Not long after that, they married and she was crowned queen. Everyone in the Crystal Realm was happy their love succeeded."

"What does the Crystal Realm have to do with Izidora?" I asked flatly.

My father opened his mouth to respond, but Viktor and Endre burst into the room, the door nearly banging against the wall before Endre caught it.

I jumped to my feet, ready to race to Izidora's side. "What happened?" I demanded.

Viktor spoke first. "We found the right passageways, but we also found another that leads to the harem. We heard King Zalan in there, speaking to someone."

That piqued my interest.

"He was talking about Izidora," Endre wheezed.

"What about her?" I clenched and unclenched my fists, freeing some of the agitation that threatened to cascade over me.

"He said that she was undermining him to take his crown, that the prophecy was going to come to pass despite their efforts, that they needed to make a new plan if they wanted to stop it," Viktor panted.

"So he knew, this whole time?" My vision slipped into red, and images of me strangling the aged king were all I saw.

My father's hands clasped in front of his mouth as he was stunned to silence.

"That's what it sounds like. We didn't hear the other person speak though," Viktor added.

"Why not? Why didn't you listen longer?" I interrogated.

"I sneezed. This damn castle and all its mold, " Endre cursed.

"We sprinted back here after that," Viktor confirmed.

This changed everything. King Zalan was more dangerous than we presumed, and he was planning something new to keep his throne. *A desperate man is a dangerous man.*

"Can you take me to Izidora? Someone needs to be with her at all times. We don't know what King Zalan could be planning," I warned.

"We will, but first we need to devise a plan," Endre promised, looking to Viktor to produce one.

"First, we need to get one of King Zalan's guards in our pocket. He doesn't take a shit without them there, that paranoid fuck. They will know who he has spoken to about this, even if they aren't familiar with the actual plan," Viktor swore.

"Ask Kriztof or the twins to find some leverage on one of them, they are the ones with the most access," my father instructed.

"And tell them to get themselves assigned to the Royal Wing's guard rotation," I added.

"We should learn the passages better, clearly there is a larger network than we are aware of currently. That might help us in the event of an escape," Endre suggested.

"We need to get Izidora in the public eye every day, so if she turns up missing the people will wonder what happened. Though she is already very popular thanks to..." Viktor trailed off, stopping himself before he admitted our plan to my father. We all knew when we swore an oath to her that that was a step toward this eventuality. That oath put us on this road and there was no turning back now.

"She needs to know all of this. Keeping her in the dark is not going to help her. I will protect her above all else," I hissed. "Any other ideas?"

"Just an observation. If you make your relationship with Izidora known, you will become a target too. Anyone will have to go through you to get to her. Think before you act," Endre cautioned.

"All the more reason to make it known," I growled.

"You know, I actually agree with this one. You are popular with the people, and if they see the two of you together it will send a positive message," Viktor concluded.

"But it will draw a clear line in the sand with King Zalan," my father warned. "We need to be prepared to react quickly should the need arise."

"We already have a plan," I admitted, finding my knuckles more interesting than the male who had given me life.

"I see." My father's lips pressed into a thin line. We did not need to say more. When I returned my gaze to him, the wrinkle between his brows looked like a chasm. He looked older than I'd ever seen him, as if the weight of everything spinning out around us was aging him years every second. I had been so concerned with my own emotional battle that I forgot to check in with him about his. It was my turn to kneel in front of him, putting my hand on his shoulder to steady him.

"Are you alright, father?" I nudged.

"Just missing your mother a little extra at the moment. She would be so proud of you." His sad emerald eyes sparkled at her memory.

I pulled him in for a tight hug, conveying my love for him in our embrace. "Do you need anything before we go?"

He waved me off. "No. Please stay safe. All of you." He looked pointedly at Viktor and Endre.

With one last look through the crack in the door, I left my father behind with his wine and notebook. The three of us padded to the end of the hall on silent feet, not wanting to draw the attention of the other High Houses that slept on this floor. Viktor pressed a brick near the corner of the end wall, and a door swung inward with a soft whoosh, revealing an extremely narrow passage beyond. With our large frames, we had to side-step to enter the passageway, my chest scraping occasionally against the rough walls. Viktor checked left and right one last time before closing the door behind him.

I shuffled after Endre, cursing the coffin walls as I went. When we broke into a larger passage, it felt like bursting from a grave into the open skies. Glancing behind me, I could barely make out the slip we emerged from; one would miss it if they didn't know what to look for. The network of passages in this castle was like being caught in a spider's web, with the tangled lines designed to trap an unwitting intruder.

Walking downhill, then uphill, turning left, then right, we traversed the maze of darkness, barely lit by our floating spheres. It reminded me too much of the cave where I saved Izidora. We hit a dead end, and I almost broke our silence to curse our bad luck. Endre shimmied between the dead end and the wall to our left, a hint of an opening barely revealed by his half-disappeared form. Whoever built these passages had been clever in their design.

This sliver of space was cleared in only a few side steps, another section of the maze revealed when we spilled into a wide passage. A dozen steps later, the spoke from our earlier trek in darkness appeared. That familiar tug pulled me left, and I rushed past Endre, knowing Izidora was waiting just down that passage.

We dead ended at Izidora's room, and I lightly rapped on the wall separating us. A shuffle preceded a crack of light, and with a little too much force, I threw the door to the side to reveal swollen aquamarine eyes.

"You came back," she whispered, then jumped into my arms. My galloping heart slowed to a trot when our skin made contact, and my nose found her chestnut locks, inhaling her floral scent. Viktor closed the door behind us, then put his ear to the door separating us from the sitting room. Izidora lifted her face from its burial site in my chest. "No one is here besides me. I set up my vase thing after you left and then shut myself in tight here."

"I'm so proud of you and your ingenuity." I tapped her on the nose.

"You forgot to teach me the locking magic," she pouted.

Shit, I did.

"I'll teach you before we go to sleep," I promised. "But right now we need to talk to you."

She furrowed her brow. "Did something happen?"

"Sit down and we will talk about it."

She nestled among a pile of pillows like a sparrow, and I kicked off my boots to join her on the massive bed. Viktor and Endre followed suit, Endre laying on his side and Viktor sitting cross-legged facing us.

"We overheard your father talking to someone about you," Viktor began.

Izidora's tiny fingers drummed across the pillow in front of her, the soft patters increasing in tempo as she waited for the axe to fall.

"He was speaking with someone – we don't know who because we didn't see or hear them – about how you were trying to undermine him and take his throne. He said that their original plan failed, and they needed to create a new one to stop the prophecy from coming true," he continued.

"He knows about the prophecy?" She pushed herself upright with eyes as wide as saucers.

Rubbing my hand over her shoulder, I relayed what my father told me. "It seems so. My father spent all afternoon searching the library for a mention of it. He found many books with pages missing or burned that once contained information about the prophecy."

"Holy fucking fuck," she cursed.

That about summed up my feelings on the matter. I dropped my voice, low enough that she could hear me but no one trying to listen in could. Viktor and Endre scooted closer, and we put our heads together, forming a barrier to the outside world.

"So, we talked to him, and we have a few plans we need to share with you. Our timeline needs to accelerate, but let us handle *that* part, okay?"

She nodded.

"We want you to make a public appearance, every day, from

now until our plans are complete. You're already doing a great job endearing yourself to the Night Realm. Continue it so you will be missed if something happens," Viktor explained.

"And I want to go with you. I want to show the world we are a united front," I added.

She narrowed her eyes as she assessed me. "So we would be public about our relationship? Didn't we discuss that not being a good idea before? Because of all the scheming at court?"

"We did, but we need to switch tactics. If your father is planning something, it will make his planning a lot more difficult if I am involved. They will have to go through me to get to you, and there aren't many who are brave enough to take me on." The smirk that pulled at my lips was sinister, and I welcomed any challenge to my claim. It would only show Izidora that I was the right one for her, the one who deserved to rule this realm with her. I saved her once, and I would continue to be her hero until I took my last breath.

She looked at the velvet canopy sheltering us from the impending storm. "You should see my dress for the feast tomorrow night. It will send a statement to the whole realm, but especially my father." Her bright blue eyes leveled on the three of us. "I think daily public appearances will help our cause, but I have one condition. I want all of us to go. I want them to see more High Lords and Ladies and Knights interacting with them, so we can build a stronger foundation to launch from."

"We will make it happen," I promised. Endre and Viktor dipped their chins in turn.

"Now, let me show you how to use your magic to seal these doors." Sweeping under her arms, I carried her off the bed, leaving a trail of amusement in my wake. Viktor and Endre excused themselves, promising to check in with my father one last time before they retired for the night.

It was late, and it had been a draining day. Izidora swayed on her feet as she sealed each door in her apartment with a pop. Her eyes were hollow as we returned to the oversized bed. I stripped her out of her clothes, then piled blankets over her and framed her body with pillows. She deserved every bit of my care and more with all that I asked of her. Working my way in behind her, I draped my arm over her stomach and pulled her flush with my chest, creating a refuge for the female who held my heart.

I fell into a dream of Izidora and I on the throne, ruling with level heads and fairness, and saving the Night Realm from King Zalan's crazed whims.

31

IZIDORA

A male stalked toward me from the shadows, his bloodthirsty glare pinning me in place. No chains held me as I scooted back, yet fear gripped me all the same. He was hauntingly beautiful, and the pale light highlighted every angle of his tortured face. Membranous wings protruded from his back, their massive span blocking out all light as he stood over me. A dripping sword scraped along the ground, leaving a garnet trail in his wake. The onyx-tipped pommel brushed against his sternum, and the tip bled red. Wickedness encased his grin, and my body turned sluggish as if I tried to run away underwater. In two steps, he straddled my half-prone form, blade soaring higher before white light burst around us and—

My eyes burst open only to be blinded by the waking sun. Gauzy curtains did nothing to block out the light glittering off the raging ocean beyond the wall of windows that separated us. I thanked the sun for waking me from yet another deadly nightmare – I had yet to die in one, but it was only a matter of time. I sought comfort from the warmth of the male at my back, his sleeping form melting the chill that wracked my spine as that dripping sword danced behind my eyes.

A hot shower would wash away the remnants of the nightmare. Easing Kazimir's furred arm off of me, I slipped from the bed, padding in the direction of my enormous bathroom. The tiles were cold beneath my feet as I stared in confusion at the multitude of knobs lining the wall outside the shower. I needed Kazimir's help.

I bounded back to the bed, launching myself behind his prone form and yelling, "Incoming!"

The sneaky bastard was awake and waiting, catching me a moment before I crashed into him and pinning me beneath him. His nose nuzzled my neck. "You think you can come in here and jump on me?" he challenged, the seduction in his voice clear as the rising sun.

"That's exactly what I think," I moaned as he kissed my neck, erection digging into my thigh.

"Plus, I needed help starting the shower... and we had so much fun last time," I reminded him. What better way to banish the images of death than to do what made me feel so alive.

"Mmm... that we did," he hummed. His arousal was apparent as he pushed off the bed. My gaze snagged on it instead of his proffered hand. It bobbed as he carried me to the bathroom. "Enjoying the view, Izidora?"

I sucked my lip between my teeth as I regarded it while he filled the tub with the handles attached to the marble wall. "Maybe."

Steam rolled through the bathroom, coating stone and glass in a watery haze. The falling water was blissful, but Kazimir's firm touch on my shoulders sent me straight into the heavens. He worked his way down my back, kneading the tight muscles lining my spine. His knees graced the slick tile as he reached my hips and massaged the muscles there before moving on to my thighs. His deft hands heralded his soft lips against my skin as they blazed a trail to my core. My leg braced against his sternum as my calf and foot melted beneath his skillful touch, and pure ecstasy flooded my veins as the tension held in my body trickled down the drain with the cleansing water.

Once his ministrations were complete, his scruff brushed against my inner thigh, charting a course for his lips to my core. My moan reverberated off the veined marble, and Kazimir shushed me before sucking my clit into his hot mouth again. I threaded my fingers in his damp hair, holding him in place as he hit the right spot and speed. Fingers circled my thigh until they stroked my core, barely brushing the sensitive and needy parts of me. They hovered over my folds, stroking and parting them as his tongue swirled over my sensitive nerves. Two digits nudged my entrance, and he slipped them inside me.

"Kazimir..." I moaned as those fingers sank in to the knuckle and curled against my walls before languidly dropping away. His tongue flattened against the apex of my thighs and synced to the rhythm of his thrusts. The shower spun around me as I sucked soupy air into my lungs, and my grip on his hair was the only thing keeping me steady. A swell of pleasure rose within me, and I ground against his fingers, trying to find my release. He growled against my core, sending vibrations through all the right places.

"Already going to come for me, Izidora?" Those sharp edges dusting his jaw tickled my thighs.

"Yes," I gasped.

His furious fingers brought me closer to the edge, keeping me there as I looked off the cliff and into the abyss of pleasure he promised. "I want to taste you as you come," he commanded, and with those words I jumped off the edge.

My walls spasmed around his fingers, and his tongue joined them, lapping at my core as he dragged out my release. My mind went black as I dove into the void of pleasure, sinking beneath the surface until I came up gasping for air. My legs shook from the power of my orgasm and holding myself upright as they slipped off Kazimir's shoulders.

His head dripped beads of salty water, the deluge above us racing down his chiseled stomach as he towered over me. Without warning, he snatched me from the ground, my legs opening for him automatically. I didn't have the chance to wrap them around his waist before he split me in two, a hand slapping over my mouth and smothering the scream from his forceful entrance into my still-sensitive core.

"Be a good girl and stay quiet, Izidora. You're only going to share your pretty sounds with me as you come around my cock. Understood?"

I nodded, unable to say anything as a gush of arousal slicked my thighs.

There was no wall to support me during this romp beneath the waterfall, and Kazimir's powerful arms gripped me and guided me up and down his shaft. I had no control over the depths of destruction he wreaked on my pussy, and in my efforts to remain quiet I drew blood from my lip, a hint of metal joining the hazy air around us. With a feral growl, he sucked that lip into his mouth, tasting my life source and drawing more from the bruise. I whimpered against his roving tongue, and my nails bit into his flexing shoulders as I found my balance. My hips ground into his stomach, providing the perfect friction against my sensitive nub, while his thrusts remained brutal and felt as if I were being impaled over and over again as gravity assisted him.

"Tell me you love me," I gasped between thrusts.

"I fucking love you, Izidora," he snarled against my neck, sucking on my fluttering pulse. He thickened inside me, every inch of him stretching me to my limits. "Tell me I'm your hero. Thank me for saving you and delivering this pleasure."

"You're my hero," I moaned, and he seated himself fully

inside me, rubbing my hips against his stomach. "Fuck! Don't stop."

"You didn't finish," he growled, stilling his movements.

"Thank you for saving me," I whimpered, trying to arch into him as my pleasure began tipping.

"And?" He rewarded me with a drag up and down his length.

"Thank you for delivering me pleasure."

"Good girl." He shoved me down so deep that he hit the very back of me, and I buried my teeth in his shoulder to smother the scream as I came around him.

He swore as his cock throbbed inside me, and hot ropes of liquid squirted and coated my walls, our combined release dripping between us before being washed away by the storm closing in on all sides. I unwrapped my legs, and he lowered me gingerly to the ground before capturing my mouth in a bruising kiss.

"I love you, Izidora, and I'll never stop saying it. I can't wait to say it in front of the whole world." He tipped his head back and let the cascade consume him until he looked like a god stepping from the depths of the ocean.

"I love you, Kazimir, and I am so glad you saved me. My life is better with you in it." His emerald orbs snapped open and he yanked me beneath the waterfall with him.

When we finally left the steamy embrace of the shower, I wrapped myself in a fluffy robe and laid across my bed while Kazimir dressed in his clothes from the previous day. "I need to check in with my father, but I will be back for you in thirty minutes so we can train with Kriztof and the twins. I'll come to the front door."

"Okay," I beamed. Releasing this pent-up tension by pushing my body to its limit was what I needed. There was no time to think when a sword was slicing the air toward your neck. He planted one last peck on my lips before slipping through the door to the hidden passage, closing it with a soft thud behind him.

Scouring my closet for my leathers, I pulled them on and strapped in. Perhaps we could stop at a leatherwork shop while we were out. A new chest plate that was thicker and allowed me to use my wings would be preferable to the basic one that sheltered my vital organs now. I plaited my hair out of my face for training, saving my long locks from accidental slices and saving my skin from nicks and bruises delivered under a curtain of chestnut. My magic had held overnight, and I banished the white outline from the doors to my sitting room and closet. Trays of food still lined the tables, and I snacked on some leftover fruit while I waited for Kazimir to fetch me. Mistik popped into my mind as I bit into an especially juicy red apple.

A sharp rap sounded against the outer door, and I bounced to it, yanking it open to greet my beloved. My face fell when Alekzi leaned casually against the wall in front of me, one ankle crossed over the other and a casual air floating about his smug face. I leaned my weight on the door, closing it slightly so not a gap of space remained around me.

"Where are you going?" he asked, looking me up and down in a way that made my skin crawl.

"To train, like I do every morning," I said flatly, unamused at his early appearance.

"And why would you do that? You are meant to be soft and pliable." His eyes flooded with black as his pupils dilated.

"Why would I ask others to do what I would not do myself?" I snapped. "Furthermore, being soft and pliable got me nowhere when my captors whipped and chained me. Not like anyone would know, because no one has asked."

He held his hands up. "Woah, no need to get hysterical now."

Hysterical? Was that what he thought of females who stood up for themselves?

Bile rose in my throat and I crinkled my nose. "What do you want?" I bit out.

He pushed off the wall, stepping forward as if he meant to enter the room. I stood my ground, not budging as he inched closer.

"Just to talk, you know, away from our parents. We should get to know each other better," he crooned.

Yeah, right.

His game was as transparent as the windows behind me. I gripped the doorframe tighter. "Well, I am about to leave, so you've caught me at a bad time. Try again later. In public."

His face darkened and a muscle ticked in his jaw. It seemed as though "no" was not a familiar word to him. He shoulder-checked me, sending me flying back into the room. The door slammed into the wall, and he stormed in my direction.

Regaining my footing, I dropped into my fighting stance, adrenaline pounding through me as I sharpened my focus on my next move. He stalked a circle around me like a predator waiting to lunge for the kill. My feet and fists followed his every move, preventing him from getting the upper hand. This was the moment I had been training for, and I waited with bated breath for his strike. He may not be the object of my pain, but he would feel my wrath regardless. Fucking bastard.

He grabbed for my wrist, leaving his side wide open and allowing me to slip right beneath his outstretched arm and circle around to his back. I brought my fists down on his kidneys with every ounce of strength I possessed, sending his body folding over as it flooded with pain.

"You bitch," he gritted out.

"You need to go," I hissed.

He lunged for me, and I kicked my foot out on instinct, catching him square in the stomach. The air whooshed out of him as he doubled over, and my blood sang at bringing this male to bow before me. But I got cocky, and he used the opportunity to grab me. With two hands, he snatched my legs out from under me, sending me pinwheeling to the floor. He was on top of me in seconds, wrapping his hands around my throat. A strangled cough replaced my breath as he crushed my windpipe, and his face contorted in a malicious snarl. "You're going to pay for that."

An enraged roar shook the floor beneath me, and suddenly Alekzi was yanked off of me by the back of his collar and slammed into the wall with enough force to send the vase beside him crashing to the floor. Kazimir held him by the throat, and the hairs on the back of my neck raised under the force of his fury.

I clutched my throat and scrambled away from them. Kazimir's growl threatened death as he brought his bared teeth inches from Alezki's blanched face. "How dare you touch her."

"She hit me first," he whimpered around Kazimir's chokehold.

"I seriously doubt that," Kazimir seethed. "If you ever lay a hand on her again, I will personally cut off your balls and nail them to the front gate with a note that says you are a female-beater."

Alekzi's eyes bulged, his face more purple than my favorite wine, and Kazimir roughly threw him to the floor. Alezki wasted no time scrambling to his feet and scurrying out the door, passing a wide-eyed Liliana, Viktor, Vadim, and Endre on his way out.

"You'll be sorry you laid a hand on me, Kazimir," he threatened when he was well into the hall beyond.

Kazimir did not acknowledge the challenge, instead rushing to my side. "Are you okay?"

I almost scrambled away, but after sucking down a lungful of air, I remained where I was. "I think the chest plate took most of the impact."

"What about your throat?" He bent my head from side to side, examining it.

"Endre can heal it," I promised. Hearing his name, he approached us, looking to Kazimir for permission to continue me.

Kazimir jerked his chin. "Can you heal this?"

"Just give me a little space," he replied. Endre touched my neck, and warmth flooded the bruises that marked where Alekzi had choked me. My throat was next, the healing magic licking along the insides and healing what was not visible.

"Thanks, Endre," I murmured when I felt fully healed.

"I'm glad we got here when we did." His voice held a hint of threat that I'd never heard from the male.

"Me too," I reached my hand up and Kazimir helped me to my feet. "Let's go train, shall we? I have some feelings to work through."

"I can get on board with that," Liliana smirked from the doorway.

I bumped my shoulder into Kazimir as we trailed behind our friends through the castle. "Thanks for saving me again."

"I will always save you, Izidora," he hummed.

The castle hadn't yet come to life; its occupants remained in the clutches of sleep. I couldn't blame them, especially as the biting wind tore into me and whipped pieces of hair from my plaits as we passed through the courtyard and into the barracks.

A crowd had already gathered around several fighting rings framed by white-capped wave surges. Kriztof, Zekari, and Kirigin leaned against the rails of the same ring, and I waved when they looked over their shoulders at our approach. They bowed to me, formalities necessary since we had an audience. It was wildly uncomfortable to release them from their supplication.

At least they didn't bow out of fear.

I spotted Ivan among the crowd, sitting with who I assumed were other would-be Knights. They all bowed low to me, Ivan flashing his white teeth as our eyes connected.

"Who is up for a fight?" I asked jovially.

"It would be my honor, Princess Izidora," Ivan called.

I scaled the wooden fence and dropped to the packed dirt, my leather boots hitting with a satisfying thump. Vadim handed me two short swords through the fence, and I circled them in an intimidation tactic toward Ivan, who held a broadsword at the ready. The crowd began shouting as we circled one another, feinting blows and feeling each other out.

Ivan swung his broadsword overhead, and I crossed my twin blades, catching his sword and tossing it to one side. I parried to my right as he recovered, dancing around the tip of his heavy blade. My left-handed sword jabbed straight, drawing his attention away from my right hand, which sliced up his center, narrowly missing him as he jumped out of the way. His weight was on his back foot, so I pressed in, my twin blades flashing between us as I attacked and parried.

Trying to regain ground, he lunged straight toward me, and I repeated my earlier move, kicking my leg straight toward his sternum. The force of the launch was enough to knock the air from his lungs as he collided with my boot. But he did not let that stop his fight. He backed away for only a moment to regain his breath before circling one way, then the other in an effort to avoid getting backed into the fence.

I continued to walk him down, my blades enough of a threat to keep him out of range as I assessed for any openings. His back was momentarily exposed after he put power into a heavy blow from left to right. I baited him into repeating the move, then ducked under the blade and launched myself past him in an attempt to take his back, just like I had with Viktor. My twin blades sandwiched him, and he had no choice but to surrender.

He started laughing. "I yield!"

Kazimir whooped at my victory, followed by shouts and cheers from my friends and the gathered Knights. I dropped a sword so I could clasp Ivan's hand. "Thanks for the spar."

"You were brilliant. The pleasure is all mine, Princess." He dipped his head and vaulted over the fence, allowing two others to take our place.

Settling next to Vadim on the rails, we watched the other Knights spar, with my teacher providing analysis. His keen eyes missed nothing, though I succeeded in pointing out a few mistakes the would-be Knights made. I cycled in and out of the ring, battling new faces and honing my skill on opponents closer to my skill and size. I won some and lost most, though I thanked each of them profusely and tried to remember their names for later. Building rapport was important, especially among the warriors of the Night Realm, for what was to come.

I chatted with others who waited for their turns in the ring, asking them about their lives and where they were from. They eked out of their hardened shells little by little, my attention and informality coaxing them to share more of their true selves and relax into our conversations. By the end, I had them joking like the Nighthounds, and I knew their loyalty was won.

I was already better than my father, and this proved it.

"Do you want to go to the range with me? I need to shoot some targets," Liliana bounced up from her latest match, strands of chocolate hair glued to her face with sweat.

"Let's do it," I replied, hopping from my perch and following her to a long range with seven hay-stuffed dummies at the far end. We joined the line of Fae waiting for their turn with the dummies.

"Alekzi is such a pig. He's been trying to get me alone for years," Liliana scoffed after a beat of silence.

"He's only tough at a distance. He was crying when Kazimir had him pinned to the wall." Pathetic, arrogant male. He got what he deserved, though I was certainly owed vengeance of my own. Vengeance I would exact when I became queen. "He also questioned why I was coming to train, telling me that I am supposed to be 'soft and pliant,'" I quoted the last words with my fingers.

Liliana snorted. "He really said that?"

"He really did. Then he called me hysterical when I told him that being soft and pliant got me nowhere when I was abused."

"He did not! What a bastard," Liliana exclaimed.

"Tell me about it. He said all he wanted to do was talk and get to know me better, without our parents around." I rolled my eyes.

"Uh huh, 'talk,'" Liliana made air quotes. "More like he wanted to get to know what's under your clothes better."

"Yep," I popped the last letter, glad I wasn't the only one who read that between his words.

The last of the males cleared the range before us, and it was finally our turn. A bow and full quiver waited for us, and Liliana grasped the bow between steady fingers and nocked an arrow with an ease I aspired to. She sunk the first, then the second into the heart of the dummy before putting the third between his eyes.

I whistled. "That was brilliant."

"I know," she laughed. "I imagined Alekzi's face and that did the trick."

With thinly veiled amusement, I reached for the bow. Nocking an arrow, I drew the string and lined up my shot, picturing Alekzi's smug face when I had opened the door. I visualized the arrow hitting him right in the heart, then released the string with a twang. It sailed down the range and sank into the target an inch from Liliana's two bolts.

"That felt good," I admitted, and Liliana laughed.

"See, I told you!" she exclaimed.

I sank two more in the abdomen of the dummy, then we wandered to the rings, looking for our friends.

After a moment Liliana said, "Most people would break under the load you've carried. But you never give up. That is a more powerful weapon than any of these males have." She gestured around the barracks area.

I wrapped an arm around her waist and leaned my head against her shoulder as we walked. "And I have a friend like you to tell me these sweet words."

"You know those are males of action and not words," she gestured again to the semicircle of males with arms crossed over their chests. "Someone has to say sweet things."

Shadows disappeared with the rising sun, and its warmth caressed my sweat-soaked hair. "Is there a place in town where I can buy another chest plate? I want one that is a bit thicker and can be used with my wings," I asked the Nighthounds.

"I know just the place," Kazimir declared.

"Oh... I just realized I don't have any money." I looked down at my feet, twisting a toe over a loose stone beneath them.

Kazimir tipped my chin up with a finger. "You are royal, and no royal pays for anything in Vaenor. The shop owners send a bill to the Royal Treasurer, and he sends them coin."

"Why don't we go now?" Viktor said. "I think the optics would be good. Izidora, fresh from training with her Knights, wants to improve her armor and buy from her subjects directly."

"I like it. Let's go meet my people."

The outer gate was thrown open and people streamed in and out, the handful of guards stationed there hardly paying attention to the throng. As we walked the streets of Vaenor, my shoulders were loose and back, and I tipped my head to the open sky. I felt safe among my people, and I couldn't understand why my father felt differently.

As we walked further into the city, shopkeepers began to notice us, shouting greetings and praise. I stopped to shake hands or wave to many of them, throwing everything I had into blossoming into a queen. I painted a pretty picture of a different life in the capital, one where their monarch knew them by name and cared about their businesses.

It was slow progress, but eventually, the scent of freshly tanned leather assaulted my nostrils, reminding me of the horses I loved so dearly. I inhaled the fragrance, then strode in the front door of the small tannery, followed by Liliana and the Nighthounds.

The shopkeep looked up from a large tome where he scribbled notes, then dropped his pen and mouth when he discovered who entered.

"Your Highness! Please, come in. Welcome to Lovak Leathers." He bowed repeatedly, looking like a pecking chicken as he did so.

"Call me Princess Izidora. What is your name?" I asked.

"Jonaz. Jonaz Lovak," he stuttered.

"Nice to meet you, Jonaz. I require a new set of fighting leathers. Unfortunately, I am unable to use my wings with this." I thumped my chest plate.

"Hmm, that is rather unfortunate and simply will not do for a Night Fae!" he exclaimed. "Do you mind if I have a look?"

"Please, go ahead," I replied.

He assessed me, lightly touching a few spots near my

shoulder blades. "I have a few pieces that would look lovely on you. Let me fetch them." He scurried around his shop, piling his arms with leather until his face nearly disappeared among the items. Once he was satisfied with his load, he arranged them neatly on the table in front of me.

"These," he motioned to the ones on the left side of the table, "are very lightweight, but they have holes around the wing area which could leave you vulnerable. And these," he gestured to the ones on the right side of the table, "are heavier, but I have magically enhanced them to allow your wings to slip in and out with ease. You will still be protected and your wings can fly free whenever you like. If I had to choose one for my Princess, I would choose these."

I fingered a dark brown one with roses stitched into the material. The leather was supple yet firm, thicker than my current chest plate, and felt light to the touch when I brought it closer for examination.

"An excellent choice, Princess. It might be a little big, but I can modify it so that it fits you more snugly," he offered.

"May I try it on?" I asked.

"Of course. I will need it on you to mold it to your shape." Unsnapping the straps of my current one, I handed it off to Kazimir, then turned the dark brown leather around in my hands, searching for the opening that appeared to be a secret.

"Let me help you," Kazimir offered. Passing it his way, he motioned for me to raise my arms. He slid the leather over my head like a tunic, and it sank onto my chest, fitting snugly, flexing and bending with me.

"The fabric is magically enhanced so it will move with you, which makes it much easier to take on and off as well," Jonaz explained.

I checked the fit in a nearby mirror. The leather hugged my

neck, creating a protective barrier against arrows, and it stopped just above my hip bones, covering all my vital organs and more. The arm holes were wide enough for me to move my arms through the full range of motion. I tested the material as I twisted and reached, but the leather moved with me at every turn. For the final test, I called out my wings, and they burst without barrier from my back, fluffing themselves merrily. I twisted to ensure my back remained fully protected.

"It is perfect," I said to Jonaz.

"May I adjust the fit?" He held his hands out in question.

I nodded my approval, and he set to work tightening parts around my upper back and loosening others closer to my hips. When he was finished, the piece hugged every curve perfectly.

I looked as fierce as I felt.

"I also have matching cuffs," he offered, and I glanced at the ones I currently wore.

"I would love to purchase those as well. Do you have pants in the same color?"

Jonaz had retreated to his notebook, and looked up from his scratching to answer my question. "If you have a few moments, I can make a pair."

"Please do. I would love to have a full set," I grinned. He retreated through a door behind the counter. We milled about the shop, and I admired the fine craftsmanship of his pieces.

The world was not filled with monsters like the ones who guarded me; instead, kind and talented and unique Fae filled my world, and I was excited to learn more about them with each passing day. Everyone had a story to tell, people they loved, and dreams for their life.

Just like me.

Jonaz returned with matching pants, the sides lined with vines of roses to match the chest plate.

"Do you have a place where I can change into these?" I asked.

"Behind the curtain there," he pointed behind him.

Dipping behind it, I quickly changed, listening to the Nighthounds chat with the leatherworker about creating a full set of custom armor for them. I grinned, so grateful they took my request seriously. It was good for all of us to interact with those outside the castle, for these were the people who mattered the most.

Kazimir whistled when I emerged from behind the curtain.

"Thanks again, Jonaz. We will definitely be back," I grinned at the blushing male.

"It was my honor to clothe the lost princess," he stammered, and we exited the shop into the waiting crowd.

"What does everyone think?" I asked lightheartedly, turning in a circle.

"A true warrior!" someone called.

"I wouldn't cross you!" another joked.

"Beauty and brawn!" another laughed.

But from the back of the crowd, someone shouted, "My queen!"

A hush fell faster than an executioner's blade. Two treasonous words, uttered with sincerity. Two words I wanted and was terrified to hear.

My heart pounded in my veins as I tried to come up with a way to dispel the tension. But Viktor arrived at his words before me and asked the crowd, "Does anyone know a good sweet shop nearby? Princess Izidora has not eaten today and would love some cinnamon rolls."

A female shouted, "My shop is just around the corner, and I baked some about half an hour ago."

"Lead the way!" I rejoiced.

We led a crowd behind us to the woman's sweet shop, where

Viktor and Endre bought every cinnamon roll she'd baked and passed them out among the onlookers. We made a show of eating with the people on the sidewalk, laughing as icing transferred from the roll to my mouth and cheek. Kazimir wiped it with his finger, then bopped me on the nose, and I scrunched my face as the icing migrated across it. My people loved every minute of it, lapping up our playful interaction.

Liliana and Vadim bickered over who got the bigger roll, as did Zekari and Kirigin. "Siblings," I shook my head, eliciting amusement from those around me.

Too soon, we had to say our goodbyes. I enjoyed every moment around my people, and I promised many of them that I would patronize their shops and taverns. I was high on my interactions as we trekked back to Este Castle, whose black spires sliced through the cloudless blue sky. Despite the biting wind that tore through the cobbled streets, the sun warmed my skin, and I lifted my face to the sky, inhaling the horsey scent of the stables mixed with the brine that drifted in on the breeze, and exhaled all my worries.

My people loved me, and I would be queen.

We left Kriztof and the twins in the courtyard after making plans to have a drink together during the feast that night. The entrance hall buzzed with servants ferrying decor, cloths, and silverware in every direction, most streaming toward the center of the castle that held the enormous ballroom.

"How many people will be in attendance tonight?" I asked.

"Several hundred, at least, if I had to guess," Vadim said.

"Well, it will be all the High and Lower Houses from last night, plus the ones who arrived today, then all the Knights, and anyone remotely noble. Then there are the rich merchants or anyone else who could afford a bribe for an invitation," Liliana listed them off on her fingers.

"No pressure," I joked.

"Who is escorting you, Liliana?" Endre asked, the slight waver in his voice betraying the casual tone he aimed for.

"No one asked me yet," she shrugged.

"I would be happy to be your escort." His voice lilted with a glimmer of hope.

"Are you asking me to the feast?" she teased, brushing her hand across his arm.

Endre's face flushed a shade darker, and I pressed my lips together, ears strained for his response.

"Yes, I am," he declared, puffing up his chest.

"Then, I accept," she said, flashing him a winning smile.

"Keep your hands where I can see them at all times," Vadim warned Endre. Endre raised his hands high above his head, and my belly ached from the laughter we shared.

As we approached the wings of the castle that housed the nobles, Kazimir stopped our group, and, in front of all the noble Fae milling about the halls, took my hands. Our group fanned around us as Kazimir cleared his throat to garner attention. With a deep bow, he brought his lips to the back of my hands, brushing them lightly across the back, before straightening. "Princess Izidora, would you do me the honor of allowing me to escort you to the feast tonight?"

His words were like water dousing a fire; conversation fizzled out immediately. Curious eyes burned my skin like floating embers, but all I could see was the male in front of me.

"I would be honored to have you escort me," I smiled sweetly. Whispers chased us from the hall as we continued our jaunt through the castle arm in arm. Our friends followed in a scattered array; Endre and Viktor split off toward the High House Wing while Liliana followed me, leaving Vadim to sneak toward the Lower House Wing.

"So, what color shall I wear to match you?" Kazimir asked.

"Gold," I replied, thinking of the glamorous dress I would don that night.

"Tell Endre to wear blush," Liliana giggled behind me.

Kazimir winked. "Gold and blush – whatever that means – it is."

There was no sign of my father as we entered the Royal Wing. I was not ready to face him after what I learned the previous night, nor did I want to spend any more time with him than necessary. But the thought of his scheming was not what set my teeth on edge – no, it was the unfamiliar guard stationed outside my door.

No fucking way was an unknown male ever guarding me again.

Stomping forward, I smiled sweetly at him. I needed information, and as much as I wanted to throw a fit, my brightness would win him over before my darkness. "Hello. What is your name?"

He glanced at me, then returned his eyes straight in front of him. "Isztvan, Your Highness."

"Isztvan, who sent you?" I asked, turning up the charm.

He swallowed, glanced at me, then forward again. "His majesty wants a guard posted at your door round the clock, Your Highness," he stammered.

Either my father wanted to spy on me or he wanted to execute the next part of his plan – neither option was good.

"Isztvan, be a dear and fetch a servant to bring us some food, I am starving," I instructed.

He dipped his head. "Yes, Your Highness."

Isztvan scurried off, and I burst through the doors to my rooms, unleashing the fury that built like an inferno inside me upon seeing the male at my door. First, Alekzi dared barge in, then my father intruded on my space too. Kazimir caught my arm before I could go far and pinned me against the wall. "Wait here. I'm going to check the rooms."

He nodded to Liliana to stay put, then dashed off into the apartment. His immediate thought for my safety did not douse the rage boiling in my blood. But he diligently cleared each room before returning to my side, just as a faint knock came from my bedroom. Kazimir strode off to find Endre and Viktor. Murmurs floated on the air but I did not listen as I stalked to the sitting room and brooded on a couch.

Servants appeared carrying gleaming silver trays, laying out new plates piled with delicacies and removing the previous day's leftovers. They were gone moments after they arrived, and for that I was grateful because my body trembled with the need to fight and there was no one to direct my fire toward. I clenched and unclenched my fists until Vadim entered the room. No doubt the newest decor at my door would inform someone later that he had arrived, but he couldn't see that Endre and Viktor were already there, so we had one advantage.

"I'm loving what you've done with the place," Vadim joked as he sat across from me, snatching a sandwich off one of the trays. Liliana rolled her eyes, grabbing a sandwich as well.

"So as your ladies maid, it is my responsibility to help you get ready for tonight," Liliana began. "And I think we need a lot of wine while we do that. And girl talk. What time can we kick these bozos out?"

I giggled and glanced at a large clock that hung above the fireplace. It was close to two in the afternoon. The feast started at seven, which gave us five hours if we didn't want to be fashionably late. "We will allow them to eat with us, then they can leave. I need a nap," I yawned.

"Allow? You should be grateful for my presence at all," Viktor mocked. The males grumbled in veiled amusement, while Liliana and I pretended like they were beneath us.

"We only allow you in here because you're nice to look at," Liliana waved him off.

In a moment of clarity, I realized we were more than a team. We were a family. I had no mother, and honestly no father. I had no siblings, no cousins, and no grandparents. Those thoughts should have left me adrift in aloneness, but instead, my heart swelled with love for the Fae around me. Families were supposed to lift you up, work together, and support each other.

Family isn't blood, but rather who you choose to surround yourself with.

My yawns became more insistent as my body lagged from the overwhelming events of the previous day, my early morning escapades, and the foreboding night ahead of us. My lids struggled to remain open, from where my head rested on Kazimir's shoulder, listening to my friends banter.

"Your princess requires a nap," I announced after a yawn that nearly cracked my jaw. "Liliana, will you stay? I don't want to be alone..." I didn't need to finish my sentence for her to understand.

"Of course. You'll never have to be alone again, remember?"

I planned on using the locking magic Kazimir had taught me, regardless.

Kazimir kissed me lightly on the forehead before he left. "I'll be back for you at seven," he promised. He and Vadim left through the entrance, acknowledging Isztvan loudly on their way out.

Endre and Viktor disappeared through the wall in my bedroom, and then Liliana and I locked all the doors and climbed into my bed. The sun looked so lovely as it set over the horizon, and I left the curtains open as my eyes drooped.

"I'll wake you in an hour to get ready," she promised. "I'm not tired, but my back is sore and your bed is comfy. Honestly, like twenty times comfier than mine."

A giggle closed my eyes, and I drifted into a dream of Kazimir and I dancing under the breathtaking chandeliers in the ballroom.

———

TRUE TO HER WORD, Liliana woke me an hour later. No one had tried to enter my apartment. I unlocked the doors to the sitting room, hunting for some wine while Liliana rummaged through the fully stocked drawers of makeup in my bathroom.

I returned victorious with a bottle of champagne and two glasses in my hand. Liliana squealed, popped the bottle, and poured the bubbly gold liquid into the glasses.

"Cheers to our first formal event together," she clinked her glass with mine. "How do you want to do your hair?"

My fingers shook out the braids as I thought about the headpiece. It was a hot mess, with tangles and kinks everywhere. "I think some soft waves would look nice."

Liliana grabbed a brush and began untangling my hair from tip to root, leaving it even frizzier after she brushed it out. With a conspiratorial grin, she said, "Watch this!" Her fingers ran across a section of my hair, and when she dropped the strand to flutter to my shoulder, it was perfectly straight.

I gaped at her. "How did you do that?"

"Magic! Here, I'll show you," she grabbed my hand, bringing it to a different strand. "Now picture what you want it to look like, then run your finger along it."

I pictured my hair straight as a board, and to my surprise, my hair straightened immediately. "I love magic," I laughed.

The giant mirror that spanned the gleaming white counter was more than large enough for us to work at the same time on our locks. Tucked beneath the wood vanities were round stools, and we scraped them back and plopped onto them while we worked magic over our hair. Once my chestnut locks were perfectly straight, Liliana teased out soft curls at the ends. The headdress would steal the show, so there wasn't much else to do.

"What are you planning to do with your hair?" I asked her.

"Well, my dress is backless, so I want to put it up somehow." She stared at her reflection, angling her head this way and that.

"Let me braid it for you. I have an idea." I bounced to her stool, grabbing her chocolate strands before she could object.

"Do your worst," she giggled. "By worst, I mean your best. I want to look fabulous."

I weaved braids around her head, working her thick locks in a spiral before grabbing a pin to secure it to the back of her head. Then I fluffed out the braid, making each piece appear larger than it was, and loosened a few strands to frame her heart-shaped face. The result was beautiful. Her hair looked like a blooming rose, with little braids woven through bigger ones to form vines leading to the flower at the center. I grabbed a hand-held mirror so she could admire the back.

"This is incredible, Izidora! You have to teach me to braid," she squeaked.

"And you have to teach me... this," I gestured to the counter covered in creams, brushes, and colors.

"Deal," she beamed. "Now sit and let me make you a total knockout."

I did as she instructed, watching as she deftly grabbed creams, powders, and brushes and began transforming my face. She highlighted my cheekbones with a shimmery powder that reflected the light. Next, she defined my jawline to make my face appear more angular. I closed my eyelids as she painted them, gently brushing different sections until I started to squirm.

"Hold still just one more minute," she instructed. She painted one last line close to my lashes, then told me to open my eyes. "Here, finish with this." She handed me a small brush covered in black paint. "Just run it over your lashes." She demonstrated the motion.

I leaned into the mirror, brushing as she instructed.

"And last but not least, gloss!" She handed me a light pink liquid, and I used my finger to dab it over my lips.

The difference between the sleepy female who had entered the room and the female in the mirror in front of me were striking. I looked totally different, yet I was still entirely me. Smoky black framed my aquamarine eyes, making them pop with a deadly gleam. My lips reflected the light even more than the shimmer highlighting my cheekbones, accentuating the pout I already had. I felt sexy and alluring, and I couldn't wait to see Kazimir.

"So, what do you think?" Liliana drawled.

"I'm a total knockout," I laughed.

"See! I told you," she laughed with me. She applied makeup across her face with deft strokes, many of her color choices reflecting mine. Instead of pink gloss, she selected a deep burgundy for herself. She smacked her lips together once the stain was applied. "How do I look?"

"Like a total knockout," I laughed again. "Endre is going to be weak at the knees when he sees you!"

"He better," she sniffed.

"So is anything going on between you?" I prodded, a curious eyebrow raised.

She sighed. "Not yet. Don't tell anyone, especially Vadim, but I've had a crush on him for years. I thought it was one of those crushes I would grow out of, but when I saw him again yesterday it all came right back. The last time I saw him, I was still underage, so of course he didn't look twice at me. But now I plan on getting his attention and keeping it."

"I think you already have it. I saw how he looked at you yesterday. And today," I shared.

She blushed, and the look was strange for her usually endless confidence. I wanted to see both of them happy, and if that meant they were together, I was all for it.

"What about you and Kazimir? When did that start?" she wiggled her eyebrows at me.

"Let's try to put on that dress and I'll tell you," I proposed.

"To the closet!" She bounced through my bedroom, grabbing the headdress and laying it on the bed before fetching the gown. I stripped down to my undergarments, and she fanned the gilded piece across the floor, creating a circle wide enough for me to step into. She began to slowly work the dress up my body, careful not to pop any seams, and I started my story.

"It all started with looks, here and there. He taught me magic, and I caught him watching me as I practiced. He watched me train with Vadim. And I watched him too, setting up tents, sparring, laughing with the Nighthounds. I never wanted to be far from him, even when I didn't want him to touch me. Then, we were ambushed on the road. I killed a man," my voice dropped to a whisper, but Liliana didn't seem bothered by the information, so I continued. "I went into shock. He washed me in a river, gave me some of his clothes, and I slept in his tent with him, but he was on the floor. The next day we turned toward Zirok House, and the ones who escaped the night before found us. I was terrified. I thought for sure they were going to catch me and drag me away from him. And the thought of that was worse than the thought of being chained again.

"So he gave me his room, and I asked him to stay with me until I fell asleep. He did, but I had a nightmare where I woke up screaming. I begged him to stay when he rushed in to protect me. And he did. The rest is history," I finished.

"So are you mates?" Liliana nearly buzzed with excitement behind me.

"How do you know if you are?"

"Every female on this entire continent dreams of having one, and if you guys are mates I will be extremely jealous. Basically, it's some Goddess magic that seals the deal once you figure it out. Fae can be mates without accepting it, but the mating bond is supposed to be insane, so I don't know why people wouldn't accept it. The bond allows you to communicate with your mate with just your thoughts, and then you will always know where they are. On top of the extra spicy sex you will have! And males are insanely protective of their mates. Lots of stories talk about males dying of a broken heart if their mate dies. Can you imagine being loved so intensely?" She bubbled more than our champagne as she regaled me with all the benefits of having a mate.

A wide smile spread across my face. "I can. I always thought our feelings were a little intense for a normal relationship. Not like I knew differently."

"Oh my Goddess, you guys have to accept the bond!"

She emitted little squeaks as she laced me into the dress, and I couldn't stop the smile that pulled up the corner of my lips when I realized what this meant for me. "Do you just say, 'hey, I accept the bond?' How does that work?" I asked, eager to seal the deal with Kazimir.

She shrugged. "I would have to ask my mom. She probably knows."

I laughed, "Just say you are asking for a friend. Don't use any names!"

"If anything, she would react the same way I am, thinking it was me," she giggled, straightening my dress one last time. "Perfection. Now for the headdress."

Dipping my head, she pinned the halo in place, then she connected the vines to the ornate center stone. When I lifted my chin, she stepped back to take me in fully, her hands clasped in front of her mouth, but they couldn't hide her wide grin. "You look like a goddess!"

A gasp left my lips unbidden as my reflection popped into the full length mirror in front of me. The whole ensemble came together perfectly. I looked celestial, glittering no matter which direction I turned. My eyes popped, accentuated by the incredible headdress that sprouted in all directions. My body was lethal, every curve highlighted by the glittering gold gown.

"Can you walk?" Liliana laughed.

"Not really," I admitted, shuffling to sit so I could put on my shoes.

"Here, let me help," she lifted my skirt and placed the flat slippers on my feet one by one as I leaned on her for balance.

"Thanks. I'm going to stand here and try to breathe while you finish getting ready," I wheezed in exaggeration.

Her bubbly laugh echoed in my closet while she fetched her dress. It was easy enough for her to get on by herself, thankfully, because there was no way I would have been able to help her. We stood together in the mirror, admiring our new dresses and friendship.

"Oh! Can't forget the wings." In a flash of silver, black feathered wings with a hint of seafoam green burst from her back.

My diamond-like feathers added to my already ethereal look. "Every eye will be on us tonight," I giggled.

"The more the merrier. They can look but they can't touch, right?" She elbowed me in the ribs.

"Right," I confirmed.

A knock sounded on the outer door, and my stomach filled with butterflies. Liliana bounced ahead of me as I shuffled to the door, opening it to reveal Endre and Kazimir standing there, both looking sharp in their fine suits.

Endre's mouth hung open then snapped shut as he took in Liliana. She preened under his gaze, shooting him a sultry look and pouting with her burgundy lips. His eyes caught on them, then his throat bobbed. My lips pressed together as Endre's mouth opened and closed a few more times like a fish. Kazimir saved him with a pat on his shoulder. "May we come in?"

"Certainly," Liliana opened the door wider, and Kazimir entered the room, followed by Endre, still stunned to silence.

Kazimir stopped in his tracks. "Fuck, I can't let you go like this," he groaned.

32

☾ KAZIMIR

I zidora was the most incredible female I had ever seen. Her natural beauty was accentuated by the makeup she wore, and I almost fell to my knees before her. Her bright aquamarine eyes surrounded by darkness sucked me in. Her full pink lips were glossy, reflecting everything. Her hair was swept back, revealing her collarbones and the swell of her breasts. Every curve was accentuated, the glittering gold fabric hugging her tiny waist and stretching over her hip bones before expanding out in a voluminous skirt covered in white feathers that matched her wings.

I was painfully hard instantly, and my mind screamed at me to lock her in this room and fuck her senseless, to brand her with my cock so every male in the Night Realm would know to whom she belonged. She was mine, but that night, I had to share this exquisite female with the rest of the world.

A halo of glittering gold and white metal circled her head and a large diamond inlaid in a swirling gold pattern lay against her forehead, the two pieces connected by delicate chains. She wasn't lying – this outfit was going to make a statement.

Once my body was capable of movement again, I circled her,

getting an eyeful from every angle. Her ass looked incredible with the skirt flaring at just the right spot to keep eyes on the prize.

Fuck, this was going to be a long night.

She stared at me with the same fire I felt for her. The world melted away as that familiar tug pulled me to her, and I captured her waist before bending her backward and kissing her deeply.

"Get a room!" Liliana shouted, and I growled at her.

I broke our kiss, pressing my forehead against Izidora's. "You are the most stunning female I have ever seen. I am lucky to escort you tonight."

She blushed, looking up at me from under her lashes. "It's not too much?"

"It is perfect." I kissed her lips lightly once more. I adjusted myself subtly before turning back to Liliana and Endre. "Shall we?"

I tucked Izidora's hand into my arm, then led the way to the ballroom. Endre and Liliana followed closely behind us, whispering and laughing together. I was happy that Liliana accepted Endre's invitation. He never said it aloud, but I knew he had been interested in her for a while. She was only twenty the last time we saw her, and she had grown even more beautiful since then. Vadim's brotherly protectiveness was endearing, but there was no better male for her than Endre – at least in my opinion.

The hum of the gathered Fae grew louder with each step toward the feast. The air buzzed with excitement, the energy diffusing from the grand ballroom into the surrounding hallways and floating through the castle. Servants ran left and right, fetching food and drink while dodging already-intoxicated Fae who weren't watching their steps.

I led Izidora to the receiving line, waiting for our turn to be announced, and Endre and Liliana filed in behind us. Only High

Houses were granted this honor, and the king was always the last to be announced – a move I was certain was intentional.

Izidora, my future queen, the female that had been my obsession since before I laid eyes on her, took a deep breath, squared her shoulders, and painted a serene yet joyful smile on her face as the massive double doors opened. The balcony overlooked the enormous space, and all eyes were on us as we stepped forward.

"High Lord Kazimir Vaszoly escorting Her Royal Highness Princess Izidora Valynor," the squire announced. I smiled down at Izidora, playing my role in our plan like a well-trained actor. But for me, it was easier than breathing because none of it was a performance; my love for her was plain as day on my face, and by the way she looked at me, I knew she loved me too.

The nobles of the Night Realm clapped as we slowly descended the grand staircase to the ballroom floor. Izidora's dress caught the light from every crystal suspended from the ceiling, and every step had her glimmering like the night sky. The large diamond on her forehead gave her an ethereal appearance, and her allure captivated everyone as we strode confidently into the room.

Fae bowed and curtsied as we passed them, whispers following in our wake.

"...she looks like a true princess..."

"...I wonder if they'll marry..."

"...he saved her and now they're together? Seems suspicious to me..."

"...and I saw her training with the Knights today..."

The judgment of the Fae around us irked me, but I kept my face impartial as we wound our way to a bar where servants handed out drinks.

A female barmaid had tears in her eyes as she took in Izidora. "Your Highness, please excuse my saying so but you look so much like your mother. I wish she could see you now. She was always so good to my family, and she got me this job at the castle. I have missed her terribly all these years."

"Your compliment is most welcome, friend. What is your name?" Izidora inquired.

"Tamara, Your Highness. What can I get you to drink?" Her hands hovered over an array of bottles.

"Surprise me," she laughed.

"We will take two of whatever that is," I smiled.

Tamara called two champagne flutes from beneath the wooden counter, a bottle of the bubbly liquid pouring of its own accord in front of us before she squirted a hint of red liquid over it and dropped pomegranate seeds into the mix. "Two Poms! They were your mother's favorite."

Izidora's smile was wide and genuine. "Thank you for sharing this with me. I don't know much about my mother, and every little bit I learn warms my heart. Would you join me for tea sometime and tell me more about her?"

Tamara's eyes sparkled as she curtsied low to Izidora. "You honor me greatly. Send for me anytime."

I raised my glass to her as Izidora returned her attention to the party. "Let's mingle. Introduce me to people I should know?"

"Great idea." I spotted Endre and Liliana speaking with Endre's parents, so we pushed through the crowd in their direction.

"High Lord and High Lady Zadik, may I introduce Princess Izidora," I gestured to my stunning date.

"Please, just Tibor and Katalin." High Lord Tibor bowed deeply to Izidora, High Lady Katalin curtsying beside him.

"And you must call me Izidora," she replied.

"We've heard so much about you from Endre," Katalin enthused. "Your wings are truly stunning, as is your whole ensemble tonight. You two are quite the pair." She winked at us.

"I couldn't have gotten into all of this without Liliana's help."

"Let me see the four of you together." She motioned for us to scoot closer to one another. Izidora and Liliana giggled in between Endre and myself, and we bumped fists behind their backs. "I wish I could paint this right now. The young are our future, and I see it clearly standing before me."

"You like to paint?" Izidora asked.

"Oh, yes, very much. I painted a portrait of King Zalan and Queen Liessa decades ago that still hangs in the castle. But I love landscapes most of all. Our family's house is quite picturesque, and I have spent years mastering its rolling hills," she babbled.

"I would love to see the portrait you painted if you would take me sometime. Who better to view it with than the artist herself!" Izidora exclaimed.

"Certainly, let's plan on it in the coming days," Katalin beamed.

"Oh, here are High Lord and Lady Adimik!" Tibor waved them over. Viktor was with them, too.

"Good to see you, Tibor." High Lord Erik clapped him on the shoulder. High Lady Renata kissed Katalin on the cheeks.

"You must be Princess Izidora. I am High Lord Erik and this is my wife High Lady Renata, but you must call us Erik and Renata. We're all family here." Erik picked up Izidora's hand, kissing the back of it as he bowed.

"I have enjoyed Viktor's company immensely since my rescue. It is nice to finally meet his parents. Well, all of your families, really." She looked at Endre and Viktor. "They regaled me with stories of their adventures and childhoods. It was great entertainment on our long ride."

"Viktor has mentioned a few things about your rescue, but I must say, I am impressed with your resilience. How long were you held in that cave?" Erik was always a talker and very direct. I cringed internally, hoping Izidora wouldn't be upset by his question.

But she seemed unbothered as she answered honestly. "I am not sure of the exact timeframe, but I was young when I went into the darkness. Before then, I was in another cave or maybe part of that same cave. Most of my life is a dark blur. It wasn't great, but I survived." She didn't go into detail about her abuse.

Erik bowed his head. "Thank you for sharing that with us. I hope we will find the ones who took you, and they receive the proper punishment."

"As do I," she returned. Liliana gave her hand a reassuring squeeze.

"If you will excuse us, I promised Izidora I would introduce her to everyone." I dipped my head to the Fae who were like family, and Izidora thanked them for their time and tucked her hand into my arm.

"They were lovely. Endre's mom seems so sweet. I hope she adores Liliana too," she giggled.

"They make a great pair, don't you think?" I nudged her ribs.

"Yes, but nothing compares to us." My heart skipped a beat at her words.

How did I get so lucky?

I spotted High Lord and Lady Luzak talking with High Lord and Lady Rass. "Let's go catch some snakes," I motioned in their direction. "House Luzak is fair-weather and power-hungry. They are recent social climbers, Vaklav's father having won them a seat on the council only a few decades ago. His wife, Ola, is significantly younger than him. She was a gift from your father to congratulate the family on their rise. House Rass is one of the oldest in the Night Realm and is very proud. They are a young couple, married only a few years ago. Lady Domi breeds Hunters at their family house. Flatter them if you want to win them over," I coached her as we approached.

The males bowed and the females curtseyed as we joined their circle. "You've caught quite the prize, haven't you Kazimir? Too bad it won't last," High Lord Vaklav Luzak sneered, not even acknowledging Izidora.

"Princess Izidora is no prize to be won. She is a powerful Fae in her own right." Powerful enough to cut the head off this snake.

"And you are...?" she quirked a brow at him.

His face darkened at her slight. "I am High Lord Vaklav Luzak. Don't you know your history, girl?"

"I know House Rass here," she gestured to the couple on her right, "is one of the oldest houses in the Night Realm. But I've yet to hear anyone speak of House Luzak."

Vaklav's face turned redder, and the Rasses sniggered. I wasn't sure which side they would pick, but they were a young couple, and with no kids yet they might be more open to change.

"How dare you!" he screeched.

"How dare I what? You simply asked if I knew my history, and I repeated what I knew," she stated sweetly.

Fuck, I was impressed by how she wove insult into innocent statements. Who knew she had so much bite to her?

Vaklav fumed, the redness on his face spreading to his exposed ears and balding head. He threw back his full glass of vodka before tugging on his wife's arm and storming away. She sighed, following him despite her obvious desire to run in the opposite direction.

"My apologies, High Lord and High Lady Rass." Izidora turned on the charm. "I simply cannot stand when people think less of me because I am female. Females can be just as strong and intelligent as males."

High Lady Domi laughed and High Lord Kaztar chimed in. "My wife is the smarter out of the two of us. And better looking.

I am simply the brawn. Pleased to meet you, Princess Izidora. I am High Lord Kaztar."

"He is a lucky man indeed," Domi said, smiling at her husband. "I am High Lady Domi."

"I hear you breed horses." Izidora's excitement was authentic – she loved Mistik more than me.

"I do, and it is one of my greatest joys in life. Endeavoring to produce the best all-around horse possible takes lots of study and thought. We keep extensive records of all our offspring, selecting the best for our breeding program. I have about twenty mares close to giving birth right now, and I am loath to be away from them. No offense meant, Princess," Domi finished.

"None taken. If I am being honest, I would much rather be in the stables right now myself. I grew fond of my mount on our ride to Vaenor. Her name is Mistik."

"Is she a dapple gray?" Domi's eyes sparkled excitedly.

"Yes! Her color is spectacular." Izidora clapped her hands over her drink as a faraway look covered her face.

Domi's expression mirrored Izidora's. "She is one of our own. I remember selecting her parents based on their incredible colors as well."

"I feel lucky to have ridden such a fine horse. I cannot imagine the others you have bred. You will have to give me a tour in the future." Feeding Izidora the tip about the horses paid off well, and I was pleased with how seamlessly she flattered the Rasses.

"Kaztar, are your lands still stocked with elk for hunting?" I inquired.

"Indeed, and we whelped a new litter of hunting dogs this spring. They should be ready to go for next season," he said proudly.

"Excellent. I hope you don't mind me inviting myself now. The last hunt I did was ages ago, and I've never shot anything as large as the elks you keep," I laughed, and downed the last of my Pom.

"It would be an honor to host you both," Kaztar replied, clapping me on the shoulder.

"The honor would be all mine," Izidora cooed.

Lifting my empty glass to them, I said, "If you'll excuse us, I need another drink."

"We'll speak again soon." Domi gave Izidora's arm a warm squeeze before the females kissed each other on both cheeks.

We found another bar, and I ordered myself a vodka while Izidora took a sip of her champagne. Her glass was only half empty. "We might have had some wine while we were getting ready," Izidora confessed as I eyed her drink.

"How are you feeling?" I asked as we stepped away from the bar. The room was loud and hot from all the bodies packed in, and I was certain Izidora had ever been around so many people at once in her life. Everyone was eyeing her, looking her up and down, assessing. No one knew much about her other than the rumors floating around and stories of her kindness to the lower class. The scrutiny was overwhelming for me beside her, and I couldn't fathom the pressure she must feel.

"I am a bit overwhelmed. I don't want to appear aloof or like I don't care about their lives. I know I am putting a lot of pressure on myself, but I just want to be good at this," she admitted.

"You are a natural. You seem to know exactly when to bite, flatter, charm, or stand firm. I would say you are on par with Viktor, but if he ever heard that we'd have to fight, so if he asks, I never said it."

"I don't know, I seem to just walk up to someone and unconsciously know how to act. It's like I can sense what they need to hear from me, or what their mood is. But I don't want to not be myself either." Her glossy pink lips pulled into a frown.

"I haven't seen you stray from the person you are yet, but I will let you know if you do. I think you have a gift of reading people easily, and your openness puts them at ease. Maybe you show different sides of yourself depending on who you are speaking to, but in the end, each part you show still comes from you. You are allowed to be complex and complicated." My fingers tipped her chin up to look at me, and her aquamarine eyes swirled with a mixture of that inner fire I loved so much, and her unbreakable willpower.

"You're right. The more I get to know myself, the more layers I realize I have. Some people get to see more than others, and that's okay." Her darkened lashes fluttered over the meaning beneath her words.

"That's because you're mine," I replied. "Now, let's see who our next victim is." She snickered as I took her hand and led her deeper into the crowd. There was still no sign of King Zalan, which meant we had time to work the room before his watchful eye followed us everywhere.

33

IZIDORA

We met next with House Volak and some wealthy merchants from Vaenor. They gathered in a large circle, fussing over High Lord Volak's daughter, Iva. Her belly swelled with the hint of pregnancy, and she glowed as everyone around her touched her stomach.

"Congratulations, you must be so excited," I faked enthusiasm. Her distended belly freaked me out, and I did not want to touch it.

"I couldn't wait to tell Havel when I found out," she gushed. "We're hoping for a boy, but we will be happy with a healthy babe of course."

The merchants' wives all oohed and ahhed over Iva's belly, asking how long it took to conceive, what symptoms she was having, and how she would decorate the nursery. High Lady Halina talked endlessly about the clothes and toys she would buy her grandbabe. I wanted out of this conversation as soon as possible.

Kazimir spoke with High Lord Jaku and Havel about the latest farming techniques their communities were trying. They seemed very wrapped up in their family life, so I assumed they weren't jockeying for power like some of the other houses. I still turned out my best smiles and flattery, wanting to win them to my side when the time came for me to take the throne. We parted ways when Iva announced she needed to sit due to her swollen feet and aching lower back.

"I never want to have kids," I swore. "It looks awful all around, and I didn't have a childhood, so how would I know what to do with children? Plus, they take up all your time unless you have nannies, and that's unfair. It's like being raised by someone else, which is basically what happened to me."

"I don't blame you. I've never had much interest either," Kazimir agreed. "I was too busy scouring every corner of this continent for you to think about it."

"Glad we are on the same page," I exhaled. "I need another drink after listening to all that. I honestly didn't know what to say."

"Let's get you some more champagne," he said as he steered me to the nearest bar. Resting atop the wooden barrier was a clock that read half past eight.

Where was King Zalan? My head swiveled around as I tried to spot anyone else I might know. There were hundreds of Fae in the room, and I was unable to see over most of them. My attention landed on that creepy glass cage from our tour, males hovering around it, their attention on whatever was held inside. Kazimir handed me my drink and I asked, "What's in there?"

"The king's harem, probably."

I knew my father kept a harem, but this was next level. I wondered if the girls were here of their own volition, if they were paid, or if my father simply took what he wanted and no one dared stop him. "So there are females in there... lounging around?"

"Some... others might be performing," he whispered.

I made a face as I realized what he meant. "And people watch that? In public?"

"Take a good look at who is surrounding it, and you will know who not to befriend."

———

THE DOORS to the balcony opened, and the squire stepped forward while blowing a trumpet. "All hail King Zalan of the Night Realm!" he shouted.

"All hail!" the room boomed back.

My father stepped to the edge of the balcony, dripping in gems, and rested his hands on his rotund belly while he looked down his nose at us. He surveyed the room, beady eyes jumping from Fae to Fae, watching to see who was not paying him attention. I sensed an oily energy in him, reeking of conniving and backroom deals. Bile rose in my throat as his gaze landed on me. He looked me up and down from his perch, taking in my white wings, glittering gold gown, and celestial headdress. I was hard to miss in a room filled with light. Darkness flashed in his eyes, deepening when Kazimir placed a comforting hand on my lower back.

He smiled wickedly, more of the deceitful energy spilling from him. "My subjects," he began. "Tonight we are gathered to celebrate the return of my long-lost daughter, Izidora." Many began clapping, only to be silenced a moment later. "I have some exciting announcements to make, but first, let's eat!" He pounded his puffed chest, trying to display the powerful masculine energy that he clearly lacked.

His guards surrounded him as he descended the veined marble staircase, and they parted the crowd for him as he walked toward the High Table. If looks could kill, the one he shot me as he passed would have left me bleeding out all over his carefully polished floor. I watched him coolly, not breaking eye contact as I sipped from my glass.

The Fae around us drifted to the tables surrounding the room. The High Table was reserved for the King and High Houses, everyone else expected to find their seat. I took Kazimir's arm, letting him lead me to the High Table in full view of everyone.

How amazing would it be if he were my mate?

Not even my father could spoil that realization for me. To be loved so deeply when I had never experienced real love before would be better than any cinnamon roll, cookie, or cake – I would forgo sweets altogether if it meant we could be mated.

He pulled out my chair for me once we reached the table, and I crossed in front of it, carefully arranging my skirt, as he pushed me in. My body went rigid beneath my father's regard as he turned to his left, assessing me again since I was closer. Kazimir took the seat beside me, his presence a comfort when I knew the male to my right wanted me dead. Dipping my head in the bastard's direction, I said, "Good Evening, my king. The ballroom is every bit as lovely as you said it would be."

He grunted and turned away to survey the room. House Valintin took up the spots surrounding us, Alekzi unfortunately sitting across the table from me, where he unabashedly stared at my breasts again. Thankfully, Cazius sat directly in front of us, so I kept my attention on him while blatantly ignoring the young male. Endre and Viktor's families were on the other side of Kazimir, followed by House Rass. On the other side of House Valintin, Houses Luzak and Volak completed the table.

Once all Fae were seated, servants glided into the room from all sides, their dance coordinated like a ballet as they carried steaming trays of meat, bread, and vegetables. There was more food in this room than I had seen collectively in my life, though everyone waited patiently for the king to take his first bite before digging into their food.

I hardly touched my plate, pushing the food around as my stomach twisted itself in knots. *What were these important announcements?*

I felt like I was going to be sick. Kazimir brushed my thigh with his fingers, subtly reassuring me as emotions of every shape and size raged a war inside me.

My father ignored me completely. That small child inside me that never got to have a childhood hurt; yet I wanted to stand against him, *to kill him*, if need be, to claim my freedom from the hands of a male that did not deserve to control it. I decided I could feel both. Simply because two sentiments contrasted did not mean they had to be exclusive.

There were so many things I wanted to say to Kazimir, but I was unable to give them a voice in our current company. Dinner topics stuck to our earlier training, the new leathers I'd bought, and how many lovely Fae I had met. The conversation with Endre and Viktor's families took my mind off the endless possibilities bouncing around my brain, but too soon, our dinner plates were cleared, and desserts of every shape, size, and flavor appeared on the tables.

The sight of the sweets mixed with their sugary aroma turned my stomach, and with the erratic drumming of my heart, I could scarcely fill my lungs with air. My father was unaffected beside me, and he polished off two slices of cake, licking his fingers with a repulsive pop at the end.

His extra wide chair pushed back from the table, and his glass of dark whisky floated in the air. A mouse scurried around the edge of the room, searching for crumbs, entirely audible as the gathered nobles and rich merchants waited for King Zalan to speak.

Kazimir rested a hand on my lower back as we angled

ourselves to face the king, and his thumb stroked small, calming circles over my dress. My hands remained hidden under the table as I twisted my fingers together over and over.

By the time my father opened his mouth to speak, my whole body trembled.

"My loyal subjects," he paused, dragging out the silence, "thanks to the heroic efforts of High Lord Cazius Vaszoly, my daughter has been returned to me. I would like to offer him a gift of gratitude. High Lord Luzak, High Lord Vaszoly, would you please rise?"

High Lord Luzak stood with a glance at me that said, 'I won this round,' and my stomach dropped as a familiar female ducked her head meekly beside him.

Was King Zalan going to force Cazius to remarry? That was sick.

King Zalan turned his attention to Cazius, whose face was pale as he glanced at the young female down the table.

"I am pleased to announce that I have selected a bride for your son, Kazimir, in honor of my own daughter's safe return. High Lady Kamilia will unite Houses Luzak and Vaszoly in marriage. "

No.

The room swam before me, and all the air was stolen from my lungs. Time seemed to slow down, and glass shattered against the hard stone floor beside me as my fingers fell away from the wine I had been holding. Gasps rose unbidden from the crowd, rising like a lazy wave and washing over my ears with the slowness of a stream. My eyes burned as I whipped my head to Cazius, hoping he had a way out of this. His thin lips were pressed in a firm line, and by the dip of his shoulders, I knew he did not.

Kazimir's hand stilled on my back, fingers bunching against the fabric as another glass shattered behind me.

Kamilia's needy eyes swallowed Kazimir, and she clapped

her hands in front of her face, overjoyed with the announcement.

King Zalan smiled wickedly, his evil energy peaking as he stared me down.

He did this to hurt me. He did this to control me. He did this to manipulate me. How could anyone be so cruel?

"And since we are all gathered in Vaenor already, I have set the date for one week's time."

My heart shattered into a thousand tiny shards, mirroring the ceiling of the ballroom, as a sob caught in my chest. We had no time to plan anything. My world was falling apart around me, so soon after I carved out this home for myself in it. My inner fire was no more than a flicker as I felt for it, a whirlpool of grief sucking me into its murky depths, never to surface again. Flashes of my trauma covered the scene in front of me, and I clutched my chest as wave after wave of agony ripped apart my soul.

Once again, I was alone and at the mercy of a male who was cruel for no reason but for the sake of cruelty, and I'd had *enough.*

"Furthermore, my doctors have declared me cured of my ailments. My sickness was brought on by the grief of losing my only daughter and her mother on the same day. Now that she is returned, I am healthy once again, and I plan to have a very long reign. There is no need to name a successor at this time."

The crowd worked into a frenzy, but their sounds were not nearly as loud as the blood screaming through my ears.

"SILENCE!" King Zalan roared, slamming his fists against the table and sending silverware clanging.

An anguished hush fell. But a lone male kicked his chair back and shattered his plate against the ground as he stalked to our table.

Kriztof!

Everyone on the left side of the table stiffened simultane-ously. I knew Kriztof hated King Zalan, but he never acted out. His eyes blazed as he stalked toward the table, silver magic wrapping up his arms, and King Zalan's guards broke into a run to intercept him. Kriztof drew a knife from his boot without breaking stride and hurled it end over end straight for the king, silver tendrils pushing it beyond the distance he could throw; but he was too far away, and the blade buried itself in King Zalan's left shoulder, narrowly missing his heart.

King Zalan's guards tackled Kriztof and wrestled him to the ground. "You no longer deserve to breathe. You are vile and cruel, and no one respects you. I am saying what everyone thinks!" Kriztof lashed against the guards, bucking wildly as they tried to pin him.

"Execute the traitor!" King Zalan roared, clutching the knife protruding from his chest.

More guards jumped on Kriztof's limbs, four pinning them down while a fifth straddled his chest, his sword flashing beneath the chandeliers as he raised it over his head, poised to spear Kriztof through the heart like I had done to the male who raped me. Kazimir grabbed me and pulled my face to his chest, shielding me from what was about to happen. The executioner lowered his blade toward a still-thrashing Kristof.

"No!" Vadim roared, jumping to his feet and launching daggers toward the guards pinning Kriztof to the ground. Liliana shrieked and grabbed at his jacket, but the fine fabric slipped through her fingers as he launched himself away from their table. It rocked as Vadim's boot pushed off of it, powering him into Kriztof's executioner. They rolled to the ground, and Vadim pounded the guard's face into the floor as he bellowed his fury.

Zekari and Kirigin appeared from thin air, tackling two more guards as they raced to defend their brothers in arms.

Kazimir and I were frozen as the scene unfolded. My mind

screamed at my body to move, to do something, but I could only watch in horror as my friends fought for their lives in front of me.

"Seize them all!" my father screeched beside me, coughing as the dagger protruding from his chest was irritated by the effort. More of King Zalan's personal guards shot away from their posts around the room, racing to the center where my friends were taking out the attackers left and right.

Chaos erupted as the remaining Knights around the room jumped into action, turning against the king's guards and choosing their brothers. Rich merchants and members of the Lower Houses fled the battlefield that surrounded them with piercing shrieks.

Kazimir still gripped me firmly, though his heart galloped faster than we had the day we raced to Zirok House.

King Zalan still screeched beside me, berating his guards as the tide turned against him.

Holy fuck, was this really about to happen?

Was this turning into a full-blown coup, the Fae of the Night Realm finally at their breaking point?

Was I about to become queen? My father only needed a nudge to find his home among the ashes.

The doors above the balcony banged open, and a tall, broad male strode confidently into the room. He wore a sardonic smirk as he devoured the chaos below him, scanning the room from left to right and up to the high table. He threw his arms up and out, standing like a god looking down upon his sycophants, and more guards streamed into the room from behind him, splitting around him while he continued to hold his powerful posture. Only these guards were not dressed in the leather armor of the Night Realm; no, they wore metal plates carved with the sigil of the Iron Realm.

They raced into the fray, some snapping whips tipped with

iron at the fighters. My hands clutched my temples as I desperately tried to regain control of the panic that clawed up my spine and into my throat. I could not lose the scream that lodged there, for I would lose these people before I even had the chance to be free.

"King Zalan," the newcomer boomed. "I believe you have something of mine." His smoky eyes landed on me, and he stepped slowly down the stairs, paying no mind to the madness around him.

Kazimir jumped to his feet, pushing me behind him and putting himself between me and the Iron Fae who approached us. His guards had corralled the room, and they stood in a faceoff with the Night Fae as this cocky male strode toward us.

"Ruslan, you weren't supposed to be here until tomorrow," King Zalan choked, blood dribbling out of the corner of his mouth.

What the fuck? They knew each other? Well enough that he accepted this male into his kingdom?

Kazimir growled a warning as Ruslan closed in on us. Endre and Viktor's chairs clattered against the floor, followed by High Lord Kaztar's. Alekzi slunk in his seat, until his head was barely visible over the tablecloth. High Lord Tomaz looked between the two, waiting for what would happen next.

"I want what was promised to me," Ruslan purred to my father. "And when I rode into Vaenor this afternoon, everyone was celebrating. There was to be a grand feast tonight, they told me, so I thought, what better way to make an appearance and claim my future bride?"

Future bride? What the actual fuck.

My jaw ached from the force of my clenching as yet another contender joined the fray of males trying to control me. "I'm not going anywhere with you," I bit out, calling my magic just below the surface of my skin. Kazimir turned animalistic, baring his teeth at Ruslan and standing to his full height.

"Oh, but you are," he crooned. "Your father made a pact with my father, King Azim, that I could take you as my bride once you came of age. He had your mother killed, and you ripped from her arms so we could mold and shape you into the weapon we needed. The prophecy says you will make kings fall, but I plan on dictating who those kings are. Iron and Night are going to rule this continent, and I need your power to make that happen. So pack your bags, sweetheart, because you are coming home with me."

I whipped my head toward my father, who sat gasping for breath with the knife still lodged in his chest. "Is this true? Did you orchestrate all of this? Did you sell me like property only for me to suffer abuse at the hands of others?" I demanded, my voice rising to a shout by the end of my questions.

He nodded stiffly.

Ruslan tipped his head back and cackled, the sound wholly manic and sending cold fear skittering across my skin. "King Zalan contributed as many soldiers to keep you hidden as King Azim. It's cute that your little friends chased you around the continent for so long when he knew exactly where you were the entire time."

His words broke the last of my resolve, and the dam behind which I'd hidden my rage burst, flooding my veins with adrenaline. With a scream that held a thousand lifetimes of pain, I lunged for my father and yanked the knife out of his chest. His lips sputtered blood, but I did not care as I leaned my face close to his, wanting the fury on my face to be the last thing he saw.

"I hope you rot for eternity, you sick fuck," I swore. I swiped Kriztof's blade across my father's throat, not deep enough to immediately kill, but enough that he would die by drowning in his own blood. Vengeance pulled a menacing snarl to my lips, and I opened up the full range of my hatred as he clutched his neck, gasping and bleeding out. I watched with intoxicating glee as the life dimmed from his eyes. His head hit the table with a resounding thud, and I lifted my gaze to the silent ballroom.

A group of Iron Fae soldiers had gathered behind Ruslan while I killed my father. The male's face was bright with delight as he took in my blood-spattered face.

"Seize her," he commanded.

"Run!" Endre shouted as he and Viktor leaped over the table to fend off the soldiers.

Kazimir grabbed my arm and yanked me along behind him as we retreated.

"Wait! I can't run," I exclaimed. He bent down and ripped my skirt high enough to allow my legs to move more freely. We raced away from the table, but my breath was hindered by the too-tight gown. I flagged behind him like in my dreams where I tried to run but could not get away fast enough. It was my worst nightmares come to life.

Armored feet pounded behind us as fighting broke out across the room.

I glanced back only to see a whip headed straight for me. The scream that tore from my throat ripped apart my vocal cords, ending in silence as the tip snapped a hair's breadth from my back. I raced through blurred vision and choked sobs, Kazimir's rough palm against mine my only source of sanity as all those scars on my back flared to life with memories. We were so close to the doors, but before we reached them, they swung open to reveal another company of Iron Fae. We were completely surrounded.

"You've got this, Izidora," Kazimir shouted, pulling me back to the present. We needed to fight – I needed to fight. I would not succumb to these monsters again. I would die before I let them take me. Kazimir and I stood back to back, waiting for the soldiers to attack. I was weaponless, only my magic and my mate to defend me now.

My mate.

"Until the end?" I asked Kazimir, my words conveying everything I felt at that moment.

"Until the end," he replied.

I called my white magic to my hands and threw up a shield in front of myself, then focused on sending Kazimir the strength he needed to fend off the Fae who surrounded us. He leaped into action, drawing the sword from his hip with one hand while flinging a dagger into the neck of a soldier in front of me with the other. He went down, and the clash of blades rang at my back as Kazimir fought for our lives. If he could only cut down enough Fae to get through the door, we might be able to make it to one of the passages and away.

Ruslan approached my shield, his blade dripping blood. "Kazimir!" My voice went hoarse again as I screamed. My terror removed his focus from the fight in front of him long enough for an iron-tipped whip to strike him, and he grunted as the tip sank into his flesh. His wings disappeared as his magic was sliced away, and he stumbled to the side but continued his path toward me. He angled himself between me and Ruslan, and I moved the shield to our vulnerable backs.

While Ruslan waited, a smirk played over his cocky lips. Kazimir raised his sword to attack, but his arms wobbled, and as he stepped forward, his legs did too. His sword clattered to the ground, and he fell to his hands and knees.

"What did you do to him?" I sobbed, dropping to my knees and wrapping my arms over him protectively. "Kazimir, please don't leave me," I begged. "I need you, I love you, please please..."

"The iron tips are laced with a paralysis potion. It's only

temporary. He will be fine in about five minutes, but by then we will be gone," Ruslan laughed.

Two soldiers grabbed me, and I gripped Kazimir with everything I had, screaming and kicking as they tried to drag me from his body. "NO!" I shrieked as the tendons in my hands popped, breaking my grip on him. White light burst from my body, blasting my attackers off of me, and I scrambled back to Kazimir. Another guard grabbed my leg, and I kicked him in the face with all my strength, cracking his nose with a satisfying crunch.

"I do like it when they fight back," Ruslan purred.

I bared my teeth, ready to fight for my life, even if Kazimir could no longer protect me.

"Knock her out," Ruslan instructed, then spun on his heel and walked away. Three males jumped me at once, and before I could blast them again, one slapped a rag over my mouth. I flailed and lashed, but my movements were slow and sluggish. Tears streamed from my eyes as my muscles gave out on me, and I felt wholly powerless. As my world went dark, all I could think about was that fucking cave and how my escape had been too good to be true.

34

KAZIMIR

The Iron Fae drugged Izidora and dragged her away from me. Inside I was roaring and thrashing, putting every ounce of strength into moving even the tip of my finger. Yet my eyelids were the only part of my body that could move as I lay helpless against the cool marble floor of the ballroom, listening to the screams of my brothers and friends, unable to save them or Izidora. A tear slipped down my cheek as she disappeared through the doors we desperately tried to escape through. I had broken my promise to keep her safe, and she was gone. Fucking Fates, I just got her, and she was ripped from my arms, returning to those who had abused her for twenty-one years. I should have saved her sooner.

My toes regained movement first, followed by my feet and ankles, and finally I was able to get my legs back under me. I crawled toward the High Table, unable to pick up my head yet, but desperate to know if my family was alive. The sounds of fighting ceased by the time I crawled up the chair at the end of the table to prop myself upright.

Bodies were strewn across the ballroom. Fae wailed as they cradled their loved ones, either dead or dying. My father laid on the other side of the table, and using it as a crutch, I shuffled around until I was close enough to walk to him. My knees crashed to the floor beside him, and I saw the fatal gash slashed across his chest. The rise and fall of it was weak, but there.

"My son..." he croaked, eyes fluttering as I pulled him into my arms.

"I'm here, father. You're going to be alright," I swore even as my chest felt like it was about to cave in.

"No... I'm not... Kazimir, you were the best son a father could have... You no longer need me... You know everything I have to teach..." he rasped.

"No, please, no, stay with me." Salty tears dripped onto the bloody tunic. "Help! I need a healer!"

"Did they take Izidora?" he wheezed, the end closing in too fast.

"Yes," I croaked, my chin falling to my sternum.

"Go, my son. Your mate needs you..." He released his last breath, then went limp in my arms.

My roar shook the room around us, cracking the ceiling with a thunderous clap and sending shards of the crystal chandeliers raining over the dead and the living. My head snapped back as my fury cascaded from my throat, and the sound did not cease until there was no crystal left to fall.

I would save Izidora again, and the Iron Realm would pay for what they had taken from me.

LINKS

Dying to know what happens next? <u>Light</u> is out now. Order today!

If you enjoyed Chained, please consider rating or reviewing on Amazon, Goodreads, BookBub, or any other platform you prefer to use! Your support means everything, and taking a few moments of your time to let others know how much you liked the book is appreciated.

Subscribe to my newsletter for a spicy bonus scene featuring four of the Nighthounds and one very lucky lady!

Where to connect with Lacey:
<u>Instagram - @laceylehotzkyauthor</u>
<u>TikTok - @laceylehotzkyauthor</u>
<u>Discord - Lacey's Insidious Blooms</u>
<u>Goodreads - Lacey Lehotzky</u>
<u>Amazon - Lacey Lehotzky</u>
<u>Pinterest - Lacey Lehotzky</u>

Links

Merch & Signed Copies:
www.laceylehotzky.com

AUTHOR'S NOTE

Trauma fundamentally changes who we are. It causes a range of issues long after the events have passed. From physical ailments, anxiety, depression, social stigma, and more, overcoming trauma can be a lonely road, and we lose many amazing people to its clutches every year. If you or someone you know is struggling, there are so many resources available.

In recent years, the conversation around mental health has shifted drastically, yet the effects of trauma, especially complex trauma, still pose a challenge to resources worldwide. New therapies and interventions become available every year, and I encourage you to keep trying until you find what works for you. I would not be here if it weren't for finding the right type of help.

Instilling a fundamental sense of safety is paramount to healing. Without feeling safe, we cannot begin to unpack and overcome what happened to us. We're stuck in survival mode, acting not from a wise mind, but one that would do anything to survive. That's why therapies like trauma focused CBT, EMDR, DBT, somatic therapy, and others are so important in the beginning, so we are learning how to cope with the emotions trauma brings us. Exercise, play, laughter, breathwork, and meditation can help us achieve and maintain nervous system regulation that will keep us out of survival mode and allow us to move forward with our lives.

The Body Keeps the Score by Bessel van der Kolk is a book that opened my eyes to new ways of thinking about trauma, and I encourage you to read it if you have questions about how different therapies can help you or a loved one. That is not the only book out there that covers this topic, but it is one I can personally recommend.

Most importantly, you are not alone.

United States
    USA Suicide and Crisis Lifeline: dial 988
    Crisis Text Line: Text REASON to 741741

United Kingdom
    SHOUT: text SHOUT to 85258
    Samaritans: call 116 123 (free from any phone), email jo@samaritans.org, or visit some branches in person
    National Suicide Prevention Helpline UK: call 0800 689 5652

Australia
    Lifeline: call 13 11 14 , text, or chat online 24/7

ACKNOWLEDGMENTS

To you, my dear reader, THANK YOU. I wouldn't be an author if it weren't for amazing souls like you, and from the bottom of my heart, thank you for reading my debut novel.

To my betas and arcs, you guys rock! Thank you for all the feedback and helping shape this book into what it is today.

Kristina – You have been a lifesaver. From jumping in with me when I was in crisis mode trying to make last minute changes, to reading this book over and over and over again, to always texting me back when I had a thought, I am so freaking grateful for you.

Stacie – This book literally wouldn't be here without you. Thank you for always giving me feedback, encouraging me to keep going, talking out plotlines... thank you for every moment you've given me and this book. You are a beautiful human inside and out, and I am SO glad the Lehotzky boys brought us together!

Kaitlin – BJJ sisters for life! What started as a random conversation after one Saturday class turned into so much more. Thank you for taking time out of your crazy schedule to edit my book. You are an amazing writer, editor, mother, and friend. Let's go get our blue belts!

To my friends who supported me along the way, letting me share my excitement with you, and who sent the word out to everyone they knew about my book, you are better than any family I could have asked for. Sophia, thank you for giving me a play by play while you read and making me laugh with your comments. Kristin, thank you for letting me talk your ear off about it once a week. Matt, where would I be without you? Melissa, thank you for being just as excited as me whenever I had a milestone to share.

And last, but certainly not least, Andrew. You are the reason I believe that humans have fated mates too. Everything I went through led me straight to you, and Valentine's Day will always be the greatest day in my life. Thank you for encouraging me to follow my dreams and telling me for years that I needed to write books. I am so glad I listened to you.

ABOUT THE AUTHOR

Lacey Lehotzky is a writer, photographer, and author of the new dark fantasy romance series, A Choice of Light and Dark. She is most often found with her nose in a book when she isn't training to be a badass fighter like her main characters. Lacey has her best ideas while traveling, where she finds inspiration for people and places in her books. She especially loves exploring the darker side of life, writing characters with deep flaws and even deeper trauma and strapping her readers in for an emotional roller coaster that will leave them breathless by the end.

Made in United States
North Haven, CT
25 March 2024

50487572R00278

PRINCESS IZIDORA OF THE NIGHT REALM WAS
KIDNAPPED AT BIRTH, CHAINED IN DARKNESS, ABUSED
BY HER CAPTORS, AND WHOLLY UNAWARE AN ENTIRE
WORLD WAS LOOKING FOR HER.

That is until the eve of her 21st birthday, when the Nighthounds, led by the
striking High Lord Kazimir, rescue her from a cave in the highest peak in the
land. Now, the Lost Princess must reclaim her power before they reach the
vicious capital of the Night Realm, where the story everyone was told about
her disappearance might have been just that – a story. Will Izidora overcome
her trauma or succumb to the whims of the madman who sits on the Night
Throne?

ISBN 9798988362012

9798988 362012

90000